J.R. Thorp is a writer, ~~…~~ Award ~~…~~
Opening Lines Prize. ~~…~~ Cambridge
Literary Revi~~…~~ ~~…~~ sition and
elsewhere. She wrote the libretto for the highly acclaimed
modern opera *Dear Marie Stopes* and has had works commissioned
by the Arts Council, the Wellcome Trust and St Paul's Cathedral.
Born in Australia, she now lives in Cork, Ireland. *Learwife* is her
first novel.

@ThoroughlyThorp | jrthorp.com

LONGLISTED FOR THE WALTER SCOTT PRIZE FOR HISTORICAL FICTION AND THE AUTHORS' CLUB BEST FIRST NOVEL AWARD

'Poetic . . . Distinctive and compelling . . . Thorp's poignant and
surprising narrative allows a character absent from the original
play to obtain her long overdue agency'   *Observer*

'Seductive . . . Gorgeous'   *The Times*

'Gorgeously written . . . artful and moving . . . a beautiful triumph'
New York Times

'Thorp's vivid debut novel gives voice to one of fiction's most
conspicuously absent women . . . Lyrical . . . Thorp's distinctive
style is heady and evocative . . . *Learwife* slots into a strong alter-
native canon of feminist retellings of classic stories'   *i*

'Original, intriguing . . . Thorp's novel is beautifully written in rich,
imaginative prose'   *Sunday Times*, Best New Historical Fiction

'The wife of King Lear is given a powerful voice in this haunting
narrative of her life . . . The writing in this novel is pitch-perfect:
lyrical, imaginative and there to savour'   *Daily Mail*

C334775787

LEAR WIFE

J R
THORP

CANONGATE

This paperback edition published in 2022 by Canongate Books

First published in Great Britain in 2021 by Canongate Books Ltd,
14 High Street, Edinburgh EH1 1TE

canongate.co.uk

1

British Library Cataloguing-in-Publication Data
A catalogue record for this book is available on
request from the British Library

ISBN 978 1 83885 284 9

Typeset in Centaur MT by Palimpsest Book Production Ltd, Falkirk,
Stirlingshire

Printed and bound in Great Britain by Clays Ltd, Elcograf S.p.A.

MIX
Paper from
responsible sources
FSC® C018072
FSC
www.fsc.org

To Eglantine

This is the story.

There was a king, Lear, or Leir, son of Bladdud the Mad. Great gift-giver, with his many knights and liegeman Kent, he ruled for decades. He had three daughters, no sons.

When old and care-bent he said to these daughters, I will pass on my crown and divide my kingdom, and give most to the one who says she loves me best. And the Lady Goneril said, I do love thee most, and won a portion. And the Lady Regan said, I do love thee better, and won a portion. And the honest Lady Cordelia said nothing, and was banished, married to a foreign king over the seas. And Goneril and Regan took all.

Alas for foolish Lear, he went to Goneril and said, Will you care for me in my age? and she said, No. And he went to Regan and said, Will you care for me in my age? and she said, No. And so he became mad as his father had been.

And Cordelia and her king returned, to conquer his land and care for him, but were broken in battle with the sisters, and Cordelia killed where she stood. And the ladies Regan and Goneril did die of spite. And Lear died of heartbreak for Cordelia; and only his liegeman Kent was left, to mourn him.

So: hearken to this, messengers, men on the fleetest of horses.

Care-bent king Lear is dead.

His two eldest daughters, the Lady Regan, the Lady Goneril, dead.

His youngest, most beloved, Cordelia, dead.

No sons.

So let it be known.

1

BOOK I

1.

The word has come that he is dead, now, and the girls. And that it is finished.

Today they will ring the bells. The priest will say four masses, for their souls. The autumn light is fragile and my veil is thick, and I must descend. To light the candles. This is just and Christian, and I am afraid.

I pause now at the head of the stair. The arc of a silvered glass on the wall holds my face, its jaw thrust like blackthorn. Through the density of my linen veil it loses its distinguishing parts, becomes mass and hollow, an unnamed plain. I trace the forehead, the lips he once called *house of all my country*, and they are foreign, without place. Hidden, like a white fox in a blizzard.

Though my sight is covered I feel the first shadows of vespers arriving. The peeling off of sky.

I am the queen of two crowns, banished fifteen years, the famed and gilded woman, bad-luck baleful girl, mother of three small animals, now gone. I am fifty-five years old. I am Lear's wife. I am here. History has not taken my body, not yet.

The lady Ruth holds my arm, her shoulder's serving thickness at my back. I lean to the wall of the stair and pitch forth, into the dark.

★   ★   ★

In the abbey chapel they are massed, waiting. Few of them have seen me; I am mostly myth, the abbess's legendary woman. Taut in herself. Their covered heads turn: nuns are not invulnerable to curiosity – they seek God in every small stone.

Shame flows into me. That the queen should be here, that she is thrown so low in the world. It makes me ache in my lungs and mouth, a pain that smothers even the misery I have been under since yesterday, when the messenger came. That was low and brutal, a keening. This new raw feeling is higher, cruel, as if pressed burning on my hand.

Ruth moves to lay my veil over my shoulder. As a modest widow should wear.

I feel its weight on my body and am engulfed with fire. Scorch across the floor. The bloodiness of my rage, the colour of it on my skin, burning all that touch me. Hence Lear would call me *storm-wife*, as he walked through the upper hall banging shutters in pretended caution, knowing that my anger could tear away a roof, strip a palace clear.

I full throw the veil across my forehead and find the light. My age-scored cheeks, the famous eyes that Lear's Fool held as 'sweet vipers' in verse: let them witness it. A queen wrapped, indistinct, is no queen. Let me be fresh to them, bleeding, brought in still shuddering from the hunt. Let them prise me from the jaw of this.

A woman's small intake of breath, at my nakedness, the raw circle of my face. Which they have never seen. Then silence.

So unveiled I take the front pew, with its royal mark, the crest of the king upon a cushion never used. The priest Manfred will not look at my face. Begins.

★　★　★

After he has done, we process down the aisle. The abbess pauses, lets me pass before her from the front pew. Rank is here even in death.

So: I lead them all out into the pale sun of the abbey cloisters. Head of the funeral column. I think of horses, of a small local animal being hitched to tiers of carriage-ponies to guide them across rivers or dense marsh ground. Pushing through mist in the royal coach, I once looked out and saw a donkey raise its trembling ears at the front of the train, listening to the air.

They are expecting me to weep. Also they wish to see me in full, the sun on my half-greyed hair, and compare my face to the circulated woodcuts from my marriages. Most had it near to the bone: a long chin, high eyes in a watchful oval under a blotted, spiked crown. Ancient blood pooling in my cheeks. The artists gave me a small mouth for fashion, but really I have a broadness in the lower lip, which Lear's braver poets liked to pun upon. *She's of good stock, she has the lip of a stockfish.*

What one remembers, what comes swimming up from the silt. I have been here for fifteen years.

The abbess comes and places her fingers on my bare wrist, then does the sign of the Holy Cross, stitching it into the air, where it hangs. *In great grief there is still the glory of the Lord*, she says, and is so deeply young she has perhaps not presided over a memorial of rank before. Even a mocker such as this – a funeral with no bodies, merely four candles on the altar-cloth, to signify. One flame, and one, and one, and one.

Suddenly my density, the anger that had weighed me to my seat, like a stone, is dissolved, and instead there is dangerous lightness, hollow, as if a child could blow and collapse me.

I take my wrist from her and give it to the lady Ruth, who grips it wholly, within both hands. She has been crying, the moist edge of her habit clinging to her neck. The abbess wants to speak, looks at my face, retreats.

When the messenger came I was rising from prayer, shaking the dust from my tunic, which has Flemish thickness to distinguish myself, my visible rank. I heard his horse stamp beside the gate and thought, *Stallion, eighteen hands, hard-ridden.* I have animal-sound in me: I can hear the brush of them through walls and know their bone-weight, how they move.

He came through the courtyard, asked for the abbess by name to give his news. Had sweat across his back down to the slick of his breeches from the swiftness and inelegance of the ride. I knew and measured men by that once.

The abbess said, *May his God protect and cherish his soul.*

A violent thing descended. Hawk-swoop. All that was raised in me, every round part, was flattened. Scraped clean. The remainder was sheer, one could not grip it. I felt slick, slipping out of palms like a wet stone. Forgot speech, forgot how to move my throat for breath.

A nun offered me her hand. In what I distantly recognised as an indication of my own madness I took it. I who would not accept an arm to aid me onto a horse fifteen hands high.

The thought surfaced: *Once again he surprises me.*

2.

Iremember the king learning: of nothingness, of the idea of being gone.

There was a noble's eldest boy at the winter court – he'd been trained in the city in the new Arabic numerals, for his accountancy. When Lear and I tired he offered to show it. Wrote it out, his strange system, on the back of a book. A family of symbols: 8, 3, 2, 5. Watching I thought they looked like animals, curled in on themselves, or stretching light limbs, showing a neck to the breeze, a tail, a tongue. The last he explained denoted nothing, the state of it, to have an empty purse or no more debt. This shape: 0. Like a mouth; like a cunny.

Lear had difficulties. *What is this, this round thing? You cannot build on a hole in the earth. If I have nothing surely I need no mark of it.*

Can you not leave a space? I wondered. Surely that was sufficient. A gap, a fall through the ink: here is naught, avoid it, map elsewhere.

The boy drew it again, larger, struggled to explain. *Lack defines plenty. It is how we know that we came from God: darkness, and then the light. So we are aware of the light.*

Lear was beyond youth then, beyond the subtleties of abstract thought on a winter afternoon in a cold hall; preferred old bloated epics, his own verse, rich food and bad sport. He snorted. *Religious arguments are perfidious. I have no pigs of a saleable size, no purple weave, no fruit left after my daughters finish with the stores. You would spend an eternity enumerating what it is I do not have. No, keep close to the real.* Hand banged on the table.

Forgive me, my king, but if you die, would you not like your subjects to have a word for your absence? 'There is no king.' Not a space, or a gap in the ledger. We must acknowledge loss and account for it safely, otherwise—

I was astonished: the daring. Talk to Lear of king-death, the end of himself! I looked then at the pate of the king, its rushed redness, the flush of broken veins around his eyes, and felt the metal of it: his will. That would not vanish; that would drive his mortal softness on, even through rot, through fields of sharpened pikes, the things that lay us low, and still push forth into the world, livid as living flame.

Ah, he said, drawing his robes, preparing to rise. Old; or feeling age, experiencing its indignities, the crackle and fuss of bones. *Your death may be an emptiness, boy, but the world would know of mine even if they were blind, or senseless. They would look at the hole and say, 'There was Lear.' That's a king, boy.*

The boy was right: it is necessary to leave a mark. To say, *There was, and now there is not.* To draw the circle, and stand within it, and hear — what?

Silence, now. The end of the account.

⭑   ⭑   ⭑

Back in my rooms, this little eyrie for noble visitors marooned above an abbey courtyard, I have taken the pins from the funeral veil and let it slough off behind me, like a skin.

How is it possible to have been married once, let alone twice? To be that animal condition *mate.* When you are knotted — and put your head to his shoulder, find the small softnesses.

Even in years alone, locked in this place, I was Lear's wife, I had threaded his body with mine, like a long needle. And still then I was another wife, the first, of the boy who died. And still now I am wife to them both, perhaps. Is this possible? Like being the mother of many different children, mother and mother and mother, all laid upon one another like layers of leather in a saddle.

I shiver, my body vibrates, a bird arranging its feathers in a new wind. I will be leaving this place, perhaps soon; perhaps in the next hours. Before vespers. They may see fit to do it then. As Lear is gone, as the protection that glazed me here, in this place, has cracked, and the clay shown through. They have no more reason to harbour me, and so.

Whom will I be out in the world now, after so long? What is my name, when the man who named me has entered the roots of the earth, and opened his mouth to the deep death-waters? Queen of no-word. Queen of stopped breath.

I am dressed in white; this is the noble's mourning-clothes. Ruth had found some paler robes and laid them in lime in the autumn sun, until they washed into pale grey. I feel as if I am wearing cloud, as if I am no longer a solid thing.

When my first husband died I remember I was portioned his mother's mourning-clothes. Lace darkened by sweat. Her arms even in age were thinner than mine, and as I prayed for his soul in his chapel the cambric sleeves split gently at one elbow, then the other, in what felt like an act of sarcasm. I thought then, *This cannot be worse*, and here I am, in bleached robes discarded by religious sisters for their threadbare elbows and knees.

The woman who gathers the funeral veil, who tends me in my rooms after the funeral, the lay sister, has never married. Will never. Her family have sent her here to shift water for the nuns and aristocratic dying, her broad back for heaving our washing, her thick wrists over our slops. I watch her and her high skull as she crushes the veil into a square for storing, and am conscious

11

of how skinned I am, how my nerves are standing thick across my forehead. But it is better than the idea of the deaths, of the four little ghosts, husband and three daughters dead, so I speak to her.

Stupid girl, will you ruin everything.

I am sorry.

Just take it away. Burn it. I will not wear it again, peevishly, knowing the smallness of this. But she goes, stolid and rebuked, and the four little ghosts recede, under this weight I have placed on them.

I do not wish them to be married, Lear had said. Half-day. Religious, to honour a saint who'd died spectacularly; a feast, dancers flickering their bells, mummers doing the saint-death again with paint for blood and paper spears. Too much ale. *They will be ruined, some useless man's donkey.*

I was combing his hair. The two eldest girls were young then, small babes. We were still hopeful of a son. Had spent the feast crushing their floral wreaths and being fed fingers of meat by my ladies. The notion that they would elongate, would unfold and harden into women with plaited hair and husbands, seemed blindly impossible, particularly in our drunkenness; of course they would be young, round as buns, for ever. The youngest, Cordelia, years away, hidden in the lining of my body.

I am not a donkey, I said, laughing. *Will you send them to the convent then?*

Nuns to pray for their old father's soul and grow pale and stupid as flapping geese! No. He was tired. Even then he had the purple circles of an old dog around his eyes. *By God's eyes I want them happy. I have always said.*

I can hear myself scoffing. *Girls like ours need men.* Think of them – each pecking at her sister. They need playthings – a house to run, servants, a husband. Alone they'd eat each other. Like lampreys.

Yes. He turned his face to me: the glorious profile, struck into coins, medals, the heart-place on the armour of ten thousand men. *Kiss us then, kiss our old face, the king demands.*

The messenger said they killed one another. The two. The pair of them, kissing each other's cheeks to lick off the sugar.

There is no looking at it directly. One must run at it, and dive, as if throwing oneself into a well. As a child in the convent where I was raised, we were told to fear wells. I would lay my head over one, dip into the black mouth for whole inches of time, then run, with a new cold skin to tell of my courage. Here it is. The well-mouth, where there was Lear, and my girls.

These rooms, the halls for rich visitors to the abbey, where for fifteen years I have lodged, as if on my way elsewhere, merely a passing guest. The falsehood that I could leave, at any time, that this small restraint was temporary.

My thoughts seem to come from a great distance and strike me till I resonate, as arrows against a shield.

It is necessary to be practical. To moor myself to an object, outside my own body, which may yet betray. To my name. Which has not corrupted, which I retained before I was wife to anybody, and keep now, telling nobody.

I kneel before my possessions. A row of white sacks, against one wall untouched. Packed in readiness for fifteen years, so that I could return at a moment's notice: *I am prepared, let us go.*

I saw the abbess looking at them once, eight years in, as we mulled a plan for an extension to the kitchen garden: maps, on my bed. *Leave them be. I am a witch smuggling my familiars in them*, I said, and she smiled and turned away.

Such ordinary things. One packet cracks at the corner under my fingers, shows its innards. Pieces I had forgotten I owned: small scissors in the shape of a hand, a folded belt. Ruth has taken care of them: the coils are still in place. They are innocent of everything.

I will be leaving once more. I lay the sacks each on the floor, with wide spaces between them that could take my entire body. Six of them. Stand above them, seeing them laid out, in a constellation: shoes in this, a travelling shawl I think in another. For a higher perspective I step up onto the linen-chest. Lear and I would do this, plans pinned to the floor, to see the fringes in the whole, how territories interlocked and moved across one another like moss. It was a trick I taught him, like so much else, an education I gave to him, as it was given to me.

I have made a circle. I may step inside it. The nothing of my life may become something, and so.

* * *

What you take when they come for you. What becomes treasure?

Fifteen years ago I took linen: bundles, some still stuffed with scent from storage. A chatelaine, inlaid with silver, from my first marriage. Hard shoes for walking – there would be walking. Furs for warmth, a black comb, a book of prayer. I gathered less than I could have, for propriety: the queen does not carry like a beggar. A small bright knife. My girls' hair, in a pocket. Cordelia's from her first illness at three days old, white wisps, barely real.

Coins loose in my bodice. The attendants strapped them to me quickly, whispering, palming them against my chemise, then dropping them down my clothes in handfuls, like leaves. I walked into the dark fearing they would fall from me and be lost in the mud, that it would seem as if the queen's flayed skin had peeled off gold.

I step heavily down from the chest and the floor shudders. The assembled parts scatter into the darkness. The circle is broken.

* * *

14

Night. I open my eyes into darkness. Which? The parts of time have moved off. I am lost in the turn. Men talk of a sudden return of memory after long sleep, in a flood. As if grief could possibly give you respite. No. It slept with me; it rose as I rose, like a well-trained dog after its master in the night fields.

Ruth breathes beside me on her pallet bed. My mouth tastes of iron.

If there were papers of law for the funerals of my girls, my king, I would sort them. Clothes, I would lay them out for the air; cool bodies, I would wash them in oil and anoint their fore-heads. Soften bruises with tallow and paint. Instead this. Space, dark, cold. Habit sews us into sanity like a cloth.

No word from the abbess. Most nights we would come together and pray, in her apartments, and discuss: *Here is the latest bishop's gossip, here is the new novice's angular misery, how can we untangle this problem of the souring ale?* Pouring my thought into her over years, the vessel of her spilling. Tonight, no. I see her podding the peas of her rosary now, her face open, waiting for obscure voices to sing out advice from the woodwork.

Perhaps she will come for me in the night, shake me out like seed into the world, as it was the first time. Exiled again. *You are free, Lady Queen,* and I'll be bundled off, and left to fend for my old self, outside the abbey wall.

I hold to my bed. She will have to fight. I will bite. Old teeth have hardened cores. I'd blind them all with a thumb before I'd be turned out. Nobody tells me to go, not now.

Where are my family lying in the ground? Had they been folded into the soil in royal clothes and thick dark coffins, or given to a hole in the earth, by the side of the battlefield, in shrouds of army cloaks? Did any person put coins on their eyes, and say a prayer for their flickering souls, or were they just thrown in a row in one rut of dirt, four astride, a family band linking arms?

15

I think of sheaves of birch, of sticks knotted in the middle. For better burning.

The messenger to the abbey did not know, was surprised to be asked. The manner of their deaths, what had passed to bring this calamity: end of all, end of life, star-fall and sun-crack. A dolt in new riding leathers, perturbed by the questions of an old woman of no obvious rank. Had his message: *Hark.*

I forgot, in the moment, that he would not know who I was. *But how is this possible?*

I am charged to deliver news of the king's passing, and that of his heirs. That is all.

And their husbands? They were killed too? Did some mad stallion come and trample them in their beds? This is – this is insanity. That was all that could occur to me. Tragic accident, a fallen wall or fire. Kent, I thought, would not allow it: his conscientiousness would forbid the whole act. *Slave, speak swiftly, I am not patient.*

The king was mad, madam. He was calm, evidently believing me strange and affronting, but withheld from smacking me. I know very well when a man's palm itches in that direction. *Divided his kingdom. Banished his youngest daughter for a trifle. Not balanced.* Cordelia, I thought. Was it my fault, whatever it was? What did I do to you?

And what? Did he take a sword to them all?

No. No, there was a battle; at the last there was terrible confusion, and by dusk the princesses and king were dead. War being what it is, madam.

Madam. Perilous territory! *Madam me no madams*, I told him.

There were gaps in this too terrible to be filled. And yet I wanted to know; I have always wanted to know, even when the knowledge damned me.

He is whispering. Has a gathering of news, wants to scatter it like salt, make the ground a misery.

They say the eldest girls killed one another.

Weak like women are. They say poison. Cool, like glass.

The youngest died in prison. Her fancy Frankish husband could not save her. She of all of them looked the most like her father, a mirror to him.

Lear died of a broken heart, or madness, or both.

Or they were all killed together. Monsieur France does not say, he is quiet.

I will give you more words, Abbess. You are amazed.

I am weeping now, and am astonished to be weeping, thinking my body too dried and painful to emit anything. Instead this wholly useless act.

Damned man, he could tell me no news of Kent, either. Kent, whom I had known since my youth, when barely breaking out of childhood. Kent the boy-page, who became the long-haired diplomat in pearled velvet. Kent who tied the flowers to my arms at both my weddings and said, *My lady*, and flushed with happiness, both times.

He has fallen into nothing. Into that hole on the page.

Lear's other death is with me, too, the planned one. We had designed it, out of caution, years ago, before I had the girls. Kings die; battle scars thicken and push out fluid; a stallion cracks a lung open, like a pear. You must be sensible. So we laid out the lines of it: the rings of thanes that would process for the funeral, the vaulting spear and sword across his breast, even the pale flowers to be knotted on shields, bone-white. (He wanted feasts and fire-jumping – he was very young then. *Get the archbishop to lay on a holiday! Make sure they bring out the jesters.* I told him they would be in no mood, and he laughed.) As the girls were born they were studded into the vision: Goneril on his right hand, then Regan on his left. The young Cordelia kneeling, at the foot of the casket.

As I lie still in the abbey room I can sense those griefs lapping over one another. Like ice-floes on the river, flanking and bruising.

A surface I cannot walk upon. And yet must, now, hour after hour after hour.

I feel blind, my old eyes are so sore; I must go through this by feel alone.

★ ★ ★

Kent. Kent, I am in my bed at fifty-five, and at the same moment I am seventeen in the garden of my first husband the young king, on my knees. Digging. My body holds both these things.

Afternoon, crushing down the camomile-paths of the royal palace grounds, and empty paths of white gravel curling between the hedges, soft with dust, and my young hands were in the earth. I had taken off the pink-laced gloves I loved; they lay on the grass.

All the grief of my self was in my digging. I had been married two months; my new king had the outrageous beauty of a fresco, and was inclined to forget my presence, when I sat beside him. I was fed sugared quinces by maids to fatten me for children, and sat and rotted with frantic love; he prayed for hours in sackcloth.

That afternoon – it was a green, anxious spring – he had wanted a purgative for a stomach-ache, *To cleanse my body*, he said; we had none. Wormwood galls, blister-bodies, heartsease, no use. The palace searched everywhere, while he lay pleasurably suffering. All his small life he would walk cheerfully into pain, expecting to be gilded by God for it.

Desperate, I had come out to the flower-gardens and looked for irises – their blue tongues.

Kent found me there, under the massed roses. A flotilla of dark scent. *Queen?* He would unfold into genteel boniness later, but then was all lean flesh and translucent veins around the eyes.

Large-kneed and uncertain. Had known me only weeks, the new wife of the boy-king he served.

I looked up, and we saw each other. Fresh as ivory struck by a knife. Weak little people, both a bit ugly.

I want the roots, I said, gesturing at the flailing plants in high wind, which mocked in their intense vitality the lush fertile pollen-heads. The petals were shocking. *The king can have them boiled in milk. The mother superior did it at my convent, when I was a child.*

Could the gardeners? Your hands— He was biting the inside of his cheek. Indeed there were gardeners, watching from the paths. Small peach-skinned queen in the undergrowth, digging perhaps a magic thing, a mandrake root. They were a contented audience: royals were hilariously unknowable and, besides, they saw my will in the shape of my body, my uncovered arms, and kept off.

I will do it myself, I said, high-voiced. He saw and understood that this was my service. I would prove my love in humiliation. And dirt to the elbows. And so show my adoration to my holy husband, bearing him the little round bulbs on a platter, like Saint Agatha's breasts.

He breathed in, politely. *I see. But the ground is hard. Perhaps a knife?* And came down into the earth with me. His best service hose would ruin, I knew, and sag at the knees.

Chipping intent at the root-parts, levering out the flourishing flowers into my hands, which we severed between us, sawing away the remarkable pale root, like an angry moon. Our hands, our hands, filling with blind eyes, the sap of brutalised iris-throats.

Occasionally a rose would burst and collapse over us, and I would want so much to cry. My love for that first husband swelled in my lungs. Already I was understanding that I could not triumph, that his frail golden body in that bed would give me only scraps, fragments, but I loved in hope. And here was a garden full of flowers, and a friend.

Kent, who came in behind me as I walked in dirt-smeared holding my crop aloft, astonishing the kitchen-boys, and watched as I fed the purgative in sips to the king, and held the bowl for his relieved vomiting. For ever ago.

That king is dead near thirty years. Lear is dead. Kent, where are you?

★ ★ ★

The wind shifts the curtain. The bells sound.

Into the afternoon I lie here and am assaulted by this. Oh, here is a woman watch her body it will not move again. Watch her head it will not crack open though the agony comes up from the root of her.

The abbess has given warning: *None disturb.* I turn from books, from food, from light, from sleep, from prayer. Today I would not rise from bed, rolled in my blankets like an infant, and refused even spoons of soup. Ruth despairs of me and lays her hands behind her back in blank defeat. The turning is perhaps the only true thing: I am a gyre, a small knot of wind unworking itself in a field. No no no no.

Dead and dead and dead. Under the crack of this grief I feel myself slipping out into other forms: animal, vegetal, sea-spill foam, winter wind, a boar roaring blue in the dark. Then at least I would fit the tales: story-woman, death's head, corrupting flesh at the touch. Oh, I know them, every ghost has good ears.

I lie and dream. I knew this place, this abbey, by writing before I ever saw it made. Shapes outlined on a map: somehow men had brought the squares and polite stone of civilisation to the Pictish north, its cool becks and white acres of cloud. Mountains that would not speak. Against that blankness, that landscape of refusal, here is drawn the blotted rectangle of the cloisters, heavy on one side with abbey and refectory. It is the centre, it buds out into other apartments: a strip-thin infirmary, visiting-quarters for nobility, a miniature garden for abbesses to pace in line with God. Dovecotes, bands denoting vegetable-beds. Around the buildings a loop of ink, a wall, hooping it inward, then purple patches signalling fields, in the abbey's service.

Over years expansions were paid from Lear's purse: a wider orchard, more stewponds, carp to be brought in wooden tubs from the lower rivers to breed. Green-eyed carp, golden-eyed, seething in the ponds as nuns scattered grain on the surface. In return for his largesse, prayers flowed, thick as honey, for his heart, his health, for his life to be brimful with son after son. I have seen none of this, except on paper.

I paid for that hanging, I told the abbess once, when she wanted to replace the old tapestry in the chapel – God, angels, various holy beings in attitudes of indignation at something, badly done – with a new, expensive working. *As I live it remains where it is. For my comfort.* She acceded. The tapestry was ugly as God's wounds but the point was made. She is a natural servant, she has always known; I am the stronger, the better – I have the greater subtlety. She has bowed her head to my will, fifteen years' worth, and come out shining.

Do people know of the place of their greatest suffering when they come to it? No, not in logic. But entering by force I should have heard some small thing, some sound, crying from the stone. *Beware, this place holds black news, beware.*

Oh, but what other sort of news is there for mothers? We create mortal things, perilous, prone to damage (Regan's long scar from a horse-fall, Cordelia with her frail skull like a boiled apple). The seed of death is on children from their birth. I hold the blanket against my bare stomach.

Goneril as a girl was quiet, with her own mysteries. Spoke late,

21

and only in brief measures, but for years in her youth would come slyly to me, to entrust me with a feather, a black stone, a husk of wheat. I was her repository for treasured things; my pockets swelled with her apothecary's store of scraps. And then would tell me, after her gatherings had stretched over weeks or months, that today was the chosen day, and process with me to arrange all these selected parts on open ground.

Little wild witch. She laid out feathers in long curves across the bridge near the summer palace, ringed them with stones. I stood guard (and the Fool, who came also, carrying the excess in all seriousness) but could not approach her logic.

She had a horse's tail once, lopped at the base, where it was bound with rope. Some stabler's cure for a mare's temper. Half hardened with mud, longer than herself, and she laid it in the sun and fussed over it. And I looked at her bending, the line of skin visible in the parting of her hair, and the soft space behind her knees, and thought, *You will die. It is inevitable. You are to die, daughter, one day.*

When she passed I took her wrist and kissed it, and she took it back from me with angry swiftness. My mother-love lapped at her body but did not enter it. She had her business, and I was to follow, carrying the horse's tail, its brute tendrils flicking at my legs like a switch.

Pain is endless renewal. Pain is a discovery at every fresh breath: oh! Here is agony again. I had forgotten. Breathe: oh! Here it is, once more.

3.

On the fifth morning, as the seal of the sun rises (which it continues to do, which is affronting, and the day pushing out like a boat into the morning), I begin to gather myself slightly, and to think: Out. Out into the world.

My bundles. I am packed, folded. I will be ready. The call has not come, out of mercy for me. But it may come at any time. I expect it and will be prepared. The abbess will say, *And your protection here is ended; the king is dead; you have served your punishment, and now must go.* And so open the gates for me to stumble out white as a newborn and gaping. Though I have been so kind to her, though I have layered my metal into her, over years, and so strengthened her, from the inside.

I wonder if the land knows. That the press of a single king is no longer on it, and so it is split from its brothers. What God imparts to stone of its ownership, to water.

The collection of lands was Lear's great aim, in the years before my exile. Rich soil, forests we would never see, stretching to the necks of mountains. He studded his counties with castles and we moved between them through the seasons: rich summers in the cooler north, among heather and the bee-wild slopes, then south for winter, in wide pale palaces that swam with sun. The populace felt us move in rhythm. There were crowds on every road: to be thrown favours, coins, sugar. Women stood among the flowering gorse with their heads covered and sang for us, in the dark evening.

To be in Lear's country, to be one of his peoples! They will not see his like again.

Lear was a lover of wholeness, of adding; I learned this quickly. Would not halve a biscuit to place in my mouth and his: he thought it insulting. Would give us both wholes, layer them with curds and meat, and let us both feast. If there was one biscuit he ate alone.

And now it's likely split down map-lines, and squabbled over. When every foot on them for years had held his crest on the sole. I think of the gorse-women, of the men on the roads, pausing at the plough with their eyes shadowed, to see us pass.

I remember the map-room, when the girls were children, long before Cordelia was born. Kent in his bronze-flecked armour, trusted beyond all else, was looking at an image of the kingdom two men wide, holding a single fingertip over an inked part. The walls were striped with shadow. *You could give a little corner here. The head of the army has been loyal.* Water, corn, air.

No. Let him be satisfied with wealth. I gave it fairly. Lear was quarrelsome.

As you say, said Kent.

It is beautiful. Look at this! Lear swept his hand across the map. *Lear's world. All the mass together. Connected. What a thing! Ah.* He had noticed me, standing at the door. *Queen?*

I had come in and was silent. Tolling my pearls in my hands. He looked and he knew. *Lost, then?*

Yes.

I could not go further. He filled the map for a son to inherit, unadulterated, edge to edge, the full swathe under a single sky. And my gut would not hold now: each fresh baby would flee, this one barely a month in. Sweet-spotting on my petticoats that morning. Hopes perhaps smothering it in the womb.

The death moved between us, split down the middle. Halved biscuit on a plate. I shut my eyes.

I heard Kent. *I am so sorry.*

Lear sighed. He was beautiful in his ripening age, thick-haired and red-mouthed. Autumn's king. *How will you administer to this leviathan country if I die? I can barely keep it in hand.*

I smiled, though my throat was full of bile. *Kent and I will keep it together.* Kent and I, brothers, manning the dispatches and hard-headed diplomats!

Lear snorted. *So you say. Or else you'll fall to some conspiracy. A little dagger in the night, and you two will be in a box, and a new man on my throne!*

I smoothed my dress and was shaking, placid. *Good luck to them who try.* He had suspicion black in him, in those days. A king with only two daughters looks like good game: plump, hapless. So plotters emerged, and would lunge, and discover in their mouths instead of placid flesh a snake-head, thrashing.

No, Lear gave nothing. Or else everything.

He was tired, now. *Perhaps you'll pull off bits and sell them. So generous, both of you.* Kent laughed at that, as he gathered the maps. It was true: the Fool teased Kent about his bountifulness to peasants, to boys wanting alms, little stable-hands. No children of his own, he told me, so the world in general might as well feel the lushness of his luck. Other courtiers distrusted it, but Lear and I knew what it was: just a good man, throwing coins.

Lear was in his furs, holding his throat. All his life he would have eyelashes that drooped to his cheekbones, petal-curled. *Do you know what they eat in monasteries on fish days, Queen?*

No, King. I had come to his arm. We were close at that time.

The archbishop told me. The babes pulled from a ewe's stomach. Tiny lambs. He showed me the size between two fingers. Barely the width of a child's fist. *Apparently their eyes are like small fruits. I would like to taste them, one day.*

25

I will ask the kitchen.

He had my arm; we were arranging our robes to process. *You see, don't you?* he said. *Taking the lambs from the belly. Killing the ewe. It's waste! To divide a country poorly produces waste.* His hand, tracing the air. As if along skin. *I do not know how to do it well.*

Yes, King. May it never come to that. I must have looked ghostly, as he kissed my forehead.

Ah, be hopeful, wench. There are sons in you yet. You'll give me four in a row and I'll have to give three to the priesthood.

I have always been the kind to turn brutal luck to a better chance. I lie, and plan.

Out.

★ ★ ★

The abbey I know is one of the biggest. As befits me, as befits my state. It is huge, white, astonishing. Walls within walls: abbey, cloister, refectory, inner gardens striped with grasses. In the dark it seems collapsible, abundant with lines, as if children had assembled a play-place of placards. *One push,* it whispers.

By daylight, as in this blooming day, it regains its solidity. Rich and thick as cake or hard cheese. Boxes inside other boxes open, reveal their intimacy; the gates between the walled gardens unlock, and sweetness passes through.

Other queens have had their initials laid in the nape of the stone in the courtyard, in iron, white as holy bone. Faces in the glass rose windows, reaching. Sweet-mouthed in painted glass.

Should they start sketching me for my window? I suggested to the abbess once. She smiled. Did not say what we knew: exiled queens are a burned-out window, a hole in a face.

I have been the abbess's friend chiefly. The nuns are known by sight from my window but I have remained aloof, a sparsely seen thing, like a rare animal in a king's forest. *Watch it pass, keep well off for fear, you may catch it again later in the season.* An exile does not flaunt presence. One companion, of suitable rank, suffices, and the servants. Ruth is a good girl.

Segments, pieces. Out of the casement one sees the curve of the abbess's orchards, the thin path to the chapel, the infirmary's high white walls with visible pink insides, like a fruit. My circled life: chapel, chamber, walks in the dark garden. As the trout in the stew-ponds, swimming in their miniature world, the span of one man's arms.

The abbess has arrived. Ruth had told her, *She is awake*, and so she has sat by the bed, with her psalter, bound by her gentleness, her etiquette. She has sweet skin, the kind that comes from full hours indoors and (I know) an occasional, secretive milk-bath. Dairy-buckets in her room, the servants haul them fresh, and hours afterwards empty them rose-scented and cold into the yard. I think of her head emerging from the white to look upward, her pale shift rounded and flush with milk.

Perhaps concealing through kindness the edict: out. Out. Not knowing that it is my own secret-self thought now, germinating. But I will not tell her. People who intend to punish you are best not informed that you desire to be punished.

She clears her throat. Nervous. *It is a rare day. This late in the year. Let me take you into the abbey a little. The wells that we planned, last autumn: they're bringing up water. The nuns enjoy them.*

She is an opaque thing. Glows, like a cluster of grapes. She is only grazing forty; for an abbess that is indecently youthful. She would have held me back from hearing the full news from the messenger – blood, ruin, my husband mad as a frog, my two eldest girls battling over something (nothing) that drew them into death – but I would not be held. I heard all. They were stupid, the girls. Always stupid.

I have slept little. I feel a different species. Wolf, dog, fox. *I thank you. Company is likely not to give me great solace. Wells even less.* Who would speak to nuns of emotions? Better argue a point on politics with a piece of wood.

Not for company. For something else, perhaps. She searches for other reasons. I know that death frightens her. Fearing a bite, that I might lunge and do some injury. *To see the places you have built. The new kitchen gardens. We plotted them well, and they bore good crops, this harvest.*

It is a tender thought. I have been an anchoress: I have ruled this abbey out of sight, crippled into silence, disfigured behind a screen. Put me in any place and I will warp it to my weight; I will shape it out though it never hears my voice. And yet, of course, it is stupid.

Rows of onions and carrots. I will be succoured of the loss of all my children immediately. You are brilliant.

This is the first of it: the grief as the weapon. I can fling out poniards, the woman on the pyre, aflame to my hairline. The abbess flickers for a brief moment. Then smiles.

You forget the lettuces. They are remarkable at this time of year.

I would never forget the lettuces. I am grave.

She at least persuades me into a dress and into the yard. Ruth loops buttons loosely, hurrying, before my mood shifts and I am engulfed again. My train is white veils tacked together from the laundry. Long rips along a thigh. Another on the stomach.

We do not talk. A cart is being unloaded and men are hauling vast cloth bundles (meat, she says; the grazing lands of the abbey are considerable) into what must be the kitchen passage; three nuns walk to the infirmary arguing a problem. They are careful to look at a place just over my head: seeing me clearly may set them alight. It is bright, and clear; the mud slips at my ankles. (Are women mud-made? Regan, coming in at the age of twelve with white clay to her neck, delighted: *Look, I am a statue. I will be beautiful.*) I stand with the abbess's arm in my sleeve. Here is a place that takes Lear's death, hears it, and throws it off, so much dross. Passages of state (deaths of kings, of the children of kings) pass through the packages of meat, without touching. They are embedded in the work of themselves. The abbess herself is meat; her knuckles show dark pink.

I breathe. I breathe the silver light, the meat-weight, the green fingers of sky. The lesson of this is obscure to me, God. You show me a place that I have never seen, that I will shortly leave – for what?

I decide it is a message for me. May I be as unassailable as the hunk of flesh hauled by shoulder down to the spit, Lord. May I be that strong, and hard, in the days to come.

That is enough.

The abbess holds me by the arm. She is distracted; my grief engulfs her, as if she has part-ownership of it. Her vision of correct behaviour and its variations, its holes and slips and violences, swims; gets in the way of the world. Her knee knocks against mine.

I feel a wash of anger, like ink over vellum. It is a game I will not play.

When do you believe the snows will be, this year?

The snows? She is looking at our feet, stepping over the mud. *Oh, early. You can have more furs. We will get a good ermine, from William's boy in town, when he calls. Or some rabbit – they had lovely rabbit gloves last year.*

Because *I should be off before they come, if possible.* Out. Out, and the landscape of bones, of scapulae. And the clearest opportunity I will have, before the winds come over the mountain and the abbey descends into its winter burrow.

Yes. Sister Maria, would you take the other arm, please? She has not heard; is still thinking, about furs, about slipping her small hand inside a fold of rabbit and feeling perhaps its heart murmuring inside. My mouth is dry with resentment. I am a parcel, which she is handing up the stairs.

Another nun comes, and raises my elbow; we ascend.

Boots, I think. Well-soled shoes.

*　*　*

Queen, they are taking you.

What?

I am to rouse and dress you. And fit you for travelling.

Let me see the king.

You shall not.

Kent! Call Kent to me. Call the Fool.

The Fool is your daughters' and will not come.

Am I to be so disgraced? No reason? No help? What am I said to have done? Let me fight in the open, as an honourable woman. Let me know the offence.

You know your crime.

On my God, I know nothing. I know nothing! May your houses feel your betrayal against your queen, to the last maggot in the flour-bin. Daughter! Regan. Regan. Look at me. Look at me.

She will not. She told of your shame.

I have none. I know nothing. Lear. Lear, come to me.

Step onto the cart, now. You've a long ride.

*　*　*

Did you want me, Lear, as you drifted and were borne towards death? Did your body betray you into primal need, for the woman who opened and gave you daughters, will, the lines and structures of your thought? Did you reach for me and encounter only traitor

30

air? I think you didn't. I think pride kept you, and killed you, and flayed you down. And you died without my grace, and hadn't even the flickering sense to regret it.

Night, again. The nuns process, the evening offices. Then silence.

If she will be a coward, I will not. There is a brave shape waiting here, for somebody to assume it, and I can form my body to fit.

By the time it occurs to me that I am leaving I am halfway across the courtyard, approaching the night gate. Its vast weight pressing against the dark.

In my pockets small coin, a candle. All my folded precious parts, looped to my body, against rib and flank and back. Veil of bedlinen. Fifteen years. Sturdy boots I found, I will walk to their graves. I will walk to where they have been laid down, and I will lie down too, and tend the burial plot, eating sweet roots and the white bulbs of grass, and pressing my hands to the earth. In the summertime the graves will attract bees like a crown.

This is what women do. If my daughters had ever listened to me, they would know.

Where have they buried them? England, England, the messenger said, far south, in the chalk. White soil that will hold their bodies until their souls turn pellucid and run through it in rivers. Here the northern soils run red over your hand. Well, and I will walk there. Pilgrims have travelled to Compostela with less fervour and more insignificant purpose.

Here, here is the gate: which I have not passed since I was first borne through it, fifteen years ago. Milk still darkening the scarves at my chest, then, for Cordelia. Weeks, before it dried up; I gave it into bowls; Ruth gently pressed it from me and buried it at night. It was barely three months since the birth, and my belly

31

barely concave and still soft as dough. I touch the gate's cool wood, the dark fastening-bar that was lowered at compline.

I have been so quiet, I have done my penance fivefold. Nobody could tell me for what, and I took the punishment in any case, because the king my love required it. Skewer through my temple, above my ear. *Outside these walls, wilderness,* says the abbess, when novices come. *Within, God.* But I want to be without, a roofless woman, alone on the heath and mountain roads, moving to her family and then past them to what lies beyond. God may find me there if He dares. And if the abbess is too milk-weak for the cut of the blade, I will reach up and bring it down upon myself.

In the distance there is a torch-flare. It throws my hand into relief, the shadow of me.

Ho, a light here!

As I turn she is coming down and there are torches at her head. The abbess, who has seen. Perhaps there was a guard, for this, to observe me in case I attempted it. She has assembled herself quickly from sleep, is barefoot; small pink feet. Pink like the underside of a hare-foot.

There are others, faces gathered at the edges of the light. Nuns. They are astonished by me, I think: the monstrous woman they have seen just once, the hidden queen. Holy girls in torchlight, scraped open with fear. Perhaps they think I have tentacles, snake-throat, a black tongue. I would bare my teeth at them; I would be mythic.

What are you doing? says the abbess.

I have no further business here. I am formal, out of embarrassment, some sense drifting in that this is not proper, to be stood slinking by a gate in the dark. *As you well know. I would go.*

The nuns do not shift. Ravenous in their curiosity, seeking to devour me gently. I cannot blame them. People would wait by the roadside for a glimpse of my golden hand in a window – a maidservant's sometimes, paraded in my glove and rings, while I rested on the carriage-floor. Queen-bodies are desired, even when secret.

And go where? Her voice is dark with sleep and something else. Slow stubbornness. *It is not a good hour. You should be in bed, you are still recovering from your tragedy. The lady Ruth says—*

A grind of anger in me that has been moving against my bone and flesh all the day. Tragedy! Naming it thus, neatly, is cheek. As if words could hold it. Language runs up against it and draws back, maimed. *I would like to tax your kindness no further.*

Fifteen years I have been with her, in my three rooms. *You are to pray for the soul of the king,* they said. *You are to remain.* Until summoned. Until the sky falls in. Until Lear is a whisper and his soul is beyond your reach.

The abbess ignores me. *You are only recently well. You should be resting,* she repeats. I have astonished her: she is grappling with an oddity, like a strange animal with unknown wants. *And you barely have a cloak! Not even a fur!*

I thought furs would be too heavy, I say simply.

And think, To crawl to my children in dead sackcloth, to grieve my king in rags, that seems holy, that seems full of worth.

Abbess, what is it? Has somebody come? A face, some stewardess or nun, swimming into the circle of light to speak. Pale carp, I think. She has a thin face, hard-lined.

None of the other women dare talk, but are shivering, bound to watch me. I think of funeral-mourners in Lear's villages, circling the byre all night to bind the corpse's ghost to earth, holding its edges with small red stones.

Nobody has come. Nobody is going, either. She stands thinking. Then looks to the women. *Why do you wait still, sisters? Go in!*

The women remain fixed, in their clot of skirts. Peering, their faces like ovals in the darkness. There is a sour current here. One

I do not understand. Then the thin-faced woman says something, indistinct but sharp as broken slate, and they bend, begin to move away.

The abbess turns her face from this, and extends an arm. *Come to my chambers. It's not long till lauds, at least.*

I am led. The gate I can hear is checked behind me. Perhaps I have gnawed it, perhaps my rage has rotted the wood. Careful, I have left a stain, I might say.

The women move away. I hear them whisper; they feel a crack in the nature of things, perhaps, seeing me in close quarters, hearing me speak. As if the monkeys and angels from the illuminated manuscripts had stood, and stretched, and leaped into the light.

You are vexed, I say, when the abbess shuts the door to her rooms and tells her servants to go.

After a public scene she seeks the safety of mutual politeness. *I am surprised.*

I had intended it to be easier. Since I must leave, and you are so kind. We have been friends.

You must leave? I did not say so.

I had expected it.

She starts to laugh. Her lovely throat rises and in that moment I see the other life, the merchant's wife, ornamental, in a salon fanning through the sultry evening. Roses at her neck. The halved self of the holy woman. Instead here; instead now. The women gathering at the gate, unlistening; a leader whose country is shifting, beneath her. I had thought her stronger than this. But no matter.

You are unaccountable. No. This is the house of God. You are welcome, as you were welcome years ago. And, she adds, *self-slaughter is a mortal sin, which is what would amount, if you started out in the night alone. For — where?*

Dover.

Dover?

To their graves. Conventional manners, I explain, in the logical voice I used when young Regan ate a bad cheese and wondered why she was ill, *dictate that wives generally mourn their husbands and children in person.* I am welcome, but perhaps I do not wish to stay.

Conventional husbands, she says quietly, *do not put their wives into abbeys and treat them as condemned wood.* She looks at my hands. *Unfit even for burning.*

Are you speaking darkly of the dead? That will need a confession. I am poisonous. Have been intimate with her for fifteen years. Only her, and Ruth, picking lice from my hair and wringing out my month-blood in the basin. So there is canny reading here; so there is a mutual language, with absent spaces, sigils for deep and unspoken hurt.

I am only ever your friend. She is upset. Between Lear and my body, then, she picks my body, but only because she never met him, never saw him, never felt the great tidal wash of his love and will. *Do you believe that I will allow you out alone into strange countryside with no map and no light, to fall into a ditch or be done to death by passing vagrants? I could not.*

At least the wolves wouldn't eat me, I say, taking the offered cup of milk and lifting it to drink; we have warmed it, as we always do together. *I have no good flesh left, I may as well be condemned.*

You are not condemned.

You cannot know that. I have shut my eyes. *We do not even know what my crime was.*

My crime, we call it, my vice; the unknown offence that led to my sentence, here. *Pray for the king's soul,* they said, and left me at her gate. No word, no judgement pinned to my heart with the wax seal of the king. The open space of it, that writhes.

No, she says. *We do not know.* Milk stirs under her, her breath.

I wrote: hundreds of letters, sealed with my ring on weeping

35

wax, to courtiers, to old Gloucester the knight with his two boys (envious, envious of him always), to the king, to the king. The blind eye of the question: what have I done? Tell me. And gathered only a crop of dead silence. As if I were burned ground, as if famine was in my body, and wind that threw dust into the air.

After five years of it — she knows — I went silent, put ash into my mouth, devoted myself to the thought of plump nuns and flourishing carrot-gardens I could not see, sat quietly. Enough time, perhaps, and silence, and Lear would forgive, and consider me cleansed. Like a rotted skull lying in the grass till the bone shone white as pearl.

Yet in the evenings the abbess and I still wore it smooth, this question of the offence. We palmed it so often that it gave nothing to the hand, like the hand or foot of a statue worn to gilt. On Lear's statues they touched the royal mouth, the tongue. So that his lips were gold. The thought pricks my throat.

You know all of this. We had our orders, to keep and succour your body and soul, which were sufficient. And no other word. You know I believe it cruel, to send you here without explanation. She was not frank when Lear was alive, but I knew that she prayed for his soul, because she believed it had a streak of blood, dark as midwinter. *This is very old meat that we are chewing.*

Well, the gaoler is dead. You may turn the key.

She looks at me. *You were never barricaded in this place. You know that.*

No. Only held by promise. The idea that perhaps this was purgative, the long scrape of whip across the back. Salt into flayed scourge-wounds.

I must strive at least to appear conciliatory, and return one of her ideas to her, as a compliment. *You mentioned furs. I do think it wise. To make the journey as it begins to cool.*

Down to England.

Yes.

And after you have seen the place where they died? She has not sipped her milk. *What then?*

I will find their graves.

And then?

This I contemplate, rolling it in my hand. An orange, a ball. Act my banishment. Do honour to the graves, find the details of how and where and when. Throw dust upon my hair. And then raise myself, and breathe, and then?

I always saw the multiplicity of things, Lear loving this in me: the many threads of event and consequence, the tracing of harvest-fail or war-victory or fall of rain, that could shape his fortune. Futures spun out from the loom of his body. Now I am surrounded by nobody, the loom is myself; and I may make a deeply rich thing, yes, I may. I am the first of my family, and last to survive, because I alone, as I always told them, was cunning; I alone had the luck.

Goneril didn't believe me. Now perhaps she would.

Kent. I think, Perhaps Kent. Yes. I may yet find him. He must be somewhere, lacquered in grief, enamelled with it in a dark wood. Or else laid in the soil, his body over Lear's, shield across the old and broken chest.

It is a gold thread through dark cloth, this idea: to seek Kent, to cup his face between my palms. Yes. It is not known that he is dead. The others have sunk beneath the earth; I am beginning, slowly, to accept this, to grasp it with both hands. I am moving into this terrible knowledge, a river flowing into dark ground. Kent, though, lived through everything, the madness and death of my first husband, Lear's wars, the careening ship of our marriage, the births of the princesses. Kent, hollow at the temples and older than I – but quick, slipping through fate like an otter. He may have survived. And be searching, perhaps, for me, in what remains.

You see there are bigger questions than furs, the abbess is saying. *Here in this place we are close, and safe. For you to consider your choices, and your friends.*

I have no friends. If I did, I would not be suspended here in agony, like a fish on a pike.

Perhaps you were exiled because you are horrendously rude.

I hit her. The flat of my palm resounds, it cracks, the sky hears it, the dead hear it. The milk is on my knee, sodden. I alone can accuse myself: I am the court of my own judgement, I hold the rope of execution. Nobody else may dare. Not even Lear.

She has down on her face like my mother, like the girls when they were small. It waves in the torchlight. Soft, smashed like fruit, her face. Blood clenches at her throat. I do not breathe quickly. I am not moved.

A breadth of silence. The milk cools over my legs. Then I give my hand. She kisses it in apology, with the grace of long performance. A scene we know: we inhabit it frequently.

We both know I would scale the wall, would raise the bar alone and slip into the dark. Order or not.

I will consider, I say. *And think of my friends. As you say.*

★ ★ ★

In my cell Ruth waits. Has slept in the hollow at the bottom of my bed these years, and likely woke missing the warm of my resting body.

Would you have left without me? Plaintive. Like all of her class, she has simple emotions. Happiness. Misery. Fear.

I choose to lie. *I would never have left without you.* And hand my cloak to her. It is kindness, it is long-worn gentle feeling, that means I deliberately do not see her face's wetness, the lift of relief in her hands as she folds the cloth.

38

4.

In the night when I wake I take the familiar walk through my head. The long day, the final day before I was exiled. At the kernel of my sane soul will still be this day, this day, the treading path of it, the little coiled ring of hours. So well do I know it that it will be the last, if my thought becomes crumbled sugar, the last solid thing to come loose and finally fall.

It was freshly spring. Cordelia at three months was ill, but moving out of serious sickness. It was clear now that she would live, but be sickly, and perhaps die later, brittle to the point of her skull. Nails small as cupped shells.

I spent the morning with her, having not slept with the king; we had separate bedchambers, had not visited each other nightly since the tail of the pregnancy. His terror of touching me for fear of distressing the cargo became a sullen punishment. I could no longer gather my girls to warm me: they were married and prickly otherwise. Cordelia and I shared a translucence, both of us open to the air, cracked in. Her mouth purple as sin.

Of course I missed him. I am too old for the weakness of untruth. To sleep and wake with a man: your dreams drift into one another, you hear his nocturnal whimpers and the soft underside of his fears. Lear asleep was still, though rusted and grizzled at the edges, thin in the shank, handsome, divested of the spoiled will that ruined our days. A night lain belly to back restores great balance in marriage.

So I was sleeping alone, and watched Cordelia. Both older daughters had arrived the previous day, avoided their miniature sister entirely, and had spent their time in their respective bowers. Regan had brought a new kitten; I remember that. I had seen it in her cloaks, small flat-faced milk-thing, and made a cool remark about the wisdom of purloining the children of other species if one cannot provide one's own. She had been married years. That girl! Her husband was young and thorough; it must have been her own doing. The kitten cried, and she turned away her face to whisper to a maid, as usual.

I have trapped every passing breath of this day. I have held it in sap, in the amber the crusading boys brought down on the trade routes from the East, fragile, all the parts of its body preserved and floating. It lies in my head; it weighs me down.

So Regan, with her kitten. Goneril elsewhere, reading. Sulking, like her father. I wove in the afternoon, listened to a cook, tossed some rope with my best dog, the white bitch Avril. (Her fate after my fate is too aching to contemplate, still. Lear would kill the horses of the men who betrayed him, lay them out with their throats exposed in the yard to scream at the sky. I told him to do it.)

And the meal in the evening was thin but placid. The girls housed in their own thoughts, Lear carousing with knights and picking at his specially made dish (a small appetite, but he could fool gluttons into believing themselves out-eaten), Kent with another courtier arguing. I wish above all I had spoken to Kent, a little. A fish day, eel in green garlic, baked lampreys in white wine.

And then bed: a kiss on the palm for my silent girls, a nod to Lear who roared at a joke, and then retreat. As I left Regan was rising, to bring the king his wine.

And in the night – this rousing. Thrust out, a cart waiting to escort me, with fresh horses. Clearly the night had been brewing foul for hours, something hardening in darkness, tightening. The maids still tying secrets to me, jewels, a comb, as I came down the stairs, one in desperation knotted a thing to my hair — what? It was lost. Ruth, new in court and crude as half-moulded coin, was lifted in alongside, shivering. Her body flat and cold as winter wood was no comfort against mine, I thought her a gaoler and would not speak.

Cordelia adrift in her sea of lace. To be alone in that house, babe — you must have grown up canny as an eel.

Has any one day been more sifted to find a point, a waver? And yet nothing. I saw a woman once drowned, the work of a moment: fine, fit, gesturing at a passing boat with a laugh, then caught under a wave and taken. It looked a trick of the daylight: we waited as if for the joke to unravel, her face to appear bright and brined out of the green waves that baffled the breeze, still laughing. But no. Out of the noonday, said my first husband, so comes the unseen wrath of God. So with me.

And old minds sway and gape like tooth-holes. Lear's father wandering the corn, believing himself a bird. Perhaps now it will begin passing from me. Amble through the grass with parts of the mind coming away. Like clothing, like shell.

I think, *Now he will never tell me*, and in the night I cry aloud, and Ruth frowns in her sleep as if at the pass of thunder.

★   ★   ★

Daylight: thud on skull. Ruth, on her knees blowing embers in the fireplace. Neat line of parted hair bisecting her flat head. Strike it just there and it would cleave nicely, like a chestnut.

Ruth! To be prised from the court was not so much a hardship in some ways. But with such a woman! Even when she arrived twenty years ago to live at Lear's court as a little serving-maid, I saw: sheep-eyed, staring at soldiers and glitter, gnawing at her own hand. Face of a fresh-scrubbed parsnip. Once in a dark room

41

I observed her lift an ivory shoe-patten to her mouth and bite it, wonderingly.

The embers defy her; she coughs. Warms old milk, skims away the skin with a finger.

Sent to court to marry a good man from the kitchens, perhaps, or be somebody's little mistress, fat as a capon. Instead she's nunneried with me! Too bad for your father's hopes, Ruth. Still, we approach virginity together here now: you preserving your maidenhead till it rattles like a seed-head with age, myself possibly thickening back into a hymen, from lack of use.

Sending me away Lear could have given me any attendant, Magdalena, or witty Emmeline, but he gave me Ruth. Clod-girl. Cabbage of the court. And so I knew my disgrace.

She comes to give me my drink — every morning, herself only just muttering into wakefulness, mouth moving. Even just-awake she has her fixed expression of anxious servitude, like raw meat on a plate. There are women like Ruth in altarpieces she has never seen, Italian. Background figures, shouldering a plough or a scythe in kerchiefs as Christ rides across the foreground, twice their size, picked in gold leaf. Women who perhaps observe the holy with gentle incomprehension, hand to their brow; or else throw their full attention into their work, sweating and shadowless in eternal sun, as God passes by. And will bear fifteen parsnip-children, the artist foretells, and so have done their debt to the Lord.

I feel incredulous pity. I am the only parsnip-child for you, Ruth, and you have served every part of my queen-body, all of its rooms. And so perhaps would earn a place in the foreground now, a fleck of gold leaf from my royal hand, which would be painted as wide as your forehead.

I drink.

★　★　★

Lear, you old ghoul, softening down in the soil, sprouting a mushroom from your eye, listen: you tried to do me wrong, you thought you'd bury me. After all I gave. And look how I took your punishment and made it thicken, made it bud down to the root with new growth, furred and greening. This abbey: fifteen years, and through the thin body of the abbess I spoke and formed it, and from my word came plenitude. Benison. Look, stupid boy, what I wrought, as I once did for you. This place hoards me like a relic, like the Cross flowing with sap! Richness that is a wise and well-born woman: they recognised it; the abbess was sensible. They see what you did not.

I am not a vengeful woman, but if you lived and knew my thoughts, Lear, you would cry out in the night, and feel fear close around your neck.

Out.

Today the abbess is persuading me to accompany her on a tour. Outside the gates. The sun, she says, the air, it is still like summer. *It will make you feel a little better, to be out. You know these fields, you have sold their harvest year after year.* As if distraction were not somehow violent! As if grief were not under my skin, bursting. To compensate I make Ruth draw the strings of my gown tight, tight. Keep the body in.

I fear – what do I fear? That I am too heavy; that I will step into the brittle abbey with its cast of serenity, its smooth nicked-lace stone, and smash it, push it under my body and watch it crack.

Listen. High-born women are not supposed to weigh like this. We are meant to have thin bones, a waist you could wrap in a single fabric-bolt. When I was young in the convent they talked about us as light objects: vases, glass and gold leaf. *She will make a good prize.* Formed out of rude clay into delicate things. Whereas I feel enormous, carrying immensity. Sustaining so many weights:

men, crowns, child-full bellies. I press the white mourning-dress on my arms. The underside has yellowed already, like a cow's tongue.

A mother-of-pearl sky. It is sext, the high point; one blinks into it. Freshness flipping the clouds, crushing the edges of the light. The open morning strikes the rigid walls, the faces of the nuns. This abbey was lifted out of ancient pink rock, hacked at the coast and hauled overland to this stark place. It glows red in most light, like flesh; the tower of the chapel gathers sunlight, flings it outwards. God's gold splashing down the stone; through the doorways, open halls seem to be fixed in a perpetual glare, grazed to their very back walls with light, tapestries sun-bleached and indistinct. Spaces without density. It makes me feckless and itches my pelt. I want angles, niches, rows of doors, moss and moist shadow.

Goneril had this too, a love for avoidance and tight gaps. Curling herself in linen-trunks, pantries, between sacks of grain. This was her vengeance, if you slapped or scolded: to disappear, hibernate with only her own breath between her hands. It was an uncomplicated instinct. To be secret.

I stand and see. Things are invariably thinner, paler, less rich than I had imagined. There is dust, seed on the pavements. Nuns processing in the inner cloister, and through archways other places, other lives: stables, the laundries, a woman raising her face to a tree in a half-glanced orchard. This place is an organ, yoked to the land along arteries and veins, men and women passing in and out (grain, news, sheep, beer). A novice crosses the yard, attempting shyly to view me in full without being seen; the half-curve of her face, its profile, the eyes sidelong as if gazing from a bridal portrait.

I sense I am an exhibition, the abbess showing me off to her women: *Look at this exceptional being, look at how she and I are joined.* As if I am a shaft of light from Heaven, anointing her head. I do not mind.

She has called a cart, perhaps slightly louder than necessary. I am handed into it by a lay woman with her sleeves rolled. See me, Lear, rising in the world! *Wrap a veil on your face. The sun is bright.*

The first time removed from this place since I came here. The gates in the ringed wall come open. This is what she says: *Look how vast, how munificent it is, to be here. Forget the graves. Be here, be in your kingdom. Be with me.*

Newness, everywhere, from the cart-top: the path from the abbey lined with green, frothing wide awake, and late grass yellowing. What one forgets, prowling a small space. The distances between things. Light pressing down into earth, so that it warms to the second knuckle. Grades of shadow when seen from leagues off, the soft pink of upturned earth, the pools of blue beneath trees. Looking back the abbey shimmers, hazy over the wall. I have not seen it from without, the mounted mass of it, raw roofs and dust-glazed iron under the squat steeple; it is like glimpsing a lover fully undressed for the first time. I feel ashamed.

The dress glares in the light. White is mourning because of its delicacy, but more because it's leisurely. The decadence of the royal grieving, to sit still and drink warm broths, perhaps, and wait unmoving. We could sit, and be mute and courageous, for our portraits. I want to grab earth, to streak it dark across the bodice. *Look. I am here. I am higher than all of you.*

I know stains, know marks, the deep language of the body. After all Lear took me though I'd once married. Knowing that I knew. It was not a blanched pale virgin for which he laid out furs, the raw north forests, coins.

We do not even know that she can still bear children, said the knight Gloucester when they beheld me first, in Lear's hall, days after the wedding. Gloucester, blowsy, cheeks reddened by hunting winds and a commitment to merriment; already fat then, his stomach leaning forward over his belt to brush against the table.

45

The ring of Lear's knights regarded me, threatened: a new acquisition, unsanctioned, brought in overland in secret from Michael's court, now standing in the queen-circlet with cool certainty.

I took my linens from beneath my dress and showed them to him. Blood warm still in my hand from my thighs and parts.

That is not the act of a queen, he said, choking. Arms to his face.

A queen is not shy of gore, said Lear, laughing. *Will you shrink from her courses like a boy? You've never known your wife, man.* Kissed me on both wind-blasted cheeks. The kiss scraped and left a whiteness.

We come to a dry square of ground. Nubbled field-edge. The workers in this place bow to the abbess and squint at me. They know their colours: white means noble, means a foaming wave, means the coming of blossom. Even unnamed I am queen, still. Nobody has called my name to me, not for fifteen years; perhaps I have none.

No. What is hollowed from me, what is taken, all else, but the name remains.

Things flare, in the light. Regan's hinge of hip that would not be smooth, and so had to be pressed to shape all through summer, weighting her small body all on one side, like a ballasted ship. Goneril weeping for dead saints, Father Wilfred finally having explained martyrs. Lear's belly, the marching-line of red across its swell. Cordelia, crying against the blood. All of them in a field, perhaps one like this, pushing up seeds from their cheeks.

I will climb down.

The abbess, who had been talking to a foreman, comes and hands me down. If she is astonished she does not show it; but the light is such — violent, coursing at the edge of every object like a threat — that her face is vague, from a distance.

You are to say a prayer, I tell the assembled men. They are leaning, in the dust.

For the King Lear, for the princesses Cordelia and Regan and Goneril. You are to pray for them. I would add my name, but I cannot: it is a still dead thing, it will not move.

They look carved, from wood, or earth; and my veil whips around my cheek. They know not to meet my eye. Do they know Lear's name? I have the sudden fear that I am speaking to dead men, that they keep their stillness because of unnatural law. Everybody may be dead. I have seen things in the smoke off burial pyres; I have heard voices in my dreams. I am surprised by nothing, Lear, nothing in this world or the next.

The abbess murmurs, at my shoulder. The startling whiteness of her, the roundness, is brought out against this autumnal sultry sky. She is cunning, Lear, she has perhaps brought me out for a lesson: *Here is your little fiefdom, here you can be a queen who rules completely.*

I let myself be brought onto the cart again. The men have moved off (real after all) and are doing the last work of the season over the field-stubble, dark sweat pressed to their backs, shadows purple and black.

I will not be defeated by this, by the coarseness of it! By the men who seemed not to know Lear's name, or those of my daughters, and merely looked at the ground. They must have known and were cowed; or unhearing, or mute. Lear's name went to the ends of the dark. His messengers told him so. They must have known.

My own name. I say it in secret on the cart, and the hanging dust moves. Power to move earth, power to calm water: the queen's name. Though forgotten. Though bloodied on the tongue.

And I know, I know, as I know the feel of my own hair on my stomach. Though this is my small kingdom, though I have tended it for fifteen years unseen, like a daughter, I am leaving it, I am already going. Listen, Lear-ghost: I'm coming to find you. Never fear.

Do you remember, ghost? First married, and you waxen as a

virgin, untaught. And so I found ribbons in my trousseau and tied parts of myself to you, hand to foot, wrist to wrist, and said, *Find me*, in the dark. So that you felt for the threads like Theseus, and were guided forth in the blind black by my voice, the movement of my warmth, and so came into me, fell over and through my neck, my chest. Knot to your knot.

So the long lash of our pairing holds taut. Did you cease to feel it? Ring around your ankle, loop around your neck, the weight of wife? I am coming down the ribbon towards you, Lear. I am speaking my name.

★   ★   ★

Of course this place has been a better daughter than any of the others, for unlike two it grew straight, and unlike one I saw it grow at all. I'll give it that.

Do you still remember your daughters? the abbess asked once, and I laughed so long she thought me possessed. What I remember of my daughters: lists and lists. The movement of eyelashes across their cheeks. I could make them out of household objects for you, Lear, walking and talking, spoon-mouths opening for kisses, and they would be perfect; such is the alchemy of motherhood. From those lists I could construct some aspect, a shape. Perhaps. *Lady, your love could move a bowl to ask for stew,* said the Fool, and wept.

Or perhaps it is a saturation, a single moment, or colour, or flick of a scent. That came closest to their essence, and in that moment contained their entirety. Resurrection, Lord, seems to be closer on that score; let me dream of it. A little, just a little.

So Goneril: small, heavy-skulled, ferine. Fitful in her movements, knotting and unknotting across the stone floors. And red, red to the nape of her neck, though she tried citrus, balmed her freckles in creams and old milk, and wept. Her plaits were the glossed orange of her father's youth, before it fell into grizzling and grey. He loved this, the undeniable nature of paternal fate. I looked at her and saw orchards, the fullness of fruit.

Tried to be graceful but had too much dog in her, too much fretting: startle her and she'd tense, motionless. An animal caught in the open at dusk. I told her, *Relax your spine, don't think so much*, but you cannot train it out of them. That hunted sense.

Regan: white as paint with coarse black hair. My own, so I taught her taming, the lines of it on her back, night-wetting to smooth its wilderness. Every morning she rose and unbound her hair, wash of dark over her shoulder, and I would think, *God help the man who sees it*. Heron-girl, full in the breasts, long and smooth with edgeless eyes. Small-featured, like my mother: pass a hand over her face and the lips, the cheeks, would barely rise under your fingers. Perhaps Cordelia was like this, when she grew.

That whiteness, that pale clay. When I slapped Regan once on the neck (some small disobedience, she had arranged my pale combs in her own plaits) the mark rose and would not fade. High scarlet, like a bite. She wore low bodices to display it, flagrant, turning to the light at dinners. I ignored her. Gave her pounded hazel for the 'burn'. Later Goneril told me (whispering – always in my memory she is whispering, smothered, a giggle in the dark) that she had rubbed and pinched it every night to keep it virulent.

Twisting her wound, bending to the glass to check its swell. So industrious in her spite.

I remember other things. You start searching for portents after disaster, you sift through old tragedies to see what they begat, a poor foundation-stone that cracked the building down.

There was the year of blackened corn. The rains smashing the crops into putrefaction. Then another year. The stores were only handfuls thick, a bare finger of grain for a day. Pumpkins wept rot despite their padding from the damp.

The girls were still young. Bone visible in their wrists and feet, hair barely thickened out of its hay-wisp. Regan brought in a crow-corpse from the palace gardens, starved and flecked with maggots, and cried when I struck it from her hand.

Lear made it a policy to give them his share of food. *I'll live to see good harvests. They'll lie out in the churchyard otherwise. Pass that tankard.*

The good beer?

Yes. We can wait another summer for a son. You'll fatten again, woman.

Goneril got at the marrow of the bone with both fists. Regan let him spoon her, lazy, her small mouth opening and shutting, sucking at the fat of the spoon.

Yes, my good babes. Who are my best darlings? My lovelies.

Thank you. Goneril wiped at her hot cheeks and offered me a piece; mindful of his eyes, I gestured it off. She paused, then fell again to it.

I knew what he did not. Feed during famine and the hunger never stops. Our hungry, aching girls.

★　★　★

When we return from the fields, their ghost-workers, I take my purpose and go to the new garden, its neat-lopped turf. *To think.* The abbess lets me go, perhaps feeling herself right: she has shown me the small round of the world, palm-size, and I am content.

No, I am preparing. Rosemary. Rue. With my own hands I will part the soil down to the rock, and plant them on their graves, wherever they are, and then pass through. Onto other parts, the remainder of my life. Prize horse so long stable-bound; I am not so old, not so old.

Fifteen years have hemmed me into a small ring of passages:

guest-rooms, abbess's chambers, the private gardens, suspended panel above the chapel through which I saw the offices. The nuns below knew. Saw the shift of a shoulder behind the screen, far aloft, on eye level with Christ. Never, never my face. Now I explore.

The fresh garden stretches. Lear cast the first symbolic seeds at sowing-time; he had a golden bowl with which he strewed water to bless new shoots. Men wrote his name on ribbons and tied them to trees. To me they gave no such work: I was not fruitful; my body's pips were all daughters and not sons. I'd have breathed pestilence into the palace garden and made all the cucumbers soft, womanly, wide-hipped. Well, there is no gardener of the realm left but me. And so.

A nun rises as I come over the path and watches me. Holds a gathering of loose greenery, which she is securing with a rope, tightening it at the waist. She is tall, but fat; the kind of solidity where the spirit clings to sloth, to its ring of wide stomach and well-fleshed arms. No delicacy. An animal, she'd be a cow — no, I think, seeing her black eyes and the movement of her jaw, she is intelligent, there lies a will. A ploughman's horse.

God bless and keep you, I say conversationally.

And you, she says. *You look calmer today.*

I am surprised. My surprise I note gathers around her easily; she passes through it. Not over-concerned with the discomfort of others. Her arm thrust into the green has one vein raised at the upper wrist.

You came to the gate as I was watering the seedlings, she adds. *Delicate, this far into autumn.*

Ah. It is one of the women who stood at the gate, staring. Possibly she sleeps under the turf itself, and I disturbed her. Sod-woman. *Yes.* I have a thought. *May I have some seedlings? I am going on a journey, and would desire some.* Going about the countryside

51

hung with bulbs, with ferns, a crown of daisy-roots, good earth packed under my arms: I can see it! The sort of pagan forest-queen Lear's rural people worshipped, leaving her rabbits, bits of meat on the doorstep to grant them good fortune. *Let them choose their gods*, he said. *Your Christ is not for everybody.*

It would be better if you waited for spring, says the sister. *You would have more choice and a better chance of their survival. Particularly to take live specimens.*

I will not wait for spring, I say.

I see. Will you hold these.

And gives me the greenery, so that I must brace my weight, it being heavier than envisaged. A child's weight, of ash-leaves and silver bark, and crumbling wood-softness, damp; damp as the nape of a neck, as sweat. To keep it taut as she pulls, I lean back. So that I am suspended, so that she is holding up my weight with the pull. The Fool, I think, would love this, would say we had a beech-marriage, a beech-birth.

Lady, the rain is coming!

Ruth had come down to meet me, and sees me here in this dance with green, nun, rope, light. She runs over the grass.

The garden-nun finishes the knot and pulls the greenery to her shoulder. Looks like a man in a book of hours, painted hauling his pack of sticks through a page of winter, while on the edges of the image a frill of flowers spins in eternal golden spring.

The first fringes of rain come then, grey-spitting, laying their small mark on my arms, my neck. The clouds are dragging over, through the light. Rain on my eyelids, rain on Ruth's bared shoulders as she raises her arm to cover me as we go in.

5.

The rain covers the evening, like a skin. One nun opens a hand, experimentally, into the open garden to feel the full weight of the storm in her palm.

Under the moving sky I assess. An old woman of no entourage but a loyal servant, alone, without family or any notable friend beyond a young abbess and her farm-hands. Divested of honour, children, husband, rank. If Lear had a bulletin of that sort he'd roar, *This is frail stuff! Put some blood in it!* so that the messenger had to scrabble for sweetmeats, some mote of good luck and fortune, to save himself from a whipping. Young Lear would have wept.

I am watching the rain. Ruth is mending the frayed gold thread of a psalter.

Well, I have come through other hells. Finding Goneril in the yew maze. Regan's bruises, across her stomach, across her neck. The early weeks of young marriage to my first husband, when I found through small increments that I would garner love and the gift of children only by subterfuge and years, years, of war. And my arrival here, in sodden furs, in a night storm (green sky, rain through to the scalp, wind so hard it bruised your mouth).

One survives. Women find small spaces, bury themselves, show green when the season betters. Kent knew it. Saw me after Cordelia's birth and said, *Ah, mistress, death never saw you but to veer aside.*

And there is the green woman. And the dust rising off the road. I will get out, in my own way.

Ruth says, *I miss the Fool.* Holding her needle between her fingers. The pause of her sadness, she is simple so that she cannot feel and move.

Yes.

He will be so sad the king is dead. He loved the king.

He did.

She looks out at the massing nuns for the beginnings of the night hours. *He will be wearing his mourning clothes and weeping at sad songs, as when the king's mother died, won't he? And wearing dead flowers in his hat.*

The memory gives me pain that hits through the body. Spearthump. At the funeral of Lear's mother the Fool strutted, pained, thrusting his chin and white face at the pomp. Lurid misery. We, dignified, folded our arms and let him spoil his jerkin with tears. Our little conscience, unfettered by dignity. Nature's grief-son.

I miss him nearly as much as I do Kent, or Lear. Bearing his wit like a lance, to prick the bloated balls of every pompous ass! He feared nothing, our fool. Bow-legged, his hair hard scraped back across a broken-veined scalp to fit his fool-cap. He'd have been a scholar if he were not so intelligent — bright enough to see behind the backs of things, and through all opaque and golden objects. There was nothing left for him, he told me once, but to be a fool, no other job.

And a king's fool sees all, knows all, embraces and reverses. When I gave him to Lear, newly married, I knew, barely, what it was I did, but I had given Lear an underside, a nonsense-man, who appeared in the glass and said, *Lo, all is mortal, none of this is real.*

I cannot think of him living past Lear. The idea makes my tongue taut against my teeth. Kings and fools are hard companions:

they live in the high absurd and look down at us grimacing. There was no fool beyond the king. His land was Lear, everlasting; he served him as long as my marriage, longer.

(Kent dives into my thoughts, clear. Moving through water: half grown, still hairless. The cleave of his back surfacing, streams off his hair like pearl.)

Perhaps I should send the Fool a letter. Will you write it for me, Lady? Like you did to my sister, when we came here?

Ruth's face is shining, old now – suddenly widely old, all her beauty vanished, as with a bird's plucking. Her age makes me furious; I rise.

We can send him no letters, you ignorant woman. Of course the Fool is dead.

Of course, she says slowly, and is silent. And eats her hurt quietly, picking at her embroidery by the candle, and will not weep for fear of my rebuke. So few people have cried in my presence.

I hope he died well. The Fool. He was the bravest of us, the most brilliant. I hope they told him frankly of death, and that they gave him mead, and let him lay a joke before the knife, as it came down to meet him.

★ ★ ★

I have not journeyed in so long. When they carried me away it took perhaps four days to come to the abbey. Travelling over what I know now to be pale brushland, cut apart into field and path and frail hedge-line. Marked on the abbess's maps, the land is unbroken, a painted limb of green. I could tell her. What appears full has fractures, hidden in the dark.

North; north. Water turning darker against stone. The light changing, stripping out of copper and gold into white.

I saw none of it, the lichen over dripping rock, the dark heather flats. I faced the cart wall, in the grip of my fury, which was clothing, which bound to my body in ribbon and swaddling-tight cloth. Ruth gave me warmth through her body, and offered food, water, once a cupped crucifix between the palms of her hands. Once a biscuit she herself (poor, weeping) had chewed gently, so that it was crumb and softness. Passed into my mouth it tasted of salt, of the sourness of her.

How can I tell you, ghost, of the dark that was there in that cart against the wall? And entered my body, as water enters and holds the hair, and weighs it down. It is dark I carry still and know as I know God, as I know my breathing. How can I tell you? First it is what you wrap between a corpse and a shroud.

And again it is underwater dark, at the place where horses drown.

And again it is the place between two praying hands.

And language falls out of it; prayer falls out of it.

I heard as I was lifted – by so many hands, hands that had in the past perhaps served me wine, or held my horse – the dogs in the kennels howling, under their taut leather, eyes orbs of gold. Sensing death, sensing the start of a journey, which must be marked.

Four days overland, the air growing thinner, as we pressed. I knew it was north from the smell. No scent of the sea. Ruth prayed aloud first, and then for the following days in silence. I refused to be seen, the shame poised to crack over my head: to be visible in the air, queen unsheathed, queen excised tooth-like from the mouth of the king, would be death.

And, horrible, against my body was the stickiness of milk. I was at that time still full of it; there was a crack in me through which leaked endless, useless streams. Yellowing beads of milk flowed down to mix with the sweat of my torso and gave me a wild, ripe smell.

I thought then it would be days, perhaps a week. Forced penance at some pilgrimage point in the mountains, on my knees, in sackcloth, knees flensed down to blood. And then taken home, broken into obedience. To anticipate the royal will is to live many lives in a single life, many words closed in the throat and unspoken. I held my fury and was mute.

Lear would leave a boy naked in a snowy field to show disdain. Locked a young bitch out of doors for snapping (his heel left flapping velvet, laughably, a mocking tongue behind him). Always acting, however, in an arc of eventual forgiveness. I taught him that: knowledge of the moment, the point in the cycle, to offer one's hand. As fortune falls so shall it lift.

Alone, un-coaxed, he would sulk, leave it too long, or weaken early. *The Lord guides my hand*, he would say, and I would say, *Oh, pale man. Oh, leaf out of a long, long book.*

The dark was as hard as any body. The milk in me would not stop. In the shadows I felt it move, and reach out.

★ ★ ★

Since the news of the deaths I have burned myself repeatedly, have lost the carried sense of the edges of my hand, my body, in the drift of rooms. Have come away from the hearth to find sore wild skin all down my back, a streak like fur. Tonight it is the pad of a finger, passed too close to a candle-flame, and so thick and white as a glove. I peel it away, revealing fresh pink skin. Alarum.

It seems fitting, as entire parts of the map are burned, too hot to place a foot upon. Old women of a certain age, breeding and thinness of options tend to strike out *towards* convents, not away; their daybreaks narrow to a slit. I am contrary, as I ever was.

Ruth pats fat onto the wound. *Mistress, do not pick.* But I will pick.

Kent! I could use your counsel so well, now. You would give me tasks. You would plan a poor-pretty funeral for four missing dead, a true one. We would perhaps scratch four holes, and pray over them, as if we were still young, and the roses still heaving over our heads in waves, in the garden of my first husband.

No man now beside Lear, you told me, when we fled overland to Lear's stronghold after my first husband's death. Rain on your neck. *I can change masters once. I will not do so again.* Wherever you are, you are not bowing your head to some new man. Men do not change as they move into age, but condense, hardening their youthful shapes into rock and substance. Death first.

Well, when we meet, Kent, when I find you at last (your shining head clashing with my white-streaked plaits, you will be quite bald by now), you will say, *How did you do this, this wonder, tell me?*

I will say, *Aren't I cunning? Aren't I more brilliant than your young men? Name one who could hide in the dark for fifteen years and come out pink and cheerful, name them. Who could battle against scheming nuns who lock stable doors and hunt you in the night.*

You will say, *How did you do it? Tell me all.*

I will be expansive. I'll say, *Yes, I was exiled, defeated, but despair had a nibble at my heart and then it saw I was very bitter meat. Have you never met a queen, Kent? This is how they live. Do I not look well? I kept my promise, that's the secret.*

You will say, *Oh, how marvellous, how beautiful, how strong.* And we will walk off, together.

Lear, you're down with the Devil, and I'm alive. Look, damn you: I survive! I'm coming to your grave to tell you, even if your ears are stoppered with moss and grass. I'll stand with Kent by your grave and he will look calm and dignified, and I will spit, and then, yes, we will move off, with our working limbs and hardy heads, and you will stay where you are.

Mistress, do not bite at the poor burn, says Ruth, in agony.

What will I need when I leave here?

I once travelled weighted to the elbow with gold. Litter held aloft by six slaves, women ahead singing so that their voices filled the purple cloth. I was to be motionless, even when the dust covered my cheeks and filled my lashes red as rust. It was my presentation, my test: to be shown to Lear's people, who had risen from their farms on the tarn and the granite-hewn hillsides and come to see the new wife, the womb of the kingdom. They watched and delighted as I processed. Fine blue day, with a purl of cold in the wind, a trick in it.

Men of Lear's house held my hounds in their train with their studded harnesses. Leather so new it looked naked. I was painted white-faced with lead, a moon rising out of the red robes, which were covered with miniature bronze bells so that when I moved, breathed, shivered, the sound of me rolled off my body and into the crowd. *What a woman you are,* said Lear, delightedly, watching me borne aloft. *They'll believe you hold up the sky.*

This sort of thing, of course, I no longer need. Though I could do it again. If I needed to.

So it is simpler. Bags of flour. Flagons, skins of wine. Dried meats, tied like bouquets. Fruits pressed and moist between leather. Knives, thin knives. Lanterns, many lanterns, and, of course, stacked gifts, boons for passing beggars and the poor, in a streak: to say, *Here returns the queen, here comes her grace, the spring comes out of the winter and breaks once again upon the land.* Hear it whisper.

My burn is dripping blood upon the floor. I had not noticed. Ruth is my eyes: she watches my body as I move through other, wilder things.

6.

When I walk with the abbess in the morning to discuss my plans, in her private gardens, I am attended by ghosts. A train of daughters, catching the edge of the sun. Lear at my back, cloud-thin, stippled as light coming through leaves.

I feel them still, just as before. Just as I felt them when they were alive. A sneaking hope. *Are we sure that the messenger may not have made a mistake? Some people of his class—*

She holds my arm in silence. My finger is bound; the grass sighs and ripples upwards. The abbess's gardens are an idea: grasses of different lengths, gradated, shorn into mazes, tiers. She had wanted floral borders at first, petals stacked hoarding their perfumed silence, but I advised this. Plainness, and in it infinite variety. The grass is an open surface, through which winds and small twists of air reveal themselves, as does the will of God.

Some gardens withhold: the square-cut yew maze of Lear's palace. (Goneril in the yew maze, weeping at night – I cannot think of it, I will cry out.) This one displays itself profoundly. We walk it often, arm in arm. In autumn, now, it is strewn: leaves, the splintered blossom of late-blooming things.

Ruth is humming behind, walking. The lightness of her, gossamer; her voice is tossed on the breeze, disappears. So insubstantial a singing voice, from a stout woman, heavy about the breasts. I slept well and the wound is pale and healing, and so she is cheerful.

I am gesturing in the wind. Sketching a map in the air. *So I will leave, once I have gathered the right things, and consulted the weather.*

And you will go to find their graves.

I will go to find their graves. I breathe deeply. *I do not know what I may find. The Frankish king may have taken Cordelia, or they may be lying in a heap, or burned, under a tree. It is war, it happens that way.*

Hush, Ruth is listening, says the abbess, warningly. It is a brutal vision.

Ruth hears her name, smiles. She lolls in the greenness of the light, I see it. If she had fur it would be prickling with happiness. I love her smallness in this moment, the simplicity of her needs.

The abbess is squinting, and now talks more loudly. *The graves may be difficult to find. It is a strange errand.* The day is an upturned bowl of blue.

It is my duty, I say. She sounds unconvinced. The necessity of it is so clear in me, the purpose difficult to explain to any second person. A kestrel's instinct, to come back to the wrist. A dog's. *I must go. And I must find Kent.*

Kent, the knight? I had heard of him.

Kent is my oldest friend. Servant to my first husband, who died. Cousin to Lear, and loved him. If he lives, I will find him.

Kent was always lovely, Ruth says, her voice disappearing in the leaves. *A very nice man.* She divides people easily: nice, evil. When people reveal subtleties she shrinks and is afraid, or spurns. My complexities she tolerates, through some logic of her own; presumably I am allowed to contradict, being made of queen-things, and not consistent flesh. I smile back at her, over my shoulder.

Perhaps we can find him, and call him here, the abbess says.

I start to laugh. *Kent in a fuss of women? He'd die.* Not a man who ever loved women. I know — so many girls weeping over him in night gardens. And yet he was placid, carved rock, unmoved. Was Lear's arrow only, for his use. He moved for no other call but the king's. *No. I'll find him. I know. Wherever the body of Lear is, he will be.*

It is so firm in me I feel it like bone. It is not until I see them, or their remnants, the markers left of them in the earth (hastily scratched graves, a heap of pale stone like a cairn), that I can breathe and sigh and forgive. I must live through their deaths to be able to remake myself; not here, with a few mumbled words from a priest, but with them, wherever they are. The girls, their bodies cracking open, letting in the winter.

And wanting their mother at the last, I know. Even Cordelia. Even Regan.

My mouth tastes of dark honey. This is why I need Kent: he knew me to the marrow, to the quick. Whatever happens to me, however I am scarred and changed, he will look at my eye and say, *Queen*, and hold out his hand.

There is a moment of doubt — myself old, fat-handed, a bent-backed woman, to go to Dover in cold winds and scream for the dead. Is it so wise? But that is just Lear, I think: fiddling with my intent, fomenting and tormenting. I shake my head. Out with you, ghost, you will not deny me. I will prevail.

Birds go clicking overhead. The thin cool air gives the sound a hardness.

To distract myself I say, *Who is that woman?* The gardening-nun has appeared, at the edge of the grass, strangely still; a ship pausing before it sets out on the curve of a wave. Leans, and begins at a frill of soil, her hands vanishing.

Sister Mirabel, says the abbess. *She tends all the gardens here. She has been here longer than perhaps anybody.* There is no flex in her voice, no warp. Whatever seethes in the nuns here, the small rotting disobediences, this woman is apart from it.

To see her bend and take a blade between her fingers, testing its vitality, there is no element of restraint. She sees the bitter earth and comes close to it.

Mirabel rises and puts a hand to her face for shade, to observe us. I receive the flicker of a sense that she can see the ghosts, too, angry and mute, massed at my back, like so many rising voices. Thick-backed woman. She has the black eyes of a person who gazes at small things, unblinking, for many hours.

Please wait a while, Queen. The abbess is quiet, and sounds hopeless; she has been so gentle, so full of giving. A streak of light in this place, like the Pleiades in the soft dark. *Just a few more days. Perhaps I can change your mind.*

You are welcome to attempt it. I am mothering. This daughter-girl, the women who pick at her with their teeth. I put my arm into her sleeve, and lean to her. Ruth walks behind us; Lear whispers, in the scrollwork of the walls. And Kent, somewhere. Somewhere.

The grass tilts and shifts. Sister Mirabel goes again to her own work, gathering her stomach to her. We go in.

✶ ✶ ✶

How can I explain this to the abbess, to any person who lived without witnessing? The shift and pull of love, and where it lies.

Lear and I were only a year married, and the horse was too wild. Had been ridden barely, and that by the horse-boy Sutton, who was unskilled; and it paced and breathed, and was a black line against the sand, and tossed wet locks off its neck. Even when young, Lear dropped our advice from him, as if it were so much ballast that prevented him from rising into air. He liked lively ones, he said. To take a higher animal and dismantle its will to obedience was a skill and a virtue before God.

We saw. He rode it till the nostrils were awash with foam and its wind was broken, but it would not give. King and horse battled down the riverbank, wrestling over slate stone, he whipping and invoking gods while the hoofs struck fire, until they rode together at a great leap into the wild-white water, where the horse screamed and fought for purchase. They rolled and cleaved apart in the arms of the river, and went under. And I ran down the bank, and Kent beside me; and Kent saw, and my hands were in the water, I was in the water, I would breathe the underside of air to save this.

It was Kent who stripped and dived and rose, streaming, water parting over his hairless body, with the dead king my husband. And brought him on his shoulder to the bank, as I was hauled in by women. Waist-deep I had gone, my legs already fins, my throat a flashing gill, death-wet to my stomach in my fine queen-lace, *Witch*, they said but dried me, so. And then when Lear rose in breath (not dead but dreaming a king-dream underwater, he said later, full of sons who gazed like coral), he looked only for me, and said my name and came for my hands, and wept.

Kent in the river still, naked to the waist, who had withstood doom like a terrible effigy, but Lear and I were locked, seen by and seeing only the other, and kneeling in the wilderness. On the grey stone by the river, while the ferns blurred. *Love and love and love.* Kent breathing unnoticed. While they hauled the bloodied body of the horse in, downstream, to retrieve the swollen leather, bright insignia of the king.

Who can explain this? Devotion to a king, in all its forms, and how it binds.

7.

In the night I clean myself, moisten my own hair with dank water from the fire pressed onto a cloth, rub down flanks and arse to my hard feet, then sit steaming and elemental at the hearth, like a witch. I may not have a bath for many days, on the road.

The abbess has gone. Veiled to her eyes. She'll dine with a neighbourhood lord who wants to guarantee his salvation, and will shiver softly in his hall, a piercing flame of virtue, as white and clear as the roast white peahen on the table, its eyes picked out in pearl. Picture her knife lifting a feather, picture her mouth taking in meat, its sour softness. Shoring herself up with the authority of men. I am not envious.

It is late. Soon it will be vigil, the night office. Ruth is smoothing my hair with cloths.

It is getting so late in the season. I do not know if I can spare the days to wait. I am not as straight-backed as I was. I lean against the chair. *Maybe we should dig a hole under the walls, to escape, or slip out through the compost-heap, disguised as cabbages.* Pause. *What are you thinking of, Ruth?*

Normally an outrageousness would make her start, or laugh, or protest. She moves slowly, is elsewhere. The cloths are soft, in her hands.

We had not seen them in so long, lady. And yet I am still sad. Wonderingly. As if misery thrusts only through the known, and leaves memories and dreams well alone!

I am stung with pity. *Yes, child. I know.*

I thought it would be easier. One forgets that the court of Lear was her girlhood, that she saw the princesses married, rings of pearl across their foreheads, and brushed their long hair in the thick nights of summer. My own hair was reserved for Magdalena, though I see Ruth hovering in the glass too, younger, her hands holding ready the hairpins and stiff veils. Little apprentice, little serving-thing.

It is different. For years the love for my girls, my husband, was binding: looped to longing for them that never quiets. Its long animal whine. Always pulling at the rope, half striking for the long home distance, for their scent on the air. Lear smelt of the furnace, of dark seeds.

But they were living, then, actors moving offstage, out of view, chastising errant servants, eating bread on saints' days, dreaming silver dreams in the same night. Constant as stars in daylight, invisible but coolly felt. And now the king is dead. Rawness has become my body; I cannot move without hurting it. The little griefs of exile in profusion.

Ruth says, *I feel I should weep but the priest says it is unholy to give show to too much emotion because women's souls are, I don't remember, like an unstable sea? Perhaps?* Her voice is thick with sleep.

You have never seen the sea, Ruth.

I have not, Lady, and so he confused me.

Never mind. Weep all you like. God sees. Her hands press against my scalp.

Outside, horses. The abbess has returned; Ruth wakes and goes to look at the torches, which she likes. In the dark I look at the gathered treasures from the exile-night, that dark collection in which so much is housed.

Unstable seas. I have spent many hours contemplating the soul, and where it lives. The indivisible soul! False, like a mirror is. We share it out, what we can, we peel off slivers and whole limbs for love. What have I kept for myself? What small flayed centre of my soul remains?

Lear was uncertain. *This Christian soul — do kings have the same amount as others? The same substance? It seems cheap.* Putting bread into his mouth.

I suppose in your counties kings have fifteen times what everybody has, including hair, I had said to him, smiling. My little pearl-crucifixes, a small side-chapel to the palaces for my prayers: he had allowed it, gently, though uncomprehending. He said something truly filthy in response, and we giggled until it was time for court: time to smooth our laces, try for an hour or two to align our rude young marriage with the compacted shapes of king and queen.

Lear's faith was profligate: for him all gods were good, echoing as they did the fundamental aspect of his being, that he was king, and charged with holy rule. The forest-deities and water-spirits of his more remote villages, their people leaving bread by the hearth for a little grey house-god, my Jesus. He'd pray to anything, he said to me years later, that might grant him a son.

A knock comes. Little rituals. After all evenings abroad the abbess brings back delicacies: vices from richer tables. She breaks into the room now: fresh, fresh as apples, as new-cut meat. She has not slept.

I say, *And how was your little feast?* She smiles and open her hands. A palmful of cake, sugared figures in the shape of a horse. Clearly a lord who provides exactly for his guests, without room for excess; I picture his face, his expression as he counts his largesse to intimate precision. Every seed, every grain.

Ruth loves sweetness. Eats with the tips of her fingers, as I have taught her. Will not take the cake until I refuse it three times, biblically.

The abbess is sitting by the fire. My neck gapes under my shift; there is smoke. *There is enough for you, Queen.*

Very little. Your friend is not generous, for all he has a pastry-cook. Perhaps too many children. Or sizeable debts.

Both. She is not surprised. Knows this: my clairvoyance, my ability to read whole lives from the small signs. *Taste, just a part. It is good.*

I take it onto my tongue. *This is a new sort of wafer.* We laugh, in the scandal of our irreverence; Ruth, deep-blooded with faith, turns her face from jokes whose stability she distrusts. Then the abbess, softly: *Come out tomorrow. Come, meet the women.*

Why? It is very late, I am strangled by my lack of sleep. Also I remember their faces at the mourning service. Their eyes like full water-pails as they saw me process. And their little ears, pretending deafness to my friend by the night gate. Who needs such humans, who know so little and have felt such miniature, such facile emotions?

They are good women. And, she adds, smiling, *I think they need to be reassured that you are not a ghost.* Her face a bowl of milk in the dark.

The creature in the tower. Yes. Perhaps beast. Perhaps long-haired bitch drinking blood from the ground. Scrabbling at the gate in the dark. Yes: perhaps they do think that.

She does not say it. She does not say, *I need you. My hold on power here is frail. Your strength will bleed into me.* But we know it, together. As in the miniatures they make here on vellum. The halo of one great saint, one queen, is painted in gold leaf with brushes of fox hair; it widens across the page, blesses the smaller figures on her left and right. Giving them the gilding of her grace.

We are quiet, in the thick throat of the night, for a long time. I want to ask, *Why did you never tell?* Why she never brought the names of women who disobeyed, and sought my advice. But some things, perhaps, are too scalded with shame. And what would I care for some silly nuns, their war for a handful of buildings, a whisper of incense on the wind?

I have been too long left without my name. *Do you know my full name?* I ask the abbess, but she and Ruth are sleeping now, entwined on the bed, two ferrets twined as if at the neck of a girl.

*   *   *

Because of the sugar-smell I dream of the smallest one, of Cordelia.

What happened to her clothes? Long white foam-skirts picked with embroidery, plums, puckers, and her cool fingers with their blue nails emerging, in the drift of the gold-dipped lace? Her cap, which was velvet-napped, patrician, her father's crest sewn over on both sides to enclose her skull, smaller than a curled hand? What happened to the teething ring of pearl and blood-crimson coral, the crucifix with a silver-tongued bird, the wreath of golden trembling barley-sheaves made for her head (since we thought she would die, and must be crowned as she went into the dark)? It was the size of an adult woman's wrist. A thousand gifts deep already as she slipped into the world, blind.

It is the cruelty of it. I struggle to explain, in my dream. To myself. That the objects of her existed after I was taken from my child, in their prettiness, their hope. Better they be burned or handed to others. Better they made livid welts on the hands of any other who touched them. Nettle, whip, scar.

Cordelia was always blameless. Had enough will only to propel herself through the days, with folded lungs, moment by moment, skimming the edge of death. Barely, barely. Three months old, aquatic. Ill as she was after the brutality of the birth, the earliness of her arrival, I thought of her as a warrior, the quiet gift of her breath surfacing. Little wonder she lasted, little wonder she lived.

I thought as they took me in the night, *It will be just a passing thing. It will be brief. I will be back in the morning, to hear her open her eyes and cry.* Could not think of time as anything beyond her next movement, the next evidence of her self unfolding. Green girl, veins astonished on her skin like ferns. Then of course I was not back in the morning; and my milk leaked through the bandages and spilled through my hands, till I was wet to the wrist, crying in the dark.

I wake with a gasp. Every waking the worst waking, the end of all things.

How, I think, can they be dead? That baby with silver folded into its palms. The girls. Heave of my breath, up, down.

It is a trick against a poor and much badly used woman, who has suffered all indignity that God could offer to a body. They are in the castle of one of their husbands. One is playing the flute. Or it is a craft by Lear to spirit them to a safer country.

Up, down.

No. No, Lear, bone-boy, had fronds of tenderness in his innards, but was never canny. I could never train him to it. Dead, then.

Up, down. The abbess comes and puts a hand upon my stomach, and I sleep.

8.

So: we descend, the abbess and I, to meet the women. I steel my back, raise my neck. I am the standard she bears into battle, gleaming. She will plant me in the ground as a signature of authority. I will play the part, for her. And in trade she will release me.

Under my shift the graze of thigh against thigh. A worn circle where they meet, smoothed hairless. I imagine these abstentious women have no knowledge of the comfort of this – the great luxury of fatness. Roll over the vulnerable parts of yourself, fold, protect the sweeter softnesses behind fortresses of flesh. My cunny hoarded up for winter.

They have had morning prayers and are eating. We will talk with them perhaps once they have finished.

She opens the door. Three racks of nuns bent at tables of pale bread. One woman's fingers are in the middle of pulling away a crust, leaving a frill of dough, a raw hole.

Nuns! Useless. Failure-girls, marooned to offer prayers for cheap fathers. *None of you know,* I think, looking at their faces. *None of you have pushed to the depths of womanhood. Put your hands in fury around the throat of the thing you love most, feel your daughter's breathing under your thumbs, and then I'll call you a woman, a proper one. The sins it gives to you.*

A woman is reading aloud as they eat in silence, chewing. Tall, with a hollow at her neck, and a smoothed voice, like a priest's. Unusually she holds her wrist deliberately under the book's spine.

The abbess was right, I have some amusement. This woman, the proud reading girl, contains so many others I have known. The nuns who beguiled Goneril, with their studied, languorous language that demanded a breath at the end of each sentence, like a tithe. Intellectual ladies in court holding their fragile poems and pressed-rose hearts, irritating others with their patience, their held-breath pose before speaking. Cruel, brains in women make them cruel, for boredom. Women fold into other women, like handkerchiefs.

Mirabel is here. I watch her, the slow procession of her jaws. Brown to the lip of her hair, the cool bronze of a much-sunned body; under her shift I imagine sickly whiteness.

The reading woman clears her throat and looks pleased to have done it so cunningly, unnoticed, she thinks. Blonde, tall. Thinner than she should be; possibly one of those women who believes refusal is erotic, or godly.

Where have these humans put their souls, Lear? Have they given so little and reserved so much for the Lord that theirs are wide and buttery-white, and buoy up under their skirts? No, surely they had a smaller portion; since kings and queens must divide their souls so cunningly, among thousands, these little people likely only have apple-souls, onion-souls. I feel pity for her, and for them, and the feeling is pleasurable and hot.

The meal is over. They rise and say, *Amen.* The blonde woman closes the book. The others move to allow her to process first, in deference – particularly, I see, the common-born ones, with blank wooden crucifixes, humble postures. They hold her in high esteem, this straight-backed girl. Small things carry weight here. A silence at the table, a hand on the book. Abbeys, courts: the games are the same. I was a good game-player, in Lear's court. I could make men who wanted dispensations walk backwards on their hands. If I chose.

She comes to the abbess, kisses her hands. *You are late*, she says. I would smack her. The abbess merely says, *Yes*. And so is a failure. Seeing her with her women I know it, that they fall away from her, that their loyalty is the thin and sour kind, enforced by habit. No deeper than paint. Any woman could walk in and call them all to her, anyone.

The sister herself knows. And turns to me, and bows. Allowing me to witness this, the fragility of the scene. It is dangerous to have so many women unsteered.

This is Sister Calyssa, says the abbess. I remember her, her voice: the woman with the thin face, at the wall. The one who cut through the whorl of assembled women. Whom they followed away.

I pray for your loss, says Calyssa, bending her head, *and hope you will now be seen more commonly in the abbey*. An abbess's speech. She is certain; she has the composed face of ambition satisfied. The threat of it.

Thank you, I shall not. I am sharp as a tooth. That she dares to be intimate with me! I will not let her forget rank. I will launch it out across the room, so that it lodges in them all, like a spear: *queen. That was well read, for a nun*, I add, and know from her face that my guess — hours practising in the dark to make herself man-like, to mouth each syllable like the priest at matins does, precisely — was correct. Nobody perhaps has pinched her in a vulnerable part, not for a long time.

You are kind, Sister, says the abbess, in the ensuing silence. Smoothing milk over the wound in the conversation. She is a poultice-person: she hates to hear unpleasantness. Calyssa, curdled and unsure now of my powers, bows and leads the women away.

73

As Mirabel, the garden-nun, leaves, she nods. Says, *I've taken the last of the apples in.*

Good, good. The abbess, subtle in her distress, holds to this offered branch, an order followed, her place as leader restored. *You've done well.*

Kindness can be insolent. I gave out rare morsels to the courtiers in Lear's orbit who boasted most about their own kitchens, smiling, my hands wide in munificence: *Here is a gift from our table, which will always be superior to yours. Here is an absurd thing, an entire goose, a whole sugar-spun palace, that I give as a whim. Take it, take it.*

Oh, they hated it. But were forced to bow, to pass the sticky gifts to their servants and kiss my hand. Hilarious. Lear protested — *My best game, brought from my own forests, and you give it as a present!* — but would admit the wisdom of it when the next year the courtiers would return with geese in kind, in excess, spilling out of larders. Regan could eat a whole goose herself.

Calyssa is a pious woman, says the abbess. Her tongue fills her mouth; she is desperate, a little. *She has a fine mind. She belies her origins.*

I snort. I have known many women with fine minds. It is blood, blood that shows.

I could tell her. In my child-convent there was an incident. Another child would not take my catechism. I was incensed. They called the mother superior.

Why do you insist so?

I am a noble's daughter with a great name and will be queen. I will be obeyed. (I caught this thought so young, barely fleshed enough for both hair and heart.)

In these walls, girl, said the mother superior, horribly, *family and name are as ash. You will be penitent, and take your orders, and so be humble in the word of God.*

But not penitent. I was queen, once and again, God's anointed

74

woman; that fate was already reaching back into my past, rippling in my humours. Humility, obedience, a fine mind. They die.

We move into the courtyard. They have begun singing; it drifts. The abbess's hand on my arm; she watches the autumn sun. It is too late. She will be felled; it is in her already, her loss of these women. To Calyssa, or some other.

If I stayed perhaps I could save her, or postpone the shame. But it is not my work, so I will not help. She and I pass on, into the shade.

★ ★ ★

Queenhood comes to you in ways that are difficult to explain. Not just a circlet on your wedding day. It was laid in me in the belly, the form for which I was made.

How did I know that my parents had great family trees, fruiting with royalty on every bough? I knew. The truth hung in the dust in empty rooms when my small body came in; vast crests of wood across fireplaces, with coiling dragons, rows of stiff oaken dogs, tongues of corn and fire. Myself the only child; presumably threads of daughters ran through our familial wombs.

My mother was downiness in sunlight, golden, positioned idly by a window. Arms, I remember, furred to the wrists, the hairs picked in gilt. Most often she kept separate, a formal presence for which one was washed and powdered and presented bleach-collared, to sweat under a brushed kiss and be sent off. Still there was the interview, where she was tawny and aloft in the light, sweetened with something (rosehips in water, I smelt it years later and felt a pull, a flick). Her dress was in mountain-folds of blue over the chair, cool and solid, removing her body elsewhere.

And so you will go to the convent.

Yes, Mother. I was young. Six, or eight, with scraped knees. I would leave days later, and the cool halls of my childhood, the shimmering threads of tapestries and bright fields, would be lost to me. My child-self must have grieved, but the memory has not kept.

It will be good for you. She was lazy; her mouth was filled with pollen; it drifted. *Your future husband is well. I had a letter this morning. A well-mannered little boy, in the court of his father.*

And when he is king, I will be queen. This thought had solidified in my small body over many years; it was developing arms and legs, like a homunculus. Soon it would start following me about.

My mother's lips parted. The abbess has lips the same colour, but not so indolent. I never saw my mother move: she was fixed, though she must have shifted to perfume her arms, or caress her hair, which was struck through with light.

Yes. You will be queen. Once you come out of the convent, and are married.

Will Agnes be coming with me? I was thinking of my companion-girl, some daughter of a good family who slept in my bed and joined me for games, though when I was piniomed in the silver-tipped lace gown for portraits, she stood and sucked her finger, or helped to pull the stays. Was it Agnes? Some other name? Faded, now.

No. There will be other girls, of good stock, and you must remember your manners, and treat them well, as your inferiors. But you will be queen, and so are marked out.

Marked out?

For a great destiny, she said. And smiled. I realise now that she thought herself gentle, despite the pointed small teeth, the will that built an alliance and made her daughter queen. Obscuring that strength in gauziness and heavy flesh. *Come, kiss my hand, and you can go.*

Her face in those rooms vanishes, is enfolded by the cloud of her, some separation. Cool and brightly immaterial, as if half ascended already, and being slowly covered with gold leaf from the feet up, by attendant angels. She was dead before my wedding, and put away in the family tomb, topped by a marble effigy (sculptor's work, expensive) with flows of silk carved across its breast. To lie still, and smile.

Rosehips. When my daughters were born I reached for their bodies, and said, *Yes.* They would know me, my milk and smell, the line of my hip; I would dip into their lives arm-deep, up to the shoulder, like a woman picking reeds in the river. They would see every line of my face in their dreams.

★ ★ ★

As the women are attending mass and the rooms lie empty I walk. I am exploring what I had only ever known by talk, by the echo of voices: the full depths of the abbey. Before I leave I want to see it, what I have dreamed.

The chapter-house is best. Wide-boned, with splayed arches. The broadness of it, the fullness feel feminine: the ribs of a giantess, her swelled lungs. The sisters are singing a hymn, and the noise touches every part, moves through the space. The brightness, the thin line of sound, over which we must all vault to get to God.

The late autumn light here is grained, pollenish; from one side of the abbey's first courtyard you can barely see the other. All is ablaze. Shafts of light striking through the high parapets onto the walkways. I move through them soundlessly. My vision flaring: white, dark, white.

In the afternoon a storm rises so I return to my rooms. The winds are coming down the hills; the abbey is shuddering and brutally squat; they built this place against the fall of weather. Yet the weather still finds it. We cannot hide from God: His wrath comes upon us. Ruth goes into the dim world for candles. I must go soon, Abbess, I think. The world outside is closing.

I sit and watch the lightning, over the wall. Have I somehow been carrying this, these deaths, hidden in the seed of my lungs? Portents, whispering? It seems impossible not to have known, not to have contained, somehow, the enormity of my loss before it struck.

Outside the wind contracts, unfurls. Fits of pique, smashing a tile in the courtyard. Winds are men: they crash their anger out.

As I sit in blank companionship with my grief at the window (hard friend, impolite guest) there are voices. Not Ruth's, others, a woman's and a man's, floating. The wind has made the walls echo; they are talking softly, perhaps in the yard. A novice and her brother-boy. Curfew is long past, she is holding a risk.

— *we never see her. Last week she tried to escape alone into the dark!* Her voice, delighted, a plum splitting to show juice, flesh.

Out of the gate? She must be mad. It's nearly winter. His less certain. What she reveals might scald him.

She is old, whatever they say she was. A queen or duchess or some such person. And the Lord has taken a great deal from her. Her tone is serene piety; her head doubtless rises, to meet a halo she has made for herself. *Sister Mary Catherine says it is a judgement for us. To show that all worldly things will come to ash.*

Though hopefully not too soon. I like the brother, I think. He is throaty, feeling out the edges of his adult voice. He may be a lover: novices are always being put away safely from lanky young men, the kind who'd find the marriage-bind a constraint to their soft-whiskered beauty after two years, three.

You're terrible. Impious giggle, then a sigh. *I pity her greatly. And have featured her in my prayers.*

You are too good, Mary Catalina. Where are the horses, this storm! I have to tell you . . .

The voices dissolve, the banging of the shutters and wooden doors increases: they have moved off, the wind has swallowed them.

I feel my body unbind, which had been held tight. as if against some assault. Which is pity. Pity! Pity for the woman who married two kings, who birthed three princesses. Benevolence for her soul!

When Ruth returns with her bundle of candles, which smell of sweet mould and darkness, she is astonished. *Lady, you have ripped that skirt quite to pieces.*

9.

My fury lasts till morning: shreds of veils, of skirts, Ruth stumble-following with apples and calming teas as I circled the room like a demon! Shouting; a wax candle spilled — it has hardened into a tongue across the floor.

This place. These women. Creatures and elements will disappoint — even when carefully kept, and managed. Fine-born horses throw their heads back and reveal whole teeth missing, or a skull misaligned, subtly, scattering the line of perfection. So with the abbey. I had fitted and built it, dreamily, in afternoons in the circle of my rooms; and in the world it droops, has corridors strangled with sweat-smell, and stinks of cabbages on wet days. The nuns show their unremarkable faces, and are grim.

From the door, aching-eyed, I watch them go in to mass. Some are crumbling into age, with white eyebrows and bulbs at their wrists, past the point where sex matters to a body. I am still heated as metal. I do not want to encounter their gaze.

There are kinds. Even here, breeds and species show, like hens. Noblewomen with their chatelaine-belts, braced by their families with lace-work and elegant handwriting and pious embroidery, against an imagined future of demanding men. Then (marriage-failure, bride-price bankruptcy) dropped like eggs into the abbey, to pray for their father's health and brothers' pockets. A little wealth, to comfort them: bright jewelled rosaries, sweetmeats at the table every feast day. The abbess herself is from a high-born family, who bought her the position in return for prayers for their souls. She allows them monkeys, sweets, long fingers of pastry, their own servants. Silk of criminal softness in the vestry. Whispering, whispering.

The shape of their noble heads is uniform; one can see the structure of them, the softnesses at key points. The women of lower stock walk with their mouths open to receive the seasons of God, and food, and work, and shelter, gratitude making them smug. So they pray, and dream perhaps of hay-beds and the smell of burning copper on the wash-fire. Doubtless they wage little wars against one another, behind the abbess's kindly back.

Even the abbey's famed glossy red stone, like an open mouth against the pale skirled sky, looks sickly today, and grips me with longing – for the dream-place, the undiscovered country. Explorers in court would claim a filled map is always preferable to a blank, but what could give more than the painted sea-monsters on their charts, riding foam-waves, magnificent fins catching the wind?

The little novice with the holy pity is coming, keen-eyed, a rim at the bottom of each socket in purple, the early mornings still strike at her like a whip. The late night with her boy must have nibbled into her sleep.

I want revenge, suddenly, a break of it over my skin.

As the abbess passes I hold out a hand for her to kiss, which she does, surprised, movement that breaks the ritual of the flow of women. A rock flaring upwards through tide, to spill spray.

And how did you sleep? she says conventionally.

Poorly. I am humble, hiding shrewish teeth. That bite. *One of your novices talked under the window till quite late. Mary Catalina. She and her visitor had remarkably strong voices, he particularly. So I am quite tired, today.* Drooping, theatrically.

The novice has widened her eyes, her mouth; shame makes

81

her look indistinct, a vibrating instrument. Like a tabor just struck, shivering through the skin.

I told you he must leave before sunset, the abbess says, turning to her. The sorrow of her plush voice, refusing fury to turn to disappointment, as her weapon. A softening thing, like smothering. I could teach her better, but I am silent.

I see the flick of it across the novice's face, contemplating saying that I was mistaken, then her eyes observing me, the line of my jaw, and knowing that I am rigid, I keep the time as accurately as any water-clock. I have her neck in my mouth.

Do not be harsh, Abbess. She is young, says Sister Calyssa. Who is, of course, at hand, prepared: to bite for power, to pull a thread so that it puckers the whole tapestry. What insolence. One of her sisters leans to talk to another, quietly, their heads meshed together in light.

Calyssa and the abbess are watching one another. The abbess unblinking, smiling. A doll, almost impervious. I am collected, and heavy, the mass of me at her back. Feel my weight. A thousand men would follow it once, running overland in my colours.

She chooses wisely. Simply says, *I am sure I am just, Sister Calyssa.* And adds, *We will talk later, Mary Catalina.* The novice ducks away and is brutalised.

Calyssa remains standing, perhaps a beat too long. Then bows, reserves herself for mass, coolly. Admitting a loss, for now. The commoner girls follow, a little goose-herd.

One murders one's children daily, the previous child cropped back, like willow, for new heads and frothing green to come out of the stump, and be reshaped. Thousands, thousands of these massacres, over a lifetime of mothering. Sometimes the stump grows dark, rot-battered; and you dig and scrape out the worming wood, burrow-knots of anger, fragile root-venoms. Though they cry, pale balm of their sap on your hands. Duty, with a shovel in its fist.

Mirabel, mute and virginal, up to her waist in branches, would understand this. I see her go into the mass last, her hands in her pockets. She at least has no pity, not even perhaps for herself.

May I go today? I whisper to the abbess. Rejoicing in our little victory.

Not yet. Not quite yet. And she smiles, and moves away.

★   ★   ★

So: I rearrange my clothes. I am a woman with purpose. Real purpose, which will take many days of journeying, and needs provisions, packed and wrapped and baked to last.

I find the kitchen quietly, through smell, sweet vegetable-boil smell, thickening the air. As hungry children in the convent we opened our mouths to wind and ate the grass, the scent of men's arms in the fields, the snatched smoke from a fire with a fish-tail in the embers.

The cook watches me with half an eye, but is engulfed in her duty, four knives, a rotating spit. A laywoman, scarf tight to her scalp. One of those women who does her craft with her whole body. The heat comes over me and pricks out the length of my skin; stars of sweat in every cleft part, over my knees.

Is it thirsty work? I say to her.

It is.

May I find you some water?

As you like.

The high pitcher has a thick lip. Must be dipped with a long ladle, and tipped; and this is not natural, I am too tall and stoop. She watches.

Grateful to you. As she drinks her neck swells with the water; she visibly wettens. Sweat like a lace veil across her forehead. The kindness has earned me a few moments. She is pressing meat into pastry coffers, each marked at the round with the pad of her fingers. Sealed in to bake and soften.

You'd be the lady, then. The abbess's one.

Yes. Imperious, which she likes. Some women hold hard to rank, in their lowness, have no desire for the white ruffles and starch of thanes and ladies to bend, and show themselves raw beneath. Instead they touch, meet the gold and steel of a greater form, and retreat — pleased!

What can I do for you? Are you wanting something? Some of the girls are sick; there's tea for them, should they want it. You look well, though.

I'll be on a journey soon. It will be three of us, perhaps others, for many days. The abbess has perhaps mentioned it.

No. No, I cannot say she did, Lady.

I am surprised.

Well. I will be leaving, and I have thoughts about our provisions. I lay out the general shape: preserved meat, good breads that stale slowly, cheeses. Fermented fruits. Lear's own entourages, moving from castle to castle in the visiting season, drove sheep in flocks ahead, for roasting in the evenings. Arriving anywhere we bore smoke and the smell of grass ahead of us.

She nods. As with many working women, the flush of her pride emerges, the deep pleasure of showing her profession's benison, her skill. *You will want hard loaves, I can make them. Oat crusts thicker than your fist, Lady. The meats will have to be last year's — they're the only ones fully cured. Where I come from we wrap hams in thick cloth for carrying. Fewer maggots that way.* Sees my face, and laughs. *And you'll need fish.*

Fish? But you have no cool-house.

She smiles. Says, *You have never seen it. Come and look.*

On the back of the abbey kitchen is a slate-house, dim and damp, lined with nets: for the taking of fish from the ponds, I think, snagging the abbess's perch and trout from their green drifts. But it reveals a secret: a set of tiered slabs, thick green as

84

underwater moss, all flush with fish – tench and anchovy and the slung curve of the eel with its pale stomach, and over them thick water flowing; freezing, as I dip a finger into it, touch a shivering scale. The flood drains through a floor-grate that shows a gloss of ice.

My own invention. The remark of every noble house for miles, says the cook. *We can smoke dozens tomorrow, and they'll be as fresh going over the smoke as they were in the ponds eating their lunch.*

She has altered a spring so that it comes down from an upper gully in the mountain through the abbey walls, somehow conveyed by force of thrust slightly upwards (pipes, she explains, and a water-wheel), and descends here, over her hoard. Coating them silver.

At Lear's household in winter the cooks would keep the meats fresh with coats of salt and submerging in the ice, which they hauled themselves, by lamplight at the river. Once, resplendently, they resurrected a boar's whole carcass, lifted at the haunches by rope and unwrapped from its sour cloth like a royal babe, born in the blue underside of ice. And disasters: improperly caulked or cased meat came up as mere bone and streaks of skin, as winter-fish (blind, I told the girls to scare them, with teeth big as a finger) found their own feast. One could not grudge them.

She is pleased with her solution. I think it well, it should be rewarded. If I had favours I would give them. My colours on a ribbon, or a gift of a dog from a litter; useful, the queen's compliments, and not massed easily. Childish; and no lace, or significant part of my clothing to cut off and bestow, and that is likely long out of fashion. Ribbons; in the hair of the sweet maids.

So I offer my hand to her. Which she takes, surprised, and then laughs. The ruthless jaws of the fish are open under the push of the water; they look as if they might speak.

10.

I am up all night, planning. At one moment, dipping into sleep over maps, I dream: I am a birch, silver-throated, sun-sap in my crown. Daughters, husbands grow as boughs, fragile and then muscular, cleaving from me and driving skywards. I witness and root them; I am the anchoring principle. Then: the winter storm presses down, and they are cracked asunder, torn loose. Ribbons of white heart-meat peel from me. I am cool, solitary, skinless, upon a plain on which nothing moves but water.

White as a stripped birch. Well, a stripped birch is a birch still. Though my head be blasted by lightning, I remain living, improbably, fat, exiled, alone, but alive.

From the window I see Mirabel outside in an old cloak, up to the wrist in soil, using the light to do early work on the physic-garden. I go down to her, in a sudden impulse. The dew of the overhanging bushes brushes across my skull; the hair seems to be folding back, leaving me plucked, open to the sky.

Mirabel bends. All that attentiveness to the garden requires a presentness. Each garden is in itself a past, a history of roots and bells, tree-rings, bad harvests from six seasons ago that still show traces through the soil. Early doves mourn overhead. My first husband, religious, loved severe paths and poor shrubs, to mimic the meekness of the human flesh. Wanted bleached grass, dead-growth hedges full of grasshoppers. He argued most years with the gardeners to make things flourish less, to pollard green ambition. *To humble ourselves before God, men, to mimic the desert of Christ.* They listened, leaning on their spades, and continued regardless. Surprise: a new crop each year, and his puzzlement at the garden's disobedience! *Must be the soil, Your Grace. Powerful stuff here.*

Lear was not a man of gardens. Horses, the dust of the training-square. Resin on a hot shield from a fresh-lopped spear, its sour honey. Give him pure elements, the moment, the thing as it was. No time, no time.

This is a garden of intent, of poised sections cordoned and controlled; a worship for God's order. The physic-garden stands apart from the vegetable- and kitchen-gardens, the floral-beds with their posies and plaited roses, the apothecary's square; each in its place. Enclosed, one enters each section and is transformed. The paths that link them throw up dust. Against the outer wall of the abbey are the lines of the orchard, the bruised fruit of summer beginning its gentle collapse. Three beehives. The earth is industry, here; it works its pleasures visibly.

Outside: marsh-heaths, endless water, fields of angry flowering barley and stone roots. Gorse and mouldering. In here the careful spoils of women's working in the soil. I think of Lear laughing about fertility, spitting on the ground to bless it.

Mirabel has her followers, on normal days. Ten or fifteen women, all noble girls, I've noticed, with pearl-studded chaplets and blood high in their cheeks. Perhaps she gathers the high-born ones out of some personal humour, seeing silken-soft hands wrap around nettle-stems, or dig out worms. But they seem loyal, and intimate, bowing their heads at her, in pleasure, and flowing with happiness when she passes them seeds, or directs their sowing. It is just another form of embroidery, this work. Today they are still sleeping. It is just her moving among the beds.

If her women were awake I'd lean closely to Mirabel, show her the closeness of attention, a touch on her arm, perhaps, or laughing loudly. And would be pinioned by their little arrows of longing, and envy. I feel them when I walk with the abbess, the nuns throwing out pinions with their eyes, hoping to prick me, hook onto my pelt. I know those glances well. They amuse me. Some women love to be favourites and react in fury when they feel displaced; others pretend neatly that they have no opinion, and only wrench themselves apart when in private, crumbling their hands together silently.

But they are sleeping. There is a cough arriving; several are ill, with hot cheeks, and are allowed to sleep through the early offices.

I make Mirabel tell me the intimate life of each plant as we walk. It pleases her. *This mint would not grow, the frost near blanched it like a lady's hands, I had to cosset it shamefully. Four years that sapling's been growing, still stunted. When I first came there was only sorrel here. That's twenty years of cabbage and radish.* Her body's softness meeting at a hard point at the spine, from bending, like a hard-fastened bunch of stems. Backwards and forwards: the plants are future-creatures, too, they promise new seasons.

I have an old person's voice, now. Thick, as if pushed like suet through muslin. I will perhaps miss this woman. She is half doughy, a plunge on one side slightly, from a palsy two years ago; thickened rounds under the eyes, and a peasant coarseness from sun. It is cruel. You would kill pigs for looking less.

She does not perceive the beginnings of my vanishing, that I am farewelling in this moment. I am the manner of queen who notices. The changing colour of rooms, the air between women when they do not speak. *You must have no back that any person can talk behind,* said Gloucester once. Get everything before you, let nothing be obscured. I was a queen who tracked things by scent, the briefest touch, an escaped sound. When Goneril passed behind me with my jewelled belt in her pocket I reached and held her by the wrist. *Lay it on the bed. Good. Now go and make your confession.* Could trace an entire crime by ear. It was the rustle of the chain against her body that gave her away. As if I would not know a foreign note on the skin of my child.

That belt. Lear, when we were first married, laid it on my naked waist and said, *There.*

I said, *What?*

He said, *There is the belly of a queen that will have sons like fields spawn weeds.* I have it still. Dogs, the crest of golden dogs.

We pass into the apothecary-garden. Feverfew, drifting wormwood. Late lavender in the borders. *A beautiful place,* I say.

With a sudden heft Mirabel mauls a bird's nest out of a bush. Tears it with the precision of a good butcher, half then half again. No eggs yet. The bird will find some other eave that hinders her less. She passes a tree and adds conversationally, *This thing is barren. I must chop it down.*

It has other values surely. A beauty. Hard wood rising, soft down on the undersides of the leaves.

A fruit tree with no fruit. No.

I am silent.

Mirabel senses perhaps that I have come across something stinging. Is not discomforted by it. Which I prefer, having flung off the soothing of others, their sops of comfort. It is better, always, to have companions who can look at your pain unblinking, without shying away.

We walk in the garden.

It is lovely. I will remember it, when I leave, I say finally. So she will know that she has my regard, and I am to go.

She is holding a handful of rosemary, now. Late-summer sprigs throwing out scent in the early sunlight. Looks to me. *It is too late in the season. The abbess will not allow you to go, I think.* Gives me

89

the crisp handful: needles falling away, over my arm. As if she had not just pronounced doom, casually. *Take this against colds. It will help warm you, the nights being so cool now.*

I am astonished. To deny me. She must have the backbone of forty thousand. Goneril told me no once as a child, only one time (a dress, she would not wear it, said it crimped her little child-belly), and I simply did not speak to her. Gave her sister treats and tenderness, while showing her blankness, as if there were a blank space where a child had lived, a nothing. Three days of this and she cracked out of her defiance, and wept on my skirt, while Regan sat on my lap sugar-smeared, playing at being a goddess.

Lear told me I should not do a thing, and I laughed, till spittle flew, and did it twice.

Nobody, I want to say, *will forbid me anything.*

But the words do not rise, so I let them flow out of my throat unspoken. Things flatten; the sun holds onto our shadows until they trail heavily down, and drag upon the grass.

★　★　★

The weather is clotting: the autumn is resolving itself into something darker, more intent. And the coughing women – I hear them, whistling in their lungs, and I am afraid. I must leave, soon.

On the chair Ruth has plaited the rosemary, in a wreath, to please herself, after I brought it in. Rosemary: for remembrance, for weddings, for death. Early in my marriage to Lear they took us to the rosemary-groves at the turn of the year. Harvest, and the wheat-sheaves heavy, dropping golden seed.

I remember the gloss of the blue rosemary-flowers in the sun-haze, as women led me to the holy well. My body first, as the wedded wife, Lear behind. Both of us bound with great wreaths

90

of rosemary, our hair spindled with needles. We were very freshly married then, still damp with it, looking at our hands together and testing their combined weight, the new bridge of their strengthening.

We left the sunshine and carried it on our skin into the shade of the forest, bees floating on my arms, my shoulders.

The well-mouth flowed green; it was hidden under a granite lip. One splinter of silver revealed the water, slipping through fern. The women reached through the moss, gleaned the water, and gave it in cupped hands. They were priestesses, bare-armed. The scene felt Greek, but these were crop-people, copper-faced from sun, one showing a blackened tooth in a smile. Lear's people.

In my throat the water felt dark and soft, bronzed, as if it had never touched sun; had lived under, sweetening, keeping itself through ages and many gods, to emerge at this one crack in the land. Lear drank from their hands, as had his father before him, at his wedding. We were blessed, in the shade-grove.

I had my crucifix in my pocket, I had Jesus bestowing on me His grace, but I knew no kind God could be cruel to this kind of heathen practice, its generosity: new-wed people covered with the hum of bees, deep in the rosemary-flowering, drinking to beneficence. My first husband would have been astonished. Lear's wreath was cocked over one eye.

In the old days it was blood. They killed a deer and left it by the well for the gods. Lear put his lips to mine to tell as we walked away. But I was serene, sprinkled with the damp of sap and new love. For my saint's day he would give me a golden frond of rosemary, to wear around my neck. A little golden deer, too, for one ear, a ruby for an eye. The tenderness of old gods.

Lear, I will die better than you. My God can do what yours cannot.

I hear the psalms roll out of my body, wave upon wave. Could recite them sleeping, in labour, streaming with sickness. Fidelity, *Domine*, fidelity to your mathematics, faith in your terrible will. Lord, you clothed my three daughters, both the men I loved and married, in the cloth of death. Help me, God, Jesus, help me now. It is my turn.

11.

The next morning the season shows its chill. Summer is leaking out of the daylight. It must be today: I must start, or I will be moving over hard ground, the frost deep underfoot. Snow perhaps to my thighs, to the belly of my horse. Mirabel is collecting thick cloth to lay over the tender shoots, with another sister, who coughs as I pass. Pale, I see now, with a ring of burning red along her cheek.

I have told Ruth, *Be ready.* I have gathered my things. By the time they awake to my vanishing I will be leagues off.

The abbey stables lean low; they smell of sour leather and soft sick hay fallen out of summer sweetness. Light splattering on the wall. The eyes of horses follow light, hands, movement, rolling under those black lashes. Regan had a horse-lash brush. Used it to dab rosewater on her wrists, her temples.

There are four. Thick-necked, not fine-blooded, with the weight of cart-horses. Heavy-skulled. A long plait presses against the neck of the white mare, which is the favourite; nuns give her flowers in their hands, I've seen it. Petals for her soft tongue.

The space between horses and men is so small, so small; their eyes, our eyes. Easy as a laugh, to slip between muscle and breath into a horse-soul, for them to slip into ours.

There is Calyssa, with an armful of hay. In her dominion. The circle of her law.

She hears me, and stands. Watchful. Blonde at the hairline, strong-cut cheekbones like the granite cliffs over a burn. Bloodless lips, freckled at the corner. How happy is she, I wonder, to be abbess in all but name?

I will need the horses, I say. *Healthy ones that can handle a hard journey.*

You cannot have these, she says simply. That mannered voice, its placid vowels.

Ah, a negotiation. A little abbess-play.

I would return better ones. Stronger ones. Which is true. I could send a whole host back, horses so divine she would die to look at them.

You can find others. Her expression is unwavering. She seems unafraid: there is no tautness in her hands. But I am no soft abbess, no commoner-nun.

In the silence I take the plait of the white mare in my hand and pull, backwards, until the animal's thick streak of neck is curved to full height. Nostrils shivering. The eyes blink and swivel. A front hoof shifts, but it knows: it is in a cage of pain, is held and will not fight. The language of a horse is fear.

She is watching this. Something shivering around the lips. *Has the abbess given you leave?*

Why would I need her leave?

Then no. You mean no.

I release my hand. The horse bends its neck forwards, quietly, quivering, in the silence. Turns its aquiline face to me, knowing its mistress. Offers its vulnerable mouth down, to be stroked, now. I touch the ears, the stippled nose, which is streaked back with cream to the great browline.

Obedient to your abbess in private, while publicly you defy her. You are an interesting successor, Sister Calyssa. She is politic, I give her that. A courtier's cunning. Works within the letter of her superior's law, but pulls apart the syntax, the seams; shows her weak, while serving her well.

Has she spoken of me so? Fighting herself to ask. Pride over decorum, her breath thickening. Sweet hay-smell, of crushed flowers, golden summer.

Is there need? You speak it so clearly of yourself.

Her full, furious blush. Blistering.

The bells begin. She moves to the door. *The stables are locked during masses now.* This is a clear order, phrased so as not to offend an idiot.

In the dark the white horse remains fixed in place, waiting for me. The wind rises.

★   ★   ★

The feeling of being thwarted. Like salt on the tongue.

I must go from here, I see, or else be swamped by human frailty. These women see only their own selves, their own God, the rim of the walls. They will hold me down until I drown. I need to escape, or I will commit crimes that no god could pardon.

The thinner nuns have white-tipped fingers tonight, and there are coughs during the holy office, shamefully smothered. Winter is rising through the ground.

Brother Manfred, who travels from the monastery to preach here, is a good man. *I am afraid it will be a bad winter*, he says to us. *I see several of you are already ill.*

His pink tonsured scalp is flushed with cold, like a baby's. What a gentle son. Perhaps in another life I gave birth to him, pulled him out from my cracked pelvis. I thought this about so many men: how they would look and grow, if they had been my sons.

He bows to me deeply, in particular. Senses that I am trembling in my clothes, caught between fury and misery. He cannot aid me. I am beyond him. My solutions are outside, in the soil, in faraway buried bones.

I am done with silent mourning, and stillness. When my first husband died I was washed shoulder to feet, like a child barely out of swaddling, and laid on new sheets, and slept in a nest of ladies all leaning to my pillow to soothe me. The rooms swam with skirts. I was laid deep with crumbs of voice for weeks, morsels passed from gentle plates to my mouth. A filled thing, softened by touching. Even at the funeral I was enclosed by many velveteen bodies, in any direction I leaned. Grief then felt tender, full of small words, a crammed place.

This grief is different. Demands space, wilderness. Or else it will crack the earth where I stand. I must out, or I will crush, or be crushed. They do not understand, there has been some mistake. I will leave. I will leave.

I go to find the abbess. She is pacing in her garden. There is a strangeness to her face, as if awaiting, and restraining herself from flight. Over her shoulder the evening rain is beginning, vast grey skirts of water moving across the horizon.

I wanted to see which way the storm came, she says. *How many sisters are already sick?*

Five. And Sister Mary Magdalene, coughing in the dark. *I must start soon*, I add. *I wished to do it today, but tomorrow.*

Why do you think so?

Because there'll be snow in a day, or perhaps less. The sky is a marble cast. Light droplets on our shoulders, pressing. *I would hardly expect your abbey horses to travel long miles through drifts. Calyssa wouldn't let me take them out to see their paces. She has a head on her, that one.*

She looks into the wind. *I told Calyssa not to allow you the horses.*

I am fixed in my astonishment. My joints move beneath my skin, noiselessly. *And why?* Perhaps an attempt to control her, but it will not work: Calyssa takes scraps of power and skins them to the quick.

She has rain on her face but will not move. The grass beneath us falls and rises, like breath, in the wind. *I need you here*, she says. Speaking to me as if this is pain to her, pure pain, I see it. A woman threatened, with enemies at her ear, who has been forced out of her rigour by my will; I am proud to have done it to her.

You are strong, you will survive without me. This is some spasm in her, some fear. I can soothe it. Calyssa will depose her, perhaps, or some other woman, once I leave; and it is shameful, but one lives.

She is not moving. *There is nothing out there for you. Nothing. Lear is gone, your daughters are gone. A world that has forgotten you. Nothing awaits you.* Nothing and nothing: the circle of ink, on the page.

The rain is pounding the earth fully now. If there were shelter we would seek it, but there is no place to move. *Lear would have forgiven me*, I say, above the wind. *One day. If he were alive—*

You would never be forgiven. In the storm-dark and rain the ground seems to lift, to swallow us. A smell of rot, of releasing heat spiralling into the air. *We were never to release you. Those were the orders. I could not tell you. But they said you were to be here until you died.*

A woman in Lear's court leaped and died one day and in her mouth they said was a sudden gleam of raw metal, something she'd swallowed, years since, provoked in some shock or disturbance of her humours to come up her throat like a fish and damn her. *So we cannot hide from our sins, but it is a foolish story*, said Kent, at the news.

My hair is pressing to my neck with rain. Crack of light over one half of the sky, shimmering white. We are full of cold, cloaked in it; water runs over my ankle, my hand.

I waited for years to hear, she says. Her sleeve is stuck to her arm. She senses its heaviness but will not move. Some hard streak of will holds her here. *That Lear would perhaps want to remarry, and I would be asked of you — but no word.*

He would not remarry. The idea swims up in me, like black bile.

The inside of my mouth is dark with it. *I was a widow, and he thought it had cursed me. Given us daughters and no sons.*

No. Widower Lear would remain chaste. Another girl, to slice his land thinner, thinner, and sit peach-cheeked at his hand and grin, covered with pearls, and give him meek babies she'd raise to dig out his heart while he slept! No: he knew the stories. He kept loyal, because of fear, which is the best assurance of loyalty there is.

The abbess and I stand together in silence. The air is full of water.

You will not let me go, then, I say.

I will not move before she moves.

There will be no horses, no food. Not from me. I will not assist. I am sorry, she says.

You are weak.

I am. But not in this. Outside the horses scream to the wind. *I have made my judgement. Their bodies are ash, their souls are with the Lord. You do not need to sacrifice yourself for their mistakes.* She is shivering. Has put her hands inside her sleeves: I can see their lines.

You do not understand me. (Goneril, shrieking in the yew maze – I push it away.) *You do not feel what it means to be married, or to have children. You think you are a woman, but you are no such thing.*

It is your choice to loathe me. But I will not let you go.

Let me go! I have been here for fifteen years. Since you were half a child with a milk-face I was here! I can give you no more! My fury is ancestral. It feels black and branching in my lungs. I see my children furious, consumed with it, as they never were in life, berating me for my failure, for my neglect of their bodies in death. Mouths like open plough-holes. Their eyes scratched out.

Old Lear turns his back, his much-loved broad back, that I stroked through nightmares and knew from freckles, its shape in the dark; he turns it on me.

Stay with me. Stay in this place you have built. The abbess is pleading. It makes her look fishlike, and ridiculous. *Where there are friends, and those who love you.*

I cannot. Here there is no person who loves me. Here there is no person who sees me to my soul, as I am, in my true self. Kent is not here. *There is no person here who even knows my name.*

Tell me your name, then. Her mouth in the dark is beautiful. *Queen, tell me your name.*

Abbess! A light. There is a nun at the gate.

What? Hair has escaped and is pinned to her lips by rain as she turns. Between us we look drowned. As if we have emerged on the tide, ringed with weed, robes so sodden that it would take five men to haul us up. Lear, we are so close to you now: the wall of rain conceals you just beyond our reach.

A novice has collapsed. They ask for you. Please come.

She goes towards them, already stripping off her head binding, the gauze at her throat. Then turns, as if some part of her is bound out here, to me, on the weakened ground.

We are friends, still. Aren't we?

Yes. To say otherwise would perform a cruelty I could not weigh out, in the balance of things. Crack something desperate. She is so young, still.

Inside I am left alone. Ruth, waiting by the door with her packages and her one good cloak, makes a strange noise, and comes to lay a fur over my shoulder. Presses my hair with hot cloth. The fur moistens and clings, and I feel as if I had grown a fresh skin, become an animal that sits in the storm and howls its heart out.

Oh, Mistress. Oh, don't cry.

12.

It was well foretold. Sickness has come to the abbey. They have dug six graves this evening. When the shovels become too cold to grasp they are kneeling and slowly pushing the dirt apart with their hands as if combing a woman's hair.

Ruth wraps a rag around her wrist and clears the misted windows, white to grey. When I come to matins the abbess is absent. The novices will not be still: they shift in their pews and press together as they sing, like bundled branches. The gates to the world are shut, while the pestilence passes.

The weather is dipping now. We are being cast slowly into the stiffness of cold, feeling it climb and grow rigid on our flanks, our stomachs. My palms turn white if I leave them out of my sleeves.

Ruth keeps me indoors: *You will be ill yourself, that nasty sickness.* So I watch, and am still as any vegetable in my misery.

The nuns' cells are baked with cleansing smoke. Windows across the abbey are thrust open to the glittering air. Ministering nuns place soaked cloths over their faces so that they appear, when they walk into the square to wring towels or take straw off for burning, to be blank, faces rubbed off a stone by an artist's elbow.

The infirmary is filling. Boiled water and blood-bowls pass through the doors. The news comes through Ruth that one is ill, that another has a rotted lung and will not last the night. What do nuns see, in their fever? Fevered cocks, the Devil rising from their bodies? I see it from this window: the lay sisters are coming to the physic-garden once more with baskets, probing their fingers to the roots for any leaf huddling from frost. They will strip it bare.

I wish them all dead rapidly, in quiet, so that I may resume my war, and break the abbess into pieces. It will dissolve: given time I can crack any woman open and spread her apart.

The cook watches too, leaning against the door of her kitchen. Like many of her class she is gruesome about death. They're gutsome – they like to follow the intimate maggots into the grave and grin at it all.

It is on the fourth evening that I hear nuns whispering. The abbess has been taken to her rooms. *She was out in the storm that night and would not be warmed. Now she raves. Her skin is like fire.*

That was an unnatural night. And has brought us pestilence. What did we do to deserve this?

I turn my face to the wall.

✱ ✱ ✱

Worship in the evenings stops. The nuns shut their cell doors and listen for the abbess's sick-sweet breath in the darkness.

On the day they bleed her I watch as the bowls are covered and carried to be emptied, out of the grounds. Mirabel tries to persuade them to slop the vegetables with it, but is defeated. The nuns pass by with their fever-steaming cargo, and leave her by the cabbages. I admire her, her frank flatness. She reduces things to their function. Body for God, blood for soil and cabbages. Perhaps she gives them her own shit, a hamper of it sticky with potato gruel spread in the darkness. I raise this idea to Ruth and she laughs with a hand stuffed into her mouth.

What would grow and knuckle from the dirt, with the abbess's blood? Mushrooms putting up pink hats and leaving your mouth gleaming wet perhaps. Fat vegetables with insides like tender flesh, running with thick veins on a strong skin. Or grass that smells when burned of fever, hair and sweat and salted mouths. I'd be a good wise woman, given the right herbs. I'd ill-wish apples as the best of them do.

★　★　★

She is fevered, the nuns say, she lies so close to the surface of her own skin that a touch may pull out her soul.

Here is what you hold to the body of the woman in sickness: poultice of fermented matter; warm dog or cat, to heat the cooled organs. Milk in bowls, curd in bowls, silvering. Oiled tapers to draw off the moisture that thickens her and makes her ribs distend. Smoke, of all orders, over her scalp. It is like luring: one bribes and sings the demon of the sickness close, to haul it free. But it can secrete itself in the body's chambers. Perhaps it hides behind the lung – I have heard of it.

Younger, I would have been crueller, and felt her suffering as a kind of gift. Designed to please me, in my anger. Enemies of Lear were driven to walk for weeks before hounds, naked, hands bound, until they fell. But I will be kinder, when she recovers. I will perhaps take her to my court too, with Kent and Ruth, and feed her sweetmeats with their sugared crust.

She has climbed out of sanity, with the fever. In the gardens the nuns raise their heads to hear her weep, then return to their work.

★　★　★

They said Lear was mad when he died. *Raving*, the messenger said to the abbess, as if the sanity of ageing men were thin, a membrane of spit over a baby's mouth. Inevitable; that he would be mad. The messenger I remember wore blue, the new king's colours, looked dazed and sun-smeared.

Mad. *Let me not be mad like my father*, Lear said in the bedchamber. When Regan was a fish in me, flipping herself in the darkness, already nuzzling for the light. A long illness, after a campaign – it went wrong, I don't remember, there were thickets of hostile letters, the chamberlains whispering in the other room. *Let me stay within the bounds of my reason while I have breath. Promise me that.*

You will not be mad.

He built wings. Did you know that? From the geese, my mother's geese, and swans' feathers. We thought it was distraction, an occupation while we ran the kingdom – a king dreams of seeing his lands from the air. It is not so peculiar. His voice with a begging note. *I saw them, before he died. Huge, bigger than a man on each side, and wrapped in silk and swaddling, like baby feet. They smelt horrific – he had caked them in stinking ash. It was Hell.*

I turned over and said— I do not know, the memory fails, yaws with air. He laid a hand on the swell of my stomach.

Bladdud the Mad. Who tried and failed to fly. His earth-bound son, who later rode a horse to death and crawled to his wife when it fell. It was his terror: *Do not make me mad.*

The insane were turned away and killed, lest they turn contagious and their breath let something loose inside his skull. His wariness at the Christian God, lest He saw something wanting and broke him.

If I am mad, kill me. Take me to a holy place and crack my head with a stone. I give you this order as your king. Every knight he swore to fealty made this oath. All of them took this strongly at first, and were wary, searching his manner for the beginnings of the named wilderness.

What does madness seem, Queen? a young one asked me, when Lear was dragging a rage around a castle. *How do we know its look?*

But fears fade; barriers left to rot weaken and fall. And one day the sea comes through the floor and drowns us.

I curse his knights, who left him mad, to die without his loved reason, and broke their sacred bond. The bells strike for compline.

I am a woman who keeps my promises, am I not, Ruth?

You are, Lady. You do. She has no interest in feeling deeper. She is blissful in agreement.

I am a woman who keeps her promises. Knight or not. If I had seen him step away from the line of reason, just one footfall, I would have kept my bond and killed him.

★   ★   ★

The abbess lies in the cave of her madness for days. Screams. Lear-ghost, I wonder. Is it you climbing in her ear and burning her alive? Are you vengeful? It wouldn't surprise me.

Ruth, to fill the hours, has asked for tales of our lives, once we leave. Once the abbess is better, once the obstacles are removed. She likes best the food, the subtleties of marzipan in the shape of men, fragile, winged with flakes of gold and almond. *I would eat so many*, she says. *I would eat nothing else and be so fat. And happy.*

Today she pauses at the window.

What?

We could leave, Mistress. Maybe nobody would notice.

Out of the gate into the chaos. We could leave and perhaps be borne on the unnatural tides that are rushing this place, over the strict rhythm of the hours, taking time apart and smashing it upon the steps, like a child dropping an egg. It is possible. The two of us perhaps with a half of bread, a peasant's cheese-and-apple luncheon, piled on our backs. Limpid stares of innocence on our faces. We could slip through, eel-unknotting, spilling, into the dust. Put miles upon the boot-leather, looking like beggar-women, tanned to the elbow. We could reach Dover by perhaps the next summer – yes . . .

Something in me prickles softly. No. A woman who would eat the first plum of the season brought to her on velvet, ceremonially, watched by bishops for the sacred spill of juice over her hand, her footsteps swept away behind her by a page, with an ivory-handled broom, and at night the prayers of thousands for her health, her happiness, flowing over her as she slept! To be small, so small . . .

And would likely die. Ruth being weak, and barely knowing outside life. Not young, though never having endured a birth. (Had she wanted a child? I had never asked. The time has passed for her, perhaps.) And I too old to carry her if injured or afraid, or to bury her body if she lay down and let the night into her through her open mouth.

No, come away. Don't be foolish. I will discover new methods to escape this place. And a weakened abbess, flesh cured to salt by illness, will be worked upon. I can get horses, anything. Yes. *We must wait.*

* * *

And in the morning we lose our chance. They have put the signs on the gate. Long ash streaks, the signal of darkness. An open circle traced. *Do not pass here. Let no man come near.*

What does quarantine mean, Lady? Ruth watching at my elbow, her quivering eyelashes.

It means we must wait until there is no more fever and illness. So that the miasma does not spread elsewhere. Nobody can go in or out.

How long will that be?

Not long. The whole winter season, to purify. They will crack us open again at Lent, they say, as is the custom. To see if the illness has run out of us like water.

So we will not go to Dover yet?

Not yet. When the abbess is well, and can order things again. Until then.

God has a strange idea of humour. To open the world, just a slit, just a miniature gap through which I could push the tip of a finger, and then to enclose it again. The ring of corruption that walls us in. Of course they will pass supplies over the wall: pallets of white bread, chines of beef in their thick burlap stockings, like women's legs. And for a fee, a high fee, old women might enter to nurse the ill, and wring out the linens in lye, faces bound with herb wrappings to stave off the pestilential air. Like mummers, a step always outside themselves. Even the thickest of membranes is porous, even that.

13.

The sickness pushes deeper. Ten nuns, twelve. Some struggle back to green health, but many now are in careful boxes, knocked together in the bright sunshine by village men, their rough angles handled with gentle hands, and left for us.

I venture out, and bring Ruth. She is so bored she at last yields, and admits that tending the ill seems godly. Their whiteness, the shock of blood in them. How it curdles in cold air.

Brother Manfred says softly in the cells, *Give comfort to this one. We have little hope.* Gestures. A pallet bed, in which a little nun whistles in her long sleep that will shortly come up over her head and claim her. Her mouth opens.

I am industrious with my face bound in cloth. I have tended children through fevers. Their pale arms thrown, to catch things falling from air, eyes streaking with heat, seeing beyond and through. Cool water on her brow makes this one whimper. Her body writhes. Perhaps she can see the ghosts, their scouring presence in the smoke.

In the night, Manfred is tending another, on the other side of the cells. The girl rolls to me. Perhaps nineteen. A girl of cornfields, apple-trees, armfuls of plenty in baskets, her hands still soft at the palms from years of milking, her hair dipping into the pail. And to come to this end, this meagreness.

I must confess. Listen. Her tongue is yellowed: she has entered into the flush of some hidden energy, which will break soon.

A small secret. Lear was given many: common people thought a king could carry their fine sins, like needles in his clothing. Bent to kiss and absolve many servant heads. I open my hands quietly to hold it, and watch her, the unfolding of her deep self.

It was me. With the bread. Tell Manfred, it will be forgiven. It will be forgiven. Her breath soft.

It is some old crime, ancient. I know nothing about it. I am filled with tenderness for this little sin, which consumes her. The fragments that make up a life, the miniature parts.

I watch the sweat cool into crusts of salt on her neck, her arms. She is giving out, now, the last elements of herself, salt and water and soul. She is releasing.

I will tell him, I say.

The abbess does not know. I ate it. I was so hungry, but it was Lent. Forgive me. Her purpled eyelids. Violets. The grip of this, bruising her.

Yes. I give her cooling pillows, comb back her hair; so that she might meet her new bridegroom prettily. This bonny body. *Sleep, now. Be at peace.* When the abbess wakes, I will tell her. I will gather this round of a life and deliver it to her. I promise it, Lear.

She dies early, in the sweet dark, passing out of herself as if through a door. Out in the world, perhaps, her mother lurches a little, rolls over in her sleep. The gates are shut. Perhaps a week will pass before her family carries her death into their midst and holds it, its full weight.

I kiss her small hands. There is rosemary on her hair, Mother, there is oil on her cheeks; the rosary is held in her palms. The sounds of weeping fever come from other places, but this cell is quiet: it collects her and delivers her gently. As milk from cupped palms, into the mouth of God.

* * *

I come back late. Ruth hears, thinks I am calling her, and stirs. I ask for some small thing to cover the accident of waking her; she leaves her warmth, attends to it, returns. It is the rhythm of her being, to move against my breath.

I want to wake her, to tell her. The girl, the bread. But leave her sleeping.

I sleep and dream of Cordelia, of her mouth at my breast. Wake feeling the weight of her head still, pressed against the bud of my nipple, my soft-beating heart.

There is, for instance, the story of the dog.

It was not one of the best hounds. I hoarded; I had no care for breeding; I kept them all in loping packs – though the long-boned hunters naturally separated themselves, were distinct, like ink that holds its worth in dense black while feebler ones sun-fade to brown. They had their strength, the mixes, with shoulders and hips borrowed askance, a head drawn on another body. Halved and quartered, hints of ancestry in a coat, the small lines of a paw.

One of that collection, then, and hardy, a good seeker, broad-mouthed for dragging pheasants and ducks out of reed-water. Could pull up a rabbit without smattering its fur. A pleased thing, ears like leaves, and simple in the round of its love, wanting a hand of food, the glory of its duty, and rest. So small and so distinct a life!

And the dog was smashed, now – caught in a toss with a stag. Smash of its bloodied mouth.

The hunters were apologetic. Regan, they said, had taken it out, loving its small skull best, and wanting to hunt. She was fourteen, lithe with a bow, Diana-quick for the pursuit. I had ordered it not to go out with the pack, but she had brought it out unseen, frothed with its fellows. It was untrained, no good for the courting you do with stags.

They brought it in on the back of her horse. Would perhaps have left it, ruined on the snow, were it not mine, were it not the queen's part, with the mark of my favour on its leather collar. On the rushes of my chamber it reached for life on my lap, and for warmth, knew my hand, the curl of my sleeve, and whined through a bitten tongue. The fine flat skull sunken by blows, and the back too broken for the tail to shift, but to be dragged behind. The other dogs kept far off.

Regan was weeping, coarsely, as if dragged through gorse herself, as if beaten. She had blood all along her chin. And so ashamed. I sat breathing with the dog-weight upon my knees. Balancing, the air seemed, in that pared-off moment of death, exceptionally still, very fine.

I had heard the hunt return, and had come down to see the prize, the ridged antlers to cut down and make into bone-handles. Instead this: panting daughter, wreck of animal. What lawn I had was wrapped under the hound's catastrophic body.

The dog will not live, Regan.

I did not mean it. I didn't. It was so dark, I could not see. Drawing in breath through her wet mouth; she sounded sodden. Her hair was half down, it told of the agonies in the field, lifting the dog herself to her shoulder. Its hot pain-whines all over her.

That does not matter. The terrors of disobedience were pushing into her. The rule flouted that had come to skewer her through. It was showing in her hands, which clutched at me, and fell away. *It will die.*

The truth of this bloodying us. I got up.

Come here. She came. Sweet dark-eyed daughter. I saw fear trembling under her skin, a moth inside glass. *You begin and so you finish. There.*

So I placed her foot upon its neck. Made her press down, until it broke.

I pray for the little girl from the cornfields. I pray for her mother. I pray for the dog. I put my head upon my arms.

★　★　★

In the morning cries go up.

The nose of the dawn rises grey in the trees, and then, as if in the same movement, weeping comes; it flows under doors, and spreads to the cells, where the nuns have waited. For news. And they come out, now; the lights are raised, they run and pass in and out of one another's rooms. The abbess has died in the night.

I know. Nobody has come to tell me but I know.

Perhaps the first time for many of them that a glorious figure has died. Mothers long dead or forgotten, or made into neat holy miniatures with benign expressions to clutch at the breast (*Oh, Mother, help me!*) in desperate moments; old nurses, perhaps, causing a spit of grief once, when they shrugged off years of service and quietly went to dust. But here is the beheading; here is the first sense of a careening into space. The moon has been cut from the sky; there are no stars; they rush into dark without knowing their bodies, their senses.

An army informed of the death of a commander is frenzied, or stalls in fear, refuses to move though the enemy are coming, coming over the plain towards them. I know. A rumour once – Lear's death – and hundreds of men sat down, in a field, bare-headed, bright in the sun with their shields and their unsheathed swords, sat down and were immovable by shouts and breast-breaking drumming, they would not. For the world was over, it was overturned by death, they were hurtling into darkness and would stay still for it, would not leave the place in which breakage filled God and spilled out onto the earth. It took Lear himself, without a helmet, to walk among them and yell, to get them up again.

There is salt in the air. We are all changed.

I close my eyes. Push home the shutters with a bang, Ruth, let them all jump and believe it is Christ shattering the windows in.

(After, it seemed, a host of them went to the chapel to see if the sound had been the drop of the wooden Jesus off his Cross, or a beheaded saint rolling his marble head down an aisle, or some other miracle, through which the abbess's loss was shown to be mourned in Heaven. And found nothing; and so walked away, looking for tears in the eyes of the Virgin, and seeing only white paint.)

BOOK II

1.

Snow falls. The gate is shut; the quarantine mark shivers in the yellow storm-light.

Somewhere the bones of the girls, of Lear, are cooling. Heat has passed out of them; even the faint memory of life. Even the scent of it, in the hollows and folds, has gone, into the ground. Anonymous soil enters them. Wind pushes out their name, and says its own.

Biers of laurel under them, perhaps, or the branches of great fallen trees; or, in the best possible world, windings of gold, at their wrists and fingers. Aureate glow in the darkness. All of it ceases to matter now, and softens into stillness. Rooks are in the black branches. The sky is ochre with cold.

★   ★   ★

We come to the abbess to give our courtesies.

The coffin is open. Around her head are three candles, for the Trinity, but one on the right is larger than the others, and so it appears unbalanced. One side of her sunken face is lurid. The cross upon her neck flares and winks with light.

The fever has flattened the softness of her lip, its sweet curve. Flakes of skin, white as chalk. And they have not done her hair. It is parted as in the sickness, down the middle, and laid under its shroud-scarf. A tendril shows over her shoulder. In the light its darkness still looks wet, ringed with salted sweat.

This is indecent. She looks unlike herself, the precise woman who always ringed her head in plaits, and oiled her temples with rosewater each morning. I witnessed it, that hidden ritual; her small pleasures. I touched those temples when they were dew-wet, still. To deny that in death! When she had suffered – and sweated away all other things in her sickness. Her hands were bruised, the attendants said, to the very centre of the palm, from clutching whole bodies of sheet, and screaming.

I want to climb into this place with her, and soothe, as I once soothed. But do not, and am immovable, in a coarse veil.

Lord bless and keep her, says Calyssa, who has arranged this, and arranged all other things.

It is a pity about her hair. I am warped, and feeling violent. I should have been consulted.

Her hair? Calyssa is holding rosaries, wrapped at her wrists. The other nuns look at me, shocked. Watch the abbess again. That loose lock, which seems to me so brutal. And she was after all only my keeper, and a silly woman, but I believe in God, and I believe in death.

Saint Peter would not recognise her.

It did not seem important. Flesh is dust.

Don't give her my corpse when I go, Lord save us, I say to the other nuns. *She'll put it out for the dogs. Or put it in a casserole with the cook.* Unwillingly they smile. Grief has made them blurrier, less sure.

Calyssa makes a furious noise.

Peace. Mirabel moves between us. She has a body like tide, sloughs off the silt of us on either side. *This is a holy time.*

She is laid with coins over her eyes as is custom, to weigh down the dead. My mouth opens as I watch them being pushed, one and the other, by the thumbs of the prioress. It is Lear's

116

profile, the one taken in his thirtieth year, and struck on coin-fronts: brute beard, a fragile picked crown, like a flower, the line of nose and chin that every hand in the countries knew by touch under a finger. On the other side, Fortune with her great horn, wedded to him in the mould, back to back.

Lear on her eyes. Lear as her vision, through which she will see the hours of her death. May he fill the edges of her sight. May he give her some morsel of comfort, in that place where I can no longer touch her.

★　★　★

Coins. I remember later the imprint of that profile on flesh, a younger one. Regan newly married, coming for more gifts, more funds for her spendthrift ridiculous feather-husband, who frilled and hummingbirded around the court for a dowry. He pressed, and she kept at Lear until he gave her strings of amber and the good lace for a kiss on his cheek!

Saw her coming out of the room flushed, with a necklace of mine at her throat: he'd had a servant get to my stores. Fresh-married with the bruises of love on her. I had a coin. I took her hand and pressed it so brutally onto the palm that her flesh, when I lifted it, had the mark of her father, his half-face, picked out in livid white. Shame. She closed her fist around it; I hope it is there still. Even in the death-hands that hold the lavender or field-rose in her strip-grave. A brand so deep she should carry it to God.

Oh, surely I must be beyond pain. Surely this must push me through the fibre of the body to something whiter, keener. To move like an arrow through the skin of the eye, and spill into the world.

★　★　★

We move out. The taste of her body, of the oiled shroud, recedes; it peels off us. I will eat with the women, as one does after death. And then recede.

The table is laid. Warm bread, a log of butter rolled in herbs. Beans in a pot, steam spilling like hair. The sisters eat now with their hands, wanting the warmth, to inhale it. Grief is greedy. Between two a piece of hot loaf passes like a kiss.

The cook stands and watches. She, like the others, is building a wall against the deaths, I think. Here is life, here is precious greenery kept from late summer, the fragrance of citrus and warm stone. Place it in your mouths. Be protected.

And yet the violence is done. We are a scalded place now, like Carthage after the salt. Seven dead. The abbess and the six others sweated out of their bodies, their lips open. Souls rising into air. I watch the women talking, the clouds of their breath forming.

Women are still dying, even now; their mouths open and release aching sounds, which float out of the cells and strike our faces till we shiver and recoil. There will be so many graves, I think, the little yard of sacred ground, with its periwinkles softening on the grave-markers in spring, and mosses flooding over the dead, may overflow. And then? There is no abbess: the abbey is a headless animal finding its way blindly in the dark.

The snow has arrived, and we are severed, as a plait from a head. We will proceed around the blank surface of the abbey by touch alone.

I remember travelling once, processing with Lear's court, both girls nearly grown. Girl-plaits wound with oil, blonde down on their brown arms. In a golden afternoon — it must have been spring, or autumn, one of those seasons where the light comes slant and gives everything its blessing, crams the air full of floating seeds — they played; and I saw them playing, in the grass, among the cricket-soundings and the crack of dead white reeds, and felt the acute sense of their separateness. I had seen them both out of my body, blue and brutal, in the first abyss of love that kills so many women, then watched arms unfold into longer sleeves and curls thicken to heavy plaits. And in that falling moment they coalesced; their general selves became particular; their boundaries thickened. Then, then, they began their descent.

One nun coughs suddenly, and starts to cry. There is silence. Another, brave, reaches a hand to look at her mouth. Turns the lower lip downward, showing its slick inner part, the apricot pink, like the inside of a cunny. She is checking for bloodied spit, for blackness on the tongue, both being early signs of the illness. A third is heat, prickling at the neck, swellings under the jawline. We all know the intimate shape of it, like a lover.

The girl's mouth is clean. She whimpers, and is comforted. I turn away.

★   ★   ★

The night is cold, smashes through everything like rotten wood. It is all lost, again. Twice in so little a time.

Ghosts, look at me. I was twice-queen, mother to three daughters, child of good birth, keeper of land that holds three good rivers and takes two days to cross. I had retinue, wealth, my pack of sweet bitch-dogs, four bay horses strung with my colours, hawks, thick veils for summer sun, a chatelaine hung till it touched my belly. I was thick with names. All gone. And I am thought to be dead! Perhaps I am. Perhaps Lear, entering the long hall of eternity, stood briefly and stroked his beard straight, as he did secretly at the threshold before he came to my room, early in our marriage. And the girls, turned young again by the grace of God, before light and husbands entered and cracked them – maybe they ran for me.

So, dead and not dead. A feather held between two pages. I am left marooned on this island with nuns instead of peculiar beasts. In all honesty I'd prefer the beasts.

The girls played at it, an exile-game, when they were small. They knew Lear always threatened banishment in his sourer moods: *Get from my sight. Let nothing tie you here.* Some courtiers, weary of his crosspatch moods and speeches, goaded him to the point for some peace; I still believe that.

We thought we were safe, the girls and I. Ducking and hurdling his dangers. Sparrows nesting upon a spike. I saw the two of them making a game of it in the gardens: *I will be queen, and I will banish you, and you must go far, far away, to the edge of the lake. And wait until I scream, and run back, as fast as you can.* They took turns, in autumn sunshine, to play out the horror of it, then forgot entirely, and ate blackberries off the hedges of the orchards, until I found them and smacked their hands for it. Little smeared animals. Berries soft-crushed into their nails, the soles of their feet.

I have no choice. I must wait, until the quarantine lifts and the cold unclenches its fist, to see. I will be perennial, formidable, bright as silver; I will flow over the new abbess like honey, and she will grant me all I want.

After a long lie of snow the ground comes fresh to the surface showing new growths, hidden patterns of swarm, of sodden history. Once after a year-frost a fen near Lear's battlegrounds grew wet, silvered, and showed old stones: a circle anchored in the grass, held for hundreds of years until the slick of rising water swelled over and revealed it. An arch, a buried thought-form. In the middle they found an arrowhead barbed like a beard. So patience shows grace, through rock.

I will show them how queens withhold. How they endure, and shine.

2.

This morning means work: cleansing properly. Sweeping, and the soft smothering noise of water. The dead women's habitats must be scoured, their belongings boiled, or burned. To push the demons out, and lay fresh rushes and prayers over every surface.

There are no laywomen now, no servants, to double the nuns, draw out their needs and free their bodies for the service of God. The kitchen is emptied. The lumpen women have retreated to their villages, to wait out the quarantine-hold on this place, with their reddened hands in their laps. Whole months the gate will stay barred, until the spoiled air is sweet again.

We have marked them on the calendars, the days we must wait. Like footprints in snow.

There is Brother Manfred, sole man remaining. Adam in a garden of angry chaste Eves, poor gentleman; he had to stay, as a necessity, a man being the only sex permitted to administer sacraments, mass, hear confession, hold funerals and more funerals. I see his dim gentle face, receding into the chapel dark. He knows he is backdrop here, pure function. His body he keeps separate from us, in the visitors' cells, when not performing his duties or oiling the foreheads of the dying; he'll last this out with as little time spent among us as possible, to preserve his own soul. I sense his fear of the bulk of womanhood cramped in with him. His tonsure makes him look, head bowed, like a full moon, hesitating in the sky.

I watch the women work, sleeves up to their elbows. They walk from the cells carrying bedding, books. Clean, mute in a line, of one form, as if printed from the same carved letter. Overflow daughters, pious children of overstuffed houses, or of poor ones.

Being of the highest rank I am not given any bundle. I stand apart with arms folded beneath fur. Illness can climb in at the throat, at the eyes. The worst of the linen will be burned, with its glut of blood, which cannot be steamed away or loosened with ash. Blood is like that, I could tell them. It resists.

A hill begins to build in the courtyard, of diseased bedding, letters, the small detritus of a holy life. Some of the dead were wealthy, and the elements borne out of their rooms are witnesses: psalms heavy with pearl, with scented oil. The pretty lapdogs with their ribbon-bows have already been killed and buried outside the wall.

The bloodied sheets are not remarkable, not in a place of women. I lost my courses years into my stay here, somewhere; the month was not marked. Fertility passed from me and rejoined the teeming world, bringing forth worms and seeds and blind little foxes, where in me it had lain useless and produced only misery. No, I did not mourn it. Relief for the lady Ruth: no more scouring the bedclothes with salvaged salt! She looks at this procedure from over my shoulder, quieter than a smell.

I follow the women's movements with small interest. They have been hammered to meekness; their obedience to God has been lashed to their will. Better. Better than wayward children, running for the boundaries.

Goneril knew the curfew and would lay bets against it: a little late, a little more. Regan, with less nerve and many backward looks, followed. I gave them a long leash but after one charmless trespass — moonrise, their hair muddy — gave no more.

It is long past sunset. You're late and you look slatternly. Come, do my hair.

Goneril was haughty. *It is not my duty to attend to you. Call a maid.*

I put down my combs. Softly. One atop the other, aligned as they were made, one ivory core slotting to the other's holes.

They were waiting, not moving. I extended it, the silence. The knowledge that they were beyond the precipice now and falling, falling through air.

Your duty is as I prescribe it. Then, when you have children, you may prescribe it to them. And may they be grateful to you for the instruction, though it is, of course, beyond your own breed of feeling for your mother.

Goneril would not move for the combs. It would be simple, it would mean peace, the disappearance of the wound. But leaned to her sister in a whisper that no husband would instruct her so. She meant me to hear it, perhaps.

You think a husband will treat you better? That you will not be required to stuff your throat and stopper down words? You whom I had esteemed for your brains. All of us are beholden to some part, Goneril: husband, father, king, God. It's best learned late than never.

I would not treat a servant as you treat us. Clear she thought herself brave for this. Little white child lit like a torch in defiance.

I raised the combs myself, put one behind my ear, then the other. Long scrape across skin.

Thank you, Goneril, for this honesty. I gave the benevolent smile that could make Lear cough with irritation. *You may consider yourself obedient to nothing, now. Not parents, name, nor train of heritage. And so you are released from all the bondage of your royal apartment, your clothing, your shelter and food, your sister and friends. Give the maid your jewels and shoes.*

This is silly. Fool, tell her. He had entered the room, then. Could sense the curdling of feeling, anywhere in the place; came to discord as a family dog, to lick the hands of the offended.

The Fool said, *O small one, there is neither mouth to spend such silver nor a pouch to be filled by it.*

I rose. Was perfectly clear: no misreading of the point. Appealing, Goneril knew, would be fruitless. The decision had been made. *It is a warm night. You may find a bed where you are granted one in the stable-yard. If you enter again obedience will not save you. Regan, come, do my hair.*

She came to my chamber again in the morning, before dawn. Smelt of horses and ash. I thought of the stable-men, mute, making the bed of Lear's girl from best hay and horse-blankets, laying her in her shame in a manger, like Christ's sinful relation. The logic of the noble was beyond their ken. But she would have their confusion as bedfellow; and the movements of horses in sleep, the dark walk of men with lanterns checking the dogs, the goose-shit and the manure.

Are you meek? I said across the darkness. Had waited sleepless, hands folded.

I confessed my sin in the chapel and was forgiven. May I enter my apartments?

I could be merciful, after the lesson. It was a hard balance, to rule them to the right, and fuss them as they showed remorse and improvement. Dog-training, morsels of sugar, of meat. *I saved your food. You can sleep with me tonight.*

Voices, loud and crude. *Stop it.*

She gave it to me. You are being un-Christian.

I slip out of memory at the sound. Two of the women have their hands on the same piece. A crucifix, looped at the top with gold. Costly, and heavy on the breast, beating against the bone: here. Here. Here.

Calyssa is trying to hold them. In the space the abbess has

left, she attempts to rise, to exert her will. *This is a strange thing to quarrel over.* She is, I see, attempting to be charming, her chin lowered and eyes too far open. As if coaxing children. When the best way to deal with children is to laugh at them, cruelly, so that they laugh delightedly back and run into your outstretched hands.

They are ignoring her face. *You would not understand,* one says. *I had one just like this when I was a child.*

My grandmother the princess gave a similar one to me, says the other. *And Sister Anna promised it, knowing that. We had talked about it together.*

In the bowels of the cells a nun is weeping loudly, and gasping, the feverish stretch of will for air. The sound moves over us; she is growing worse, she will die. The knowledge has made these women whippet-scared and ferocious. Terror, and the sour scent of evergreen wreaths on the graves of the freshly dead, is changing them, shaping them into dangerous things.

I cross over.

I will snap it in half, I say. *Here, it is easy.*

I lay a finger on it. A crack in the ivory, the weakest place. I have a gift, can always find the point where things are easiest splintered, or riven into parts.

One cries out and puts a hand over mine, over the crack. Closes tight. If I broke it now it would throw upwards through the thick bottom of her palm, perhaps through skin. Something else rises in me, a dizzying thought. My vision crushes at the edges.

Did you know a man came to Lear's court once with an ivory woman? I say. *Anatomical. One could lift off the carved stomach! He had painted all the bowels red, and the womb had a tiny child inside it. The heart was a little jewel. It was a pretty toy. A physician who came to tend Lear's mother, he was.* They are watching me but I view them through the blur of it: the physician unfurling the naked ivory woman the size of a forearm, her pelvis showing its curls of purple and scarlet. At

125

that point I had no children. The child in the ivory stomach was wax, yellowing inside her. Growing old.

I look up. Nuns, crucifix, closed hand. *Of course this will not interest you.* Release the ivory at its bending-spot, the nun still holding it.

She's played Solomon's judgement on you, says Calyssa. She has lost the moment, her power diminished, but at least she can acknowledge the trick. She smiles at me. And, like many women who carry their intellects like thorns on their heads, is suddenly beautiful. Or at least has a freshness; but it passes, as she moves away, to untie other gnarls, other arguments.

The nun who had protected the crucifix twitches a smile too, and takes it, pinning it to her pocket. The woman in the cells continues to cry, as if newly born. She will die hours later, and be wrapped, gently, her mouth cleansed of blood from her bitten lips and tongue.

I want to say, *It is not fair.* Since I would have broken the crucifix to make two new ones. Since any actual mother, meeting Solomon, would perhaps look at the child, look at the hovering sword, look at the open mouth, red and cruel and wet with demand, and say, *Do it.*

3.

The meals are disordered; the steaming plate is late to my rooms. Several nuns were late to vespers. The abbess, the dead women are still working their way loose from the world, still fading. We had all heard their screams when the pain divided them, as a butcher cleaves a breastbone. Human from animal.

And the abbess was young. She had had barely more summers than the novices. A handful at most.

I soothed Ruth; she has not seen death, she is afeared of ghosts and the nasty thorned tales of the kitchen-wenches, who see her pale spaces and see fit to fill them with ghouls! She was shivering in the bedchamber, like a cat frightened by a fire-spark. I told her old goodwife tales, to spit upon her breast if she saw shadows, to hold some salt close by against fairies.

My girls feared ghosts too, but were comforted in Lear's cloak, smelling the sour strength of their father, against whom no unnatural force would dare an assault. Ruth sleeps, and I am alone in the whittling dark.

There are lights in the courtyard; I come to the casement. They are bearing the abbess's body out late, to be laid swiftly in the ground once prayers are concluded. The bearers, all women, are moving within the thin torchlight; it must feel to them as if the world is small, closed within this one globe of pale light, their feet and the lit stones of the path, and the weight of the abbess. In their world she is the largest thing, a greater burden even than sin.

I watch until the lights cast around the side of the inner wall to show they are moving away, burying her in the sacramented ground of the crypt by the river.

*   *   *

One of the novices weeps in her sleep. I hear her, the high note that thickens out of a girl when she is past virginity, when her hips have cracked open to admit life, men, the weight of afterbirth dark and purple as a cabbage. This is perhaps her first abbey winter.

Dreams are walking all through the abbey tonight. The abbess's burial has washed into many corners. I can sense many women awake on their pallets, breathing into the dark, or caught in some disturbed place. And the fires burn all night, to clear the air.

They are so young, Lear. Even from a distance I see their youth. When I married my first husband I was seventeen, late, the threatening time in a girl's life: that hysterical bloom. Before the rot. Beauty that is painful for its faint smell of putrescence. The second I was twenty-five to Lear's bare twenty, and hardening; he placed his hands upon an animal that had its second age, its mature teeth, no baby pearls in the jaw. I have entered doors at both times and I know, Lear: old is best. Let me be old; let me be wrinkled and winged, and fly about at night bewitching milk. Better.

What did you see? I asked Lear, freshly married, uncertain of my appeal; a widow, rich as Croesus but with no children, with years on him in age. And never beautiful.

Precision. He rolled over on the marital furs.

Precision? I thought of scales for flour, shears at a spread of cloth.

He considered. His head lying on his crossed hands looked broad and unweathered. *You lay your cup at table and know its position always. You move through a room aware of every man and their mood, their scruples, their gods.* When he was tired he stroked his hair back from his temples in long, fluid strokes. *I saw a fish once with huge black eyes that never shut. The fisherman who brought it said it was famous, that it could see a wolf's jaw gleam on the bank on a dark night. I thought that would be a good wife, if she were pretty.*

A fine thing to say to a bride.

He looked at the ceiling and made a grin. *I am ugly, the lucky son of a lunatic, and you are a widow rumoured to be barren. Honey-soaked speeches will do me no credit or you any compliment.*

You are ugly. But you'll grow into a happier look when I give you sons.

Precision. Even now. Precision is my great virtue, if it were to be so defined. I leave no element. I am unrelenting.

Suddenly there is screaming. Repeated. A weep, a tear in it.

Ruth is still sleeping, and I contemplate waking her, but instead come out to see. There is some strangeness in this that she may fear.

A cluster of noise reveals the solution: a monkey, a nun's fresh pet, in a jewelled collar, crying in her cell. Promised to the girl by one of the dead, a noble widow. The nun had smuggled it out before it could be given away or killed, folded between her habit and flesh. I think of it prickling, livid, its sights contracted to this circumference of cloth and women's skin. Dank and sweet and airless.

Meat is missing, several eggs. The cook is furious in her boiled, white-eyed way. *Rats, they are. Holy women and all, but give them a nibble and it's rats.* And pushes her hard hands against one another as if cracking them out of a trap and smothering them.

Now in the passage we see it, lengthened into a bright-furred thing. Fine red beard and a pot-belly, like an overfed country parson. Gold at his neck, like a slipped crown. Vain little man! I start to laugh. The Fool would know you, would cosset you down from the high rafter with croon-songs and a darting piece of fish on string.

The Fool had a monkey for a time, miniature, in a little jerkin. It was dead by the time our first child arrived — Goneril, named hard, like the prince she should have been. The Fool never took another companion. *Never share the stage, my lady*, he advised, wondering as I swelled and became the twig sustaining a peach. *One tip is sweeter when not divided in twain, eh.*

The monkey-offender is tearful. Her acquisition screams ecstatically from her shoulder, delighted. Brother Manfred arrives, shocked: to him women and monkeys are likely much the same thing — tempestuous, full of vice. He'll shift the animal into a sack and throw him over the wall. *Such behaviour*, he ventures, but can summon nothing else.

We see the monkey's fine fingers, the white blaze of his tail, his testicles purple as sweet grapes. Looks at us from the corner of his golden eye. I feel a rush of desire for this creation of God to stay here. Let me wash his feet.

No. He goes. Sack-bound head first, he gives the assembly a long blazing howl of fear, and leaves the slop of his urine on the straw. Manfred whispers a long stream of half-muttered Latin and departs; passers-by will find a small, shouting sack by the gate, in the morning. The nun herself is consoled. *What a lover you picked for yourself*, I say to shame her into self-forgiveness, and she laughs, the bruised laugh of a tired woman.

Poor fear-animal. When she wakes, I scare Ruth pleasurably with tales of its tiny feet, its tail that might curl about her neck in the night and tickle, gently, her jaw.

★　★　★

The day is the vivid blue of lapis lazuli. Purpling shadows slide over the snow, behind the holy women who move, bearing sheets, boughs of herbs for the sick-rooms. Praying under their breath.

I am out: I have numbered the days, I know what the dawn signifies. I must breathe its air, feel the weight in the back of my throat. Ruth knows too. She has let me go.

As I walk ponderously, fur-burdened, I see Calyssa, alone, by the barred gate. Its quarantine mark. From her sleeves she spreads something that glitters, that I cannot identify. Small whorls of it, settling on the snow. Salt? Ash? Her head raised, watching the blue over the gate-posts, the print of them on the skin of the sky.

Ah, she waits — to be anointed abbess. We all expect it, now. But these things are done by the bishop. The abbess will have laid things in train, committing herself to heirs in writing, weighing their value. We must have the pronouncement under his seal, but it is a long way; the news of the abbess's death is likely still streaking across the land, like an arrow shaft, to hit home at the bishop's heart, behind the rosary, the heavy embroideries.

The office will be hers, but she has to watch. For a letter over the wall. For a writ struck out of the sky, a shaft of gold. And she will not lunge for it beforehand. She wants law, this Calyssa, the weight of the bishopric on her forehead, anointing her with the proper oils. So she reserves her hopes, and tries to be patient.

Though I see wistfulness. In the pause of her neck, its lines against the winter dark. Before she puts her hands into her sleeves once more, and moves away.

A day for hopes denied. Goneril was born this day. It was cold. Both she and Regan were born winterside, composed from our two bodies in the early bounty of spring, and carried through the frost. She, Goneril, was late. Took days, was hauled out blue and open-eyed but steaming into the cold. Yelled like a farmer finding wolves in his field. Regan, when she came two years later, lay flat and would not be tempted. The midwife padded the bed with sweet-smelling cheese to lure her out for milk, and at last one arm came from me, the sweet star of a hand, reaching for a hold. Greedy, always, looking for her reward.

A girl, they said both times, and I said, *Check twice*, then *Comfort the king.* Who had been drunk both mornings, sweated out of his wits at the glint of death, the fragility of lineage. Kent had kept him out, sweetening him with winter ale, to stave it off. The seam of madness in him surfacing, its thick glint in the pale sun.

Neither time did he curse me. I curled with my babe in the nest, like a badger in briar, and felt destroyed, all my control come to this instinctual mystery with which I could do nothing. He came to see while the sheets were still bloody, and kissed their eyes, and said, *A great queen she will be*, and then asked was I well, was I healthy, could I perhaps have more, a son? So soon.

And I was eager, yes. If my womb had not just fruited I would have laid him then, to prove my duty. I said, *Yes, of course*, and he said, both times, *My bold hag*, and took my hands.

I tried to make a wreath for Goneril's soul, but it unplaited itself, quietly, back into sheaves of sorrel and golden grass. I left it on my bed, for Ruth to burn.

I move to see what Calyssa had spread before the gate. Seeds. Little grains, gold and pearl, for the birds. A woman of gifts, then, for smaller things, if not for herself.

4.

Ruth whispers the next night, *They wish for you to come after the night prayers.*

This is surprising. But perhaps we will be speaking of the bishop's letter, or of the monkey; and it will pass the time. I wrap, in cold colours, and the white furs.

The chapter-house is full; they have left a space for me on a bench, warily. The cook brings chestnuts to pour over the embers and pick, smoking, with the pads of fingers, till the softness is burned out. There are no servants, no maids to pick out their lice; the evenings are bereft, hovering with the abbess's pale ghost and the many women lying newly in cemetery grass; and there are still sickening women in the cells, who lie and wail. So they come to me, for entertainment.

It is war, in subtle shades. I had forgotten. One must not, living surrounded by ladies. The nobles, the common women: the two groups pull and fall apart, in arcs. Without the common bolster of something to hate, or the soldering presence of the abbess, they sit separately this evening and look askance at one another, and at me, who belongs nowhere in particular. I think of parliaments, the gathering of thanes. Politics slicing the halls of power, end to end. One could not move one's seat without declaring a shift of allegiance.

Calyssa is quiet, by the fire. We are ungoverned, for a spell.

At least the feeling is intimately familiar. All my life: serving-women at the tables, in clusters while I walked the gardens, plucking the lute in the solar. A padding of women; quiet, passing lawn from hand to hand. And watching, watching. Lear's queen must to visitors have looked impossibly multiple, feminine beyond the bounds of a single body. Bursting.

I knew some names then. Genevieve, who tasted food for poison. The Lady Evangeline who took the summons to the king about my labour, each time. Spanish girls, Germans, sent to court to serve and learn noble pastimes: how to peel a fruit, to dance, to send erotic messages embroidered on a belt. Many left pregnant or otherwise happy; Lear kept handsome men for knights, all merry and mostly red-haired. They filled us out with twins of ourselves, girls and boys mirroring and swooping, pecking at our hands and flitting to the rafters.

I force my attention back into the room. The women are telling the story of Lazarus, who was laid dead, grey-bearded, and Jesus stood above him and said, *Be living*, and he was alive, at the click of the fingers, and rejoiced. But what good was it, this miracle? Lazarus had not known his death, was not lying within it in regret. He lay neat as a bread loaf, clean, his shroud dusted by the Jerusalem winds, and his hair dutifully oiled by a daughter-in-law. And he wakes and is given the knowledge: dead then alive. Would it now not be a discontented life, with a bite take out of it? Give me back my death that was whole, and ignorant, and did not desire.

They speak of Lazarus's wife. Her surprise! Her delight!

But perhaps she had become used to sleeping in the thin bed alone, I say quietly, *and now there is her husband and she must adjust again to his sighs and sleep grumbles.*

They look at me. One says, *Oh, but it would be a wonder to her.*

Have you ever shared a bed with a man? It is sweet perhaps for a while

134

but they sweat and stink out all their sins in their sleep. There is laughter. I open my hands. *And she had cleaned the house, and bought mourning-clothes, and perhaps sold all of his things, and was used to just a small bowl of grains in the evening; and now she would have to stock the larder again, and be a living wife!*

The two sides think me amusing. The common women titter over their embroidery, thinking of brothers, fathers. A few of the noble sisters have had men, and are sighing over them, over letters with their wax-printed seals (like a press at the nape of the neck, Lear always said, *I feel your touch whenever I open your seal*) from successful sons. Widows I have noticed have a settled look, pulled into themselves, the folds of pale flesh. I am still brittle, flaming. I am twice-widow, now. I will ride it all the way to the outer edge.

I'd have turned him out. I say this to shock. *A man who can't be trusted to stay dead — who keeps himself miraculous — can't be trusted at all.* Several of them laugh. Calyssa makes a hilarious distressed noise. Lear, I trusted; and look what you did with it.

Mirabel in the corner is listening but heavily. Even this act in her seems weighted and slowed. I see her portion out her attention. The livelier part of it roams out in the cabbage-garden, pushes into the dirt to see moistened salt and cool stone, a nosing and nuzzling thing, stoat-quick. God is in frost and crimped roots.

There is another fault. To give that Lazarus-luck to a man! Women are lucky — full of luck, round with it, resonant with the wavering of God's will one way or another. *To judge a farm's health, look past the farmer, look to the wife.* The men at court taught me that. The man may have padded his jerkin and hoisted his hose to look well done-by, but in the woman's body, the waste of its muscle, there is truth. An unfed woman can't make herself bloom, like a chicken-breast. Fate: there it lives.

And women last. Men rise and fall in sheaves, every season shaving down a new crop — war, honour. Women are weaker but we last: we sink into age, grow long bones, tell stories, hoard four score and ten. We get old and hairy and forget naught. Provided you survive the bone-cracking of the births — but beyond that it's easy.

I am roused. One woman has asked, daring, moving closer, *But your husbands, God rest their souls, both of them have died. You wouldn't have them again? If Our Lord laid His hand on the head of one or other, and said, Rise?*

Which husband would you have me endure again? I am bitter as citrus. I curdle all their milkiness.

One of the noble lot. I have begun to note them, their packmarks. The abbess mentioned the diversity of her flock with pride: *From laundries and the continental courts, my girls, and burghers' homes, and all else.* A sunny thinker, but without her their rank flares out, becomes visible. Jewelled chatelaines hanging at waists, warped and worn prayer-books, held piously to the Lord.

Whispers. Darting, under the surface, their fingers darting. They know so little. So little. *Your first husband was a righteous man,* says her friend, hesitantly. *So I heard.*

So you heard, did you? I forget: I am not real, I am bound into a thousand songs, I am four parts legend to one part solid stone. This the fate of queens. They see me in a frieze of other thoughts, other stories.

Well, who can it hurt? To be intimate with them, to pass the season till they have an abbess, and the quarantine lifts; and so find out their hidden parts, the secrets lodged under the pelvis, in the silver bone under the eye. In place of handmaidens, these women: less luxurious perhaps, but proffering entertainment, more elegant at least than a juggler.

And their idleness is dangerous. I broke a necklace once just to give my fighting daughters something to do. Bead-gathering they were reunited, palming the things in small hands.

I wonder, Will Calyssa thank me? For calming her troops, while she waits for her crown. Perhaps not – but I can lead, in the floating space, one abbess in the ground and the other unnamed. I can have this little kingdom, for a spell. Yes.

Would you like to know about my husbands? Would you like to know about my life?

Yes. Please, yes.

I think of the old story of the fishermen, one each side of the Avon perhaps, who each believe that they have a great trout, and haul and play out the line and tauten it for luring, hours on hours; and are in reality snared to one another, the hooks lashed together in the deep water, as fish look on and chew the water-weed. I will play the trout, be hooked skewer-through in the lip, allowing a giving and going of line, yet pulling their hands down, down, into the white water. Desire opening them like windows.

And I have known all the shapes of it. Desire, the burn, the lithe rabbit flicking from your hand. And what the poets called holy love. How Mary looks at the Christ-child: bored, beautiful, yet incapable of freeing herself, her hands from his navel, her gaze from his gentle oversized head, like a peach.

I was married at fifteen to a boy who would not fuck me because he was a saint. He died of saintliness, and I ran across country to marry the pagan Lear, and gave him three daughters, and so he hated me. And the Lord will not raise either of them, ladies, because He has given me the sufferings of ten husbands in the bodies of two, and that is quite enough.

I smile. There is blank shock, spilled on the floor. The chestnuts are oiled, black with hearth-ash. I put one in my mouth and it reveals itself, steps from its skin and is creamy, reborn.

★　★　★

Their faces! People always think I will talk like a bird. Sweet short chirps, snippets, laced bits of sentences. The frail song of a seasonal animal. I astonish them, as I did when I was married.

What do you mean you don't have the men? Show me the maps. Push the boundary here. You will fetch the iron and you will do it by winter. We conduct it this way here. I heard you the first time.

Man-language. Straight, thick, pillaging and forcing through. Gloucester, he of the multiple sons and belly wide as a fishpond, said, *She should grow a beard on that tongue, for its coarseness,* when he thought I couldn't hear him.

And I'd still speak clearer than you, I said back, loudly, and heard him start and cough with shame. Likely Lear thought this was a good place for my man-tongue. Perhaps he thought regimented prayer-lines would strap me back into some kind of gentility, like a girl tied to a chair-back for posture. More fool him.

Goneril said once, *Must you talk like that?* after I swore in court, and I laughed at her.

Said, *I'd rather speak more honestly than you do, all finicky vowels and fine vocabulary you don't understand. I know the governess is a pretty woman but this is not the way to impress.* Watching her flush pink to the dip of her young neck. We had to send the governess away, blonde women with soft-tipped eyelashes being chronically poor at discipline, it seemed.

They were bad with language, my girls. Thought it was a servant, when really it was power itself, the pull and hold of it. The Fool knew. Forming his puns in the shadows.

I have been thinking of my numbers, I say to Ruth in the morning. *Married twice, three daughters. Perhaps I should marry again now so that the daughters and husbands match up.*

She is as startled as if I had thrown her a cat. Then she laughs, with a kind of hysterical relief. She has not heard me joke much, perhaps.

It is true what I told the women. The shape of my life is not complex. Like an otter's spine or some other long animal: many knots, in succession, held together by a thin taut line of blood. Born, sent to the convent, married once, married again, mother once, twice, three times, then laid here. And yet such flexes and agonies, in that one whip of line!

The window is snow-drowned. The nuns are hiding, quiet; no deaths today; perhaps we have survived the last of it. Crouching, in hope. With Ruth I am going through the bed for lice: pick, crack between fingers, throw into a pail.

I may tell them, night by night: little nicks, little mouthfuls of a queen's life. They are begging for the taste of it. And we are so sparse, here, there is so little to sustain us. No abbess, shut walls, the wash of the tides of death. Simply the hours, and the work of prayer, living at the hinge of God.

Before my first marriage there is sparse material, they will not want that. My parents' house with its huge stunned rooms, placid serving-women moving in and out of shadow, a single white dog sleeping in the sun of the long hall. No.

I have something: doves. They kept hundreds of doves: the rustles and wing-beats of the dovecote, sweet crumbles of sound. High-born families kept them, in those days; it was a noble's privilege. Out of fashion, now, I think. You cannot lure a dove but must seduce it, careful, hands underneath it as if cupping milk in your palms, lulling it out of its smothered dark.

Once in my early girlhood a high grille was left open in the dovecote and they flew upwards. A thrust of sound into the air, and a vanishing. I thought they would be easily lured back, would hang like white pears in the trees; instead the forest gulped them down and gave out, over days, blasted corpses. Guts in glossy mounds. Eyes stolen by rats, ants seething under a wing. I cannot tell the nuns this, though I feel Mirabel perhaps would understand.

My parents knew obedience, but also saw its limits. Girls are fiercer birds, egg-stealers, rimmed at the eyes with bone. They sent me away when I was still dove-small, white and tender, but beginning to show adult plumage. A thickness across my chest, long silences at midday when my tutor could not make me attend. Their knowledge had reached its end. I was unfolding – I had streaked past the last forest of their boundary. I was sent to the convent.

This feels healthy. To revisit these old places, which even the abbess never saw. I feel strong. I push further. A louse between my fingers is black, and small as a seed; Ruth takes it from me, to put into the bucket.

Should I talk of the convent? No, it was not like this place. There was no gentleness; the nuns wore darker habits, and kept the flesh of the Lord under their tongues for hours. We learned Latin, embroidery, the nipped steps of chaste dances. All of us of wealth, brought to be trained and moulded to the bridal veil and the chatelaine. When we grew into womanhood and had our first pomegranate-cluster courses, they shamed us in sermons: *the curse of Eve is upon you.* Eternal sin smelt like underarm thatch, like the sweetness of girl-fat thighs sweating in darkness. We ate cold bread and were silent.

You learn to lean close into hunger. To sop it with other senses. Crushed flowers, the feel of air, a cold press to the throat to stop constant swallowing. Hunger was our first little fool, our animal, following us in train. Girls ate petals of the rose crowns at Easter, threads from the floor, their own dark hair.

You will have rich lives, the nuns told us. *You come from great power and will be wives and mothers to noble men. We are teaching you to suffer like the Lord suffered, and be obedient.*

It taught badly. Hunger teaches hunger and is never sated. I consumed men and their love and their sweetness with the rage of the starved, and was thirsty beyond the reach of rivers, and

140

needed fucking beyond the strength of rutting deer. When rich-ness touched me I clung like the Fool's baby monkey.

Kent, when he came, saw my appetite through my clothes. Would remember my starving for the rest of his life. Would that it had taught him better.

★   ★   ★

In the end, that night, I decide to give the listening women the garlands of the history, not its meat. Old friends come drifting, over the smoke. Ruth has packed me in furs, and the women are silent, sewing. They wait; they are hungry. I am in command of the room.

I was married to the wrong man, first. Did you hear that, in the gossip? No. The first husband to be suggested had been an older brother — crowned several months earlier. He had a great coronation. Rumour said that as he laid his hand upon the golden sphere a part of the coronation tent collapsed, and he laughed. But he died. The illness that came up through the ground in those years. All of you are too young to remember. And so I was passed in betrothal to his younger brother, poor boy. An accidental king.

It was not like this one, the illness of that time. It entered people's throats, their lungs, blackening them from the bones outwards. One saw dead frogs clogging the reeds; one saw babes bubbling at the mouth. I tell them this, and they whiten at the edges.

In the convent we were safe, and the world outside simply shifted darkly, and rearranged. What were men? Things with downy parts between legs, as with dogs, or bullocks. In youth you accept everything, take life into yourself. Of course a royal husband, of course a woman giving birth to rabbits, of course.

The nuns stretch their hands. Sparks emerge from the fire, then fall. Alike, noble and common-born, they are imagining themselves princesses, married to kings. I am a vessel for their dreams.

So I was taken from the convent to be married. I was seventeen. The nuns had sent the new king a sketch done by a novice, and it was said he approved. I know they are looking at me, at the spike and wrinkle of me, turning me backwards into my first bride-self, and failing. In the portrait I had lips bowed at the meeting-point, a hairline out of a fine Dutch textbook: a dream-girl.

Though I will not tell them this, it is also the beginning of Kent. I first saw Kent when he came to gather me from the convent for my first marriage. *You are ill* were his first words. *My lady, I come with an offer of marriage from my cousin, your father's cousin, great prince. But, Lady, you are ill, you cannot travel.*

She is not ill. She has a strong will; it marks her face. The mother superior was disapproving. I had refused sleep for several days for some small infringement. Sleep was the only currency, the only portion of our control.

A will in a queen is a good possession. He bowed and gave me my first bridal-gifts. Had they been selected by the elder brother? The circlet with the white stones. The loop of long gold inlaid with dark crosses. Still I can count its links, move it through my hands.

There is a silence. Without an abbess, these women are reaching for some greater feeling or idea; and I appear to be solid, or at least unassailable by any forces they understand. I am mythic: I represent politics, and lines on maps, and long-dead courtiers rotating in ballrooms. I am, I know, proceeding through this place increasingly laden with these women's dreams, holding me with small hands, like so many ribbons, flying off. Ghosts, do you see? A queen is multiple: she holds – she is a vessel of seeds and potential. She grows and grows.

One of the nuns says aloud, faltering, *But it must have been strange. To be married to the wrong one.* One of Calyssa's, the common girls. Puncturing her own envy.

Who are we to say whom the right men are? These things are decided for us, another says piously. *By God or by our fathers. Or so they are in families of quality.* They are prickling, snide. I sigh.

Despite the later rumours, Kent had eight women with him. Who would send a young man alone? They were fat; they pinched and kissed me. That night they bathed me in milk and huge looped white herbs, as the girls watched, crowding the chamber doorway while I had scented oil combed through my hair. I gathered my hands to my face: I smelt unlike myself. Nothing animal left on my skin.

I remember. Kent rode ahead with the standard. I lay in the carriage, gorged, was delighted by light, by the horses' white feet. Small things. The women fed me cakes; the court had sent mothers, vast-bosomed and full of soothing. A canny act. To lure a chick you click and coo, lay crumbled corn.

We paused several times, to rest the horses, and in my rich new gowns (too big, I was thinner, had eked myself down out of stubbornness) I would clamber out to look at roadside flowers, and be quietly sick. Kent said, *You swear you are not ill. I will not take you to the king if you are.* He saw I thought this a threat, and recovered himself. *We will find an inn; you can rest.*

I am not ill. I will recover my looks.

I am sure you need no repair, in that particular. And he bowed his pale head in the sun, already balding though only eighteen. The women were present for all of this.

She is a sweet-faced child but I am not sure she has become a woman, one said to him later as I tried to sleep. *She has a slim waist and no paps.*

The king has scarce become a man so they will be slim saplings together, Kent replied.

The women are still squabbling, like a group of little birds. I put my head on one side and fall into sleep.

143

5.

The next night it is the same. They have perhaps processed through all the hours and masses under the stagnant eye of Brother Manfred for this, for the royal audience. I expand to fill the room. I have courtiers; I am delighted.

I met my husband and he was very beautiful. But very young.

I waited for the young king. The ceremonial rooms had a painting with one rotted corner; I watched it, its blackened part, which was shining with new oil, as if they were rouging it back to health. It seemed hopeful, a hopeful gesture, and yet here was this gawk-boy, all elbow and throat, stunned still by his fall of fortune. He looked as uneasy as a hare in a truss: hurt, shocked, exhausted by his failed thrashes for freedom.

I had been told here was a monk, trained and cloistered for the Church, at the very rim of taking ultimate orders, before death had laid his beautiful older brother at a stroke and drawn him to the crown. He was freshly tonsured, still. It seemed raw, like a bruise.

What they had not said: he himself was a wonder. No grace of form but the face of a girl or a spectacular child. I stood in the ceremonial room and saw the Godhead in his flesh, his vulnerable lean to arrange his shoe, and loved, with a stunned suddenness that flushed my throat. Poor little virgin!

You ride? This I suspect being all he may have known of women.

They ride; they eat sweet foods; they produce children, and sin, and die.

Yes.

I have a fine pony. You will be happy here.

May I keep dogs? Had several at the convent, long graceful hunting breeds shared between girls.

Dogs? I do not like dogs. In the Holy Book dogs are an insult, or the eaters of human flesh. Matthew said, 'Give not that which is holy unto the dogs.'

But in Ecclesiastes, Lord, it is written 'A living dog is better than a dead lion.'

Hm. Yes. I will consult upon the point. Perhaps there are holier forms of dog, breeds that more closely approach the Almighty.

I, too, would like to know if that is true, I said gravely. It seemed auspicious. There could be no disaster in dogs, in the discussion of them. He turned, made the sign of the Cross on me, and walked away.

He had a stream of names, passing over his body, as was the fashion of that time. Tied and trussed to him, the ancestral sediment of emperors and old princes, their oak voices still pressing from the walls and shadowed alcoves of state. *King* fitted him poorly. He was lost. For myself I named him Michael: archangel, flaming guardian of death, his beauty burning out to the edge of vision, like a star.

The women here want to know of the wedding, and I tell them: a hundred waiting-women in proud colours, the lightning-crack of trumpets, great visions of holy portent, gold and gold and gold. The nuns want to bear the scent of the triumph as if it were their own, as if their bodies processed towards the holy king, and were anointed with the bishop's oil on their hair, so I give them detail, all that I remember. Pearls, spread at our feet, crushed.

They are besotted, or judging, tutting at worldly weights. I see a novice turn to her friend, whispering. A high-born girl. She must think my ears and eyes blocked, or corroded with age.

I felt this with my girls: their dim and hidden language, in gesture and nonsense-words, and once older in the movement of a hand, an eyelid, even in crowded places. Whole narratives in a dropped fan. It darkened me with frustration then, I would try to crack it open like an egg.

I say, *You have a thought?* My voice is thin as glass: it slices the room. I know what she said, but now she is caught: she must renounce, or declare.

She holds a stammer in her voice, but her head is cool. *It seems ungodly to talk so much of gold and wealthy things. For we are not to set our hopes on the uncertainty of riches, but the rich provisions of God.*

I cannot help what was, little one. Little donkey. *But, as it offends, I will retreat. With apologies.* I adopt a gently humble air, covering my head to leave. Furs over my hair as their faces show alarm, and turn in fury to the girl who's engineered such a turn to my feelings. The entertainment leaves, the jester is upset!

The Fool would throw mock-tantrums when Lear was lacerating in some sadness. Haul himself over the tile, sobbing in dust, for any paltry thing: a cloth animal apparently done to death, a hazelnut crown not fitting his head. And would not give us succour or dance, until we choked down laughter and soothed; he'd lay his grizzled head in Lear's lap and coo like a bird as we stroked behind his ears. Goneril, older, scoffed, but the Fool knew: sometimes one withdraws, refuses, theatrically, to heighten the delight.

I look up as I leave and Mirabel is smiling, behind her hand.

Other, more hidden, things. My father came a month after the wedding.

So. I will depart. Hail the king.

Do not leave me here. God save me. I was quick, I kept my voice quiet but ardent, like a child's arrow. *Let me come with you. Let me come home and be with you. He does not love or want me, please.* I had his hand in both of mine. The two together would not fill his palm.

He looked at me, at the tiny mass of me, small bones and less flesh and a golden gleam at my waist, my betrothal belt, weighing me with white stones. His gilded thing. Prize bird.

Hail the king, he said, and left me.

★　★　★

I wonder to myself about the monkey, whether it escaped, whether it slung out of the bag and was reborn in the broad silver reflections of the winter plain, and rioted up a tree, and is waiting there for spring. Or shivering, under a hedge. Or dead.

Monkeys. There are some things you cannot explain to nuns. Old jokes, nearly half a century gone. Kent asked, *What did you think of your king?*

He is very beautiful.

He is immensely pious. I have known him only slenderly as he spent his youth in a seminary, but a holy man will make a good king.

You are hopeful. I have not met any kings.

You will meet a great many. The nuns tell me you are well trained for court. He will have his own rules. It will likely be more restrained than his father's. But restraint may suit you. You have led a quiet life.

On the contrary. I demand riots and firecrackers and at least one monkey.

You will be a very popular queen but a very confusing wife. I wish you luck in your monkeys.

He would always leave with that expression. Even long after I had become Lear's wife, and changed all of myself, shape, name, the hold of my body. *I wish you luck in your monkeys.*

The Fool wondered at it aloud in facetiousness once, and Lear in capacious mood said, *It is their language. Let them have it.*

She has had Kent near as long as I, and long association breeds its own dialect.

What was our own language, then, Lear's and mine? Snarl and whistle. Teeth and snap. Oh, for his nuzzle along my flank, oh, for the warmth of him in the mornings when the sheets cracked with frost! I am here; I speak; and yet I am unheard, except by useless women. How poor a fate it is to be a woman finally without a loving tongue.

★ ★ ★

I am told by Ruth to wake early: an event is occurring.

A dark morning. A woman is crossing the yard, a nun with sweat at her neck. Still with the stable heat on her — you can see the cold part before her body, the steam from her mouth. And carrying pails: hoisting them at her waist, pushing her cap back with a wrist. Another comes over to her, a young one.

Oh, give it, give it.

Hush, you'll have it presently.

The weight of it pulls all the nun down on one side, so she carries at front, like a great belly.

In the chapter-house the bowl of milk goes round. Every woman takes a little dip of it, on their littlest finger or the pad of a thumb. Fingers go into mouths, tasting the sweetness. In this soft grey dark they share the milk reverently, in a hush, sucking, wiping their sticky hands.

At my turn I dip the crook of my small finger to the first knuckle and lay the cream under my tongue, for a longer pleasure. A deep intake of breath, as they observe.

They do this, they tell me, most winters. The fresh cream of the cows at first milking, before light, seems a holy thing, sharpening the edge of their deprivation, the winds down the length of the halls. Many of their tongues when they whisper are tipped with white.

Decadent, I say.

Oh, no. No, never. The bishop would allow us. Only one bowl.

It is their apology, their coaxing: forgive us, take the gift of this into yourself and continue to share. I am theirs, now, marked with their love of a small thing, even if soon I will leave (they do not know it). And both sides claim me, as their figurehead, their gift. Well, I am everybody's queen, I do not need to be divided like Solomon's baby.

Still, however, there are gaps in me that will not be filled by God, by sweet milk.

The messenger did not tell me how they died, the girls and Lear. Only that it was terrible, that the calls came too late, that Fate at last released Lear's grasp on its white luck-hand. Turned away.

I have sketched them in my head as they aged: the girls thickening, Goneril's hair darkening and her cheeks filling, Regan turning down at the mouth-corners, both of them still with the dark dip at the point of each collar-bone. Lear's skull emerging further from his crust of hair, the red perhaps receding into a wash of yellow and white, his circlet flaring on a whiter forehead. For them, perhaps, I retained one figure – still slackened after pregnancy, turning for a piece of meat at the table on the last night – and never aged.

I clear my throat. Perhaps it is best I do not know. If I knew how their bodies had been cracked and beaten, it would leach into their best memories, the ones I preserve. Eight-year-old Regan, shining in her shift from an illicit river swim (how we beat her!), would have a bruised mouth and bloodied hair. No, let them be perfect, still, and angry, and sob in the bath, and watch me from the stairs; oh, let them be alive, and loathe.

The woman who takes the bowl at the end to return to the kitchen looks at it, in the hidden part of the doorway, and licks its last parts clean. Does not see me watch her.

★　★　★

Two nuns pass me as I walk through the cloisters. I feel their envy, rising like heat. They push into my life with little fingers, they touch the icons, the pearlescent ermine, and they take it into themselves: queenship, the root and loam of it. The noble ones are perhaps more arrogant with it, imagining themselves so close to queenship, as if they could have had it by a hair, one rotation of the wheel of Fate. The common ones are ardent, suspicious of their own desire.

Calyssa, I notice, envies nothing. Merely listens, and scolds her women if they spill pearls of candle-wax over their shoes, through inattention. The arc of queenship is outside her ambition, and so simply unreal: she is waiting, poised to unfurl in her own season. Mirabel also shows no movement. Is a creature of necessity rather than appetite. Everything weighted according to need.

And so few know what it is. To be married to a monk who regards your body, your smell, as a quiet snare that will damn him.

In the early years at least he assured me that it was not myself but my essential nature, my feminine parts, that could not be endured. The helpless accident that meant I was born with breasts and no cock. I was still thin from the convent and had barely hips, barely shoulders, almost translucent at the neck. He said that this had pleased him, when they told him about his bird-girl bride: that I would not be fleshy and lascivious. He patted my hair as he would the fur of a dog.

In bed he stiffened. Laid a sheet between us, bolsters. *I am not strong. I do not know what to do about it. About lust.*

It isn't lust in marriage. It's love now.

I do not love you yet. Brutal as a falling stone. He was careless with it. *For now it remains lust. For an unknown woman.*

May I see it?

Unwilling but without comment he unwrapped it. A contracted softness, like a closed paw. I wanted to touch it but could not, seeing his anxiety, the turn of his eyes. *I see. I think I can do without that, for the present.*

My ladies knew. That Michael would not take me, that he refused congress. *Take care and remember your prayers,* he would say and kiss my hands, and leave me at my door. Even when we had been roused out of the banquet-hall, newly wed, by drunken courtiers, raucously calling for torches to lead us to bed. His face cool and enduring.

I became a sneaking animal. Barely aged, scarcely blessed with hair across my intimate parts, I shaped myself into a bartering, smaller thing, begging and slinking myself into his blankets. And what to do then? And what to lure him, what to repay my covenant and bring forth more men, more men, to populate the earth?

Ruth comes down to me in the cloisters. *Lady, you are standing in the wind. Are you well? What ails you?*

I am well. You are kind, lady Ruth.

She bows as if struck, and retreats. Little sweetnesses when I remember to give them shock her intensely, like having water thrown at her face.

★ ★ ★

In still pools you will do almost anything to create movement. Loose an arrow. Prick an arm. Stir a little fight, then arrange its reconciliation.

Ruth will have to be taught: she is as new wood, she has no sleekness. I look at her in the evening.

Lady Ruth, show me your curtsey.

My what?

Curtsey. You know, bob at the legs. You can do it.

Well, Mistress.

That! You look to fall over — what manner of work is that? Were you never in a court at all?

I am sorry.

Kent will be ashamed of you. The knights will die laughing. Her bobbing head; and she crouches over herself, as if punched in the stomach, falling backwards. The head of a puppy, contracting at night. It is the act of a wounded thing.

Michael, I want to tell her, could not bow at all when we met. Out of fear at the ceremony I watched his feet: long, golden as pears in the wedding slippers. Saw that they turned inwards towards one another when he bowed to the priest; the knees came together in communion, and swayed. Poor-grown. I looked up, saw the little tongue that licked up the host, and was lustful and ashamed.

A thought: he is alive solely in me, now, little first husband. I imbibed whatever part of him I could, put hair under my tongue, his old clothes next my shift, lay with his cock between my thighs all night, still as a fish under a stone. And Lear, and my daughters! How much of them had I eaten and drunk, skin and wound and breath, lips to scars and childhood bruises, mouth to cock and nose to sweet sleeping bellies? Have I taken it in sufficiently to produce them again, as copies from my own body? Women past the point of children must carry that in them, a pear-tree from a seed, a bird from a swallowed bone, soft, flapping against the spine.

Could I do it? A click, and out they would flower, all the parts I kept, building them anew.

What would you have me do? Ruth is still standing. Abashed, graceless.

Oh, learn, learn! I will show you. I get up. If I cannot learn the trick of making, I will shape what I have. *Stand here. Straight. Yes, at the spine. No, don't fiddle with your skirt, stupid girl. Now fold at the knees. Exactly as you see. Hands out, palms forward, as if you are bearing a candle in each one — perfectly still. And now we lower — our — heads — shoulders — down — and — up — up — and there. Good!*

A string breaks. Goneril, curtseying, after we told her she must marry. Precisely done, as if performed to drums. The stillness of her an insolence; the implications of that perfection, the down-bent head, in deference a beat too long. Lear did not see but I saw. Timing, the angle of a hand, everything can show hatred, once you learn how.

I release my own body. Come upwards into my rightful self, straight-backed, bowed to nothing.

That will do. Get me something warm. I will die of the cold.

6.

I come to the chapter-house every evening now, regularly. Drawn by their hunger, the whites of their eyes, drinking me. And I feel old, though their presence is comforting, in its own way. *A sapling in an open field catches lightning,* Kent said. *In forests only the top branches burn.*

Old and old. Age makes its marks, cool hollows under bone, the skin around the nipple crinkling; and resounds, in discomfort on the chamberpot, or bizarre pain for no good reason. A crack inside a jaw or knee. My body, I think, is receding from its young dreams: it is becoming conscious; the thinned hair exposes us to the sky.

And youth is whole. In the memories I give them, which dip back past the midway of my life, I am always all present. Thighs rustling within dresses, the weight of plaits or pearls on my hair, clutches of sweet humours in the gut. The memories have a milky thickness. *Tell us of the court where your first husband lived. Were there great ladies?*

Now my senses have thinned to sharp poniards: only the frank and obvious starts them. If my liver burst and my nose itched, it would be a struggle indeed for me to feel both simultaneously.

Then, however, I was seventeen. I moved across to Michael in the dark. I whispered, *May God forgive this.*

I am telling the listening women other lovely things. I describe lanterns strung in the trees at parties, and how I wore crushed heartsease and lilies in bouquets upon my breast. And the flutes and sweet singing of young boys as we danced at court. Those songs! As if they were softening the very air so that we moved deliciously, as if through honey. I can make it sound like Heaven. And it was.

But through this, the other half of my life runs concurrent, a vein alongside flesh.

Sleeping, Michael in darkness was beauty itself. He rolled and found my body, and discovered appetite in his sleep, the lure of my stomach's curve, and holding to the curls on the back of his neck I mouthed prayer upon prayer, laying them upon the rhythm of his body.

Luck meant that he did not wake. I passed his bed-attendant, who looked away from my sopping shift, and fled to the light of my own rooms, the girls who had been waiting, who had perfumed my neck before my journey. All of us were traitors, night-watchers.

I remained, of course, as thin as a fish. One learns. The vigil was a cursed one, the seed I tricked were turned.

And what honest child could you have had? the Fool said to me once, when I spoke lightly of it in Lear's solar, among women. He had fair passage, was a eunuch of humour, could walk barefoot through any solid place between us. *It would have been a weasel-prince, snuck from the hen-coop, having to be lured out of peculiar burrows . . .*

True, of course, though I slapped him. But we were borne by hope, us dark-women. What babe I procured from Michael may have been jaw to feet in sin, but his pate would have been glorious, trusting gold.

What a shame that lovely man gave you no children, says one of the common nuns. Sideways, as if attempting a spear-throw, to see whether it wounds. A high-born one gasps at the effrontery.

Have you ever met a saint? Their eyes swell; they are silent. *You would not know. Be quiet.*

*   *   *

But I cannot deny the women the pleasure of it. I am their new green thing, glimmering like a bud. And I miss the abbess; perhaps twenty of them, massed, might add into one of her.

It is grim, here, for all of them, noble or common. The smoke of the burning linens all day in blistering wind, and paths taut with ice overnight, then loosened every morning, till everybody steps through mud, and is dragged. Heaviness, heaviness; stagnant water, ink needing thawing over candle-flames. Fever-weeping. The new graves are naked: the flowers laid have gone to rot and slime. The fish under the cook's sluice are the only comfortable things, caged in eternal coolness, awaiting devouring. The cook herself attempts cheer with us, honey in the gruels, whitening fat on the lips of the bowls, but it is a moment of warm joy, which passes.

Michael would love it here. Michael delighted in the stories of holy men who became hermits, rejected human companionship and society for four walls, bread supplied by the kindness of others, and contemplation of a single problem. Humans rarely provide a single problem. I (very young) wondered what would happen if you solved the problem before the end of your life. He said it was therefore the wrong problem, and that you had either to take the duty of the Lord for your revelation of a solution and spread it among the faithful, or to examine it better to find a less facile answer.

Or, I said, *pick another problem.*

Yes, he said.

Mirabel, having picked her problem, is out every day in the

winter garden, breaking ice with her feet, snapping frostbitten twigs down to nubs. Throwing her entire weight against the season. Isolation for her seems like a clarification. You can see the sweat on her, the pinkness of her neck and arms, as if she is forcing herself in dark places, like rhubarb.

And it moves in interesting ways, which show development.

Today three young common ones gather in the square of the cloister, laughing, briefly. I am passing an upper window, and pause to watch. They have something; they are passing it. One sees me and turns away brightly, concealing some innocence, a piece of sugar, or a little treat stolen from the kitchen. There is no shame in her: she shares with her shoulders that it's a transgression, yes, but one I would not begrudge.

Another, older, sister passes — one of the noble-born — and sees, and begins to berate. I hear nothing clearly but the oval of her face shows vivid against the snow. Pious, frantic. The sin of luxuriating, the sin of indulgence, of allowing temptation to pass the lips. The abbess would simply observe, and smile, leniency giving her more weight for greater censures; Calyssa would half lower her eyelids and whisper through teeth, enforcing in secrecy that felt somehow more shaming. This woman knows no such elegance, no twist or strategy, and is simply bludgeoning. A fighter, she'd be an axe-wielder against nimble pikemen, whipping away, clean out of the circumference of her rage.

I wonder briefly how Mirabel manages her noble garden-girls. Sheer force of attention, perhaps: I have never seen her bend into anger, or show the venom of a disappointment. Merely turning her body away, then, from a crestfallen follower, and moving towards other trees, other things requiring her thought. She takes their devotion as written, and so they continue to give, without doubt or consideration, and are likely sweeter for it.

The three girls are Graces; they move against the fury of the angry woman with apparent gestures of humility and compliance. Three saplings overweaving, bending to a force of weather, but preserving, I know, their green sap, the resilience of their boles, that will simply reshape around an obstacle, and crest in fresh directions.

The nun moves away, her vitriol gone from her; and likely feels relief for it, the bile released in the blood-bowl. She has reoriented herself in the world; she must feel as steady as the North Star.

There is a patch of ice upon the path she takes. The girl who had turned away looks back towards me, with pretty black eyes, places a single finger to her lips, as if pressing a host up to be kissed.

The furious nun falls, and is splendid, spreadeagled, a star of limbs. She shouts on the descent and then is entirely absorbed in her own robes, as if underwater.

The three women move forward to help, all cosseting and concern, and will poultice her vanity, until she cannot doubt their souls, so suffused with tender intentions. The nun with black eyes has not looked again. I duck away so that I cannot be heard to laugh.

They have decided I am a prize to be fought for, then. Well, let them try. Yes, little sacrifice. I will accept you.

★ ★ ★

Mourning takes many forms. Tonight I dream of the best parts. God grants me them: it is His gift.

Goneril in love (always in love!) at five, at four, with beautiful knights, with the swelling pink-cheeked Mary shining at the door of the chapel, and demanding coins, posies, gifts to tear from herself, or else following them in silent piety. She and Regan stealing cheese on winter nights through a device of strings and hooks, curd swinging up to a window, as the kitchen-women carefully bit their hands to swallow laughter. The girls' father-love, which formed one day into the decision to make him honey, and so into his cupped hands 'as a present' they delivered a pot of wild bees, which pursued him, yelling, as the Fool lay on the floor and covered his head! We caught them – creatures of burning summer, clotted in an upper corner – and turned them out. Dust-gold on Lear's palm. *Midas again, mind your fingers*, said the Fool.

Learning to ride upon the hounds, saddled and leathered for the occasion. I learned equality from them. They nipped, they tore small wounds; fights over evenness, the precise halving of plum-cakes and bread-bits. Always dividing, down and down and down. Goneril dosed with wormwood after swallowing, in wild misery, a whole unripe pear to avoid the ritual of her sister's wet mouth.

Girls who could apportion crumbs, in silent war. We gave them a cake in thirds, watched the battle and laughed. The Fool: *Who's going to tell them? Divide a buck in equal weight and one poor 'un's got the antlers.*

Old words, out of the dark.

Mother, I can't do it. I do it all incorrectly, it falls away.

Hush, sweet. Give your plaits. It needs steady eyes. Cool those tears, you'll stain your collar. There. Now bring the glass and watch. I'll undo, and you provide the same on your own.

I'll do it wrong!

Whatever you make will be a great fashion, your beauty carries it so. Now try a little, slow, and slow. And here is a pin, and one more pin, and the last. Is it not a sweet confection? And all of your own, with patience and calm.

I wake up calling for water, in the weight of my love.

Ruth brings it, soft between her hands, to my mouth. I desire Lear now – carrying the pitcher from the sill in the chamber,

159

playing the old game. Daubs from the clay lip on my knee, my ribs, both my shoulders. *Oh, I cannot see, where is your mouth? I am blind as a stone I tell you.* Laughing, pretending his infirmity, smearing me with wet till I capitulated and cried, *Here, here.* Mirth weakening me from the inside.

When I cried, *Water*, in the night it was not for the thirst of the body.

★ ★ ★

In the chapter-house I am watching the women and see their divisions, their gradations. Dress lace, the show of a wrist, white stone. Their voices are a loose jumble, like coin, but their differences have shifted, background to foreground. The curdled whiteness of a high-born sister's forehead, sweet callouses on a commoner's fingers, small as shell. Separations, subtle but burning. Something to be toyed with, perhaps.

I have a gift for perception: to walk into a chamber, a merchant's parquet lobby, and see – here is the emerald earring, the gossiping servant. Things that could be useful, things for gain. Power is inch by shivering inch, building a skin out of fine scales.

Lear wondered at it. *How did you know?*

He put his hand on his purse as we left. The plate is poor. Not difficult.

Where did you learn that, witch?

Being a young wife, looking to learn a man's mood when he will not give you a trace of affection, that's an education! How Michael dressed, the lie of his face in the morning: I could build an entire day from a droplet of a glance, where I would walk and wearing which flowers. Clues, like seed in the snow.

So: I became the type to pick. Out of a field of wheat, one poppy. Out of a row of heads, one eye with a disloyal cast. Out of the sky, one star.

Tonight two women fight in the corner. A little noble woman and an older common girl. *I will tell Brother Manfred,* says the common-born one, petulant. The other pouts, bridles. Each performing their righteousness.

Calyssa says, *Peace,* her voice nicked at the edges, but they do not attend.

Whoever thought that gentleness is the nature of women when it is such violence that we come from, that we live within? The swift crack open of hipbones, month-blood, bruises from hard lacing at the waist, teeth marking our nipples red, smack and sore and night agony under a husband-weight. Even the holy women ache: the saints have their breasts cut off.

A fight can be amusing, but I have had enough. I say, loudly, *If you'll be quiet I'll tell you a secret.*

They are silent immediately. One stares, the bottom of her eye-white just visible, a slice of rind.

I stage-whisper, *The abbess bathed in milk. She did. Up to her neck.*

A laugh. We are bound together in our knowledge, the slyness of it. Both sides are drawn together; they pucker. I am skilled, still. Outside the wind, outside the night tightens around us.

Calyssa says, *Do not slander the dead.*

I saw it myself, I say to her. My friend's rising skull, flowing. As if her hair were white, as if she were four hundred years old, a being of chalk. *Do you question my eyes? They remain sharp. They see such things, Calyssa. You would be astonished.*

Calyssa's eyes pull away. She has her own bruises, perhaps. And cannot quiet the whispering women. Not like I can.

★ ★ ★

Of course I know how to calm a room. My political education was practical: I came at it as farmhands learn the lines of a cow's

161

body, the shift of its limbs in the warm dark before dawn. They give the boys books. Lear had books, and learning from good masters, and whatever he'd gleaned from his father, that half-starved field of grain picked over by birds. He would, he said, rather be hunting, pale boy streaking overland away from court into the wilder version of himself.

Girls are formed by increment. We deepen our knowledge slowly, by parts. I was dipped again and again into the substance of it, until my colour darkened and the shade stained through the bone.

Kent attempted to teach me; and would give me small pieces of knowledge. Twisting his fingers under the lap of the trees he said there were rules: service, and obedience, and care of secrets, and rigour in God. *I have my code*, his mouth open to reveal austere small teeth, *and it has served me, but as queen you must make your own. Form a rule and they'll follow.* Light through the leaves threw us into relief. But I was too young, and rattled in my power, like a badly scabbarded sword, and was awaiting deliverance.

Four years married. Michael had gone on pilgrimage, crawling over hills in some distant direction with bloodied knees. He would kiss the ring of a relic, I forget now the point. Had watched him go, moving from the door of the palace at sunrise, on all fours, sinking at the hips, like a thin cat. Lanterns held by servants all the way to the ridge of the next county. Laid my veil over my eyes and turned away, in weariness.

And we would wait, held until the session was over, and he came back brittle and happy, praising the saints. The rhythm of the marriage had laid itself out. I knew it rigorously by then. The plot of every day worked around faith, the shift of it under his skin.

Eighteen, twenty, twenty-one, I would not yield: I held his house, his fiefdoms, his line. While he indulged himself in rotten

162

sackcloth I collected rents, spent days with cooks and angry thanes, flushed and furious to be faced with a queen so small at the waist you could join two hands around it. They were discomfited, I threw their planets off-centre. Wiser ones knew the king was no help, and I at least had open ears. I made victories through accident, or colossal luck. God having given me a husband devoted purely to Him was at least granting me beneficence in other areas. Long lists, dark oaken chests, the exchequer. I forged the king's signature, carried his seal hidden in my chatelaine, swaying at my pelvis. Things within things within things. Transparent ivory, money in cool palms. Fronds of ferns, quivering in the afternoon conservatory, when I should have been lying with the king, but instead wrote legal letters, stained my mouth with wine.

So: the king had vanished. Then, trouble.

Diplomats had arrived. Kent in the corridor: *What will we do? The king is not here — they cannot follow him to the monastery.*

The Fool: *Yea, and would have to go like dogs just to catch 'em, with tails lashing their backs.*

Give them to me, put them in the hall.

They, the four of them, thought me a poor thing. At twenty-one enough to flourish and yet no children, and a king absent, off biting stones out of hills instead of performing on me in a bed! But being odd I charmed them. That advantage, the strangeness of it. A thing to tell others, *The queen is alone with eight hounds, the boy's a pilgrim or likely dead, but the house holds, who knows?*

Late, drunk, they rolled their sleeves to their elbows and told me indecent things. The silver thread in the cock of a current prince, they said, to keep him virile. Looking to see if I'd shift, if a blush would rise to my hair. Instead I asked them for help.

I needed education on matters of state, I explained. I was so

163

young, barely out of a convent, with a king (they knew this) weeping most nights and exhausting the priests. Could they aid me?

They saw, I knew, a weak spot on the map, and reached to touch it. So they were generous with their advice. *An audience is a weapon: do not give it freely. Ignore the first visits of a person who intimidates. Spy on friends more than enemies, and keep good spies, well-fed. Build sober armies that love your king. Befriend ruthless men through their soft wives, hawking, hunting. Give sons, give sons.* I had the heads of my dogs in my lap. The room turned green with the dawn, slowly, as if peeling off the top layer of skin on the world.

So I was blooded in. And I worked, slave-hard. Candles in the halls, a council that wrote well for the will of the absent king, who moved deeper into his God as into moss, a soft working. Took a whip to a maid myself one night as the others watched (a small crime, but persistent, and needing to be wormed out); he passed at the door, saw her bared back and the blood and his dark wife standing astride with a lash, and moved on, without remark. When my father passed away he came to kiss my forehead. *You have not wept.*

No. Weary, and the harvest to count, and still several miniature scandals to care for; and the fire banked high so that my cheeks were scorched; and I had known my parents so little, had seen them all my life at one remove, as through thin gauze, moving in circuits of their own mystery.

You grieve little as you are the Devil, he noted serenely, and left me.

I had gifts, and luck; I had the width of myself and other bodies, strong men, and the grace of the Lord between myself and ruin. Kent, coming into beard then, drilling the armies under Michael's colours; the archbishop, tender for the holiness of the king, and bunkering the edifice of his God-given command. And no children, no children! It was a rare doomed thing: it was like riding an animal as it was hunted, hearing the yells of the pursuit in the trees.

It ended as it had to. Death was in it — we were carrying it at our necks. It could not be repeated, that terrible court. If you told me of it now, I would not believe you.

7.

The feast of Saint Nicasius passes, with its prayers for cities and for the decapitated saints, and then the feast of the Immaculate Conception. Our Lady's scent fills the chapel, fills our throats: rosewater, incense, burning green wood. The illness runs still, but its floodwater has thinned. Barely brushes to the ankle.

I am offensive to Ruth. Smack across her collarbone. She had been feeling along my veins, the pocks along them from past blood-letting, like holes in the earth. At the birth of Cordelia they bled me so vigorously I thought I would be dried, husk, rattle-bones.

Why are you so hard, Lady?

I am honest. *My life has been poorly balanced.*

A life lived with two weights upon it, kings, has no true centre. It cannot be still, or even. I am haphazard, so I swim in incomplete or incorrect emotion. I am a vision half sketched by a stumbling painter, insecure and feeling his youth, in bad light; in the one clear hoped-for shaft of sun it would be clean and properly wrought, but at other points it shows a viciousness, a capacity for teeth.

A witch on the pyre, a woman told Lear once, will burn tongue-first. You will open her mouth to find blackened teeth, a palate of ash. Women lie. Women are unbalanced in their souls. And daughters worst of all.

I kiss Ruth upon the forehead. *Let us be at peace together.*

Tell me again of what we'll do when this is over, Lady.

We'll go south, where it's warmer. We'll find my old friend Kent, whom you loved so much. Such a gracious man. When the quarantine lifts, when the gates are open. Kent, who will know the graves, and the right places: to restore myself, my name. To re-enter the high bright places of the world, to the sound of trumpets, battering drums. *Here cometh the queen.*

When will it be?

When the season of illness is over. Soon. There will be such happiness.

Such happiness, and I sit with her, stroking her hair. When was the last true happiness, the last feeling that the world was good, and honest, and white as apple-flesh to its deepest parts, and that bad luck and bruises were just illusions? It was Cordelia: Cordelia's first whisker-scratch against my stomach. Calling, with her small mouth. The memory is a flood: it dives over my head. I am overflowing with pearl.

Kent. I am with child again.

Is it true?

I have not told the king. Kent — I'm terrified. What if I bleed?

You will not bleed. If it is a boy and lives, our fears are gone. You are a remarkable woman — and you're sure? It is not just the end of your courses through age?

Quite sure. I'm widening like a tupped sheep.

Ha! It will be his greatest happiness. May God keep you. He embraced me suddenly. I felt the hold of his breast across my stomach; he was shaking. I held his neck with a hand, the fraying curls of it, suddenly concerned — the man is ill, perhaps. But no — and he was gone, with a frantic kiss to my hand that left it white with force.

A rustle of sleeves. *Magdalena.* The maidservant was on the stairs above, fixed at the landing: I knew the shape of her, the angle of her head, though it was in darkness. Pressed into shadow. *Come, help me. I am disarranged and must appear before the king.* True, for Kent had crushed the silks on my bodice.

And yet she did not hear: she ran upwards, without pause, gathering her skirts, to meet Regan, on the upper floor, whose hands I could see clasped under her ribs, poised for some event. *Her hair is thickening,* I thought. *I must tell her it looks well.* Even in the torch's dimness, I remember, the caul of my happiness made her and all other parts astonishing in their beauty. She in her woman's height, watching the stairway, shoulders bared, was radiant, the shadows beneath her cheekbones sepulchres, crowned plaits waiting for the wreaths of sacrifice.

When I see her it is this vision, of her in her most incarnate self, that appears: full, at the height of her beauty, and silent.

My apologies, Mother. I seem to have interrupted you enjoying yourself.

Regan, come, I have news—

But they moved away together. I was alone.

Further. I tread into the trail of happiness, feel it crushing under my feet.

That evening was like none other in my life. Lear thought me a liar, until I laid his horned paw on my stomach and let him feel the warm, the rise of this new sun between my ribs. So old, both of us. He lay in silence with it, and I saw he was weeping generously; and would have forgiven him then, forgiven him all and anything.

It is a blessing from God, he said dimly. *He gives miracles arduously, but He gives them nonetheless.*

It is no miracle, Lear. I was laughing. *It is as ordinary as anything.*

You think you would have struck a seed in the belly if it weren't for God's great will? Woman, you're all chin-hairs and warts, and here you are blossoming as if it's May. It is a sign of Lear's righteousness.

Yes.

There is something lacerating in human happiness, I think now. In the rise and swing of it; a punishment. The Fool knew. He was an artist of self-brutality. His grasp for our laughter, as he feigned shaving in a mirror with a feather as the blade; when the real, savage edge was us, our clapping hands, pouring over his head and nicking holes wherever it fell.

Lear held a feast, to celebrate. Garlanded me, rose-petalled, his blossoming girl. His delight, my delight, like golden rain, showering us. The girls and their husbands came, as ordered. Their cool hands pushed close to the orb of it, the last child in me. *Is it not admirable?* He was dizzying, he boasted. *That I am so thick with seed I can fatten a dried-out bag such as this! I have even outrun your green-grass husbands! Well, your children and mine can be playmates together.* I was holding his hand. We were lovers again, then.

Regan said quietly, *A seed-victory indeed, and most improbable.*

Hmm? What was that?

Her curtsey. I held my own glowing prosperity and would not let her touch it; the sense of doubt in it. *It is a great blessing to our mother the queen, and we may pray that none goes ill.*

Ill? None will go ill. The worry across his forehead washed me with love. *But you did not desire to upset me: you are a gentle woman, and a loving daughter.*

So I am, Father. So I am. Kissed his hard hands, and handed him a drink. *I may prove that loyalty in great service on a future day.*

I reached out. *I'm hot, Regan. Fetch a fan or a cool cloth.*

She turned. *Magdalena? A fan or a cloth for the queen. I am indisposed.*

★ ★ ★

At last the final nun heals. She walks, wavering, into the open gardens, the fever having released, and rolled away from her body. Boulder from Christ's tomb. She looks resurrected, an Easter-woman; her face sallow as greenery. Calyssa glows, as if it was her own miracle.

In celebration of recovery, to dampen the fights, I pick out the best stories of court for the sisters that night. Dances, fans, pools of slow golden fish that lay glossy in sunlight. Stillness, languor. The Fool, tinselled and belled, lolling on a cushion. In the chill of the chapter-house they step into the haze of a hot summer, and breathe in perfumed air. I show them the meeting with Lear.

The court of my first husband: hot June, women in linen pacing the parquet, dampening their necks with perfumed water from bowls held by servants. My first encounter with Lear: sitting with Kent. We exchanged nothing. I barely saw him.

This is my young friend, Queen, the Prince Lear. Kent put down his pen, had been inscribing. Maps, letters. Like a diplomat he wrote himself in and out of the world. After fetching such a respectable young queen-bride (*a good girl*, the court shadows said, *and sensible*), his value was high. Lear bowed his head in the accepted manner. *He was kind enough to visit me at court, while I do duty.*

You put a good sheen on it, Kent. My pursuit of employment.

That's my office.

Not a pretty princeling. Not good-skinned or well-clad. Half broken already in the right thigh, a riding accident's deep puncture I would later lay my lips against. Altogether – and he would roar at this, later, well into the marriage – not a man to be remarked.

I had heard of him occasionally. His mad father, the lands lost. He spent years in skirmish, running a taut line, inching back land his father had relinquished. Peasants liked him for his youth, his freckled head, his penchant for ducking into village brawls and cuffing all offenders. Soldiers too. Seeing themselves in him, barely a skin-width from a child, and yet thrusting himself over precipices; they laid their loyalties in hundreds.

Was still 'boy' in court, youth still burnishing him for mockery. *The ugly boy is amok again.* Though by the Archangel Michael's last illness he was king and high thane, no longer a child.

Strange, but I would not lie in the cool of my own body and think of Lear, or desire him. Nobody believes this now: they think the net of his love was thrown over me long before. But saintly Michael was all to me. I was his mirror, his faithful animal. Lear, the freckled young fighter, was just a part of the landscape.

I saw Lear only in flashes, in segments, behind Michael's aureate glow. Red-headed. Burned cheeks from riding with the hordes daily. Chewing as he turned to watch me process with my women through the throne rooms to the lower garden. Michael was not ill yet: I was still caught in the struggle to bear a child with a man who refused my body as a temptation from Hell.

We were at Michael's winter court. Some graceless remote castle, chosen for its proximity to shrines, holy waters. His advisers would prickle constantly at his tendency to move according to the geography of faith, rather than political expediency. My lady's voice at my neck as we stood at a window, wrapped in furs. *The young foreign prince, the poor one. He's caused some trouble.*

I remember her voice. Thick, with an intimate solidity. Later when I needed to be statesmanlike I took on her voice, its small confidential vowels, like gifts passed between hands.

I laughed. *How troublesome can a poor man be?*

More than a rich one. She rolled her eyes. Pale blue, glimmering, like a wren's egg. *He has barely a strip of land to manage and so rides around prodding others into fights.* Curled her slim hands, their pink-scrubbed nails. *I don't know why Kent welcomed him. Perhaps some debt.*

This stung. *The king's knight has a good mind. Perhaps he believes the prince to be useful.*

She snorted. *Kent likes to find useful people to galvanise us.* Sarcastic. Women so rarely loved Kent, his faithful bald head bowing before the throne, his elegant distance. I never wondered why this was so.

At least the new prince will have little entourage to burden the kitchens. I did not care. Michael was praying in sackcloth all night again, his skin blue with fervour and cold. I suspected perhaps he whipped himself, though I saw only flicks and flashes of his nakedness, interpreted it in the dark. Reckless red-headed boy-princes hardly signified. The wreck of my marriage was all-consuming.

Do you think we'll move on soon? This castle is so cold.

Not until Lent is over. The king will not be moved before his penance is complete. And if he sits in the cold for it, so much more pleasing for him. Bitter, even then, the sourness beginning to filter into my skin, my flesh.

I tell it lightly for the nuns: a stray little boy, causing trouble in a court of gold. Who'd thicken into a rising king, red-headed, blazing with laughter. They take it, and smile conspiratorially. Well, it is a history, of a sort. I lived through what came next – Michael's illness, the country of his plague, his death – and I look at these holy women, their limited thinking, and I cannot make them endure it. Even in story. Even in dreams.

★   ★   ★

The Fool came to me before Cordelia was born. The bottom of my stomach was bruised, so I did not swallow what he gave me.

I do not speak plain, it does not suit the cut of my garment. But let me lay a word for you, Majesty. Blood is not speaking well of blood, in this place. The savvy animal sleeps out the winter. Do not taunt the blizzards by wandering naked. His plain face, his hands upon my wrists.

Fool, I am eight months with child, I do not understand you.

You are beautiful as ever, Queen. May all be well and end as well.

And left me. I was not alert: I did not see what was breeding in the water. The fate that was coming from the depths to drown me. I was fat, and happy, and thought it was all charmed. When there was such a seething thing underneath it all.

8.

The end of the illness seems to release us from some unspoken bounds. In the morning a nun comes to the door and says, *Do come and watch Sister Calyssa. She is birding.*

Birding?

Come, watch.

Is she hunting? There are no prey-birds here: the abbess disapproved. Though the bishop himself had a goshawk he called Lucy, brought to the king's feasts, and loved like his own fat soul. I do understand this. Hawks are not luxurious but they move against civilised sense. Have no regulation, will be quiet only by forced hooding or after a meal, not by delight in God. This place filled with the cries of some hungry birds in the mews would feel vicious, as if somebody had hung it with legs of meat. This is why the young should have no hunting-birds: one needs to know lust, and the body, to read their gluttony.

In the open courtyard Calyssa has laid a noose, a thin string. It has become an arrow, at its end is a swift: the head of it, beating and beating, tracking the straightness of the line across the air. Its shadow on the grass like a sundial, marking time. Calyssa is still, laying a trail: a handful of gold, some seed, crumbs. Waiting for terror to lessen into curiosity, a captured thought.

Gives the swift a little, a little. Bread crumbled from the long loaves. It hops to the feed, lays one wing out, turns to regard the light.

A fox could lift it out of the air, that bird. Too small.

Sssst.

From the postures of the other women — many of them, massed at the windows — I know this is a frequent piece of theatre, though I've never seen it.

It is resisting. Listens to the wind. Pick pick.

And what good, I note quietly, *is a swift? No practicality. Unless you want to draw a carriage made of acorns, like Queen Mab.*

Sowing myself some seeds: the thought of Mirabel's disapproval giving me a brief charm of happiness. Watching the lure and the bird she is unmoving; she keeps her counsel.

The bird, however, is not a good mummer in the play: unpicks the knot, flickers, streaks away. Calyssa's white hands still full, at her sides, of hot grain. Perhaps, I think, it comes daily, allows itself to be caught, wooed — and then a vanishing, like any coquette.

Failure in Calyssa makes her movements stiff. Gathering the twine, the knot. High colour on the visible planes of her face. I lean to look: penetrable, perhaps. This could be the dark gap through which I enter, and divine her, the way she is laid.

The swift's loss is no anguish to me. I have no tenderness for small things. I was built for the broad, the outsized. My birds were bigger than Lear's, and hunted more hares. My horses outpaced Michael's at a pursuit. I never took a lesser portion, or let my king have higher ground.

The common women watching whisper lovingly. *Her cell is full of wings. White reed and rope, you can't move for millet or seed on your foot. Thrushes, a fat dove she spoils, and one other, exotic, I think a parrot. Blue like the sky. And two parakeets, and crows. The abbess would let her keep them, but only in her cell.* The women pass it to me, this knowledge. They like to give their own secrets; they like to imagine a trade.

I think of her hidden place, with bread-white beaks, a flash-cruel parrot on a windowsill, the bluster and boom of big black birds. Wings rattling like shields. Full of sweet-singing in the dark.

It is logical. We all have our own armours, our own courts.

*   *   *

When I mention the birding in the chapter-house that evening one of the noble women laughs. One of Mirabel's garden-sisters. *Her father was a bird-trainer in a hunting-ground. Or something. Though she does draw beautiful birds in illuminations.*

Common I call it, says another, quietly. Rank breathes in the room. It is another self: it sits on all their shoulders. If asked it would probably have its own voice. I remember the seed by the gate, its gentle fall upon the snow.

When she is abbess, comes the voice of a common-born nun, shrill with disdain, *nobody will call her common.*

They will. Another nun's voice: casual, cruel. *She will be the commoner abbess. People will be proud to see her, risen so much from her background. Wherever it was.*

Still no letter from the bishop, but the truth of Calyssa's rule hangs, an axe yet to be swung over a bough, a plait of hair. The noblewomen seem to feel it as a taunt, this elongated wait. They begin to shift, to pry. Thwarted vines regrowing in another plot. They know Calyssa will outrank them when she takes the abbess-crown, with the smear of scented oil on her hair; the head of the abbey ascends, leaping over the things she could not have by birth or fortune, to sit closer to God, virtually in cloud-cover. I heard once: a daughter made abbess while her mother remained a nun, in the same convent, her name lagging far behind, in the ledgers. I wonder if the mother ever spoke again, or if it was the consummation of all her own desires, if she was the keenest, the one carrying her daughter's robes, smoothing rosewater into her hands.

But the noblewomen are beginning to reshape the future to suit their structures. Superior before God she may be perhaps, but Calyssa's weak blood will never be forgiven. They will remember.

I will not deny that there is a difference in temperament. Though royalty has its own fragility. Lear, Michael, the royal blood relations of my past acquaintance, all having a certain sensitivity, a breadth to them. Perhaps they were made of finer material, to switch and waver at slighter breezes than the harder-hide lower orders. Lear snuffled after scents, knew apples coming into ripeness on the precise day, could pick up the touch of his own musk on my belly a week after we'd last made love. Or perhaps he played at it, to please me. I loved it, to be so marked, under the starch and brushed linen.

But people would always want to look inside us. Thinking there would be holiness within, the drip of pure water, to inspire them, or else decadence, with gold-dipped peaches and saffron in the baths. Of course it is neither. What they pin upon us is so much what they themselves require, and we are false as any other man, and fighting drunk at table, and full of wit and salt, like fishwives.

The knight Gloucester warned me of it, early, in my days with Lear. *He feels strongly, Queen. No ordinary dullard, this one. A passion's got him by the throat for days.* His way of ingratiating, thinking I had no such strain of my own, that sought it in others. When I had seen early, in the convent, that I was a more subtle and delicate creation than other children, who snotted and wept and were happy in thick shades. No mottling to them. Hurtling from sense to sense, without discernment, like trade-winds.

Common. There is so little variation in it: between the noble sisters, the nuns. Though they believe it to be a gulf parted by Moses, a mile-wide stretch of silvered sand. They have the same hungers.

The passing of the illness seems to grant permission. They all begin to make havoc, now. Common, noble girls. Creating miniature insults, like mice. Sent to nip at toes. The long quarantine broods, and they seek little fights to fill the evenings, to give themselves their own entertainment — and, perhaps, to win me, to claim me to their side. The older nun, tripping over ice with her breast puffed like a goose. The girl's laughing dark eyes.

They grapple and make stabs, for and against, then look to me, judging my face. If I approve I'll foment their little games; if I disapprove, I can slaughter any of them, at a whim. They know. They fear me.

At court, lazy, made fretful by the length of afternoons, I invented wars of my own. Ladies in waiting: I set them sparring, sly, a hand in a pocket, grazing a remark on the skin like a brand. *Helena thinks you uncouth but I like your manners, Margaret. I shall keep you close. Do you not think Matilda heartless for her remark? You are my most comforting friend, I must share all your confidences.* Notes, tears in closets. I was clever and bit nobody twice.

At present this seems too small to concern me. Years of Calyssa as abbess for them, while I break out afresh into the new world, make my own way, and die independent of this, the enclosing egg of this world, that smothers. Well, good luck to them. The atmosphere grows dank with grumpish women, their nicking voices, and I am yawning when Brother Manfred appears.

We are silent, as if caught in a crime. I blink at him through the blueness of my lashes; he bobs, seems scarcely real.

I was passing — such noise! He opens and shuts his mouth. And has chosen, perhaps, to expend his authority, feeling braver. *I remind you all that the hour of vespers is close. Perhaps you should rest.*

The sisters are meek. And united again. His bald head glowing with cold makes us remember: the land of women has many divides, many landscapes, but the border with men is the thickest of all.

They murmur apologies, exchanging cunning glances. Manfred nods, hesitates, and vanishes, perhaps sensing the words held in throats as he opened the door, the white teeth lip-softened. To give him our blank and pleasant acquiescence. More likely, though, he is satisfied that we are obedient. Men always think they are the architects of women's actions, when we can slip under their demands and flee, away.

I think, *If I had been in a monastery with an abbot, I would be almost to Dover by now.* I could take any abbot, any archbishop in high pomp, and reshape their will in two afternoons. Three, perhaps, if I were tired.

One nun turns to me, flushed with the feeling of camaraderie. *Tell us what happened to your first husband.*

I am saddened suddenly. *He went mad, and died. There is little more to tell.*

When I was a child in the convent, a girl beat herself to death upon a wall. She was twelve. Commoner's daughter, who'd come up to money. She'd been sleepless in the heat; we had tried to tempt her to rest with soothing and milk, though I saw the white of her eyes as she rolled in the night, and was afraid. The nuns gave her draughts of dark stuff that stained the corners of her mouth. On the fifth day without sleep she took her skull to the hard slab and cracked it into bloody moss and paste. It was a raw death, and her eyes open throughout, though they closed them when she was put into the earth.

I had been a companion to her previously; she taught me her

mother's foreign songs on slow afternoons after catechism. One learns. The dangers of closeness with a rough mind that will condemn itself.

Still. Temperament does not save. The deep blood-legacy of sense in my girls, the vast thrum of their veins as they were exposed to the world, did not breed sense, or gratitude. Lear's face, in the end. Fringed with the feathers of swans.

Went mad how?

There is no how. Mad is mad.

★　★　★

Kent, haggard, said, *The king is growing mad.*

The archbishop was dismissive. *He is increasing his devotions. Piety is a thing to be admired in a king.* Sunburned hands and thick nails. As if he had spent years labouring. A man who had scaled up a hard rope to finery and suckled to it firmer than a babe at a breast.

I was furious in terror. *Yes, and you benefit well from it, you and your monasteries. How much has he promised you in the past months? What price have you weighed on his soul?*

Kent was cooler, always cooler. *I respect your judgement, Archbishop. In your wisdom you must acknowledge that the king's frenzy is neither natural nor balanced.*

No. He has great strength of will. I have attempted to make him consider—

What?

Moderation. But he is my king. None of his wishes have been excessive. Extra masses – perhaps he neglects his court duties, but he has good workers—

He has spoken of flogging himself. I was loud. *Of penitence, walking the pilgrimage trail, unaccompanied. He regards me, all the household, as a corrupting influence—*

I was so young then. So intent on truth. As if the revelations were solutions, as if throwing open all the windows could burn every miasma from a room.

The archbishop shook his weighty head. *It would have been better if his brother had lived. Existence in monasteries is conditioned to prevent these excesses, which are prideful in their basis. A king cannot be a monk entire.*

He will drive himself to ruin. Would wear a hair shirt if I didn't prevent it. He will look ridiculous. My voice a shard now, thinner. *People will pity me.*

Nobody pities the queen, Highness.

9.

The cook comes to the women after the meal one night to say it is pig-killing time, the blood-month, and there are none here to help: all the men are out and won't come in for the disease, and she can't blame them, but the pigs need to be killed. *Will there be helpers?* she asks. *Will anybody aid?*

I come forth with some others. There is surprise at this – it rises – but rank does not hold you above knives and the smell of white fat. Being a guardian of all the country by the grace of God only brings you closer, to the swelling bodies of criminals swinging on the pole, the bone you pull from the purple flesh of a deer.

And it has been so long since anybody showed me a new part of human thinking, some freshness. I know all these women, the codes of them. Whatever their birth, however they bicker. Visible even through their habits, even through their subsuming faith, the daily shift and tide of it, their souls. This one punishes, or is a hard mistress to herself. This one wants so much. This one lies. Maybe when shown blood they'll venture into new patterns. It is entertainment.

The pigs are glowing rounds of good meat, almost gold along the backs, and too intelligent. White-lashed eyes. Watch them pursuing their want of food, grain to hand, hand to pocket. They can follow the line of their need unerringly, nuzzle at the cook's emptied palm and scream. The strongest, which is Mirabel, slams them on the head with a hammer. As if beating in a stump, or shaping iron. The skulls split and swim apart; the weight shifts under the crack and rolls to the side in the straw. One spits and shows its tongue, purpled, with yellow tushes. We have to hold it, foaming, as the jaw is hit, the dark of the ear.

Pig-soul. Silver, shimmering with hunger. Instead of rising it burrows to the earth, snuffling, seeking acorn-smells, the undersides of mushrooms.

It takes three women to knot and haul the bodies up at the back legs. Ankles finer than a dancer's slip through the rope. At last the bulk is aloft and the throat cut, and a girl lies underneath with the bowls, gathering the steaming offering. Along my hairline and the ridges of my wrists speckled blood gathers so that I resemble an egg, or a flecked beast's stomach. I feel young.

One woman hangs back, but the one beside me moves forward on her elbows better to hold her bowl, and is knocked gently at the forehead by the hanging snout, in a kind of blessing. I am reminded: get to the animal heart of anything, the fur, the temperament when kicked, to know it. That's the method. Most of us are born and thicken into one form. Wolf, soft-bellied lizard. Lear could buck away from it: be deer, bird, stone. When you put out a hand expecting solid flesh and found only feathers, perhaps, a gliding rage that spun off into the dark. Lear, surprise-boy, menagerie of a man. Marriage is husbandry.

Later we boil the blood dark. The cook, to keep us awake in the sweet-heat swelter of the kitchen, blood-fat drunk, tells us shocking stories. A pig so fat a mouse, unnoticed, made a nest in its teat. A woman who gave birth to piglets, one after another, pink and squirming from the bedclothes. We scream and pray delightedly, and are all adrift separately, on the blackened rushes, as the carcasses swing in the smoke like bells.

Mirabel rested after the hammering. Has come up by me and taken a chair.

You do not mind the blood.

No. I am cool. *We handle blood as much as anybody else.*

I am surprised. I thought you might be squeamish.

You do not know much about royalty, I think.

Perhaps she thinks her bluntness may be winning. They will think this, some of them. But there's no trust in it; honesty is still choice. A simpleton lays his trust with a fellow who claims to wear no mask. It is all the hunt: one knows.

I give her a long look in the silence. *How long have you resided here?*

Oh, years. She makes a heavy gesture with her hand: months in it, decades. *I was not to be married. A pity. But the abbess gave me the gardens, the one before this. And so,* a shrug, *it is not a waste.*

Your family had prettier girls? Oh, cruel, but to the point. A bridle and she's vain, an acceptance and she's false. The cook makes a smile and looks away.

One. But stupid. Married and died. Her husband's in prison. I was given to the abbey with the dowry money. It was better.

Shame has no hold on her, then. She is not fine-boned, does not let it resonate. What happened has happened and passed on. It must be fine, to be that ruthless to one's past, like a cherished crop sent to the scythe.

How do the other women see her, this Mirabel? My girls gathered strays, wet-mouthed cats going blind or toothless, rabbits too skinny for the pot, once a foal badly born that died in three nights; they gave it blankets, held mash to its snout with wet palms. Kept their power of youth as ointment: it would heal. They had beautiful round faces and sweet pockets of acorns: it would heal. And Lear no prize himself, the runt with the freckled neck and Kent's old boots, running around on borrowed horses causing fights! Oh, the Lord knows the power of the rejected and base, from whom the great turn their gaze.

So Mirabel, with her power; I lay my hand on her arm. Not destined for the abbess-crown, perhaps, but a friend; a woman I may miss, when I am gone.

⋆ ⋆ ⋆

I could tell her. Death is about waiting for the denial of language. How it falls out of the body. So the pigs; so men.

When my first husband died I wanted to lie inside his language, to nestle in it, curved against the hard S of a prayer, a syntactic echo within the chants he said in the evenings over meals. They were his real body. What he gave me piecemeal of himself, crumb and skin and scrap, was illusory: the real ken of him was not the suckle of his shoulder or the lie of his back as he slept. It was his voice, praying, and I would knot myself inside it. It seemed possible.

When he lay dying and could no longer give out the call to his Almighty, I took it up for him. Repeated all his liturgy, even his upswing of hard breath before a plunge into deep recitation. I knew it as well as myself.

It was a kindness he did not take well. *You are not my confessor,* he said to me.

No, I am only your wife.

You smell like wine. Will I go to Saint Peter salted with sin from you? Do you promise me you've done all your penances? Please.

You're weak. Rest.

You will not promise? I am not angry, wife. You are a flawed vessel. I was never a mate to you, not as I promised in the holy ceremony of our troth. I will not apologise. The Lord understands. Still in him his lack of forgiveness for my love. That was bodily and all-encompassing, and crawled into his night bed to give him pleasure.

I am sure he does.

Yes. I have arranged the nunnery for you. With the archbishop. You will live out your days in the light of God. Remembering that beatific face now I can see the fullness of the smile. Its selfishness. That hoarded me to him as Regan hoarded a cloth doll, imperiously, ripping the seams through her absolute possession.

So it would be a nunnery, then. And pale, barely twenty-five, to retreat.

After you pass to His kingdom you may have no further care for my soul, King. Its burden will be beyond your blessed attention.

You are corrupt and faithless. He smiled, gentle, neither accusatory nor pained, merely self-proven. *Your sins will eat you like dogs. So many dogs. Heartless.*

You have my pity. Go to your destiny in peace. I will not sully it.

Michael. I believe they call him a saint, too, in the place where he was buried, a small monastery he had endowed. I passed close by it once, on my way elsewhere. It was covered with white flowers. I cannot remember its name. Was another queen, by then.

Our entourage did not realise we were grazing so close, touching the hem of my vanished life. I heard the name of the town and cried aloud, but said it was my stomach, and they left me.

The flowers were beautiful, abundant and chaste. *I salute you,* I said in my head. *I salute you, husband, in your place of death. May it garner you all the rewards of Heaven, since so little of Earth gave you pleasure. It could have been long and happy, our marriage, but you have passed, and I am alive. Rest well.*

★　★　★

There is a cat that joins us in the evening. Thick-furred, with a white breast. Somehow slipped through the quarantine, and now pads across the floor, long-whiskered, as was fashionable among gentlemen twenty years ago.

They always said to me, *You think too much of your animal. That thing.* But I have gone through life partnered and buttressed by beasts. Needing their heaviness. Long spine of the hunting beauties, pale paws crossed, at the bed's foot. White horses still and steaming in the dark mews. An aviary once, in a northern castle: flickering, the click of wings, a place to plunge a hand.

My favourites: a cow kept for milk at my childhood convent, blowsy-eyed, its huge hasps of shoulders sidling through the reeds by the river. A kitten for the girls, who kissed it even when it grew to a fat tom and spent its days lying belly-up and undignified in spots of sun. Five peregrines all small and vital in my jesses, green and white. The hound Lear killed.

Even the blind stagger of the Fool's monkey, stinking.

So when the cat comes I know how to caress it.

Bub, bub. The ladies are pressing their hands to the cat. *Bub, bub, nickety cat, you want a nice thing, who's a soft sweet.* Animal-talk. For children too, though I do not believe in it: I talked to my girls as adults. Full-blown as glass, even in their swaddling gowns. I talked to Cordelia while she sat with the wet-nurse, and she raised her flattened forehead from the breast to watch my face. Dull eyes. Thick, barely penetrated by light.

This one's a sickly thing, said the nurse. *Takes milk badly.*

Her hands were blue at the nail. As if held underwater. They clipped her hair at three days, thinking she'd drown in air and fluid. Her mash of mouth took in so little, barely enough to fill a palm, to blow a scrap of wheat across a room.

Smother it. It cannot live, whispered one physician at the birth, and I was awake, white with pain, and said, *No.*

How could a girl with straight limbs grow from that pocket

of skin? Little fish-thing. Blot of blood. Half of a daughter, heaving every breath up and down a ladder in a bucket.

Here, cat, I say, in the good fresh tone of an official. *Here.*

It pushes beyond the ring of women and knocks its flat head against my knees. It has a knuckle for a skull, ridged at the ears, jawbone fashioned to a point.

Good cat. They shrink and look sulky. It winds up to my side. Secret, with a cunning hand, I gift it the usual thumbful of fish, out of my skirt. Loyalty is sweets, fish, gold. Mirabel alone sees. I envy this little animal that knows only smells, the blue ache of hunger, and warmth in the paving-stones. It waves softly at a moth, in the light.

Calyssa is reciting her psalm to a small circle of her women. I see now she has caught her swift, cunningly, and sits with it, a small chain about its leg, hooked to her finger. Grain on her thumb. The small greying body beats and glints in the light. It bates and dives once, twice, the arc of its forked tail striking against the shadow like flint. Each time the line brings it up sudden. It is testing its freedoms, the games of its new world.

The abbess ruled against this. Pets must be confined to cells, their small eyes winking in the holy dark. Ribbons massed at the necks of little dogs. She is beginning her reign, then: the swift is a consort, a prince for a new future.

But the crisis is coming, of nature. I see it.

The cat's long body is slack, it is gathering inside a movement, towards the glinting bird. This cannot happen, my voice is in my throat. There has been so much blood at the mouths of these women. So much they have suffered.

I am old, but quick; Mirabel less, who tries for the cat, casting her wide arms. I move, I catch the swift, by the leash, which is glittering like teeth. And throw it forth, from the reach of the cat-body, which has thinned into a line, gathering the firelight into its fur as it passes, so that the pointed head is almost a comet. Calyssa's hand bursts and the leash parts from it. All this in less than a breath. Released the bird dips, flies. Into the rafters. Where it screams, a long scream in which its small bird-heart is almost visible, beating.

Ah! says Calyssa. She is gazing at the rafters; the cat hazards a movement, then realises its flight has been into disgrace, and moves off.

Can we lure it down?

Oh, your pretty pet. What a pity. That nasty cat.

One of the sisters may even dare to touch: a hand upon my arm. As if we were clustered together in this trouble and of equal weight. I pull myself away, but as if to move closer by the fire, violence already being in the room.

The screams of the swift trail through the dark.

Capturing that swift took hours. Calyssa is speaking to me, gloomy, her finger showing the score of the leash. Rawness.

And you bring it out of your cell, I say, disgusted.

She is wilting. The bird still carries the golden chain — we can see it winking from the beams. She had wanted to appear regal, perhaps, with her little prize looped and darting at her fist.

It is the fault of the cat. One of her women wants to be conciliatory. Calyssa will not concede, and stays looking at the fixed star of her lost delight, scratching the roof.

I am furious. *Did the abbess not say you could keep them only in your own rooms? Why this fresh rule? You are not abbess yet.*

She looks with stark misery. Her mouth is a slash of blood. Has held her patience so long, and slipped just a little, just a little. A single weakness that whipped back on her, like a rope released.

A quiver of regret in me: is it fair to slip into their souls like this, a finger into a white glove? Like the whisper in every marriage: is this too intimate to be just?

We have no abbess, says Mirabel. Slow procession of words. She would not be hurried by God or the Devil. *Not until the bishop's letter arrives. And no cat, and now no swift. It has been a bad night.*

Then perhaps we should keep to the will of the old abbess. My teeth are iron. *Given that she is barely cool.* And her thought flowing out of her, into the ground, through the rock. *Until she is succeeded, at which point everybody may carry birds everywhere, if so ordered.*

The reminder: not yet. The flood of power is at your neck, Calyssa, but not over your head, you are not permitted to dip your face below the surface. Remember that.

At this rate she will give me all horses, all loaves of bread, just to be rid of me when the gates are opened. Well, so be it.

Later Ruth binds my arm: a long cat-claw scrape, as if I had passed through the humiliation myself, and come out with the brand of it upon my skin.

What a horrible thing. Were you not afraid, Lady?

I am not afraid of anything. And feel in my body the truth of it shudder, dully, like hammer against skull. Mirabel with the pig, crushing.

10.

I dream again. Long silver hooks along the inside of my soul, which moves, and is pulled, out of my mouth, along the outside of my ribs, and aloft, up, up, towards God. The raw parts are dangling and I see them rise towards the roof. The pain lifts: I no longer miss my children; my body does not weep; my eyes are silent. Snip! A bird comes, into its beak the excess goes, stringed, silver-anatomical, gullet-feed. Such good food, so white with fat and selfishness! And leaves my little body, divested, pooling at the corners, dead, quite dead.

I must have dreamed them, their deaths. Following, touching their skulls, ringing their wrists as they reached for a jug, a book. How could I not have sighted it, around these centres of my fierce love, circlets of portent-light saying, *Here is the measure, the manner, the very date and star of your demise*? I knew their most intimate skins: how could this be a part I failed to see? Or perhaps it was a sound, a whisper that came. *You and all your kin, dead, bad, cast deep, end of your line.* I could not catch it, I was not sufficiently keen-sensed, so it has hurtled past and caught me.

Lear put his faith in fortune-tellers, after years of mere daughters and no further children. Kent found old witch-women with hands dipped in purple dye past the wrist. Forests of dried crops in their larder bottles, winks that turned milk sour. They'd burn wattle for Lear, and rattle out bones on the earth. Where was his heir? Why, he begged of them, did it elude him?

Still, then, the son thrummed in our dreams. The ghost-son, a sweet thing with Lear's white eyes and my dipped back, running over water, sailing on ice, an impossible, vanishing thing. I rubbed musk on my stomach and breasts, the women fed me wormwood and rubbed my temples with stink. One simply said, *Age. Elder women have daughters. Sons are for the young.*

I had her whipped and she promised sons to fill our halls, sons to glut the very roof and coo, like pigeons, in rafters. After that the women were not useful to me.

*   *   *

No letter, still. Calyssa is no longer apparent, in the evenings. Has retreated, frustrated, to her cell. When she passes in the cloister I see she is watching herself, how she holds her body, standing distant from it, to ensure it is lofty, and has the architecture of power. Hands stiff at the hips, like the abbesses in the portraits, as if distributing grain.

I feel for her. The office of abbess is so near she feels its warmth, waits for it angrily, like a lover. Looking back she may remember this time as a blur, before she settled into her true self and could be still. Her followers preen.

Above us the swift is still rising; caught in the high winds, so that below it the circle of the abbey walls is printed on the landscape, like a shape on parchment. An O.

Still a friend of hers, or ally – one of those common women who, being pressed under a stronger woman's will, feel it as tenderness, and experience cold at its removal – seeks to wound me, one evening. For vengeance, perhaps. *The chapbooks said that Lear stole you. Straight from the grave of your first king.*

Yes, I know. Passed around in drinking-places. My own face a smear of ink, Lear denoted by a wild flash of red hair, at his head, at his crotch. Our crowns oversized, our genitals frizzing over the page. The idea! That I, innocent and wide-eyed with my hair down over my breasts, was meekly scooped onto a steed and led off, weeping!

I make her repeat it, then laugh till my belly aches. *Stolen how?* I say. *Stolen from where? Did he lure me from my mourning chamber and come across me conveniently in a wood? In front of four hundred lords, heave me into a basket? He was a child.*

It is better for your modesty. She looks scandalised. Somehow lower-born women have the greatest view of shame, the tenderest ability to assess its shades, like gradations of lace.

I won't pretend my second king was not my choice. It would be insulting. The first died: they would send me to a convent or marry me to a puking child, so I laid out my own way.

Obscure nephews. Bridegrooms they offered me, in the meeting-rooms, as Michael lay dying. They were kind. The pictures were clear and on heavy paper. I could take them and touch them to my lips in my chambers, see if they presented any marital emotion. All so young: six, eight, seven. The artists were faithful: the sketches showed the down on their cheeks.

Lear was twenty. He wrote letters sketched on glass. Presented me, through Kent, with dogs, two bitches with soft necks, to succour me in my mourning. Under their leather jerkins bearing my colours, pressed into the fur, a painted message.

THE WIFE OF LEAR.

I remember unwrapping those jerkins, gently, in the darkness of the mews, to make the dogs comfortable. And seeing the message, swiftly laying my hands upon it as if it burned the very air, as if it would be visible to the bishop and his men above. Breathing. Pulling my hand slowly across so that it revealed one letter at a time, across the bristling hair, the dog turning and nudging at my hand, whining softly.

What kind of woman is it who plans such a thing? The disgust of the woman curls.

And he knew what would speak to me. Animals. Their streaked fur. The hounds' wet noses against my hands. Love, and all its surprises.

★   ★   ★

I go to bed, in the sheets where Ruth has laid the copper pan of coals, the evenings being blank with cold. A lid of ice, shutting upon us.

For my first wedding there was white rice. Incense, a hundred-guard of horses, pipes and tabors. Long plaits, knotted while wet by the mother superior, hanging thick down my neck and spine. Their swinging sweet weight that left damp on my back.

For my second we hurried overland in the wind. Grasped flowers from the gorse for my bodice and arms. Thistle, maiden's slipper.

As we came to the final moor before the church Kent said, *There will be others following us.*

Then we pay them. Or I pretend a marriage and fall miraculously ill at the final words. This is not a new game, Kent.

How do you move an animal to a new place?

Wrap it, hide its sight. Fool it with old smells: lay jackets under its haunches, daub scent across the carriage roof. And let it come to its changed settlement only slowly — letting it roam a new room, a corridor, a windowsill, gradually expanding its world, as the glass-blower slowly fills the balloon with air from the pipe. Why would we think humans are easier settled, more conditioned to brutal shifts?

In the church he laid a palm along my shoulder. Bared skin where the lining of my shift had split apart with the ride. Said, *Greetings, Lear's wife.*

Greetings, husband.

Warmth of his hand. I thought, He is so young. He barely grows a beard.

Won't you wear the wreath?

I am too old for floral frills. I'll tie it at my waist as a favour.

Not old. I'll teach you youth again. Our sons will cancel out your years successively until you are back to a girl, eating blackberries by the fist.

And how will you enjoy a babe for a wife? No, I'll grow old.

In the bed he laid his hands flat. Said, *I do not know how.*

I said, *I know. Do you want me to show you?*

Took his love in my hands. He regarding me. The scream of the greyhounds in the mews. Under the embroidered thickness of his robe the milken whiteness of his salt-scrubbed skin.

What had I thought, moving overland, migrating myself as sweetly to another kingdom as birds find warmer spaces? The act seemed easy, the offence transitory and unfelt. The new place and its rules were the real texture of things. Old oil lanterns in the evening, the stockyard feel of Lear's father's court, its pigs grubbing in pens in the dark, barely a foot from the chapel door. A king nonetheless, but only bronze-crowned at that time, still hauling himself into light and ease. I called him boy, he called me wench and hag and witch; we were happy.

Tonight I lie and think of his face as he beheld my body. The low tilt of his eyes, his leisurely contemplation of his pleasure. His lust was a curiosity: it took adventures and was restless. There was no gratitude or gloating over another man's spoils. He looked upon my body simply, as a deserved happiness.

And yet even after two children there was wonder. *Look at this body, my wife's. Look at this possession. It is infinite and self-enclosed, and yet*

I own it, and its intricate parts. Let any man see this and not be struck with awe at life's gifts to Lear.

How can I live with this cold and whittled thing, which was once such a glowing feast, a dark happiness? I turn in the night and touch between my legs, and move softly. There is no pleasure now, a mere scratch at the corner, half remembered.

11.

Well, well, there shall be some fever here after all.

The fires are over-banked; I sit nearest the door, shaking my chemise off my wet neck and back. Sweat here is a mark of distinction: its salt ring shows your favour – closest to the hearth, the broth, the rising steam of a boil-bowl. Everybody has their hair showily bound off their necks like servant-girls, tucked in nets, even those who must be cold for it, whose ranks hold them far off. Vanity.

The bishop has written. Calyssa has the trick of waiting until the sound dissipates before striking a new sentence. Threads us all along with her, her needle of thought.

She has the letter, the rare thing allowed over the walls, with their bare quarantine circle. It must have been thrown by some messenger, his face wrapped to protect him: the smell of women, of illness, of rotting materials.

I settle to hear her proclaim herself, and be congratulated. An end, at least. But it is not that.

He requires us to decide it for ourselves. Her face is a raw thing, still scalded with the news, rising to shock her with its wave. And now vibrating, as the idea ripples, and the still surface of the room becomes a pool in rain. Voices crash and murmur. *For ourselves,* she says again, perhaps with the idea of calming, of being an unguent, but is too hurt for that, the edge of it still

197

cooling on her face, that she was not the immediate natural heir. Well, sing that ditty to me, girl, I've heard it a few times in my life.

He writes, she says, with a miniature tremor at the edge of one vowel, and talking louder to compensate for it, *that it is the most appropriate procedure. Even in our case. With which he sympathises.*

And he is glad of it, I think, having met many bishops who are lapped in their piety as a carapace, harder than baked clay. Sealed as any ham. And will not move beyond the requisite acts, as a preventive to cracks.

The women glow and whisper. It has thrown them apart, this new shock. I must watch and see how they fall, like Calyssa's seed, onto the snow.

We're for a fierce time now, the cook says afterwards. Escaping the heat, I had come to watch her and her fish, what I find (I have told her this, she laughs) to be their fundamental honesty, the running water slow over their bright mouths.

How?

There will be a contest to be abbess. These women, she said, taking a knife and folding it wrapped in its leather, *do not like to lose.*

No. They will hoard the offence, until it darkens.

She looks at me. *Will you put up your name, then? For the position?*

I contemplate. There could be a whole body of women moving under me. Estates to manage, and an abbess's duties. Rings of faith around me, forming and brightening.

No. It would be an admission, it would be a final sink into the ground here: *this is my place, I confess it.* The abbey is the prison Lear made for me, the bridle so carefully constructed for my face. Forcing down my tongue.

I take a piece of offered biscuit. *I am too old for the running. Like an old mare. Can't make my way over the fences.* The cook snorts. *Then we will see,* she says.

They may play prettily for this little position. Myself, it is real power, or it is nothing.

★　★　★

It comes to the abbess's own saint's day so we go to lay what flowers we have (dried late-winter roses, sheaves of new mistletoe seeping sap) on the drift of her body, and pray, and look for her signs of favour.

Calyssa still bright-edged with hurt. Her mouth moving over the prayers, at the altar. We are all watching, perhaps, for a signal of the abbess's abiding choice: a scatter of petal from the mourning-bough, fallen over Calyssa's hand; the blink of water-drops at her feet. That death might break its vows of muteness and speak aloud, declare her still beloved. But nothing: the chapel gives nothing but the scent of itself, the sour scent of broken wood.

The common women mutter, and would clutch to their leader, to give her comfort. But she stands apart from them, brand-bright. The contest comes, and she will throw herself forwards, a burning line of fire. Who will rise to meet her? Who will dare?

Brother Manfred chants. Mourning, we seek to touch the abbess through veils, through the air. She is so recently dead she must hear us, nearly, a murmur by her ear, that she cannot place. My old friend. I want to gather her to me, like a bouquet.

And death seems so ordinary. That Lear, freckled boy of a mad father, who came to me on a wedding-day with his hair full of gorse-knots, even that King Lear could dwindle, could diminish into nothing. Ridiculous! I am holding roses; my joints are clicking in my clothes. How soon before all men who spoke with him, all women who ever heard his chain clink or watched the move-ment of his shoulder under his cloak, are gone into the ground?

Lear worried about this. *Tell me. You're wise. What carries on of me without sons?* His bitter voice when the two girls were married, and my belly remained placid as a stone year after year. *What lasts of Lear if not a legacy of kings? My father would laugh. He'd look at this whole pack and laugh at my life. He was mad, but at least he had a son.*

The injustice hurts, even in this dull crypt-light, with neatly behaving corpses all in a row, smug in their blessed beds. Lear was vibrating with life – his veins leaped to meet you. Even after fifteen years without seeing, I'd bet on it. A man like that deserves, if not immortality, then a stronger grasp on the fragility of history. It should please him better. *Lear!* men should say, a century, a thousand years from now, *Lear!* as if they knew him as a brother, as if they had seen his procession in the street: vital, solid, raising a hand to the thinning pate inside his circlet, squinting at the clouds.

★ ★ ★

The cook and I have chewed and swallowed most of the women. Which is salt, which is bitter, which would give thick blood to be abbess. Small-thinking, but she sees. *No, she'd be poor, she never finishes a platter, sends everything back with a bite in it. Weak-minded, I call it.* Few women's palates suit her purpose: poor teeth, a brackish mood that sours the mouth. Discarding specimens.

Meat-woman, rippled with fat: I think of her strong cool hands on the flesh of the man she loves. Has been locked in here with us, *You'd starve without.* That is love, its own species. She favours Calyssa, of course, but thinks others will not. *Low-born. Princesses are respected. Family crests and that. Though the noble girls do some work, I'll grant them. Mucking in the slop to pick radishes. You must be everything to everybody: that's an abbess.* No face swims forward. Perhaps it will be an election of one.

I educated Lear out of meddling. *Choose the best and let them govern themselves.* Young, he would be in everything, hobbling horses and poking at the laundry-cauldrons, charming the smallest army recruits. *Undignified,* I explained, *and it will be too vast. You will cripple yourself. Pick deputies, attendants.*

You will leave me with nothing to do, woman.

I leave you with the best things. Government while harassing the bread-makers in the kitchen! Leave off. Have a king's system, where the particles of the household and the country have their own heads, and come to you to be managed.

His father, I wondered then, must have had a strange household indeed. Mad early, they said, and so unbothered with king-stuff, wandering, possessed of his loves and minute explorations, fiddling with bird-down, while around him chaos broke banks and swarmed the edifice entirely. A royal house constructed to ignore the will of the king, to doddle and divert it from the places it could most bruise. So Lear never saw command, only a train of men adoring his father, quietly holding a government by will and silence.

Kent will arrange it, I suppose.

Kent, then.

And Kent did well. Gave him masters, and good whole men to run the parts so Lear could fold up, and give the purity of his name his whole attention! All the world should have a Kent, who is before and behind, laying the road, carrying the train, and loving, ever loving, wherever your foot fell.

Kent at his door, at night. When Lear woke screaming. Ripped sheets. The servants and I had to fasten him at the arms while I laid my head by his ear and whispered, *It is not real. You are living. You are in your bed. Sssh, I am your wife, I know you.*

Is Lear well?

I looked at him through a veil of my own darkness. *He is well. It is a bad dream.*

Lear had dreamed of thrones of blood, he said. Of lightning striking his member and making it charred flesh. (I touched it to show him it was quiet and unchanged.) He lay beside me dizzy, and was still hurtling upwards through the night, though I put my hand upon his chest to hold him down.

You can go, Kent.

I will wait, Queen. Until the king wakes. And was found, by the servants, in the yellow morning light, curled at the door asleep, dog-body, soft in the limbs of his own armour. Willing to patrol even the edges of his king's dreaming to cull the ghosts that came out of the marsh of the dead.

Lear came then, white-faced, and kissed him on the forehead. As when he had been a young king, and Kent had sworn on his knees to fealty. Kent closed his eyes.

There are places of honour, of service, where even wife-love cannot go. I have seen and not begrudged, all loves being needed to sustain a king.

★   ★   ★

The cat has been allowed back into the chapter-house in the evening. It lodges, and ingratiates, the swift having twinkled into vanishing, bearing its scream, the beautiful mathematics of its body, through a window, a door, and the chain along with it, like a war-banner. Calyssa may still keen its loss, but has not birded.

That cat grows fat. Mirabel watches it evenly. *It was meant to catch rats.* The intense practice of her that must find *use.* An exhausting position! To coax from everything a requirement, some strong thread of rational value. Presumably she attacks sleep as with any other practice in pursuit of worthy dreams!

What is sin, to Mirabel? A misuse of an instrument.

Some of us are too lazy for rat-catching. I yawn.

I would be a good farm-cat, Mirabel says. The image of it. I agree it suits her. *A decent worker. Which is why I am going to be abbess.*

Says it simply. Does she know she is heard? She is, and the texture of the room shifts, under the weight of it. All the bowed heads of the women move, like flowers, to follow her.

My eyelids move woodenly; as you age the humours contract. *Why do you want to be abbess?* I'd have thought the gardens for ever, for her. The rule of the seasons: culling the rotten wood, the failed bulbs that never fattened. Her hammer upon the head of the pig. Stripping, stripping away what is not of use.

As I say. I am a good worker. And come from a good family, she says solidly. Ah. Well-born Mirabel, I think, of some strong stock, gold-hammered faces! I imagine a marriage portrait in oils, with mother-of-pearl daubed on her painted cheek. The patrician thud of blood in her neck. This is the challenge to the bird-catcher's daughter, then. Surprises, and where they fall.

All things aren't gardens, you know. I'll be a little vicious, I have time. *You can't prune out the silliness of novice nuns. Or tie the cost of meat to a vine-post.*

All things are gardens. She carries on her impassable look, but may well be laughing at me. *Tend them long and intelligently and you create growth. Neglect them and they turn into blasted heaths.*

Like children.

Perhaps. She smiles briefly and leaves. Had I said that aloud? It appears I did.

So there will be a challenge. The cat-girl and the bird. Wash of blood against blood. Somebody will end with their eyes pulled out.

★　★　★

There was Lear's rage early in the marriage. A damaged hunting bird. He flooded with spleen, whipped the boy, and then was mild again. A child's inconstancy, flippant.

You are no longer angry, then. I poured his wine.

It was only a hawk. He took a long draught. *He will not do it again. What was the fault?*

The boy let the dogs get at it. The left wing is twisted near off, and it is likely blind. He gestured.

Cruel of him. I crossed to the low window. The raised hall looked onto the courtyard and mews. *He is laughing now. I wonder what he has to joke of.*

Is he?

Yes. In the yard. The ostler, a few others, leaning on spades and bundles, had come doubtless to comfort and jostle the stable-boy back to good humour. The boy was trying to be ribald but I could see his cheeks, his neck. Still bright white.

Lear came to the window. I moved out of view to his shoulder. To be merely voice, unbodied.

It is a pity, I said. A pause. Beside me his ears red with winter burn, as he watched the joking boys. *He is laughing at you.*

Nobody dares laugh at me. His voice trembled.

He does.

The men's laughs rose then. In them the clear streak of the boy's voice. Attempting to clamber back from weakness.

I moved off. Too close and I would be seen to push, or scold. Also I would have been tempted to bite at that ear, its delicate pink thinness. *It is not his fault.* This was my play.

No?

You are weak as a woman. I smoothed my dress and looked up at him. His black expression. *They make fun of you for it. You must be harsher. Harder. Or treason will creep up.*

Yes. I trained him to harder angers. Years later, when our sparring became intent, I could blame only myself that he could cherish offence over whole cold weeks. He'd carry a single rage for miles. A pilgrim of fury.

12.

News of Mirabel's intent has passed around. The cook, as with many low-born women, pretends that this emergence was clear to her days ago, and that she was waiting to release it to others. *I said she was clever. Strong too. Could pull us all around by a rope.*

You should market yourself as a fortune-teller at fairs, I say. She laughs, rises past offence and cracks a humble loaf with her fist. Ruth, her fingers covered with late honey, licks silently.

Better the future than the past I always say. Content, flour-dusted, her body's boundaries are blurred; she melds with her cloud of white. *Bread tomorrow does more good than bread yesterday.*

The place feels taut. Rustling. A dovecote in the dark, bracing against the coming wind.

★ ★ ★

So: the election, and I am to be here. I watch. The nuns are arranged in crusts, fine layers, stretching and building to the back of the chapter-house; a single heard sound will cause an outward ripple — all heads will turn and absorb it. They are part of a frill, as if around a child's neck, in their white habits.

The abbess, who must now have another name, and pass under it as if it were an arch, whispers in the ground. The air is leaking out of her side. I have seen the dead: the wetness leaves first, then the expanse, the fat, the air. We breathe her in, in the dust. The wax of the candles from her service has been scraped off the chapel surfaces, leaving them nude and shining sharply.

The factions are no surprise. It is a matter of instinct; what they believe to be intellectually judged is merely their sense, an animal idea of grouping. A fox sees another fox and knows it, even if it has no sense of *This is myself, it has my smell*; power plays itself towards those who look and move like each other. Reasoning cannot fight that allegiance. Lear I taught to watch and imitate, like a player, the people he desired to impress: the soldier shoulder-roll, the noble stance, standing with a heel cocked over an ankle, like a dancer. And, yes, the Fool did it but imperfectly, cruelly reflecting, as if in a broken glass; all enlarged, and mocked.

Thus the ardent noble ones with Mirabel, the quieter, brushed-down ones with high eyebrows to Calyssa. Seeing the hidden part of themselves, something they know to be virtuous but cannot amplify in their own person – the lettuces of Mirabel (who is sweating quietly but serene), the quickness of Calyssa (silent, undulating with discomfort, almost laughing in distress) that they can press to their hearts, like a saint.

I float, seeing the parcelling of these small countries. It is like little marriages, without the snoring and the sore parts.

Women! Men think without them we go hard, dry up, become brittle as teeth, and chip. Or rot, plums at the bottom of the barrel, in an excess of soft sweetness. Neither is true. We simply form ourselves around new hungers, new holes in the soil. As babies in the convent we all pissed upon a seed, and gave the fresh free mustard that grew from it to the visiting bishop, and felt holy for a single day before it was told and we were all whipped to pieces.

This is the new mustard-seed, two of them, many fingers pushing them into soil, many hands moistening the earth.

They perform a count, hands above heads. One pauses at my seat, I wave her off, this not being my land, not my map to divide. I came here unwilling, and ruled without any need for a vote. I will observe, be gentle, and unspeaking.

The count is redone, then a third time. There is a split: a tie.

A remarkable work! A miracle. They lie stunned, like flies caught in the flat of the sun. All the work run out of them into the floor. After Lear said, *War!* the men looked like that. After I said, *No dowry*, Regan too, and Goneril. Flush against a truth with no air to move.

One woman clutches another's hands. The air is brutally hot. I find faces: there is Mirabel, quiet, as if submerged, holding herself. And Calyssa vibrant, flashes of emotion on her cheeks, like shadow from passing cloud. Ardent beyond the violence of her dignity. Could cross the room now, press my fingers to her skin, and feel them whiten with heat.

The rigid parts loosen; it has collapsed; what I found so enriching, the row and fold of them, is now muddled. One removes her shoes, touches the yellow sole of a foot slowly, as another whispers close to her neck. I feel a sudden contraction of disgust: my humours have risen. Bile yellow in my throat.

When I remove myself they are still padding around on the wooden floor, holding candles, fussing, putting their robes over their arms to pray for a solution. Lear in his age despised the frailty of wavering men, who swung between so-and-so without taking a choice. *Just throw a spear and make done with it*, he snorted. *Work with where it lands.*

13.

Days pass. I stay in my rooms. Ruth brings the body of the news: no movement, the sides on a still plain, staring without shifting. Thinks it sinful. *They say such things to one another*, she says, pouring water from the jug. *That God will bless the abbess and her right followers, and hear their prayers. It seems not right.*

It is the wickedness of politics. Stay clear, girl.

One senses it in the day work of the abbey. A vast place can fill entirely with the whole thought of two persons, or one, and press at the walls. Lear and I watching Cordelia alone, after she was born: the room river-full, overflowing, our sadness and sudden strangeness to one another.

It will crack. We are not created for the indefinite. One knows. Michael left heretics in the white square shivering and astonished for hours before their execution, in agony, naked and open-mouthed. Told me (eating breakfast, slowly) of Christ's greatest horror on the Cross, that He hung so long in waiting before His death arrived. My men, my cruel and darling men.

★ ★ ★

It cracks. They have come to ask that I make the last vote.

I had not expected it. *I am not well for this.*

My daughters would ask me, *Which of us is prettier?*

Neither. Both of you look like foul little pigs after such a day in the dirt.

No, Mother!

Ugly little pig-girls! I should put you out for the farmer. And then he'll take you to market and sell you!

Well, I should fetch the highest price anyway.

Ha!

Oh, girls are cruel, and women grasping, and all concerned with vanity and violent jostling for position, and men would be best served to keep us all in separate mounds like hermits, daubed with pitch and too far separate to talk to one another, and visit us occasionally for coupling and witty remarks.

Calyssa, of course, expects that I will take Mirabel, and is spurred by her honour, which is a cage of thorns, to accept; she is wearing her sackcloth, grinning with the high pain of such decency in my rooms. And may even be decadent with it. She says, *We will respect your choice,* with a harsh loudness that makes Ruth watch her in a kind of awe.

Mirabel is picking stains from her robe. She has, I think, no smugness. It seems discourteous. To be so sure of victory, so stolid, that it pushes nothing from her body. I had wanted some sign, a vigour. The spoils of triumph come to meet her and find no echo, a hole in the earth.

They wait.

I must think on this. Come back — come back after mass.

*   *   *

Lear would have swung immediately, put his axe in the stump of his choosing and walked away. Selected pages, men at arms, by look, by the shape of their skulls, of their walk, some other distant, vague note of merit. And so was surrounded by incompetents with no breeding to spread on a piece of bread! Said he knew a man at a glance, even in silhouette, even underwater. Gloucester, hearing this once, added, *And I know women by the shape of their shift*, and all laughed.

What a waste, a mess, what he threw to the gods, what he strewed on the floor in a rage. Killed, in fits, and then would weep to me of it, as I lay and held his head upon my belly. I had made him thus, I claim it. I am too old for falsehood. We move through the paths we carve.

I am not an axe-thrower. I am intimate. I weigh and work. I have been granted several turns, round and round on Fortune's wheel. This is perhaps another chance. I stand to look at my relics: the unwrapped knife, the clasps of child-hair in a bowl of stone.

Ruth. Ruth, where is the white belt?

Here. The leather is old, I was working it.

Bless you. Here. Place it round.

Oh, it is a beautiful thing, Mistress. And you have had it so long.

Such white pearl-stones. When young, when hungry and alone, I would place them in my mouth and taste the roundness, the salt of them. Wanted to weigh my body, to give it heaviness in the world. Still they hold their thickness at my hips, like moons.

When they return I will be ready.

BOOK III

1.

I have begged a day.

 The following evening is the Feast of the Immaculate Conception. The nuns are setting the wicks of the beeswax tapers, left wrapped in paper and cloth since summer, still with their faint, anxious smell: honey, dusty glades, hot shadow. They stud them in the dark halls, across every beam in the chapel, till the mass of lights seem like glints on the fur of some gigantic animal. Moving through the darkness.

 Mutters. Abbesses waiting, massed in the shadows. The women think I'll come to it tonight after prayers, throw out a name, a coin.

 I want, suddenly, my women with me, the long blue lines of their throats, their paces behind me in procession, rustling, carrying my book, my fan. Where are they now? Genevieve, the Lady Catherine? They will have fallen out of youth and beauty long ago. Fat, somewhere, in knitted caps. I hope, I hope. That grove of women, that garden. Instead I am alone with Ruth, and a crushed elderly ermine at my throat, so far from its animal birth it must be now at least half wax and camphor and stultifying oil.

 Still. I can make the sound of a retinue with my own body. Can boom into a room as if sixty passed before me.

 Tonight we eat well: good wine, bread yellow with saffron and lard. I grind my teeth into my jaw. When the girls were small we watched the goose-herds lead the best birds up to the courtyard for the cooks. Geese fattened by best grain and cloves till they were cushion-birds, barely balancing, rolling on the slope from foot to foot like indignant nobles. The cooks came into the melee bare-armed, leaning, cocking a white breast with a finger. My gluttons loved it: screaming fowl, the enamelled sky of early winter. Under my fur cloak, my hand on Regan's head, the other around Goneril's shoulders to pull the sable to her skin (being thin, being raw-throated every winter), they would bet: picking the fattest, the one for the pot, soothsaying the cook's choice. *That one there, Mama, it's so round it can barely walk.*

Later at the table they would squabble to say the glistening roast bird crowned with plaits of herbs was their choice, then fall asleep in my lap with hands knotted against my stomach. Lear filling their pockets with gingerbread and sugared stars.

After prayer I tell them clear. Mirabel and Calyssa watch silently. There will be no slips, no rumours beneath the skin of things.

I say, *I will tell the bishop my decision when the quarantine is done. When he arrives before Lent, as is customary. No later. No earlier. So is the will of the queen.*

Best to make it finite, to put a round on it, as a rope around a horse's neck. Give them a defined place, a scope and distance, and watch them fill it. Here is your allotment, what will you grow?

A few months. Not much. Wars are, of course, waged in less. And that with more waiting and frivolous nonsense. Still it is sufficient, to be diverted, and see a little further, a little deeper. Also it is winter, and we are all in need of some entertainment. Truly I am a generous woman. I move out of the chapter-house, smiling.

★   ★   ★

They have asked you to judge, says Ruth.

Yes, Ruth. Who else could do it? Myself: power, power in the streak of my chin, the slant of my wrist, my dark mouth when I open it to pray. Visible, even to these small women who have seen little. Queenship changes the taste of your body; it is an imprint in air. Once had, it will never leave you; divorced, deposed queens retain it, though it blurs, or spills away.

But how will you choose?

I do not know. Not yet. But I will.

I must design a competition, then. I have known so many. Men crying out broken-armed in bloodied sawdust. Girls in the child-convent battling silently over a hoarded knuckle of bread, fingers in each other's eye sockets. Women on thickened court afternoons, not touching, rolling insults from within their nests of silk and crushed organza, like eggs. And the girls' husbands, each holding one of Lear's arms, as he descended blearily the steps to the garden.

There are rules. Cain to Abel, Abraham to the angel: there are rules.

A thing I overheard, once. *Run to me, see who can kiss Lear fastest. Who is his best wife?*

I came to this game late. Small girls, still, carrying roundness at the belly, a lily softness under the arms, still hairless utterly. Their cries of delight working into the stone. Dig up the paved floor of that palace room in a thousand years, there will be laughter out of the hole.

They were poised in a corner; and ran to him, shrieking, his open arms, like a bowl. Veils on their heads. Little brides, white as biscuit. Kissing him through the gauze. He played at eating their fingers. *Such good queens!*

Their joy held me still, in a net. Wrapped thick in it, and distressed, in a point of my body I could not ascertain, something distant in the abdomen, the part that would not give sons. It now whispered, *Pain.* Rising he kissed them still, clung to his chest on either side, best girls, with bouquets I saw at their small breasts, soft and crushed. Would leave dampness on their bodices.

May I join the game? I said.

He dropped them down.

Mother, look, we are having a wedding. Goneril showed her bundle, the dried bunches of herbs and old buds put in the linen to keep it sweet. *To Daddy.*

I will attend you, then. Are you both marrying? I will carry the skirts. When you marry as ladies there will be maids to carry your skirts, you know. I spread the veils behind them. Through the white the floor's pattern, visible, the bright arrangement of stone, Lear's crest at the centre stamped in red clay.

Stop.

Lear had turned his head slightly away.

Oh, Lear, they make pretty brides for you. They dress so nicely. I was sweet; I packed no malice in it. It needed none. In innocence we can make as good a parry as in war.

He knew better than not to meet my gaze direct. Would not show shame in the shift of it. We held each other firmer in this than we had in bed for months, years.

We were in a race. Goneril is pleased. *One of us kisses him fastest and she loves him the most! I won three times. Regan is slow.*

I am not. My dress is too long. I kept falling. See. A patch of dirt-bruise on her thin arm. And the drag of the veil under her foot, a long tear where the shoe had gone through.

A handicap! Then you both love him best. It is a draw.

I will prove it better, offered Goneril to her father. *In other times.*

Yes, he said.

Perhaps you will, I said. Passed my hand over her head. Lear in looking away from me showed the back of his head, the dirty

216

ponytail. Thread of silver in it. Age leaking into him through rock.

What will you make them do? Ruth, asking. Scraping oil through my hair, gently.

I would not make them run to me, the would-be abbesses. Gasping, the muscles of their legs floating, and their nun-girls lighting a track, Roman, with torches. Round and round the abbey. No. But how to measure the worth of a woman?

I could measure every part of Lear with my mouth. Isn't this marriage? His knucklebones, the line of his arched foot, the mossed curves of his pectorals. This was our evenings, in the early days: myself seeking the whole of him, the dipped scars, the parts of the back rubbed bald by armour, with the gentle mapping of tongue and lips. So that I could find him in the dark, so that no man could come disguised and claim to be my king. If I were blind now, and put against any part of his skin, sagged knees, raw testicles, the sunburned scrape of his neck, I would know it.

Useless knowledge. Lear, I would rid myself of you if I could, but you are bled into me, I know your shape as I know my own. And it is instructive, in its own way.

So: there must be thought in it, this race. The silver line in the centre of a tadpole spawning; the shiver of it. Life, directed. As I think, the women are outside, gathering for vespers. The office at nightfall: the lighting of the lamps, the carrying of faith in a flame, cupped in a hand.

★　★　★

The last scrape of the knife against the stone: heat. Unseasonal warm cracks over our heads in the morning; we are submerged, sleepwalking. It means more snow. In this inch of grace they have decided to do the shaving for lice; and the novices are in the courtyard in rows, each leaning their head for the close crop of the medicinal scissors.

I would louse-pick the girls myself, and Lear: finding the twitch of a thin thing in their hot hair, lifting masses of plait to finick with thin fingers. And afterwards, like my mother had (one of the sole memories, reaching out of the dark), I put their whole scalps under a cap of lard and honey and egg white, to suffocate the last and soothe the wild skin. Posset-hats, little white bonnets of babies, layered on with thumbs, a maid at the back and myself working from the hairline, away from the eyes. It set hard, to knock upon with a nail. I told them I would cook them in it, that this was crust. They grimaced and were wild, and shrieked! And loosening it with milk to scrape it off took hours. Their hair shone afterwards, as if licked.

Here the solution is starker. Well, they cannot spare such fat.

And they will not mourn it, their hair-glory. God could drift closer to them, without its gold thickness, its skein of dark wave in the way. Threaded with ribbons, some of the plaits in the bucket, as if dressed for the fair. Most, however, are plain sheaves, wetted for the razor. Russet, black. The girls raise their heads without the weight, test their new lightness.

Perhaps we should tether them, I say to Ruth, as we walk among them. *In case they fly away.* She puts a hand in her mouth and bites to stop laughing. Mark of teeth a ring around her thumb.

One girl is crying at the fat loop of hair, thick as pig-haunch, that has been lopped off her. Laid in her lap. The nun stooping is whispering comfortingly of Mary Magdalene, of the deep sin of carrying this jewel-length, this voluptuousness. She could smother herself from storms in it. Live out wild, like a fox on a heath.

What do they do with the hair? Ruth is holding herself, as if from invading scissors that may press through her veil.

They use it instead of sugar. Cover it in spice and set it in the shape of swans. She looks pale blue at the thought. The girls moan. *No, you fool, they burn it.* The stink of it, pushing through the evening, which will likely be cold, and so hold scents hard. *Maybe they should give it to Calyssa for the birds.*

Calyssa – who is now at my hand and strolling as if in conversation, as if at a pause when both parties enter an easy silence, from long acquaintance!

She even looks away, as if not to require my attention. To watch us would be to see friends at a promenade. And we are watched. Her impertinence is astonishing.

I stop abruptly. I'll talk at length with one novice. Calyssa must in her performance of mock-friendship walk on alone, or else turn, shamed, to wait for my attention in full view, like a lit taper in a dark room.

Green, the girl's skull. Though the remaining rim of hair is a soft stubby field, it will still move slightly in wind. Blood beneath it is already rising to the surface, feeling the heat. I look for thoughts, to see if they show themselves on the new-shorn parts, swelling underneath: letters, shapes. But no sign.

Your name?

I will be Sister Mary Ursula. It is the black-eyed girl. The tips of her eyelashes are blonde. The pertness has run right out of her, like water.

A good name. Your hair will regrow. By summer you will look like a pretty lawn in a nobleman's garden. Full of flowers! True. They come out of winter sprouting, softly, thin at the temples, and gradually the growth climbs towards the light. In spring one sees them finger the new curl at the nape of a neck, and wonder.

Thank you, Lady. She is wilting – with shame, or with the weight that's just been released.

Calyssa has waited. Must move away as the nun bearing the

219

sheets that gather the hair comes through. I can see her throat, shifting.

Did you have something to ask? I extend a hand: false courtesy. The palm of the mummer in rouge, mocking a king. She knows.

I wondered if we could talk a little. With her mouth almost closed, as if brazenness fails her.

Fetch me a cloth. A cool one.

She looks. Grey eyes, the long look of an archer, surveying a horizon. Then turns and finesses a cloth from somewhere. It takes some moments: they must dip it in water some way across the courtyard.

When she places it in my hand I pass it, once, around my wrists. Bracelets of wetness. The hot air is already moving downwards, the cold rising from the ground.

Thank you.

Ruth, I know, will replace the cloth in her hands. I have already moved off, down the path, back to my apartments, leaving them in the growing shadows. As if it would be that easy.

2.

Inevitably, as I said, the warmth falls out of everything. It comes towards snow again; the light is thick bronze.

I move through the chapter-house, thinking. Evening.

The women have wagered on me. On my breaking out of my fine silver ring of separation and giving my gesture of approval to one or the other. I can make no innocent movement: a reach for a churn of butter or a shoulder rolled back from the body will be seen as signalling favour, as if it were erotic, as if I were giving out my politics with the line of my flesh.

They have no sense of a queen's control. I can, of course, align myself cunningly, give hints and darts that seem to cast motes to each side. They think I operate in such thin things. Queens would not survive with just that lean language for their work; the obvious ones do not.

Well, and how are deliberations?

It is Calyssa. Lowering her head cheerfully to me, as if to joke, and to separate herself. Is performing relaxation, ease, while tense as rope. I give her credit for pushing forwards, even after her humiliation in the yard, which I know hurt her. I am dignified, sallow in my furs.

Listen, I say.

And pause. What can I tell her? I am blank as clay; they attempt to read me, and cannot.

I speak louder. *Are there none here who wish to change their vote?* I say. *I will ask just once.*

Seeing, at the last, whether one of the women will crack, and change. The will of a woman may be paper, thinly pressed – you may see your face through it. But no person moves. They are fixed in this frieze and will be obedient to it.

I am creating a contest. I find my voice again. *It will be fair, and clear. Do you agree to abide by it, the two of you?* It is formal, but there will be deep dyes here, that stain. I must know. My mouth is cracked at the corners. I must seal it.

Calyssa and Mirabel agree, aloud. Astonished, perhaps, but not displeased: it is order, obeys some kind of rule. If Lear were here he would make them swear a blood oath, sacrifice a fingertip, humiliate themselves; a tithe for the king, for fealty. I am kinder. I take their oaths, and I hold them and smile. Slivers, scraps of light.

I say, *Tomorrow we begin.*

I am ready to teach. Whether they are ready to learn remains to be seen. When I go inside my hair is so cold that you could press your lips to it and see the mark they left, written in heat.

✷　✷　✷

Blood oaths. Court life with Lear was violence. Not just from him, it was everywhere. It seethed. Hidden wounds under plates of gold. A bruise floating, in a blush.

Once four courtiers dressed up Goneril as a little boy and set her walking across the throne room, to her father. Barely three then, an age at which sex is fatness, is softness and curved bellies. Where they found the clothes for her I still do not know. Little breeches, a toy sword. Some old clothes chest perhaps, an outgrown son who'd stepped out of these little parts.

She spun out of their hands and came marching, delighted, while somebody called, *Hail the prince*, and we all looked: this other future, stepping barefoot across the floor.

Beside me the Fool said, *Oh, this play's a cruel thing.*

What did they want? To shame Lear, who was already then becoming irascible and blowing wind about, for his daughter-plague? Or else to please him, garb up his eldest inconvenience and say, *Look, it's easily mended, here is what you want!* Like binding a wound.

Lear would not strike her. He stood and saw her across the floor, adoring, walking into what she thought was ruffled hair and kisses and sweet biscuit, and waited till she came to him. Then he took her by the neck. The fat white neck. And turned her back, her bare feet wet on the floor with sweat, and yelled until she ran, weeping, *Get hence! Little beast! A pox on the sight of it! And who thought this was mannerly, who believed it well? Come out and let's parade you. I shall have it!*

The little boy-girl. I found her in the scullery, blind with misery, being fussed by our old cooks (they're the best with children: they hoist them up like legs of meat and wrap them well). I stripped her gently, could not move fast for she was a solid ball of woe, her chest collapsed. She would not touch the stuff, though I let her keep it all.

The courtiers were young, at least those who claimed it: boys up to a jape, not seeking to light on a dark thing. Though there were perhaps other hands in it, older ones, greyed old nobles who'd touched my fingers in tribute at the wedding, then said to one another, *It will bring grief, stealing a wife.* I had the young ones whipped; they regretted; they said their pieces before Lear and were dismissed.

Later, in an intimate joke for me, Lear made her a child's armour: gold-hammered, every plate a sigil, with small pleated folds at the knee and elbow and waist out of thin bronze, and a full helmet ablaze with inlaid flowers. In her stiff finery she was as hard as a star. She wore it little and was soon grown too thick for the arms, the waist. I had it packed away; perhaps it is there still. Little boy-girl in bitter gold.

I wish for that armour now. I wish for her body within it, small, vanishing, her eyes dark between lids of metal, running through the yew maze with her sister, the sun drifting behind a cloud. The percussion of her limbs, clicking, their movement audible even when hidden.

To be a queen is to be armoured, even when you are naked as daylight.

★　★　★

Night. I cannot sleep and have come to the kitchens. My belly moves under my dress as I reach for more bread from the cook. I am, for a moment, aware of my body, of its slowness and heaviness, and it seems like a luxury of suffocation.

I am fat, now. I have been climbing towards this solidity and roundness for many years, from angry underfed youth to the fullness of pregnancy, to the downturned breasts of late woman-hood, bottoms still hemispherical but the tops flattened with weight. I feel the whole of me pushing down into the earth. I am growing into the goodwife queen, the harvest goddess. What use a fine waist?

Perhaps I should charge that whoever can lift me longest, hold my whole rolled self in their arms and not bend or topple over, should be abbess. The two women with their sleeves rolled, ribbons at their arms, hoisting till a vein bursts! Mirabel would win.

The bread swells in my mouth, the crust loosening.

I must design this contest. I must make an abbess out of these women, out of mute flesh. I must set small battles, and see them won. I do not know how to begin.

What makes an abbess? I think of my dead friend, of her failures. Softness, capaciousness, distraction; sugar in her body, in her lungs, which lit up with sickness, like blue flame. Abbesses are very like queens. Their dominions are small, ringed around, and less inclined to be bothered by men, so their intimacy is a privilege. Though men are amusing, they give much less than they think.

If it were my court I could teach these green young players such things! There would be letters, miniature rings, tokens of threat, the dress and dowry of a proper fight for favourite. Genteel, close-mouthed. Breathing behind screens. Archery, dark-cut claret. But Mirabel and Calyssa are not court women. They would be pecked to death by one in ten minutes. Naive as bald babes.

The cook says, *So you're to do it, then.*

I am.

What are you going to make 'em do? Jump through a hoop? I'd pay to see it.

Perhaps. I grin, she grins.

They think they speak of power, these women, but power is not one language. It is diverse; it works its way under the tongue.

Fortunately I've taught before. Lear had no patience; I gave him instruction, showed him the rules. *Watch me.* The white hall with the yew floor in our palace, I built that, for courts to parade and perform their orbits. Against the pale wood, which concealed nothing. Hundreds of lessons, thousands.

One divides one's opponent's court against him.

One shows obedience to the highest figure in the room.

One's first obligation is oneself. And one's family. That is the last rule, but also the first. I should have taught him *Do not exile your wife*, but perhaps it would not have taken.

The cook passes me a cake. I am thinking, chewing. Cud-woman, hearth-girl. There are so many lessons, we would be here a lifetime, a marriage-length.

I could just ask them, *Who will free me? Who will let me out and allow me to vanish?* But they would say yes to all things, both of them; they would promise me the impossible. I could ask for a monkey. I could ask them to layer praise on me, my hair, my cunning, my hands, like the old troubadours. Mirabel handling a compliment, thrusting it at me like an onion! No. I must have better methods.

I think of Kent, who would not eat cake, who was wheat and salt, all his life: plain-browed, unadorned. Instructing me under the waving roses of my first husband's garden, as I struggled towards queenship. Drowning, my throat full. I had said, *Kent, I can't. It is too difficult. I want to go back to the convent.*

And he said, *Let me tell you what I know. In the court you have five occupations. You fight when you must, you serve your master, you are honest, you consider secrets a virtue, and you fear the judgement of God.*

It cannot be that simple. I was young, the roses were crushed underfoot, their tenderness ghastly. Michael would not touch me though I loved him. I wanted to be destroyed too, and left to rot on summer grass, at seventeen.

It is always simple, Kent said. His severe shoulders, which bent slightly. *I had it from my father, and he from his. Five occupations. Remember. Recite them.*

Kent's five lessons. What it takes to be a queen, an abbess.
War.
Obedience.
Honesty.
Secrecy.
Fear of God.
Yes. I nod to myself. Of course. In hunting, one pairs need

with style. Thin-necked hounds for fox-hunts. White ferrets for rabbit, diving through soil in pursuit, a lightning-body in dark earth. My father's hunters had one, gold-leashed; as a child I watched it. Luscious snake, I thought, a land-eel, precious fine teeth in its soft mouth that knew the shape of rabbit skull intimately, could curve around one and hold. Troubadour songs were made for animals like that. Beautiful like women.

I will go ferreting, I have the white gleam of it, and I work underfoot: one contest for each rule. Five times these women will show me their weaknesses, and I will assess. I will be the scales of Justice; I will find what is wanting.

The cook has turned her back. She has sensed I am elsewhere, in some place where I have no need of her. Crumbs through my fingers. Honey at the corner of my mouth.

I hear Regan child-sulking, whispering at my ear, *You always loved Goneril more.*

And my reply, years distant now, over dark water, *Do you know your father's two maps, hanging on the wall of his rooms, that are identical, and show all his lands from here to the horizon?* The height of two men, those maps, with curls of forest like boys' hair and identical stamped crests, commissioned for two high walls, so that he would be mirrored always by his country, no matter where he turned. *My love for you both is like those maps. The same in every detail. Not a brushstroke of difference, and stretching from here to for ever, out over the wall, to beyond the sunrise, Regan, where the birds go to sleep.*

I wonder if she ever believed it. I wonder if I did.

★   ★   ★

Morning. Lambent light spilling over the wall.

I come to prayers. I am still in mourning white, moving among these dark women; a line of flaming thought, a banner glittering

227

before a parade of black mares. Indecorously my sleeves are yellowing now, coming into rot. Perhaps I should ask for the cook's pale cheesecloths and be bound up like Cheddar, to see out the season. I will ask Ruth, to see her laugh.

I could come out of mourning for you now, Lear, and terrorise them all in my old robes: velvet and purple, worn down to the nub. Old brocade. I contemplate throwing all the white stuff out of a window, watching it curdle into a puddle, and emerging in pink, aged green. Fresh in a new spring! Ruth would gasp; Mirabel would likely ask to have the petticoat to put compost in it.

But white is a helpful colour, Lear. It marks me out, makes them see my colossal presence clearly, like a swan. While they are peahens, clustering. No, I'll stay white-headed. Not for you, you old bastard, with your smashed-up head, dooming me to live in this little pink prison. For myself, for the whiteness of my own plans, my intent. And for my daughters.

During prayers I wonder about the plans I have made overnight. Five-pronged, like a hand. Like a wheel. Have I done right?

You know nothing about a human's weaknesses, the humours that run back from their skull, until you sleep with them, or glimpse their nakedness. Chaste or not. Poor Gloucester, fingering the edge of a smock, diving bosom-wards, sought to know himself, and came back with the same mirrored face each time. He had the game backwards: women arc the world out from themselves; they crack open at the hips like fruit and deliver it forth.

After prayers the women assemble at the chapel door. *We are ready*, says Calyssa, to me.

I watch them. Mirabel passive, solitary; a rock in a river, around which matter passes. Calyssa sensing that the moment requires poise, and smoothing herself, so that she looks distinct, and historic; it fails, and she is young, over-bitten with cold.

I do not think you are, I say.

What? Calyssa looks strange, as if the lines of her face were sketched poorly, and shivered.

Not ready, not quite. But you will be. I will test you, as I was once tested, as an old friend at court taught me. It is a good way to find an abbess.

But this is not a court, says Calyssa. She is impatient.

It is the court of God. And both of you are poor courtiers, at the moment, but have good potential.

I turn to walk away, and I fall.

It is the lack of light — grey, across the slate, with tapers throwing only a wet glow that draws in dark — or else this confusion, folded together with the women in accordion pages, but I go forward, and down. Dragging, and pulling another woman half prone, to one knee, heavily. We are scrabbling. The frozen path against the heel of my palms. In my whiteness I must look like a trapped swan.

Calyssa has her arms forward already and is diving. Feels to some extent the hurt within herself, the blow against the stone, and is disappointed, berates herself, for her perceived weakness, for not fitting into my suffering that she could see it from the inside and comfort it. Wrings my hands, a little, and is too shrill. In her own eyes she fails; and in her anxiety loses track of her feet, which step back and onto the woman forced to kneel. She is caught between perceptions. And, when she realises it, is unkind. *Get up now — help her. What are you all standing around for?*

Mirabel waits, sees which one shows most pain: myself, or the old nun with the hurt knee. And angles that woman's leg back, perhaps against her wishes, to see the mark, in those hands through which passes all life, all earth, and says, *It will heal,* and *You should go to the infirmary. I'll come with a poultice later, takes out the swelling.* Myself, judged only lightly damaged and so capable of self-healing, she hauls to standing in gentle insistence, then ignores.

You think this does not matter, I mutter, to the ghosts lying by my ear. *It matters.* It was men set up the divide between the ceremony rooms and the women's quarters, and thought they had divided the world. Only men. Who else would be gullible enough?

The nun, mouthing in shock, is taken away, and is not so injured, not so. Will heal, with lavender, and steaming tisanes. The arranged nuns murmur the sympathies of people who have escaped bruising through chance, and so believe themselves moral. The Fates do not care, I want to tell them. They kill all.

Was that a test? says Mirabel, suddenly. *The first test.* Looking at me as I judge the rip in my skirt, wide as a mouth; as if I shed, as if I am an insect. Soon I may trail my old white face behind like a grasshopper, too. My new body may be dark and glittering and hard.

I smile at her.

Perhaps.

And walk away, strongly, without hesitation.

First lesson for them, from Kent: war. People are testing you, always. You must forever be prepared for the arrow-rain, the shout of fire at your boundary, and rise to meet it.

3.

I am a woman who enjoys the drop of shock onto a face. The stun, the awe. From bewilderment you can raise such prizes.

I remember. *Return the wife of the king.*

A rim of them, Michael's men in the rain. Behind them the long flat of Lear's land, peat and bald rock and strips of fog at the heath-shoulder, and massed in them his family's ghosts. Ancestors whitening the light. They had walked over the graves, the cairns. Who silvered the ground here, the thin air? Who patrolled the wind?

The bridge over the thin-dug moat was raw wood. I had a forehead bared for the rain. I had my circlet from the wedding. Flowers, falling.

There is no wife of that name here. I am married to another lord. Use his name. Had come out alone, deliberately. A single sign, a feather in water: the mark of magic, come no nearer. My dragging coat darkened and slapped at my calf.

There was one speaker, head of the guard. *You have betrayed your honour, or been forced to it. You should be ashamed.*

I mourned my king fully. If untraditionally, but I would not allow that. *I am by law free to conduct myself at discretion. My conscience is my own affair.*

You choose this? Sniffed at the smoke rising from the peat-fires. A blasted place. It fitted me: I was radiating, happiness and fury;

there was no hiding, the land was open as a face. *And where's your master?*

Not aware as yet of you. You are my remnant and I face you thus alone. I extended a hand. I knew he recognised the gesture, militant, a man's signal of formal honour to his foe. *I know the court lost the chance to pair me with an ally of their choosing, and thereby have a pick of my wealth, but it was fairly done, and the play is closed. Tell them to curse themselves for slowness, not Lear's wife for pursuing other courses.*

He shrugged. *It was the propriety.*

Return, goodman. Tell them that you were forced to retire. In disgust at my conduct, I added, holding out a smile, *and protection of your virtue.*

He laughed – relieved, and amazed; eyed me with confusion. That I could lay a stratagem like a parkland and watch the riders blunder in the copses. The bride-earrings curled at my neck, lightly.

They may not like you better for it.

I don't mind.

No. I suppose you wouldn't. He placed his hands in his belt and bowed. *May God lie in this path as well as the other, Queen.*

Yes. Do look horrified as you return. The soldiers talk.

He and the pack moved heavily: they could not be graceful on this land. A virtue of it: sucking full water-holes, sheen of moisture on rock, hiding its densities. Under the angled sun it could all shine, to be plunged into, to swallow.

Lear arrived then, bedecked. Scarlet hammered into the brass mouth of his guard, horsehair crest alarmed, assembled in haste. Was shocked. White spear of wife, and the open plain, singing of water. No men.

They are gone.

Yes. I sent them away.

I would have done that. I was preparing.

It was only a small matter. I could do it myself.

232

He was beautiful when ridiculous. My unclothed monarch, slipping on a mat and banging his balls. The boy couldn't last – vulnerability like this would kill him, but it was so precious. Young Lear, tough as a day-old calf.

Our son will be like this, I thought, and love bit down so fiercely that I stopped breathing.

★   ★   ★

The next day dawns fine, and we are walking, in the new fresh-crush sun, to the river within the abbey walls. This is an act that holy women do when they are not spinning, or embroidering, or drifting through clouds towards God. It is a ritual, as we woke today and the countryside was streaked white and blue, and no person for miles; a few black figures in the fields, bending, but elsewhere wide roads, empty. A map dipped in water. The knowledge of it rang around the abbey: alone, winter is here, we are alone.

So we are going. I am in my pressed white arrangements of cloth, and Ruth comes, in blue, and the nuns, to remember that we are alive and God favours us, in this desolate place, with the quarantine on the door like a bitter mouth. We cluster and pray as we walk. Calyssa suggested it. A little excursion, to see if the river had frozen. To pass the graveyard, with its small flowerbeds, and kiss our rosaries.

And it is time, I think, for the second lesson. Obedience. The pull of servitude.

Knowing they are being measured, somehow, the two women want to be useful, to woo. Mirabel keeps back, waiting her chance to fold a veil or lay a carpet. Calyssa dashes ahead through the shrubbery, and fusses, till at last Ruth tells her to be peaceful: she is upsetting my head. Ruth is better than a brach – she circles and bites intruding feet.

233

To win my favour has never been a feat for lazy men. The boys who swarmed Lear hoped to charm me, to dandle me off with songs and little gems. I gave them to the servant-girls. Watched them wear their nobility like a sore. To be won with so little! I could make a frighted badger come nuzzle in my sleeve. I could make these two swim in the winter stream. Could make them climb a tree, bring down a boar with their bare arms and teeth, anything. Anything.

The river has frozen in parts but in others there are laneways of green water, flourishing their foam. The banks are stippled and branched with frost, and the women go to look, to lay out stones and test the weight of ice at the rim.

I sit on a part of the bank. It is too close to the edge – the mud bunches beneath my weight; when I rise there will be bleached-dry patches. The green water clarifies. I am so flooded with self now, with happiness. Why should I not lie here, in this expanding day that touches the undersides of the sisters' clothes, with the lichened rock, and be content? I could become a web of flesh and green bone, for eel-nests and leeching fish. Little frogs could sing in my pelvis.

The ghosts are in the greenery, in the slant of the sun. Lear is here suddenly, kneeling at my knee, I think, and then know it is not; but it is, in some way – my husband crawls to me, and will cry. After the horse, reaching for me from the riverbank, and weeping. My hands on his hands.

Are those late blackberries? says one woman. Some on the far bank, others ahead. Somehow not killed by frost.

They are. Ruth is excited by sun and sweet cool air.

I would taste some. I say it to Ruth, who moves, obedient immediately. Knowing the love and release of serving. Behind her the shadows of my own girls, who would not, who would fight or dawdle or lay the berries under their tongues and pretend they were furred with blight! *No, none left, Mother, not at all.*

Calyssa, attentive, says, *I'll help.* Has taken Ruth's wrist and pulled it back, holding hard at her side, where she believes I cannot see. Is rising on the top of her feet to get the highest sweet ones, the most drunk on sun, dark as sloes.

With both hands cupped full she comes back through the brush. Ruth follows eating, sullen, black-tongued. Sits and will not speak.

To seem less heavy with ambition she offers them widely; the others take perhaps one or two but know she is playing a point, and steer off. I take a choice few and smile. She had read the bush incorrectly: these are green still in the top bulbs, with bitter liquor at the back of the mouth when crushed.

Mirabel, I know, has not moved to help, and I think, *Tut.*

There is a crack, a smash of sound. We turn: Mirabel is wading out into the frozen water, hip-height, brown as ale, her habit silvering out behind like a tail.

Her body in water, the sight of it, shifts under my ribs. Lear dragged back to our rooms muddied and sluiced, dredged from the bottom, like a fistful of gold, after the horse threw him; old, coughing silt. What was the horse's name? It has gone.

I say, *Stop.* Nobody, I think, hears.

She has reached the far bank, hauls, and is on shore, wearing four skins it seems on her own, the square hollow above her thick thigh under her hip revealed on both sides to be the size of a fist. In the white sun, and we have all risen, there is yelling around me like horses. She has broken off from us: she has been born again through this dip in the river; we no longer know what she is.

She leans to a blackberry bush. Breaks off a branch.

Comes back through the water, bearing it overhead like a torch;

slower this time, as the robes are a heavy train, laboured against, pulling back from her chest and shoulders like the harness of a cart-horse. As Kent returned, as he came back bearing the body of the king.

Calyssa and four others pull her out, gripping at her through her clothing, which has become a shell. She lays the branch in front of me, then sits, removes her shoes. Breathes soft through her mouth. *Cold*, she says.

The berries are glorious, waving in splendour. The nuns eat in silence. She has brushed us all with some darkness, some element of will. We are awed.

Later, returning, I think, *Did Mirabel mean to humiliate me?* Watch her moving across the flat land in front of me, hands open at her sides.

No. She would not. Not for my rank. It was directness. Was taking the shortest route to the greatest gain, like a child (Goneril, putting fingers through the bottom of the feast-cake to find the lucky silver). She has won, and she knows it.

When Ruth walks up to put a folded blanket in my hands I suddenly reach and pull her head close and kiss it, upon the forehead: damp, sweet-smelling from the ring of sweat at the hairline. She makes a pleased noise. Calyssa had turned her head and watched me walking, hand over her brow for the sheer sun; turns away.

4.

In the dark of early morning the women are singing, singing, the plunge of their hopeful voices into the night.

An abbey at matins is a vessel filling. In the night, still grazing the edges of sleep, these half-roused women are walking towards God: stripped of language, appetite, thought. At the beginning they move between notes by memory, are waking into prayer, firming into the full shapes of their bodies. I am still awake, I sleep less and less, as I age; the habit has fallen from my body like hair. In my rooms I hear them. Snow is falling.

I am hunched in my furs. Grief is a kind of snow-blindness, snow-deafness; the world departs from you, behind a wall.

On an impulse, wanting human voices, human forms, I wrap up and go to the chapel's upper part; the small window high in the wall, where I can listen without showing my face. Built for visiting kings and bishops, who would not want to take mass with the unwashed nuns, but to listen with their heads level to the rose window, on speaking terms with God. An ivory screen, picked with holes, for eye-peering.

I want to pray, but I am distracted. The women are tensing, puckering; I know the shifting weight and tenderness of a place as it changes, the taste of misery in a room. This contest will hurt them. I wonder if they know that, if Calyssa, Mirabel, their mouths open for dawn, know it. Little novice Sister Mary Ursula, with her shaven head nude as a moon under its cloth, yawning.

Brother Manfred sees the movement behind my screen, I know, but steadies his head, and propels the service forward, away. He does not understand.

Perhaps I give them all too much credit, these women. They look like wood, or stone. How can they feel hatred, or pain, as I do? Perhaps it is too strange for a noblewoman to make a contest for nuns. Lear thought that as you climbed up the chain of being, senses flowered: kings felt more deeply than the peasantry, who had hot muscles and little else. Lear's body, he said, did the work of thousands, for whom he intuited the world. I may simply be a different being. Rank will always tell.

But I have seen peasant women straighten in the fields and narrow their eyes into the low sun, raising their arms above their heads for shade, and they looked as if they understood. I do not know. There is something, but God has divided us, noble to slave, perhaps not to know, but to accept.

Calyssa's fine head bows forwards. It is well-shaped. She is a classical animal; the Italians would love to sketch her. If the Fool were here, I think, in this brooding atmosphere, with the straight-backed disapproving priest, he'd drop something. He'd throw a candle, an apple, out of the little window, and aim for Brother Manfred's perfectly circular head, and claim that it was a miraculous summoning and everybody should pray!

I drop nothing. Tempted though I am. But I smile.

Fool-ghost. You were mine, to begin with. A player in a travelling troupe that performed in Michael's court, who dared strike at my childlessness onstage. *The lady's an untouched pan that would boil a chicken of any size, if the cook were strong for't.*

How you could read it I don't know. The courtiers were livid, and you avoided being set in the stocks only by swift feet. I felt — seen, understood.

So I sent my own man, and a bit of coin, and lured you to court, which you proudly acknowledged. *I have a high bride-price to marry this queen, though marrying may mar the taste.*

He is so brutal, said the courtiers. And it was true: you saw no authority beyond the hand that gave you food, which was usually mine, and all else was a shade to be pissed upon. Privately I asked, *Are you so irreverent really, Fool?*

Madam, I was not born into reverence, but on the other side of the sheet to't; and having seen it askance, I never could look longways, but always have my eye at a crook.

Exceptions. You were kind to cripples, pedlars, those bestowed with fits.

You'd make a poor king, Fool, with such favourites.

I know, madam, but chance is blunt: it has no sharpener to give its blade a wit.

And children. You had no mockery for children, but aped and jigged for them; the girls tore at your clothes and batted your face delightedly, and you batted them back.

The Fool-ghost whispers. I do not hear it: the words fly up to the top of the chapel, and are lost in the snow.

Matins finishes, and the women beneath me rise to walk out of the chapel. From separate souls talking to God they retract, their unfurled selves roll back and they become one great body, many-wrist, many-face. Chilblains on the fingers of one novice, every woman feels the prickle.

I am floating above them, like an angel, which amuses me, and would doubtless make the Fool choke with mirth and make some horrible pun, about heavenly bodies. The contest will separate these women, briefly: their nun-body will be pulled apart, as neck-bones break in the hanged. But they will clot, they will coalesce, around the new abbess I give them. Everybody will heal, in the end. As ordinary women do.

Ruth is at the window when I return, comforted. Says, *It has stopped snowing.* Yes, clear, the dawn sky still gleaming with winter stars, the Bear over the abbey roof.

★   ★   ★

I lie awake. I wish I could explain to the women what I was doing: what obedience means, the anticipation of wants in the powerful. How it can save you.

A day without meat. The cooks had stuffed an eel and it sat with its pale eye on us. Regan would not obey. She had unaccountable fits of refusal: would not lie still to feel the tension of a room and wait. She would walk right into rage, which we all knew intimately, that could fill open space like scent.

He was already in a poor humour, Kent had warned, with the pass of his hand at his chin as I entered the chamber. There are rings of language for kings, the one taut around him — counsellors, intimates, favourites — then wider spools, passing through the corridors, transmitting the shape of his mouth, how well he'd slept.

And she strode into that, to the red glint of his face, and angered it.

Some remark he passed. Her dress, something about lateness; in this mood he was inclined to be rude to shadows on the wall. One rose, one took it quietly, one walked on or took a little quiet breath in an outer room, hands against ribs. She was poorly herself or else would never. But said instead to Lear, *Do not speak to me like that.*

Mmm? Repeat, child, I caught it wrong, I think. He would pretend careful deafness. It was dangerous, a feint to show she should back away.

240

Regan drew breath. Brave. *Do not speak to me in that manner.*

Do not! Lear blinked wide. *She orders, did you hear her? Kent, am I raving, did you note the miracle also?* Kent would not be drawn. *Do not! Go, Regan, tell me 'do not' again.*

I would not wish to displease you, Father, but you are distracted and spoke too harshly. I was offended.

Distracted! He could spit. Servants would hover with new collars, take the old ones to bleach dry under the ovens. *Am I a buffoon, Regan, that can do but one thing at a time? If I say before all the assembled court, that you are a foul, corrupted whore, then it is as I say! Tell me 'do not' once more, Regan, I'll crack you like a witch under a wheel.*

I am not myself, I must retire.

He wanted a thing to whip, he found me. *You call these daughters? What have you provided me? Skunk-pups, that's what.*

Hours of this, beaten upon my back. He would not rest until he felt himself acquitted, until the pain ran out onto the floor. I bowed and left to find Regan.

She was in her chamber. Eating a biscuit. Cruel, I thought then, astonishingly cruel.

How could you leave me, Regan, to face his wrath alone? What manner of daughter are you?

I could take no more. Is not eating. Merely putting the biscuit into one palm and the other.

Take! You take all from us. You are bedded by us, your linens and horses and fine plaits are our gift. I could cast you out and leave you roofless. Oh, naughty, naughty girl! You forget your duty.

They owed us all. They gave us so little, and would scratch out everything, our blood, our very eyes.

Take what you want from me, I shall not be subjected to these indignities. She was, I realised, talking as I talked. As if the fit of me could work on her. As if her raw bone could support my structure, the thing I had worked forty years to build. Infuriating.

Indignities — oh, child. You are so young. Come here. Come. She came over to place her head against my stomach. *I forgive; you are so callow.* And still had hope then. That it would break into them, the pain they gave their mother, that it would knock down the door and cleanse the place from within.

Obey. Obey, obey, obey. God, your masters, your controller. Whatever is above you: obey, and you survive, and you are received into the bosom of love.

5.

The winter days have a scalded, glaring light; the sun is all yolk and blood. A time for wanting. I feel the rhythm of the contest rising, now, its next stage: are they honest? Can they lie?

Ruth is vivid, banking the fire, her cheeks a splash of white. I drink broth in a cage of sunlight, and think. There is a line between my eyes; it burned in during my first marriage. Lear would thumb it when I was tired.

Kent's edict demands a test of honesty, but he was thinking of men, who lie about honour, sin, the appearance of shame. Women are darker-coloured. Women lie about desire, about what they want. The tests must be different, here.

I have had to teach dishonesty too. Lear was a man born without a second face. He walked into the room and I saw all his thoughts before him, streaming. Had to conceal, to cut pockets in him, to show him how to slit and hinge himself. An entire carpentry of state. I have always been thicker, denser; I can conceal countries within myself. Whole men. Lear, you never knew the half of it.

And I know how to pick it out in others, that hidden thing. Some girls carry it in their eyes, their hands, glove themselves in it and walk about, burning. Others make a hole in the ground, push its thickness in and do not visit. Though it grows, though it turns its roots into a snare at your ankle. Trap.

Goneril, whispering. All her sister's secrets falling out of her mouth.

Ruth passes, carrying folded rugs. She is worried about moths, about winter's harsher tricks. I can always see into her mind – she is pellucid; there is no part of her that dissembles, whether through the force of my will or the thinness of her own energy. There is one aspect of her life, though, that I do not know.

Ruth.

Yes, I have cleaned the rags. You may use them. Ruth has a habit of moving to my needs before I voice them, not with irritation, merely as a matter of efficiency. I look at her face: long, without the push of any inner sorrow or impulse, though with lightly scratched wrinkles now.

Ruth, do you remember the night we came here?

She looks, momentarily, astonished, and the change on her features is rousing: she becomes an animal, a huge-eyed rabbit. *Yes, Lady.*

What happened to you?

As an order she must follow it – it is her nature. She sits and clasps her hands. *To me?*

Did you know you were coming with me?

Oh, no, Lady. They roused me from my bed. Two of the knights. I was frightened to see them in the sleeping quarters – they were big men. They told me to gather my things and come down, for I was to have a long journey.

Why you, Ruth? I have wondered. I had my own maid, after all. Or at least Magdalena, who knew such secrets!

I think, Lady, the other women in the room told them to take me, as I was newly there, and not so well-liked, and when they came looking for a waiting-maid, the men, the others said my name. This old betrayal still stirs her: she looks down at her hands and pinches the fingertips close, till they show white. *And so I bundled up my cloak and Bible, and put on*

*my clogs, and all of my skirts for it was such a cold night, and came down;
and there were you waiting, on the back of the cart.*

What did I look like?

*I don't know, for I didn't know it was yourself: you had a veil on, and
a great many things, and I had no person to ask, so I perched alongside you.*
After a silence she says, *I thought you were ill perhaps, and being taken
to be nursed. It was a long journey.*

It was.

*And then we came here in the north. And they told me I was not to go
back again, but to stay and be at your bidding for a servant, and—*

Surprising: she is crying! *You do not like being my servant, Ruth? Or
perhaps it is this place that displeases you?* It having never struck me
before to pity this woman, who has had body's comfort, and
good food, and only this small room to neaten; and a single quiet
mistress, rather than many who might pinch and be cruel to her.

*No, Lady, no — you are a good mistress, and it honours me to serve the queen,
in whatever condition she is found.* She adds the last part as her own
thought — I sense it is one she says to herself in privacy. *I had not
considered,* she says more solidly, *that I would be taken from court and placed
in an abbey. I am accustomed to it now, but it seemed solitary, for a while.*

I pat her hand. *But you will have life beyond this abbey, Ruth! We will
go into the world, after this little winter. And you will live long beyond my
death, and can make a good match, perhaps.* Old though she is, she'd be
a good wife for some gentle widower, fussing around his blankets,
kissing some seamed forehead, clasping a brittle hand. Yes.

This, unaccountable creature, makes her sob! *No, do not speak of
that, Lady. I have no friends save yourself.* Little marsh-rabbit.

*We'll show you to all the men we find. One of them doubtless will think
you charming.*

I would not want such attentions. She is terrified.

God help me! *Then they'll all ignore you entirely and put you in a
basket with the onions. Would that please you? Woman, you try my patience.*

Yes. She breathes more gently. She finds my irritation much less dangerous than my pleasure, which is a very sensible outlook. *Here are the rags, Mistress. I hope the winter is over soon. It is so long already it seems.*

No longer than any other year. But that itself is a lie; and we know I am making it, a construction to soothe, and are both comforted.

Nuns are honest. Nuns sit before God and are naked to the soul. But every woman has a hidden part, a thing she cuts open, her own flesh, and plants.

In this contest, Lear, I will find it. Wait. Watch.

★   ★   ★

After the prayers of prime finish, the winter sun has come into the corners, pale as honey, and the women eat. The spoon goes into the soup, the bread crust breaks and spills steam across their hands. Under the dining table they push their hands beneath their thighs for warmth.

I am seated between the two contenders, for policy. Had come in furred head to foot, like an elderly badger, and insisted. I feel condensed by the curiosity of these women, on all sides. Isolated people will fasten on an object, and hold, as if it anchors the whole, and is critical to the walls not falling down.

A nun is rising to speak from the Psalms, as the women finish. I say, *No more of that. I would hear other things, now.* And shut myself up, in portent. A door, snapping. A child Goneril, saying, *I know a secret, but will tell you later,* in terrible mysteries, haughty as a page.

The nun blinks. The two contenders look at one another and are surprised, and perhaps a little inclined to smile, but must acquiesce. This is a new turn, and I have caught them off-balance.

What would you have us do? says Calyssa. The cook is in the corner, holding the bread, smiling, her hands wringing in her apron. She is fond of me, I have decided.

Sit over in this dock, I say. Gesturing to two chairs I have seen, against the wall. *We are going to have a trial. These excellent women here will be judges with me; even if we are not allowed onto the councils and commissions of justice, we still have a need for fairness.* Smiling at them. To join the joke.

There is a murmur. Cow-eyed, the women stare, and do not understand. I am irritated. Did I not tell you, Goneril, that it would be like this? Like being eaten alive, and finding yourself in the belly of the leviathan with a hundred stupid women in the dark? Your mother knew. Girls of Lear's blood don't become women of God. We've lived with a god, and that should have been enough for us.

We were not warned, says Mirabel. The pelt of her is moving to the chairs in gentle obedience, but there is a twitch in her voice, a click. Regular parts, disturbed.

The better for your answers. It is crucial that you be truthful. Or you might try to lie — but we will find it out! Won't we?

This time one of the girls accepts, nods smiling. They have understood, now, that it is a game, and I am entertaining them, as the Fool would, in a mock-court. The two women sit. Calyssa looks stark as death, as if her throat moved under a rope. Condemned, I think, and then I think, You at least have the benefit of answering your accusations. I had none.

Let us deal justly, I say. Loud, light. Seeking not to humiliate, but to anatomise, in the soft room, with the light trailing in corners. The ghosts are gathering, at the women's eyes, like flies. *First question. Have you ever sneaked into the kitchen at night to filch extra cake?*

Never! Calyssa looks scalded with astonishment.

Oh, I have, says Mirabel. *But not for some years.*

The cook laughs, and verifies. The room cracks, and pleasure flows in; shoulders are released, and the women begin to move forwards, and form their jury with me, assessing the two contenders, who are seated. All their mouths still smell sweetly of soup.

This is a space, I tell the holy women, *in which to ask all questions you have desired, but cannot, since they are bound by the law to be honest. Abbesses must be clear as water, you see.*

This is a lie, but nobody probes it.

So many questions are asked. Questions of religion, past sins, small incidents, some impertinences, but nothing that can rip a soul. The women for both sides are striving to be fair, and spreading their interrogations evenly across the ground. They want to luxuriate in their moral goodness.

Calyssa, I note, tightens her muscles around a lie. Will dip into falsehood if she fears being brutalised. Otherwise she is a martyr to honesty. Mirabel flows simply between truth and untruth, so that the two are blurred, and often fails to see the distinction. Silent women are easy liars.

The two would-be abbesses also begin, against propriety, to enjoy the attention. Most people believe that they are fascinating. Only hermits and the very rich can claim the privilege of stating themselves boring.

Is it true, asks one woman of Calyssa, *that you once saw a relic? A real one. Or did you make it up?* she adds, as if to press the point.

It is true. Calyssa is hesitant. She is struggling with intensity, her feet kicking her dress to pieces. *It was the foot of a saint. I saw it as a child. It was so beautiful.* She is threatened by her own passion, by its unseemliness. *It lay within a silver box, and the priest opened it, and we saw.* Her voice has anger in it at its inadequacy, at the falling away of words.

What did it look like? The novices in particular are breathless;

248

their faith is pushing through them, and makes their faces a little beautiful.

A bone. Just a grey, yellowing old bone. Like you'd give a dog. But in seeing the bone I thought of God, and it was like a shaft of light in my mind. Calyssa's voice is lifting. Looking not beyond me but directly at my face, embodying in it the past, the intensity of her vision, that it is not vanished but here, now. The relic in its oiled gold box. *I knew then I wanted the life of the Lord.* Her lips are desperate. I want her to look away. I am not a relic in a box, not legendary bone, not yet.

I feel in some part deceived. Kent, your rule is failing: the contest is not about honesty, any more, but about revelation. First Mirabel and then Calyssa is courting the room. The shape and cadence of interrogation have gone.

I am determined suddenly to be cruel. I will push us to the sticking-point. It is my own body I throw upon the spike, to bring forth some kind of truth.

I will ask a difficult thing, I say. *The abbess, God rest her, was flawed. How would you be better?*

Silence. I am humped in my oiled furs.

Mirabel considers. Head low, pursuant to her thoughts. *I have seen three abbesses, and their weaknesses. I have been here a long time. The last was the best, but I would be stronger.* I wait, but she lapses into silence, which is her true self.

Calyssa, striding into the gap, is affectionate, as a mark of her rank. *She couldn't make a plan to prick a boil.* The grasp of a familiar relationship has made her happier, her own visions torment her.

She was perhaps not full of plans, Mirabel says. *But she did good work. Was too kind sometimes.*

Kindness is a virtue before the Lord, Calyssa rejoins.

When you manage so many women it is not sensible. Mirabel is simple, but not stupid, no. *You are not kind. Neither am I.*

I am sure I am not hard, says Calyssa, peevishly.

The mood has disintegrated, the women are suspicious of one another once again. Mouths are hardening against teeth. I am satisfied.

I want to ask, *Did the abbess love me?* The question comes and is a deep temptation, and I would ask it, but it trembles and vanishes, in the green sunlight, and in its wake I see it was a ghost-thought. Naughty abbess! She has joined the crowd of ghosts, now. Sat on my back like a pack: two kings, three daughters, one abbess — you will all make me a spine-bent beggar. No, I will not ask.

The bells break over the women, for the next round of prayer. Calyssa and Mirabel rise, and move together to the door. *I hope it was fruitful*, Mirabel says to me, as they pass. *This contest. The seedlings will have to wait for watering, now.* Not resentful; merely fact. But I am thinking of the abbess, her pale hands, and of the ghosts. And cannot answer, before Mirabel has gone, and the other women, into the cloister.

★　★　★

Did you get what you wanted from that? the cook asks later.

In a way, I say.

What do I want? I've always wanted everything. Even now. My old body is unfair. It retains its richness; it has not corroded into a late quiet. Where is my own third age, the crone, small and dried as apple seed in a palm, loosened from the treacherous wetness of marriage and desire? My body curls at the corners but still retains a white sweet core.

Perhaps after all I am made for men. Perhaps my lush dead body will refuse the virginity of a winding sheet and spill, sleek as guts, pelvis-first, to the floor.

Measuring desire in men, changing it, is no difficulty. *Desire,*
I warned Lear, *makes you terrible. Look inconstant. Don't let them fix on
your tastes, your flatteries. Be distant, untraced, a bird escaping a hand.*

Lear and I were locked in a dance. His cock through a coat. A
flash of tongue at him within a veil. The sweet smear of him on
belly, neck, in the dark of my hair so that I had to draw flower-fat
through it in ivory combs. He was young and knew little, only
what a woman's parts are in poet's words. Flower and shell. The
real he had not touched or smelt. I taught him part by part: foot,
heel, knee. How to touch ribs as if playing a lyre; without seeing,
know where the arrow falls. Women are more difficult.

The cook is speaking, gathering the bowls. I enjoy her, her
rude shape, her willingness to be obedient, and find joy in it. *I
wish I knew how your minds worked. You noble ladies.*

Why do you say so?

Her eyes peering like berries in dark bread. *These little battles. Is
this what court is like? Trials and fussing and tricks, and — and occupying the
time?*

Yes.

I'd hate it, she says decisively.

Quite probably.

*Give me a fist-fight to sort things out. I saw a trial by ordeal once, Lady.
Now that was a way to determine a winner. Two men standing in the sun
for ages, days and days. One dropped down dead at the finish.* Her lip is
curling.

Court is like that too. I have flour on my skirt — it makes it whiter;
the underside is blond, now, like a bad bruise. I brush it away.
Except that we don't die at the end. Which is worse.

But you enjoyed it? She sees my face, shakes her head. *There, you
see, you did. I'll never understand it.*

I did enjoy it, of course I did. The victories. The one of the
sleeves, for instance.

Some foreign women appeared in Lear's court, with wide slits upon their sleeves, bare to the skin. Thick lace surrounding them, and beading, but still an instinct: that flesh was present, that it breathed. Men contrived to pull their arms, to see a hint of cunning shoulder.

Dressing, Lear said, *I hate the open sleeves on the new courtiers' girls. Cheap. Letting their skin brown in the sun.*

You've been listening to the preachers. It's fashion, it's harmless. And let them be beautiful! Let them glory in the cloudless noon of their loveliness, and have it win them husbands; much good might it do them.

Harmless! Thunder and lightning, it's terrible. My girls would never be so immodest.

Girls have a propensity to be immodest. It is no harm.

Pssht. Perhaps you were, as a girl. But my girls have royal blood. Puffed-up prince, little frog-face, pushing out his lip in the mirror! *They know the value of their bodies as symbols of Lear's grace. They are good, good girls.*

Oh, I could carry fury as a weight, a ball of resin in a pocket.

It was a week later I said to Regan, *Did you not like the shape of Anne's gown? I thought it very pretty. The foreign ladies always look well.*

Yes, Mother. In gowns and headpieces they trusted me. I knew the proper appearances, the shapes of maturity and density that signalled nobility, womanhood, wealth. Regan at thirteen had a tooled leather over-jacket with a sheath for her little hunting-knife.

Would you like one of your own? Goneril can too. Your father loves to see you dressed in the latest fashion. It reflects generously on his taste.

Can we? Pretty birds, liking to be observed; in their finery in private, thinking themselves unseen, they turned and sat for one another, to see how best to lay the cloth. The maids who lay at their door at night told me they whispered themselves to sleep, often in the same bed.

Of course, I said.

And these good, good girls of Lear's royal blood were fitted with sleeves so slit you could pass a kitten through them! It was fresh to them, free, to see their own bodies in court, which were so often laid over and over with smocking, dark lace. They touched their skin and giggled; Regan licked Goneril through one of the openings at her elbow, when she thought I could not see.

So proud they were processing to show their father! Who saw the spaces, the open pale parts of their skin, so young still that the hair upon it was blond, and was astonished.

He ordered them out. Before the court, before the bright foreign women who turned their faces so as not to see. *What is this pestilence? Your arms! Get from my sight until you learn not to dress as whores and slatterns. God help me!* They left weeping. And I was victor.

The girls disrobed themselves, would not wait for the maids. I came to them later, when their faces had been bathed.

The king is angry but has agreed to forgive you.

Regan snivelled. Small thing, putrid, like a curdled apple. *You said the king would like it.*

I said no such thing. Apologise.

She stood straight. I remember her lips, strangely white. *I apologise.* Goneril said nothing.

It was a good little battle won. After that, Lear would not talk of the triumph of his blood over mine in the character of his daughters. Though he always wanted to make them saints, for small gifts: that they came when called, that they made him feel adored. And the girls healed. They always did.

When the cook and I leave the hall the weather has changed and the sky is suddenly dark despite the time of day. She is caught in it, the coming storm, her body thrown almost to the ground by wind.

6.

The wind is hard in the afternoon, so I am trapped indoors, with Ruth and my thoughts, and my view of the waving, struggling branches of the orchard, tearing at themselves to get free. I feel for them.

Ruth oils my hair, and I tell her of Calyssa's relic. She says, *Oh, a nasty bone. I would not like to see it.*

Possibly it was a man's ankle-bone, barely a decade old. Unlike Calyssa, I know sellers of holy fragments. Michael adored relics, carried them tied in many ribbons on the inside of a cloak, close to his skin. A mouse-bone said to be the finger of the drowned Saint Florian, its holes sealed with gold. Fragments of the hair of St Cecilia, like a lover's locket, looped by his nipple! Really just rat-bone, death-head; Kent and I knew, but kept silent.

I have a relic. I can show you. It can be educational. It is wrapped in one of the bundles and I bring it out, clothed in its slip of wool. Though Ruth shudders, and hides behind her hands, for fear of what it might be, I unfold it: a reliquary, plum-sized and prickling with light, built out of crystal and ivory. The Lord's grace, rendered miniature and open to understanding. Worn at the neck it gathers sun, warms through the bone.

It is beautiful. Ruth appears to have believed I would lug a full severed head from the bag, skull-heavy, trailing blue hair and sharpened teeth. Perhaps a mossed eyeball. But, no, instead this tiny city of God, the top a pierced cathedral-nave of gold.

What is inside? she wants to know. I have passed it into her hands; she holds it against herself as if to hear it, as if it might speak.

Nothing of significance. It has no real purpose. But it is a very lovely thing. Brought hastily with me to the abbey, expensive, with enamelling. One of my ladies had dropped it into a pocket as I was taken away, hoping perhaps that God would sense its presence, and give mercy.

These objects trail hopes, and hold them. I remember.

Lear and I went on many pilgrimages in search of sons. We did rituals, laid waxen images of babes at the foot of saints, offerings I'd had made and then carried next to my breast. Bit the tips of our fingers, then placed them together in prayer. Under the white round of a dozen temple roofs we made the same whispered demands: sons upon sons, please, lining my womb, overlapping on my skin like feathers. It did nothing. The gods' ears were stoppered.

One day Kent came to us. Court in session, high summer.

The Princess Regan says she has found somebody. With a holy relic. I do not know . . . Bless him, the memory is filled with his love, his awkward shoulders. He wanted as much as we did. His desire for future boys, for the happiness of Lear, streamed through his body. Light through stained glass.

Regan, twelve then, or thirteen, rising into her beauty, but years from inhabiting it fully. The shape of it glimmered like heat-haze, but in angles and full light she was raw, all neck and elbows. She and her sister came to the temples too, dutifully, laying down their wish for a brother to any comprehending god who might be listening. *Bring our parents princes, many princes.* We thought it might be prudent — maybe smaller, sweeter voices would be more pleasing, maybe their smooth hands scattering water would bring gifts.

Show her in, the woman. And Regan. We sat in state. I watched Lear's face, his weariness. So many children lost, to blood and darkness, mere weeks after taking root. We were desperate.

How did she find the woman? I never knew. Court streamed with people, the supplicants of kingship, demanding succour, grants, grain, vengeance. The many arteries of Lear's love. But Regan discovered, somehow, and brought her out, before us.

The woman's name, her stranded face, have disappeared. Old, I know. Some good family; perhaps in court as an entourage, rotating on the parquet, chaperoning a younger girl with camellias at her throat. But here the old woman was, and she held the relic, pretty as spring, and promised thickly. Sons, wealth, rampant horizons full of blazoned standards with Lear's face. It was a fingernail of Christ. It was a hair clipping. It was some aspect of a body, that we might carry, and deliver ourselves.

A gift, she said.

Lear had the screwed-up forehead of a puzzled newborn. I looked and was struck with love, like a bell, but could not touch him.

It will help, Regan said. *It can do miracles.* Young enough, then, to believe that miracles were free, that they were not paid for in men, silver, charred meat.

I looked at my daughter.

Oh, Regan's face. The graze of pollenish freckling on her cheeks; she'd blot them out with white paint in a few years. I saw her standing by the woman, a lady of a foreign court with excellent posture, and curtsey, and heard her say, *She has told me so many excellent things, Father, about what it has done,* and felt shrillness, a dark paw rending my ribs. Their hands, their wrists pressed together, Regan's worshipful eyes tipped down to this noblewoman barely to her shoulder; flowing with adoration, with the kind of frenzy unique to young girls. The steaming, scalded love of youth.

No new mother shall mother you, Regan, I thought. No mother but your own.

We took the relic, bowing, and Regan left with the woman. Who reached, as they left, to smooth Regan's royal veil away from her face. We were alone.

Lear sighed and walked to me. Put his hand at my neck and pressed our foreheads together. A Roman gesture, a man's bond, skull-brunt preparing for war – but I met it, and would lay my head as hard into the embrace. Fist at his hair. Two implacable forces forming their own arch.

I was fresh from another miscarried babe. So little seemed possible, or real.

We must get rid of that woman, I whispered. *Who knows what she's telling her?* I was his wise wife-queen, who could dive into the thick of manhood like a spear. He trusted me then.

Perhaps. You keep this. Released me. The relic, looped into my hand. His bleared eyes. *I do not know. There is the astrologer; he says we should couple under the right moons.*

I'll try eating the moon, Lear, if it helps.

Ay, madam, eat the moon. The Fool, slipping in sideways. He would find the hurt part in a conversation and slip in it, fill it with hard sense. *It's made of good strong stuff, to be struck up in the sky. I would like to have some of that moon.*

It likely tastes most bitter, Fool. That was Lear. Smiling.

That is true. But bitter's no butter for me. I need make no sons from my churn.

We laughed. Regan would weep, later, after we cast her friend out of court. Scratched at my arm; her nails, long from picking thread and harp-work, left a star-shaped wound, which faded to white. Shredded herself, her hair.

But it was done, it was done from love, Regan. No traitor daughter, no false mother. The real, or nothing. All else is a waste.

I grin at Ruth, at the ghosts. I smash the relic upon the floor. *That!*

Lady!

She gasps, for loss of beauty, and possible sacrilege. The cracked crystal on the stone is glorious, like a sugar-sweet. I laugh. There is such joy in destroying a thing so that nobody else can touch it. And it was useless: it fulfilled none of its promise.

It is nothing, I tell Ruth. *See, it means nothing at all. Just dust.* Sparkling glass. In our hands, as we gather, it burrows. It will be in my body, Regan, like you, shivering.

★　★　★

The storm hangs over us into the dusk, threatening. Underfoot the frozen grass throws up the smell of black earth. A deep smell, with heat beneath it. Crush of darkness into it with every step.

Mirabel and her women moving between them, making preparations; branches may fall, the frost has made living tissue brittle. I see them, their heads among the bare wood. Their words are being snatched from their mouths and taken into a rising funnel of wind.

Mirabel: hard woman, purposeful, devoted. Perhaps too single in thought, unable to hold two halves of a concept in the same hand, like an apple. Calyssa: rigid, punishing herself, but driven by ambition, by passion that bites down. I see them more clearly. I am understanding.

It is the fourth contest, now. About secrets, and their concealment.

The man who survives in court is the one who says the least. Kent told me that. I sat in servant-silence with Michael, curbing my tongue, holding my own glittering bridle. Later, beside Lear, I realised that this withholding could be for more than my own conceal-ments, and became the spy-master. Hundreds of men, half mercury, thin at the tongue as serpents. And women, small-boned, many of them, slipping in sideways, mopping up talk. A good monarch makes informers of animals, wind, high lightning.

And I gathered everything. How the crops were running. Brewing marriages, sour ones. The money in sleeves, under the stair, secreted, sewn into dark linings to multiply. Turn of talk in five armies. The inside of every pomander from here to the Holy Land, and the back of prayers for double the distance. What Goneril was reading; how Regan whispered in her sleep. Every truth has an underside; every deal has a golden element that can be coaxed or bribed or fucked loose.

Lear himself had no stomach for it. Arms and trade alliances he'd take as instructed, but information was womanly, wormy. As if all the talk came from between thighs, smelling of dark sweat. Well, perhaps it did. One fishes where the streams are likely.

The branches are screaming. Mirabel's women do not seem concerned. One has a loop of wool, perhaps meant for the tender beds, something vulnerable. Instead she has wrapped it on her head and is walking, and I recognise: she is being Calyssa – she is acting. The stillness of her posture, nose thrust upwards through the folds of wool. The wind is attempting to throw her over but she stands ruthless; and her witnesses are laughing, chaotically. It is a very good likeness; Calyssa might be feeling it, and burn.

Mirabel has not seen, is hefting something – some bowl of soil – under her arm. When she turns the performers and audi-ence scatter, as if the weather threw them into the air, as if they are falling to earth. I would pay to see Mirabel disapprove heavily of anything. Would she lay a hand on a neck, or smack? Or simply move into their shadow, and give her level stare?

I lean out of the window further; my hands fill with wind. If I could fill my skirts perhaps I could float over this wall, and be deposited by the storm in some tree-top, and be regarded by a bemused farmer as a miracle.

Well. I must remain in the present, and contemplate. How do Mirabel and Calyssa hoard their hidden selves, their politic misfortunes? Can they keep a secret? I miss my spies. Give them three days and they'd fillet this place clean, know where all the bones were and how they joined! I could sit and be fanned, drink cold wine that tasted of stone, and wait for them to come.

Instead there is this, here, now: the women, clutching their secret mirth, moving in the garden; Ruth, washing my white veils, as I stand in the window and watch the lid of storm clamping on the world. More than ever, I feel the limits of myself: one woman, old, and seen, always seen.

Still I'm doing rather well, considering. Think of Lear dead, green at the temples, maggots for teeth, slapping his knee in hilarity. *Eh, wife, you'll find your way out of any hole I put you in. I knew you for a lizard.* Yes, perhaps. Wait and see.

★   ★   ★

In the night the storm cracks open. The wind is vast: it hauls against the abbey. To be caught between such forces! It pushes my tower, forces it to maintain its thickness.

I am like a cat: I sink into small pleasures. This bed, these furs.

The abbey is alive, it works, out in the dark. I hear the wind moving through it and finding new places. The stables, the warmth of the kitchen, the orchard, the chapel, the stores and cellars. No knowledge like a storm's, which breaks things apart. Tomorrow we may wake to see the walls blasted, the eye burst open, like Jericho.

I'm caught in the first dip of sleep, now.

Why can they not have everything they want? Lear watching the girls. Making rings in the dirt, with their two pups tied to their waists by long ribbon. Alive, alive, with their necks in the sun, and freckles bursting on the backs of their hands, and budding openly before us, passing through time. Goneril had knotted her skirt to her, to run.

Because it will make them sour. Like when the cook put all the spices on the meat, that week, because the batch was on the edge of rot, and it made us all scream and reach for the wine.

We are at the bottom of the wheel, now. Fortune has rolled us on the rack, and the circle has broken, leaving us ungathered. *Sum sine regno.*

Things are becoming disordered. I sense it. Memories are pouring out of me, and there is lightning, breaking across the room and leaving a stain on my eyelids. I struggle to keep hold.

Even in a storm one must retain one's name, one's place in the cosmos. Lear, I would structure the world for you on nights like this, as it is in the Gospels. Would tell you the outer layer first: Heaven, God's sweet girth, echoes of cloud, buildings strung out of light. Hell, buried, like an inverted nipple. And then, travelling inwards, the stars, the planets a belt of diamond luck. Under that the earth, breathing, huge waves of air, in which birds were suspended, and smoke from distant fires.

And the solid, soft depth of soil; and the animals, men and fish and beasts, flitting and raising their heads; and at the centre of it you, the king, pulling it inwards, like a pucker in a seam. *You vanish and there's naught, a hole, nothing,* I told you, *no point to hold the world and heavens in place; it is all confusion. Rightful king, God's lynchpin.* Whole atmospheres and planets spilling from your body in the dark.

And now you are dead, and our marriage is broken, and everything is falling.

Lightning, pooling. The world is collapsing. I grip the sheets. I may be mad; I may well be mad. This. Now. Here.

The storm cries out, blistering. And my girls are here, in the room.

By Hecate, I whisper to myself.

Goneril, Regan, Cordelia. Ghosts, out of the bracken. Bright against the wall, so that I blink to see them. Their spirits not yet filled and light but still half earthen, bloodied. So recently dead they can still smell the soil that covers their mouths. I have birthed them between my hands. I have magicked them out of air.

They are beautiful; they shiver like grasses. Cordelia, whom they say had a face so much like Lear's: mouth, chin, like a moon to his sun. She is a mere shade (bricks visible through her gut), and silent, but I hear the other two, older, on the verge of speech. Well, why not? When a queen summons, death is no excuse.

Ruth sleeps at the foot of the bed. Against the thunder she moves tighter into a ball.

Have you come to help me, darlings? I say to them, in my head, which is the same as speaking out loud; the tongue is nothing, the intent is all. *To select an abbess. It is a momentous decision. They have left it to my judgement, and to God. Show me.* As if Mirabel and Calyssa were here too, in the room.

Goneril, serious, her hair thinning back from her forehead now, moves without haste. She likes stateliness, a tall back, an impressive voice. (The voices of the nuns who seduced her – a thickness, like resin warmed until it slid and shone.) So Calyssa, then – but Goneril has also a strange streak of pity. Would gather broken animals, the maimed mice from a stable, and nurse them as they died. Mirabel may then be her choice.

I turn to the other. Regan despises, swiftly, Mirabel – had no patience for the slow or fat. A skater tumble on the ice-lake earned her cruelty. She herself was swift, on bone-skates, twinned to the ice. Unhesitant: her ghost sees Mirabel's plod, her ponder-ousness, and dismisses her, like paring skin from an apple, snick. Calyssa does not earn passage either. Too nervy, not sufficiently settled within herself. What could fragility offer my Regan? Only indecision.

Cordelia silent. Cordelia abstains; Cordelia floats free.

I am dissolving into river-water. Map-lines, the wall that keeps apart past and present, the membrane separating a babe in the stomach from the air of the world, pressing; we believe that they signify, that they order. They do not. The world is an O, and is outside and inside, falling through itself.

I see, and do not see. The lightning is falling, like lily-petals.

Daughters, you are poor compasses, you fail the point! Give me your hands—

But, of course, they are vanished into thinness. My daughters. Useless, at the finish.

7.

In the morning Ruth is crumpled with sleep. *Oh, I dreamed we were all underwater.*

Did you dream? I had no dreams.

I am shaken. The storm has passed on, leaving only puddles. I look from the window: there is one half-fallen tree split from itself along the trunk, as if weary, too long at the dance. Thin and blue, the wind on the day after, and bashful.

There are tiles, strewn on the grass, catching the light. Little scales off this gigantic fish; we are Jonah, we travel in its gullet. Lucky there are no roof-holes, or the women would have to haul up the scaffolding themselves, and hammer a hat back onto their world.

You have not slept, Lady, I can tell, Ruth says, and fusses, holding warm water to my neck, giving me scent. Lavender on the temples, for wakefulness.

It is a passing strangeness. Were my girls here? Were they not? Grief is plundering me; it is burning down the walls. They crack, and hard-held things spill through my fingers. Many things may come rattling free. The morning light after a storm is always the most honest.

My girls. My beautiful girls. I want to tell Ruth about it, what I saw. Built out of the shimmer off a feather, the light that passes through a fish-scale, iridescent; the passing shine of a season, all things visible through it. I may be mad but I see the dead; I may be crossing a river I cannot see, but on the other side love moves closer, closer. No wonder Bladdud was always so happy.

Though, of course, they were useless. As usual, as they always were. I snort to myself (Ruth looks up, looks away). Children! What is the point? When I took Goneril, breasts still aching under my bodice, to her father, to greet him and be anointed, she lay upon his chest and was ill. He still looked at her besottedly: barely even a creature, surely half plant, breathed. So little effort it took for her to gather love to herself, merely to be pushed out breathing. You'll learn bad habits, babe, earning such regard for so little, I thought. You'll spoil. But I'll teach you about deserving.

Bring them to me when they can talk, I said to the wet-nurses.

Ruth brings me stewed fruit, the nub of a loaf in bed. Bends her head to arrange my blanket. I could tell her. I could. She knew them, the girls; she may rejoice that I am becoming something else, that all the honeycombing in me is being knocked through and the honey coming clear.

Before I can, she looks up and says, *Oh God, you are bleeding from your nose, Lady. Hold still.* And gathers my blood in the cloth in her own fingers. As it flows over my lip.

Well, there must be costs. There are coins you have to pay to cross the Styx. This is my payment, spotting on the floor, streaming through her fingers onto the neck of my white mourning-gown, so that I have a necklace of burgundy, of royal vermilion.

★   ★   ★

I pass through the day, attempting to look and move as normal. Some energy, some nerve, appears to have fallen from me. It seems transparent, capable of being ripped with a gesture of a wrist. This abbey, this contest. And past things are more vivid.

Husbands, daughters, hopes of sons. Regan's face on the stair. Feast days. Weddings, in the halls. Feeble, feeble, the stuff of a life. But solid as a stone.

Outside they are paring back the split tree. I watch, from the window. A woman's wrist turning as she strips the bark so that it peels away like oil. The white of the revealed wood in a streak, the tree unknown to itself. They will smell of sap, now, the women, its honeyed bitterness on their palms and the exposed parts of their necks.

There are some parts of the immediate that will not fade. Lust still rises. Brushes the inside of my pelvic bone with its gold tail. The turn of a servant girl with her breast twisted in her tunic; some masculine part, a flower's pendulum, a horse panting at the abbey gates. The scent of crushed parsley, which I rubbed on Lear's breastbone for bruises. Running hands over the house of his ribs, the long sweet dip above his heart. Unknowing, years ago, I walked past the point where no man would touch me any more.

I know I am clouding at the edges. The past is filling me. But there is still life to be had, here. There is a contest, a prize. I must do as Kent says.

★ ★ ★

I will mount an assault, to find the secrets here. It is direct, unexpected; the best spies were forthright in black rooms and behind doors, opening their hands, *See my play, now meet it.* First Calyssa.

I visit her in her cell. It is unexpected, awkward, she is not in the habit of bending out of routine. Places a cup on her table, moves it elsewhere. The birds are quiet. She shows me their cropped shade-cloths, the ways in which she dips them into darkness. Parts of leather, salvaged hoods; bells, bells for ankles, small as a child-hand. Her bird-world.

If the ghosts follow me, I must bid them be quiet. I have a job, here.

I am polite. *And you are here — how long?*

Since childhood. Likely her family knew restlessness. Likely they put her here young, for safety.

And you want to be abbess. And not to go out into the world, and be a wife.

She makes a face. *I wouldn't be a good wife.*

You likely couldn't make a very good match, no.

Calyssa flushes. Cruelty can be tender, carries the same vicious pleasure as unrequited love or anger. *I have things men wouldn't like.*

You don't know men. A merchant's wife, somewhere. Skirt-deep in accounting, running some pale boy round the house for ink. An honest man would welcome it. *You seem unsettled,* I add.

I slept badly in the storm, she says. Then, suddenly, *How many contests are left?*

Insolent! *I will not tell you.*

Then the women may believe you have no system, and the judgement may be random. It is not usual. She is angry, and flapping in it helplessly. Not a woman who understands how to modulate her intensity, by pressing down on her knees, or sucking comfits.

You will not protest my system if you win, Calyssa.

I will not win. She is sulky. Has decided to laden me with her honest thought; and see, sullenly, what I will do with it. *You do not like me, and Mirabel has been your particular friend. Kings give their best positions to their favourites. I know.*

If you had no chance, I'd have crowned Mirabel weeks ago, and wasted neither my intelligence nor your time with the rest, I say, annoyed. *I am not cruel. Or not cruel enough for that.*

She is silent.

Let us trust one another, I say.

I trust you, she says quietly. Small mouth, hard tongue. I do not believe her.

I have come for a serious question, but if you cannot be in temper I will not ask it.

This works: she is ashamed by the idea of being seen as irritable, that green womanish emotion. I know she is merely chafing under the yoke of my strange direction – and, I realise for the first time, may have loved the abbess; may also be carrying grief, in her small reddened hands. Though she would not admit it, would rather swallow knives. *I am in temper, I apologise. Do ask, I will answer.* The bells on the ankles of the birds distract; bells, bells on the ankle of Goneril, on feast-days, casting out music as she danced, generously. No, I must stick fast.

You worked with the abbess, and so were privy to many parts of the abbey and its workings. You know its secrets.

I am not the confessor. That is Brother Manfred. We sit and contemplate Manfred for a beat, then pass over him, his milky head, the humility downing his cheeks, as he will be passed over all his life. *But I suppose I know a little.* Carries her pride warily, in a sealed box.

Is there any concealed element in Mirabel's character, perhaps, that would make her a poor abbess? I am keeping my eyes open, fixed upon her. *Anything she would not tell me. You must be frank.*

She is, I know, the kind to pry, not out of the power of slyness, or of withholding truth, but for knowledge, and for pairing the faults of others against her own sins and measuring them on pale, hard nights, to find herself perhaps the worse. Secrets for Calyssa are self-punishment. She studs them into her belt of weaponry against her own soul.

She looks out of the window of the cell. *She is a good woman,* she says finally, without malice. *We do not agree on some things. How to discipline the novices when they are children, and finances. But no. I think she is very much as she looks.* Considers, doubtful. *She spends a great deal of time down in a hedge at the bottom of the garden and will not tell me what is there. But that I think is spite, against me.*

I see. I attempt to consider this hedge, Mirabel pointedly not telling Calyssa what is under it, and not laugh. Girls!

She looks at me, her thoughts turning; I see them in diversion, a stream redirecting its coil around a branch. *I know something, though not of her. Did you know that you are not in the abbey records?*

I? I am surprised. This falls on me unexpectedly.

No mark of you anywhere. You are simply an unnamed guest in the best rooms for years. Her face does not demand explanation, but is simply pleased to have given what was offered: a secret, an oddity. The birds shuffle like cards.

How strange. And am exhausted. Leave me to talk to Kent, I want to say. I want Kent, and my Fool, and some oranges.

Of course I am unwritten. Of course I am hacked out of the book. It would have been part of the banishment. Lear would have splintered me from his family tree, so that his girls came from his own body, without wombs. Such was his anger. So nobody could find me, no person track me if he did not bestow his granting.

After a long pause she shrugs. *You do not have to speak of it. Your crime is God's business, not mine.*

As you say, archly. It is God's business only, in fact. The ones who know have died, and no prayers will make them speak. Well, I will die, and Saint Peter may charge me with it honestly. My tiredness bows me. I say, *Nobody knows my name, you know. Nobody alive.*

She is confused. *Nobody?*

No. I was born with one, but they change them when you marry kings. Rather like with nuns. A pause. The room fills to the brim with ghosts, with Kent.

This moves her. A woman who colonised loneliness and made it profuse, rich with wings, but feels it as worrying in others. *You could tell me. I could call you by your name.*

The tenderness runs a split down the centre of the room. Perhaps after all it is not grief that folds up time but moments of gentleness.

I sigh. *No. It is not for anybody now. Only for myself.* I rearrange my furs, so that she sees I am not being spiteful, merely maintaining a distance: I am island, continent, scratched out of the maps but still there. *It is getting dark.* Winter hours, the sun lessening and losing its hold, rapidly. Shadow coming to the windows. *Your birds must be hungry.*

In the rafters their opening beaks, the soft punctuation of their tongues.

*   *   *

The whisper has gone through the abbey. The nuns demand parity, the equal slice of myself down the centre. Like a martyred woman.

So Mirabel asks if I will walk in the gardens, after prayers. I go, though I am so tired.

You gave Calyssa a task. I would like to do it too, she says. Has no intention of dancing around the point: she knows. There was an exchange, some kind of measurement, in the dark of Calyssa's cell, and she wants the same.

I wonder what she will do. *Do you know anything of Calyssa, any secret, that may warp her suitability to be abbess?*

That is all?

That is all.

She lines her robes with silk, she says unhurriedly. *And spends part of her dowry-money on those birds, though it should go to the abbey.*

I want to laugh again. Some women are bowls of oil. Whatever falls — bread, stone, meat — settles, and the surface unbroken. Mirabel may have entire meals concealed! But will give up anything if asked, if given the right prize, and is that worthy? Kent, is it a valuable element? *You do not approve of these little extravagances,* I say. *But this is an abbey that allows such things, I think, outside quarantine.* Sweet sugar in the pockets of novices, wines thin on the tongue as a lover, perfumed dogs. Under the rigour of the hours, these gifts.

And Calyssa in her secret silk, which protects her against the chafe of her will, and shames her! I cannot blame her for it. She is close enough to God to be scalded. *It is the will of God that we mortify,* Mirabel is saying, *not carry flibbertigibbets. The illness was terrible but made us at least gaze at ourselves more clearly, for a while.*

You would cleanse us, I say, and look at her face, and see the calm, intractable force of sainthood, and am for a second afraid, but also loving: my own girls carried that look sometimes — Goneril had it when she recited the Psalms. Goneril would slip her fingers into my palm here. I must stay present, I must not drift. *Calyssa said you were hiding some secret pursuit of your own under a hedge,* I say idly. *A lover or a silk robe, perhaps.*

She takes me to the edge of the orchard. Through the snow she is a witch from the deep bog, turf-cut, made of mud and sweet rainwater.

At the edge a bundled thicket. She lifts, gently, the hem of the hedge, still with its dark evergreen cloister. Releases smell: cold earth, sap, mottled close damp. Young berries showing themselves, raw. And yes, and yes.

Hedgehogs. Hibernating to outlast the year, in this softness of fur and moss. With (I see now) the small pink young, feeling for the first time the wind, their blind faces upwards. These filmy skins carrying already the idea of hardship, of weaponry, which they will grow out through their backs. They will awake armed. Good, good children.

And I am overcome, by the penetrability of things. The hedgehog is a daughter, blind, at the blue nipple of the wet-nurse, who curses her, thinking I cannot hear, is the bashful belly of Lear freed of its breastplate; is shorn skulls of working soldiers, is sugar-mice at feasts that crumble under the thumb, is (further, further) the plaintive neck of Michael, vulnerable, reaching out of its hair shirt.

Life is so short it is lived simultaneously. One thing is the other. Folds and folds. In Heaven Lear must look back now: *Ah. All of that, was it? All at once? Yes, I see. How strange to have thought it to be any other way.*

Mirabel's face is all pride. As if she'd birthed them herself.

8.

The women of both sides, Calyssa's, Mirabel's, are bringing soft things, now, gifts: offerings to my favour. Knuckling them against my steps. *Give her something she likes.* Ruth is becoming accustomed to her new ritual of opening the door at daylight to gather them into her hands. Carved ivory, seed-pods like teardrops, a pressed blossom powdered with old pollen. They lap against my sides – I could build myself armour.

The givings are anonymous; they have the shame of that at least. Knowing these are small things.

Unusually I nap in the afternoon. I feel sleep is settling in me, gently, after my long night. Wide drifts of dreams, through which I push easy, weightless hands. Landscapes seen through veils and cloud. Pad, pad, through the last day before the exile; pad, pad, and Ruth wakes me. Hair across my mouth.

I have a scorecard for the contest in my mind, though it is obscure to them. Values, victories; Kent's face, hovering over his system. Five virtues, stratifying this. It is all tallied, everything, even their faces at prayer. The lines of their mouths. As yet they are evenly balanced: their weights in each scale tally exactly; there is not one fleck of gold between them. I am a good apothecary, and my scales are true.

What the girls could give me that might sway my thinking is not possible. Ribbons from weddings, weddings; Goneril's,

Regan's. The pomander inlaid with green glass that Kent fastened to my belt, dense with scent. Obedient children. Michael, in his beauty, loving me. And boys, and boys.

Ruth at the door says, *Oh, beautiful.* And turns, her hands open, to show me the newest thing, but I am not attending.

★ ★ ★

I should be thinking of the next contest, but I cannot. I am waiting for my girls, secretly, every night. Hours upon hours. But they do not come.

I cry, a little. Heartless girls, heartless daughters. Is there any pain like a child who does not want you any more?

Lord God, I have failed so much in my life. Lear raving at me, once. *And Gloucester comes to it twice! Not once but two sons, born so close they are barely severed by a straw! True, one's a bastard, but what calls God's fortune to lie so awry?*

Would you have me take a lover, then? Shame in it. *Give you a host of bastards?*

Do not count the fault as mine. The turn of sex lies with the mother. The midwives tell me that.

Midwives! Would worship whoever said what he needed. Later when he turned away to other, pagan, gods, it was their silence that lured him, their black-blood hollowness: he who by that stage needed only himself.

Then your God condemns us for past sins. I took another man's wife, and look how the world punishes Lear.

This was the pain that hit so hard as to let in daylight. Myself a curse, my widowhood a stain upon his nature. I drew him to me and said, *Let us make another, let us prove it wrong.*

Afterwards I called Magdalena to rearrange my hair: tumbled, pulled out of alignment. While arranging my plaits she said quietly, *You could hide your courses. We could find a babe, a boy, we could say it was his. It has been done.* They could hear, all the servants knew — we had voices during fights that could carry to Jerusalem.

I hit her then, hard. *You think your king would not know his wife with child after seeing her twice?* She had the mark of my hand on her face. *And you, what would you? To be my gaoler, to hold the secret at my neck? Peace, I know the game.*

As if I had not thought it! As if I had not looked at every small flaxen head presented in court or hauled at a breast in the yards and thought, *One small move, a few coins, and there we are.* I touched the foreheads of Gloucester's little boys and wondered at their price.

There are miracles — we hear them from merchants: babes found under the bark of oak trees, washed up on the sand in cradles of weed. What price for that sort of kindly gift? But no: Lear wanted the legitimate, the king-queen heir, by my body or by nothing.

Do you have any more delightful ideas? I asked her.

Other queens would take a lover. Have a son, any son. So that their lineage would last, even beyond the kings. She was watching me. Careful, her dark skull.

I am not other queens. Now, shut your mouth.

Forgive me, Queen, it was kindly meant.

She left then. I fixed my hair myself and, once I had bathed my face, was none the worse.

* * *

There are screams offstage. Ruth arrives. Says, *Come. Oh, come. There's a fight.*

The sky when visible over the walls has layers, as if painted; like a dome I once saw, its fresco falling in, the white plaster

275

leaching to grey with damp. We look down from a window at the heads of moving women, circling.

There is one at the centre in her black winter cloak. She has been scalped; no, just her head cloth, pulled off, revealing sullen red hair, a slice of white scalp at the parting. There hasn't been violence, not yet. But the women are gathering. A parliament of crows on the white ground. Their feet drag the snow clear and leave dark prints.

What happened? My breath comes out as cloud.

They said she tried to betray her side. Mirabel's. And wanted to break the tie by allying with Calyssa, instead. Ruth hates bearing gossip, I've noticed. Something in it makes her wooden, heavier.

Silly fool. We are too far down; the dive is too deep. The faces around the woman come from both camps. Mirabel's women are pompously furious – their skirts in motion form small whirlwinds – but Calyssa's mutually wounded; the simple solution of luring an extra woman is not clean fighting, not now. They are affronted in their dignity, which in common women of ambition is the holiest artefact.

I cannot see her face. Whether it registers shame, whether it bears the right conciliatory cast. They are shouting; parts drift up to us.

You are false, says one.

Shame. Shame, says another. Opening her arms wide against the white. The weight of disgust in her voice would drag a mortal down. Pin her to the earth.

I think of the milk, pooling around a hand, its bowl open to this rusted angry sky. There are others here, in the windows. Mirabel and Calyssa themselves are not visible, not yet.

This is injustice, says the first. Appealing to us on the high walls. Then reaches, suddenly, for the woman's cowl, her neck.

Hold! The black wave crashes. The fury that runs within it is fluid – it spills. They have their hands on her, others are pulling off, she herself is flapping her white hands like a fish. Behind me Ruth has her apron in her mouth. The cook appears at the corner, bellows, plunges in knees-first to batter them all apart; her hands crack against skulls, the whack you'd give dogs. They will not relinquish their hold. *Gentle ladies!* she howls, both to appease and to condemn.

I laugh aloud. Put a hand to my mouth. Nobody has heard.

Oh, they will kill her. Ruth moans at my shoulder.

Many voices, above and behind; Manfred has come through to the corridor and is calling down, astonished and angry, but his admonishment is lost in the hurtle of sound. Mirabel herself arrives, shouldering into the cloister, and I look at her. She is motionless, pails in each hand, caught on her way to another place. An entrance into a scene in which she is not an actor, wandering onto the wrong stage. I see her face, and understand she does not know what to do, how to move. As if a hive had cracked open, and the air around her head were now swarming hot with wasps.

Enough.

I look at the eave nearest me, its thick weight of snow, borne upon its back. Two hands high. I move closer and hit it hard, once, twice, with my fists. Ruth notices and follows. Mystified, but obedient. She has tighter fists.

The snow moves, then booms over the edge in a mass, one white hand falling to clap the other. Swallowing the world.

The women are hit so smartly that some of them fall. Bruises on their legs later, perhaps. The sound dissolves in them, knocked right out with their breath. Ice in their mouths. Looking up to see the judgement of Heaven, and seeing me, Ruth, the ring of other women still shouting, leaning and slapping their hands on the wall. The woman herself is dazed and shakes her head slowly, like a bad-born calf, as women rise around her, dusting off their sudden weight. Blood on one temple.

I think of Goneril in the yew. And would call out to her – but she is gone.

★ ★ ★

The black berry of blood on the woman's face does not feel real. I think of the waving boughs on the river, with their purple globes; platters of crimson meat, on tables. Colours, fragments.

And I laughed, in the moment. Why did I do that? It was ridiculous, the black women falling against one another. Their clumsy grappling. (Regan, Goneril, fighting, tearing at baby-flesh, over a toy, a bangle. As punishment I pulled their soft-sprouting hair at the ears, made them sleep apart. In a day they were reconciled. Like weed in water, they tangled, drifted, came together again, in the tides.)

This is so small, their little world. Gash above one eye, it will barely scar. Only Ruth heard me laugh.

I have other matters tonight. I kneel. The nuns, their miniature wars, will keep.

Regan, my bloodied girl. Why do you not come? Why one visitation and no other? You have been severed from me so slowly – like your sister. Clipped clear like hair.

Stages and stages, in which you were removed from me. Your marriage. You and Cornwall had been married months and still you were being kept in the court, Lear throwing up amusements to lure you: saint's days, special feasts, hunts on new horses. Cornwall was thin-faced and would not raise his opposition, not yet.

You were speaking to Lear of your husband. Sunlight streaming through the halls. *I have not spoken to him yet of servants. I would like Hana with me, and a cook who knows my favourites. His kitchen folk may*

*make bitter food. And horses, whether we will have a carriage, and if the horses
could be bays. Remind me.*

His face. Beneficent, a saint's face, shorn of a halo but doling
out grace nonetheless. *I have a surprise for you. Infinitely better!*

Father?

*You will not be leaving your father, whom you love as the very line and
centre of all your doing. You will be staying in this court, in your house of
childhood, with your husband.* He reached for her. *Is it not a fine thing?
Come, kiss me.*

You were still. The corners of your mouth, only I was close
enough to see them, had turned sweet white. Your hand remained
in mid-air holding the silver tassel of your gown. Lear's hound
whined, and you smiled, you returned, moved like a wooden doll.

*Forgive me. I am — overwhelmed by your generosity, King. I had thought
I would be far from you, in a strange new home, and now am told I will
stay, and it is more than my small woman's heart can bear. It may crack apart
from happiness.* Measured your voice in small steps. Like drops from
a cup. Not a shiver in it. I placed a gentle palm on the base of
your neck; you were cool, you had caught yourself as you fell.

You may leave us, Regan.

Was she not pleased? He was a beam of light, ricocheting around
the room. Leaned to ruffle his dog's ears excessively, to demon-
strate this great glowing love on everything.

Surprised, I believe. I was slow.

*I must give her another ermine. She seemed cold. But she was pleased, yes.
I saw it in her.*

Yes, King.

Later I went to you. I wanted to be sweet and soothe you,
your old hopes, but it was stuffy, and Lear had been over-charitable
all afternoon and ruined several delicate affairs (sent one peasant
off with two pigs from the royal store, and roared at the boy's
surprise!), so I was thinly tempered.

279

You were raw. Goneril stood away from you, as if frightened to touch you.

I have had to explain it to Cornwall. He's gone to his horses. Do not give me harsh words. I have had a surfeit. Had evidently wept but was done; your voice had glass in it.

I was soft. I stood at your back and smoothed your veil around your shoulders. *Your husband will have his seat, but your father expects you both to be based here, for most of the year, and to partake in the life of the court.* Your hair was in thick plaits under the married woman's cloth veil, nicked at the corners. Your husband must have demanded it so because of fashion.

You could not persuade him?

I did my best. Your king has his will, you know that. I was touched that you both thought this, that I could have hauled him backwards out of this new desire.

Goneril says it was your plot.

Goneril looked at a fixed part of wall behind my head. I would, I thought then, rather have you both running like wolves on the moor and living on rabbit-flesh than keep you here, muzzled and sworn. Better bare ground than this.

Aloud, I said lightly, *I think it would be best if you went to your husband. We will prepare apartments. You will be well-kept. And when you have a child you may speak again.*

How can I soothe Cornwall out of this? You sounded so weak. Had never yet lured any man out of poor temper, except your father.

I kissed your cold scalp and relaid the veil, pinned behind the ears with twin clips. Bears made of gold. *You are his best-loved thing; be mournful and let him soothe you. Make him one of your poultices. Go, run. It will be well.*

You rose and left. Your shoulders were higher; perhaps you were feeling comforted. Your neck had always been bloodless: there was no emotion to be read in it. Goneril stayed, still watching the wall.

And so. I attempted brightness, a let-us-work-with-this solidity, like good plate. *She will reside here, with her court, and her husband's men.* I smoothed the front of my gown with both hands.

And myself?

You will sleep in our bedroom, or with your sister. As you choose.

A slender choice.

Don't be insolent, Goneril. I do not have patience for it today.

She raised both brows. *No patience! Remarkable, a condition unlike any other day.*

I was so suddenly tired that I laughed. This surprised her. *I know. It is what it is. We will find you space, girl. I will make you a set of rooms above the stables, eh? Magdalena, get her good gown, the one with the birds.*

This at least bought a smile from her, a little bargain. I thought then it could be balanced: two girls, the husband, the many desires of the king. Great vanity! But we passed through the doorway into the inner room, undoing her stays.

★   ★   ★

And then (time slips) — you had been married years and came to see me. Spoiled, hardening at the edge of the mouth. As women do when left too long without occupation, direction for their will.

Your husband is well, Regan?

He is. He thinks too much of horses and the cost of things.

In charge of curtailing your expenses? He has my pity. Extravagant. Always, even small, layering yourself in laces.

You told me a queen should be extravagant.

You are not a queen, Regan. You are a little lord's wife of a little breadcrumb of land.

If Father would give out the dowry——

Your husband took you despite it, in the hope of future grace. It is a proof of heart, and of patience.

Yes, eminently patient! But you smiled, knowing your beauty, and the captivation of your husband, who still escorted you off your horse like a young page. You could always be soothed through your vanity, Regan. Goneril through her intellect. Lear through his prowess, his knowledge of men. Small keys to many drawers.

If you had the dowry you'd spend it on furred gowns and monkeys, anyway.

Monkeys! You turned, in your yellow gown. *I miss the Fool. Where is he?*

In the garden entertaining the king. Goneril, would you fetch another linen? This is disastrous. Goneril looked at it, laughed at my puckering stitch, left.

I would take him with me. Father will give him. I must speak to him on it.

I placed needles one by one in my shift. Lines of silver, surfacing, holding hem to body. I said, *Bladwen tells me you still have your courses.*

I do.

Don't cast that foul look. This is my household, I will command its tongues.

I had no look either way.

I did wonder if your husband were well.

He is, as I said, well.

That is good.

It is.

And you?

I am sound, Mother.

Of course you are. You are healthy, and well-provided. What kind of woman are you, Regan, in your bed? Do you kick him on his heel and force him out to sleep nights in the snow, if it pleases?

Mother.

I merely ask. As it seems you forget all your duties.

Oh, are we having a party? I should call for trumpets. Goneril entered. Skirt, swimming over tile.

Hush, Goneril. You'll be married soon, too.

It is not so simple, Mother. Children are a blessing's burden. A larger dwelling, well-provisioned—

Oh, plead to your father. He has a new child to provision. He'll doubtless have time for all your woes. Poor Regan. You spent your life in pursuit of better, thicker, sweeter.

It was a bad stratagem, Regan, said Goneril.

Have you brought forth a child in some secret way that wins you superiority, sister?

I was tired. *God save us. How did such fair advantage breed such weakness?*

Luck, madam, and too much meat i' the evenings, said Goneril.

I am not weak, you said.

No. No, you are not. Forgive me. I am old and just out of childbed, and may well still die, and your father crawls towards his final age, and neither of his daughters prove their love by any provision of an heir.

Mother, Death couldn't find you, and if it did you'd beat it off with sword and shield, said Goneril. And you, Regan, were silent.

What was it that you said of Cordelia, to yourself? *Fie that a child of mine and its aunt may be years or so apart. Fine indeed. Oh, give it away, it cries too much. Sickly thing.* Not knowing that I heard you. Cordelia was dark-eyed, spitting. The next day I would be banished. Fie, fie.

It is long past midnight; I have poured myself through darkness to find you. But you elude, daughter, you escape every time.

In the morning I am angry, and sore. Exhaustion runs from the corners of my mouth. Ruth comes to say, *The woman from yesterday has repented. Brother Manfred says she must be pitied and all need to confess today.* Then says, *What is it, Lady?* Can read me easily, like a map, like the crossed anonymous wood that marks a grave.

283

I miss my girls. I am honest, the truth breaks off from me and floats.

Ah, Mistress. She will hold me, as a child holds a dog. I will surrender to it.

How can I have more tears, Ruth? How can I have any more sides to pierce?

You will survive this, Mistress. I have faith. And kisses my hair, on the balding pate where I once had a plait thick as a sheaf of wheat; and we are weeping together, in the quiet grey daylight, as the nuns sleep.

9.

I am awake. Slept all the next day, but sleepless now. I want to mount a contest today: these women are clawing into one another; without activity they're squabbling. It is a waste of energy. The snow-hit girls will be feeling their bruises today, and finding themselves foolish. After a rush of primitive emotion, people return to the surface, breathing, pretending they were never raw or furious. Reclaiming their better selves.

I think, I must redirect it, somehow, this brutality. Before we see more pain. But the chance, it seems, has been taken away from me.

I hear the notes of matins, in the dawn air. Something strange: the notes are veering, the singing distracted. It bears the marks. An event.

Well. I rise, dress, and wait.

Presently the brush of the hands on the door: a congregation has arrived, with the sun. The whole courtyard grows like the inside of a rose.

Sister Mary Luisa has had a vision, in her sleep. An angel came to her, messenger of the Holy Virgin, and told her that Mirabel be anointed abbess.

A visitation! They crowd through the door. The nun herself is flushed, has let herself show sweat. She has a thick chin, with a pleat in the middle, like pinched dough. Calyssa comes behind, and waits.

I am grinning, careful. *You dreamed of this?* God help us, women and their dreams!

I dreamed that the Virgin Mary came to me, and she was so beautiful, like the statue in the chapel. This being a statue in wood that the abbess had privately repudiated, wondering why the Virgin had to have such pronounced lips, such a sensual smile. *She told me of God's wish for the abbey, for it to be great and last a thousand years, and that Mirabel would be abbess.*

I smile as I would at my girls, at their frail wants. *A lovely thing to dream.*

But Mirabel's girls are pushing. One has her ardent hand on another's shoulder. *It is a sign!* After the fight, with its animal feel, they think this is something else: a gentle blessing. When brutality and God are the same, the same thing. I know. The Lord wants blood for sacrifice: no meagre fruit will do.

I am pleasant. *Dreams are not miracles; you know the Church's view on this.*

Calyssa says, *Precisely.* They give her mute stares. She exhales with restraint.

One says, *If it paved your own path perhaps you'd be kinder to it!* Stupidly, some of them have begun to sing, beating their palms against their sides, stirring the early grey air like dust.

Peace! I say. Too late: Ruth is waking, by the fire. Looks at them with small, confused eyes.

Mirabel has arrived up the stairs, moving slowly. The girls reach for her. Her confusion in the fight has been forgotten. They could forgive her almost anything, I think. The contest has become less about her, more about their own fervour, their desire. She will be hoisted on their shoulders like an object, to be covered with flowers.

Sister, she has dreamed of you! As abbess! Clearly they think this decides the matter; that I will take the fancy and give her the abbey-keys there. She is not fooled: she sees the circle, she sees the women preparing again to sing, something moving out in front of her, expanding perhaps beyond her reach.

A kind dream, she says to the girl, *and I thank you for it.* Dark, still water in that voice. *You look feverish. Go to the nurse; tell her a cooling draught and some feverfew.*

Mirabel wants to lop off the end of the thought before it can spread. Careful, careful woman. Is she pleased? There's no pleasure on her. If she ever becomes a saint it will be a great artist who can give her face lightness, serenity lifting. She squints; the nuns, silent, rebuked, recede.

I think of her standing in the cloister yesterday with her buckets, a visitor from another world entirely, as women tore flesh for the sake of her. I press my hands to the corner of my lips, to feel the line scoring them into the skin. Ruth, coughing, has come to assemble me, my morning parts. Rubs her eyes like a child.

Prophetic dreams. Calyssa has clearly fallen entirely out of temper. *What next? As if we're all children.*

Kings have fortune-telling dreams. It is strange that I tell her this; it drops out of me without a thought, as if it rolled free from a pocket. *My first husband dreamed once of a lizard creeping over his head. He said it was a sign of the Devil. Then the next day a spider crept out of his hat and bit him.*

They look at me sideways, as if there's some portent or lesson in it, but I am thinking of Michael, his thin face in utter astonishment. I was twenty-one, I tried very hard not to giggle as I bound his pink ear.

Mirabel laughs, suddenly. *I am at least grateful for the lack of prophetic lizards, then.*

Are there lizards here? Ruth is fearful.

In winter? No. Calyssa is irritable, and still strained. *Let us hope that ends it. Who screeches so in a courtyard out of hours? I have a chamber of birds to settle.* Of course, the birds, I think, must know the pattern of voices, matins and vespers, night and morning.

Whistle at them, says Mirabel.

Calyssa gives her the look of a person searching a merchant for a fraud; sees nothing, is dissatisfied. The Fool called that expression 'smelling an orchard for an apple-john'. She goes. Mirabel looks to me.

You were awake early.

I was. I have the all-awake look, and my face still has the singe of painful places. *We should all sleep now. One thinks clearer in daylight.*

She nods and departs. When I dip into sleep for the first time, a little later, my daughters are absent, but the two contenders are visible, looming: Mirabel potato-fleshed with hot steam across her scalp, Calyssa fringed with feathers, great pinions from her neck and spine, pressing close to her skin, the secret soft down.

* * *

By daylight the dream of the Virgin has gone everywhere. It moves through the nuns as if they themselves had known it; by the night perhaps it will come to all of them, in its own shape.

I cannot harness it, Kent. This hare moves away from me, out of reach.

Mirabel and her followers are in the garden again, after a small snow-melt, pushing at the soil. Bulbs, for spring. Her women look at her with maternal pleasure. Calyssa's women are scalded, muttering. Several leave anxious tokens at my door, including a text on the treachery of dreams; bless them, bless them all, I am benevolent. Ruth tells me to go out for the air and I go, floating, bearing wisps of dream behind.

I am in the cloister-garth, feeling the white air; sleeplessness and ghosts have made me fretful, I have come for relief into the cold, which is inarguable. Mirabel is pressing bulbs, holding each in her hand to smell for rot.

Kent, your last test is fear of God. Was this dream sent to try me, too? Is it the Lord's decision — or Lear's last gift, daunting me from the heavens? It all seems possible. Though, no: Lear wouldn't have the wit to be so frustrating.

As I watch, three of Calyssa's women move across the garden paths, and say something to Mirabel as they pass — it is tossed away in the blue wind. I do not hear it. The grass is sour and dark.

From the expressions of Mirabel's girls, straightening from the ground around her, I know that the words were cruel. Their faces are locked things: they have heard something coming and risen grasping their armour. One speaks angrily, and holds out a hand in retort. It is a stark gesture: hand, woman, white bulbs, black ground. Their heads outlined in silver against the light. The memory of the brawl restrains them, but the thoughts are the same.

I turn towards the locked gate of the abbess's grass garden, and unlock it (I have a key, she gave me one once *for your solitude*), and move through, clicking it behind me.

The grass is snow-covered; it is quiet. There is a bench by the wall. I sit to pray for a while.

Nuns! I should pity them but cannot, there is no bend of my heart that will do it. Goneril, do you remember? In another life — alongside this, spooling out its ribbon — you are a nun, and I visit you in your abbey; we sit strained, in the receiving-room, as your austerity sweeps all before you into deserts. Instead, instead.

I think I see a glimpse of her in the dazzling snow, and close my eyes. Daughter, I remember.

Your beloved nuns, Goneril, who arrived in Lear's court after

Regan's marriage. They stayed a month, petitioning for something; and you found them, Goneril, in their brief streak across your sky, and followed. Astronomer-girl.

Lear had no concerns. Though I saw you together walking, you and the nuns, touching hands, and your face, and observed in you a flash of some ardent thought, like desire. *Oh, of course let a princess talk to nuns, and learn their self-rule. Better that than men.*

Better men. When will she be married? Her sister's bound up with the marriage-rope, and she being the elder . . .

When we command it, and she shall be consumed by our will. He could double himself so easily in speech, by then. In first marriage the plural of his tense had been weak: he could not see himself as the flush of so many hopes, the multiple parts of the crown, land and sea and sky. But the habit came upon him gradually, and so by Regan's marriage he was *we* – his will had easily expanded to twice its size, thrice. I had turned away, snorting.

It was perhaps my doing. When young you and Regan had asked, *Tell us of your first husband, the pious one, the one who was a saint;* and I had embroidered Michael for you, pruning his sins, pluming his righteousness. So that he was as he had deserved to be, not as he was. Regan, ghoulish, had found the thought of widowhood appealing, as you could be married twice and have many nice dresses. You, Goneril, clearer, had simply loved: Michael, folktale, saint, golden man. May we all live so well in the minds of children.

It was before a procession you told me; it is so clear in me, it runs like water. An anniversary of Lear's accession, we had made it a carnival. Wheat for the serfs from the storehouses, entertainments in town squares. Striped silks, sugared sweets, hot plums. The whole country was merry-drunk from skull to shoes.

And we were to process before the people. Thick in our furs and painted leather, upon horses so hung with medals and veils that they looked like us, or we like them. A bastard-animal of bare skin and bridles, gold ropes and braids. I was preparing your hair, I remember, cursing it for it would not lie, and cursing for a maidservant to make you look proper. *Magdalena, that hairpin is a crime. I will skewer you with it myself.* You sat quiet.

The quietness was a fresh thing. I had seen it enter you softly, from the bitter arguments of your youth, and foolishly thanked God for it. A muteness that was not defiant but a withholding: a still held breath. As if a thing lay to be said and would call upon you soon.

Mother, I will not do this again. Under the weight of the headdress you were rigid, Goneril, like stone. The gold pulled the sallowness from your face, so that you looked metallic.

Be quiet if you cannot say sensible things.

I am being sensible. I am decided upon my course.

Regan, fetch my combs, will you? The wood with the ivory bells.

I have laid myself before God, Mother. I have heard the angels. I will follow His call to be a bride of Christ. Beatific. Your face like a horizon after a battle: serene in beauty, uncaring for the havoc before or after, because it was not its business.

So. How dare you do this now? You picked your time correctly. Just as we process. To embarrass me before all the highest people on my most important day! You are conniving, I see your design. I had thought you better, Goneril, far better than such a humiliation.

I have no design to humiliate.

You are a fool and a liar. God will not have you, Goneril. He has no desire for servants with forked tongues.

Your sly white face, performing innocence, lying that you were not cruel, that you did not wish to see me red with rage and misery in my highest crown. That you had no wilful need to punish me. And the nuns! Why did I trust holy women? I should have learned.

The garden is breathing; the light will consume me; I will be devoured.

Goneril, I had raised you and your sister to turn to each other, to be twinned, like two lines of light. And still it was Regan who came to me and said, *She is gone.*

What?

Gone. Goneril. With the nuns. She went hours ago. Pale, and so still, when in this moment she was casting off her sister in flame, and burning all the small tendrils that knitted them together! As if flinging it in my face. I saw Lear in her lips, the line of her chin. Defiant, like wearing a crown.

I hit her, as she knew I would hit her. Then I sent out guards. The stable was full, no horses gone: she must have left on foot. The sentries were roused. Regan daubed her face, held her tongue till I saw the edges of it turn white between her teeth.

It was the Fool who found you. Occasionally I believe that it was I, and that we alone saw each other, in the yew maze. But he was there, and had held to your sleeve, and asked, *Listen, Mistress, oh, it is so cold this hard night, let us back to the hall.*

You had packed so paltrily, my girl. Barely half a loaf, and coins that no merchant would take, being round fat gold and ceremonial, Lear's coins for the giving of alms and honours. You picked them from the purse, perhaps. A peasant's clogs, a cloak from the stables. I wanted to laugh, seeing you.

Coins. Coins in the dark mud; coins in the bodice, sewn tight as scales.

The yew maze was thick and severe in the heavy dark, steaming with cold. You could take it with your eyes closed, could navigate it as a child with Regan hand to hand, blind and deaf, all in the shade. I pretended then to be lost for you – *Oh, find me, I will never get out!* – but in the night snow I walked without a lantern. The black walls rose. From here it was as if the palace, the lights, had never existed.

I found you in the centre, clutching your cloak, the Fool holding you fast. Or perhaps you holding him. The two of you struck together.

It is my will to be gone. It is my royal will. Against the dark branches you were a hare, a deer, a white apparition. Your voice throttled, so tight. The walls high as a man closed against the wind; the air was still. *I wish to be a nun, and to serve God.*

You will never be a nun, Goneril. Though in that holy dark you shone, and looked like a saint's icon, one circled face painted in black wood. *Your service to God will be through marriage and your king.* And added, irritably, *And no nunnery will shelter you without our command: you are known, you are the king's child.*

I can be disguised. I can mutilate and scar my face, and sever my hair.

It is so cold, Mistress, said the Fool.

My fury rose, then. So little you knew. So much we protected you. *And will the abbey accept you then, a dirty lack-girl coming nameless to their door? And how will you pay for your novice state? Sell your signet ring? You are out-thought, child. Your ambition runs far wilder than your possibilities. Tame it closer.*

Men had arrived then.

I moved to you, to give you the rawness of my sympathy, to make you understand.

You were wild, you showed your fingernails. *Have pity, Queen. I cannot stay here, laid next to my sister's marital bed on the dog's cushion! Where is the part of this vast palace that could be declared Goneril's? There is no place for Goneril here! I will eat the yew berries. I will eat them. And I will die.* You wanted to crawl without a name, beholden to nobody. Your arms clutched at me, you threw away my comfort.

Bear her inside the house.

When Lear was told he would not believe that one of his girls would leave. Of course he turned it backwards so that it was my fault. *Your Christian God! Turning girls against their loving fathers! Get those nuns out, throw them into the river.* And kissed your hair, Goneril, and I saw you retreat, into mute acceptance, into the middle distance. Held in his arms, under his beard, as he gave you a new ruby ring, and told you he knew how to make you happy, never fear.

And he did, so he thought. A week later he said, *Albany has raised his hand.*

For her? I thought he'd never wear a bridal crown. Bachelor for decades. Gentle, yes, and with speech that calmed hot mares.

That one — no. But he is an honourable man. Has served me bravely. His beard may no longer be full red, but—

I thought, But he is so old.

I have given him no answer, said Lear.

No. Not yet. Good to make him wait.

I thought of the yew maze, of the flailing wrist in my hand. You crying, *Have pity, have pity.*

He is an honourable man, I said. *Let him wed her.*

Your wedding to Albany was farce, Goneril, you knew it. He laid your hand upon his to take you to the dinner, and you accepted; but at the feast you turned your face from his conversation and laughed indecorously with companions, passing musicians, any other person. Accepted his remarks with the briefest of replies. He ate quietly and with quick appetite, a stunned man, still shaken by his blessing. Had never thought to marry, Kent told me.

When they departed he took some rice from your hair. You moved away, swiftly, as if ducking from a gust of rain.

A cruel wind's coming, said the Fool beside me.

I open my eyes. There is no Goneril: she has been lost, the light has gone from the garden. Blue shadows are cutting it at the edges. The court nuns died, or else were banished, I do not know. They walked out of the story and vanished, as if through a gate. Women flowing out of a hand, into the forest. And my girl, who could have been a nun, yes, and lived still, and been hungry and delighted. But was it not better, Goneril, to live and die royal, than to sit and crumble towards God without a name? You will thank me; yes, I think so.

I gather myself and move out of the darkening garden.

★   ★   ★

In the evening Ruth finds me painting my face. Putting my hair in thin, thin plaits. I am dressing, in case they come back, my daughters. I want to be ready, to look masterful, a filled-out woman. Have unwrapped the royal circlet from the packages, which I have not worn in years. Wheatsheaves shivering in gold, against the candlelight.

I am seventeen again, I am just-married, I am perfect, awaiting my king in the dark.

Ruth is confused. Her hand on my shoulder smells of mallow, of grasses; she has been sorting sweet hay for the floors.

I promise I am not mad, I say hurriedly. Thinking of the hedgehogs, eating, blind. Thinking of Calyssa, her sweet lining.

No indeed, she says, and is troubled, my sanity, the plane of my exacting thought, being the place on which she puts her body. Which could smash, she thinks, which is made of earth, of fired clay, tiles that collapse under a foot-weight. She sees this suddenly. I bare my teeth, to prove I'm still balanced.

No, truthfully, I have all my wits still. I will hold together.

Yes. She moves carefully away, as if wondering.

The girls do not come. I wait; I wait all night. I wake with the circlet fallen into my lap, its sprigs and golden harvest crushed, against my hands.

10.

There are to be flowers; the last of the season, gathered up for the Advent.

John the Baptist, my favourite: animal-man, relinquishing women, stepping fresh from the water with his body bound in skins. Like Kent. And born to the elderly Elizabeth, whose womb itself was a dried river, which the Lord shifted aside, and let through the flood, and darkened the silt with tides.

I am plaiting an Advent wreath out of slack flowers in the chapel. So little remains: little folded dry hasps, burrs, petals crackling like fire. I am quiet. I cannot see the cold brows of my dead girls under their mourning crowns. I cannot kiss the chin and the eyes and the fingers of my king. No night visitations; no shivering gifts in my sleep. I am lack and lack and lack, barely a soul at all.

Brother Manfred is here, so I rouse into politeness. *Are you well?* I say to him kindly.

He has a mouth with an unwieldy bottom lip. Drooping, licked at the centre with pink. Biting, he hides it: this evidence of body-want, the fragile pink of his self. He is, I think, a soft man. And women frighten him.

I fear this is becoming unholy. He is speaking to me as an equal, as if we contend with the same problems. When all he does is tie their little sins at one end and send them off to Heaven, and read services in his quiet voice, and sit in the sacristy with wine while the women do the work of loving, grieving, building and rebuilding belief. He sounds concerned. *They spend so much time thinking of their competition. We are here for the strictures of God, not these tussles for power.*

Ah, but God knows power and its tenderness, and where to wield and fold! Did He not lay a competition among Cain and Abel for His love that led to a bloodied skull, and push Abraham to the darkest part of himself at his son's throat? (Though perhaps it would have been different, had Isaac been a girl. Daughters being lesser, bringing fewer gifts, in the desert, and generally.) What's holier? And I ask for so little. No smashed brother-brain, no hands dyed with son-blood. Just pledges, small tithings, proof of their desire. Crumbs.

I smile. The wreath is full in my hands. *It is a dark time, Brother Manfred. So many dead, and the abbess gone. Without an occupation I fear they'd brood, and become melancholy.*

That terrible fight! He is self-castigating. As if he could keep forty women under his own power, in such a season.

I shrug. *Isolation and grief will cause extremes, naturally. But I think a new abbess and the opening of the abbey will cleanse us. Like a bloodletting.*

Yes. Yes, I hope so. He looks to the ceiling: the painted stars, their wheeling circuit.

I want to flatter him. Little boys complaining to the bishop when he arrives would be distasteful. *Brother Manfred, I wonder: how does one judge the piety of others? You must have thoughts on this point.*

One cannot. He looks perturbed by the idea, if pleased by the change of subject. *Faith has no earthly mathematics. The acts and deeds of any soul are measured only in the ledgers of God.*

And we cannot peek a little at the page?

Men of the cloth can, perhaps. Who have been trained in the point. Smug, smug. Like a little rooster, fluffing his chest feathers. *But the rest, no.*

I see. Well, I must create my own ledger, Kent, woman though I am. Swiftly, before I dissolve.

The women process to the service. The one who brought forth the prophetic dream is last, and nods to me. I am possessed of a sudden desire to be kind to her. Pain gives out these moments, grasping hands in the dark.

And have you had more visions, child?

None. She looks at her hands. Is young, still. Given to holy orders with her pup-fat still on.

But you are not sad about it, I think.

They all treat me so strangely now, she says, almost in wonder. Well, this is what one gets, I want to tell her, when marked out, the gulf that expands between you and your fellows, that new country. Queens know.

I am sorry. Would give her the wreath, but it would be interpreted as a sign, a weight on the scale, so cannot. But my pity is sincere, for her. *I hope your dreams give you no more messages.*

She bows her head. *All I dream about now is fire.*

⋆ ⋆ ⋆

We had been a brittle group, the factions souring at one another. But it is the season of feasting, now; and I relent for twelve days, for the birth of Christ. There is shrieking: one novice chases another with a whip of dry wheat. Resin in the fires. Indecorous! I look out of the window to see several women with hoisted skirts, grappling up the orchard trees to cull the halos of gold mistletoe. Singing. They could be fourteen, or forty.

The feast nights are extensive. Pig-blood sausage, the wealth of our work, and fish, served to me as the cook smiles. Every evening I withdraw early, prominent with my bare head, a woman beyond pleasure, scalding their happiness white briefly with shame.

But it passes. Conscience does. And they go on singing late; a sugar-house is carried to them; the novices break off windows and panes. The chapter-house is dizzyingly hot: the atmosphere thins, till a person seeing another observes only scraps of colour, a flicker, each alone in their wild joy.

Truthfully I am sitting with my own feast in the nights. Memories. Lear coming back from war into a hot winter hall, blue with bruises. Taking water from a bowl in my hand and pushing the whole fistful of it back off his forehead, till his skull became a tilled field of dark red, upturned soil. Cordelia, with her soft mouth against my heart as the fires banked and spat. The education of a queen is slow, but it forms hard; I am the sum of all my secrets, and I forget nothing.

The ghosts do not come. I grow desperate. On the last night I tear apart the bundles. Perhaps you want something, daughters. Perhaps I can lure you.

I never told you what I kept. The scales you both dropped: teeth, ribbons, dark tears of stone from a pocket, split child-skirts messed in play, ruffs made for a kitten all afternoon and abandoned, the cool pomanders hung at your necks as babes. These pressed hearts of childhood, folded smaller and smaller; I kept them. In the white parcels I still carry them, brimming; I could not leave them behind. My children, my gifts.

My fists push through, and these hoarded pieces fall apart. Bead, crumb, threaded dust. At my touch they unmake themselves. Everything, everything is nothing, daughters; I see. If you come it must be for me alone.

If anybody comes and sees me on the floor with this destruction around me, and says, *What are you doing?* I will say, *I am killing the ones who killed my babies.* I have my thumbs on their eyes, my fingers down their gullets, crushing their tongue and palate. But nobody comes. There is torn paper, leather straps; there is very little, in the end. I pack it again as best I can, so Ruth will not see. When I leave I will have ghosts at my back, little else.

On the last night they make Ruth the lord of misrule, crown her with sweet bay and old rosemary, and caper her around the room; she is weak with laughter, but tossed so often she is bewildered, weeps and runs to my door.

Do they mean to make fun of me? Are they being cruel?

What to tell her? That, no, these people rich with the love of God adore her and wish her pleased; and would not tease her. But this is not strict truth, for they know her different; the lady's maid suspended between layers, in the regimented rows of lace that lead to Heaven.

Yes, child.

And comfort her as she weeps. For the sake of her soul.

* * *

The next morning the dawn cracks open. Epiphany. Salt crust of a day.

I am not sleeping at all now; I have a hidden pin to prick me. If I fall and miss one sight of my visiting girls, perhaps a glimpse of Lear's face — and they would do it, they would come just as I tipped over the edge into the bowl of sleep! So I am awake. It is my penance, but it brings terrible, deep clarity. I walk in the garden and listen to the sleeping abbey.

A pack of snow falls. Something holy in it, to be hidden so far under ice. Transparent spears of light perhaps, but no sound; and far above us the pattern of footsteps, of children walking and birds in search of food. Here I am, with my dead. Here.

Do the nuns sense? That in me the past and future are eliding, coiling together, thicker than umbilical cord, made of the selfsame substance? Perhaps. But it does not matter. The quarantine will end at Lent, and so the bishop may come, to bless us and hear the vote. The infirmary has emptied. There has been no sign of other illness; the tongues that were black are buried, and whisper to other bodies, under the winter ground. So there must be Kent's final contest: of piety.

How does one measure the piety of nuns? Shall I measure who can say the Pater Noster fastest? I rub my hands together, my wrists, for warmth. I am frustrated.

Goneril, you taught me this sort of thing. Every woodcut in your book of saints: you were as loving to those saints as a bride, even at six, at seven. Your favourite saints' days were holidays; you would tell us their great histories and victorious suffering at dinner, your cheeks suffused, blushing for their horrors (severed hands, heads, wrists, breasts). And hoarded gifts, which you left upon the chapel altar, pagan presents, acorns and candle wicks and your father's favourite ivory whip, the chaplain coming to me with them gathered in his vestments saying, *The young princess is so generous.* The pieces in the bundles, which have come apart and cast themselves into dust, on my floor.

I am a mass, daughters, I am moment upon moment; my skin contains years and shows them all to the light, all at once. I am trying to remain solid.

My hands are numbed. I had forgotten my gloves, which are dark leather, given to the abbess, but too big for her fingers. I lift my palms and I smell her, just for a moment: soap, cambric, the sweat of prayerbooks, of wooden rosaries and ink. It fades, it fades. My friend, what weather you left behind! You would know how to lure my ghost-daughters, how to pardon myself for them. How to be shriven and full, so that they forgave me.

I bite a finger; there is no feeling in it. There is a snowbank, which presents an idea. I plunge both hands into it up to the wrists and resemble a saint with no hands, martyred thoroughly by a heathen!

My hands are now hot with pain. I return them to light. They are slick-wet and red to the tips, the age-lines scored white. Somewhere my pious daughter is proud, and smiles. Suffering. Piety is suffering, Goneril. So you assist, at the last.

11.

So: suffering.

I begin to fast decorously, obviously: sit at meals without tasting, with an abstract face. *I fast until Candlemas, for the memory of the abbess,* I say, when asked. A full twenty days. Rituals: oil on my cheeks, obvious praying. Ruth thinks the concept ridiculous for my age and health, and wheedles me nightly into a little broth, a little secret bread. To her this is no dislocation with God. I sip and do not contradict her. The Lord knows what I am about, and Goneril will be pleased: she will be watching, and know I love her.

It is meant as a beckoning to a challenge; and the abbey knows it. Something real at last, something tangible! It excites them. The nuns fly around, speak late into the night.

The competitors make their bids known. Mirabel will be praying in isolation for twenty days. The plates of her knees will turn white under her robe, the bruises pool around her feet. As she enters the cell I flex my own toes.

They feed her bread through a hole in the door – she has become an anchoress. I imagine her tilling the soil of her prayers, running lines of seed, prodding the crop with hard wet hands. When she comes out what will she be? Will she have left her skin behind, moved out of a chrysalis into something smooth, without hair or softness? She will be thinner, daughters, that certainly.

Calyssa must meet the bet, and leap over it like a high wall.

Eventually her plan comes. Will undertake a pilgrim's crawl, bare-headed, in the mortification of the snow for the abbess's soul, her girls tell me. Round and round the abbey. A saint's move, a push towards holy pain, her spine a whip. Michael would love it. He is blue in the shadows, breathing his approval on her. I tell him, *Quiet.*

On Candlemas Day we are none supposed to observe. It is meant to be done in the privacy of her own holy suffering. A ship of her own passion, her anger. But, of course, none can resist. Mirabel still in her cell, rolling over the stone of her own voice. Otherwise, most of them are in the cloister, or upper windows, observing.

Calyssa removes her shoes, her stockings. Has let her hair loose – it is surprisingly long; in a plait it must roll past her shoulders; undone it runs to the waist. Not heavy. In the wind it does its sovereign best to escape her head and be carried off, small animal-fur, to bury itself elsewhere, but is thwarted and streams, a standard, for this war. She kneels in her smock, presses her palms together.

Pilgrims crawled to Lear, to me, for the curing of their illness, for the touch of a royal hand as a blessing. On their knees up to the throne steps. If they were too covered in buboes and scabs, washed to the necks with illness, we would kiss a medallion, lay it on their palm. Thus the golden peal of God upon them. Miles they had come, muddied copiously, made into stone, into hard ground, so that their lips when they parted were like cracks in the winter soil through which green shoots come.

I watch the white of her face as she crawls, bent-backed. Snow parting around her like a skirt. Her lips moving always, with high prayer for the abbess. *Her desire*, I think, *is keeping her warm.* And the incandescence of her purpose, livid, so that she (I see it) is just an outline with light in it, a lantern for her own will. Stained glass. The hair darkens with the sleet.

Hours and hours. Forty turns. At a distance in the cleared snow of her pathway her women, so that if she dies they may witness her, may pursue her into the closing mouth of her death, and find holiness. None touches. I go in, where there is heat and Ruth has banked the fire, and wait. Suffering being absorbing to feel but boring to observe.

On her final turn I come out to see. Ice has formed on her skull like a coronet and weighed the wet ends of her hair. Spindles gathering white thread. Shift ragged, through the pressure of weight on ground; it trails behind, greying. She is a pathetic comet. Blood, there is blood. The finale is a fixed, brutal moment in which she kisses the Cross on the chapel door, lays her head upon it as if it radiates, like fire.

Then she allows, with a movement of her body, her acolytes to approach. They come to comfort, they bind her hands, which are not moving. As she stands her knees are visible through the ripped shift, blots of purple on them like violets. Blood to her feet, the skin must have broken apart. She looks to me, to the balconies, and I know the expression without seeing clearly: the arrow shot of love, the request open as innocence. Beseeching that she might have done enough. A daughter-face.

I nod to her gently: she is shriven; I grant her mercy. She smiles, and goes within, and is folded by her women.

Mirabel when she emerges the next morning, on the brink of Candlemas, is a surprise. Not a silvered, thinned thing but sodden, dirty in the cracks of her elbows and the broad plank of her face where she pressed it on the ground. Her women speak of radiance, of something inextinguishable in her expression. She resembles to me a partially rotted vegetable, harder, more resistant to light. Something has not fallen away but clarified.

She will not sit though I reach for her hands (I would kiss it, this head that has gone through so much, that has shown obedience to the violence of will), but walks, immediately, into the garden, to put her body into its old custom: bending over a bed, straightening to hear the rain come over the wall.

★ ★ ★

Calyssa's hair must have taken hours to warm, spools of it suspended over fire, part by part. Mirabel now moves slowly, a hanging cloud of bruises at her hairline from her days of prayer. And they watch me.

A squall of rain has cleared the snow in the evening; the abbey is washed cold, a baptisement.

Candlemas night is the brightest of the dark season. We have made candles for weeks, bee-smell on our fingers, the wax rolled over palms. Scents of spring, of hope. Novices bring their hands to their mouths, to catch a hint of it. Not all life here is about contests, I remember. Behind the warring women, the background moves: meals, sleep, little prayers, nuns in the kitchen curing fish with salt.

The chapel had been filled with candles. Crowds of them on the altar, in the vestry. We have all come to pray here, in the sweet smoke, and will leave the whole host of them, to burn through the night. The shape of light on the chapel ceiling has no shape or border: it is a simple field of gleaming, into which God might peer, and see Himself.

The smoke rises to my little window above the altar, where I would hide myself and pray. I see it, as I blink in the darkness. No, I will be among them tonight.

The nuns below me are tired; their prayers are fervent – they light the air with need. There is a peace that comes with exhaustion.

I can see that Calyssa in lighting her candles trembles, and must be supported, though she is furious at the help.

Which can I choose? I light the candles. I am desperate. They are both so young: how can one choose between daughters? Kent, they have betrayed their excellence in every particular according to your laws. Shall I not elect both, and have them twinned in God? No, there must be a victory. The women are massing: I feel their weight. They cannot live without a single leader, one choice. I appeal to Jesus on His statue above the altar, but His green mouth remains pale, unspeaking, and I retreat. We leave the chapel, and hope for clarity.

I see as we leave that some distracted nuns have left a pile of tapers by the altar. Leftovers, perhaps. The bundle is the weight of a small child. We made so many. But we are all too tired to move them; so they stay, held together with straw, as we walk out.

We are listening to a reading in the chapter-house later when the cry goes up. *Fire! The abbey is burning!*

The women whisper, and are uncertain. It is not real; it is real.

But there is the fact of it, as we come out, to see. Fire has spilled out of the chapel door, and onto the massed blankets of manure and straw laid down to protect the bulbs. Haystacks ablaze. The ghastly green fire that comes of burning wet things is rising in the night; already rampant, grasping at all the walls. We come out and move through the smoke, like ghosts, calling, holding hands to reassure one another; it is weighty, it pushes deep into the lungs.

Mirabel's fresh new shoots in their banks of earth are shivering with heat. Branches become silver and white. A seed-pod has cracked; my tongue is hot inside my mouth. There is a chain of water now, rapidly, pulled in buckets from the wells and hauled hand to hand by the nuns. Knees and hands are wet; the paths between are soaked stone.

Ash floats past, holds to my hand. I watch it burn through skin, redden the layer. The pain will come later perhaps. The windows of the chapel are an open eye, and glisten.

A great sigh seems to rise as the first of the orchard trees begins to burn, the upper branches full of lifting sparks.

And then the birds. Alarmed by the smoke and darkness, or with some logic of their own, Calyssa's birds are escaping. We can hear them before we see them, screams in the green dark. Her door must have been left open – she is tired – and the cages were shattered: they rocked themselves loose. I see the spread of two white wings over the tops of the orchard, then the three blue parrots streaking through, parting the smoke.

Some make it over the wall. Others do not. Oh, ghosts. Oh, they are my ghosts, my girls, standing at the top of the stairs, I see it now.

Seeing wings on fire is a deep horror. The white-red rot passing through the outer feathers, blackening, eating and eating them. The birds are beating themselves against walls, the roots of trees, thinking themselves snagged; their tails shedding light, howling.

We see Calyssa. She is too bright a thing – she must be seen by many at once. Would scorch the eyes of one woman. At first I think she also is on fire, the light in her skin so dazzling. But she is merely running through flames and uncaring, stripping ash and sparks from her clothing, as she calls to the birds. Her voice sucked into the smoke, into the torched trees, that whistle and crack upwards in the flooded night.

The glowing birds will not leave the trees, though she cries, and holds open her arms. They know only themselves in the dissolving brightness, the fulgent world that announces their becoming: they are breaking out of their forms. They are nothing, nothing is consuming them, screaming.

Some of the women come to her to hold her as she is attempting to climb a tree, where a small one is red as a coal, and already bursting at the chest, unable to fly. The heat is on her hair, her hands are powdered black. I run to help, to hold her.

Then out of the dark there is a whispering, a cry. From the chapel. It is my daughters; it is a nun, perhaps, trapped. I turn and push through, to the chapel, past its open door.

Inside all is smoke, all is dizzying and sucking, and folding at the edges. No women. Single candles flicker in alcoves still, but the flame is in tides, rolling across the roof. The Christ-figure has fallen away in a train of sparks; pillars glow red, their insides burning out. The corner where the pile of candles lay is all hair-licks of fire, so thick and yellow they could almost be plaited.

There is no voice: it was a trick, a fluke of whistling wood.

I stand still, wondering. Daughters, were you calling me to this? This death? The heat enfolds. I feel as if I pushed the fire out of my own body, I gave birth to it, like a burr of holy lightning. Bouncing ball of light: I saw one in the convent as a child, a metal wheel in a storm singing with sound and fire.

Behind me Ruth is pulling, is saying, *Mistress, this is too dangerous.* I yield; my hand is in hers, I am being led.

Then the chapel roof makes a wild noise, as if released, and collapses inwards, in a billow of sparks; and we are engulfed in clothing of fire.

I have never been on fire. It is delicious. My daughters appear at the edge of the flames: I am alight on a pyre, I am a saint, Goneril, I reach out to touch you. I see your faces in the smoke, pushing through. Yes. This is how I will die.

But no: it is not myself afire. It is Ruth, her shift moving alone as if an animal, in horrible light, and her mouth open, but not screaming, only open, only a small hole in the heart of the world.

It is Mirabel who takes Ruth's shoulders and rolls her in the snow. Gripping. Till her skin smudges and is revealed, blackened, steaming. Around us the ash falling. The fire goes, my daughters vanish — though I put out my hands to them, which go through Regan's white beautiful head.

★ ★ ★

In the smooth morning dark, in my unlit rooms, I take off my mourning clothes. Off the cloak, the veil, the chains. Grey now instead of white, and smoked through to the bone. The thick robe in folds over my head and shoulders. Unbutton and unbutton the under-shift, which is sulkily loose at the bodice, across my breasts. They lift, they seek the air.

Ruth is in a corner, silent, weeping. Scrabbling at her face.

It is exhaustion: the skin itches, wants to rise, to be full and honest. Like pulling weeds away after hours in thick river-water, diving for stones. Oh, a body can radiate its own hard white truth.

I take off my shift and stride into nakedness, my cool self, awake to the world and the cold. God's eye will find me at my Eve, at my most honest; the dark brushes me down, as a groom brushes a horse after a long day's sweat, and soothes, and says, *Good girl, here's a girl.*

★ ★ ★

I wake to find Ruth's eyes are inflamed. Ash, or the falling cinders that clung to lashes and burrowed into the tissues of her body.

She cannot weep, bites on a small rag as we paint up to her eyebrows: ointment with violets, lettuce hearts, cool yellow cups of fat. The cook brings up milk from the cows, which we use to bathe each eye. Ruth's face shimmers in the light and becomes

310

another, a changeling, something unformed stepping out of the candle-shadow.

The pupils when her eyes are opened, cracking the dried fat at the corners, are scarred into whiteness. As if the milk had wormed its way in, spread open like a star across the iris, and engulfed all.

O heavenly God. She is saying this to herself. *O Father have mercy, O God, O God. Help me bear this.* Can navigate largely by touch — and such a small space to hold her. For fifteen years she has been in this room, or fetching things from outside it. In the sudden fall of her blackness there is at least habit. I will not let her touch my face. I draw apart as she leans, pulling my skirts out of the way of her outstretched hands.

It is so unfortunate, says one of the women to me, quietly. *To be blinded late. And she is not strong.*

Yes. When I leave I must leave without her.

Fortunate that she is not sharp-hearing. So I move to the outside room, and hold a thick robe to my face to quiet my crying, and she knows nothing, but moves in a state of fixed concentration, praying constantly, reaching with her feet for the next piece of solid ground.

12.

Afternoon: the fire has stopped, the chapel gives out smoke but is quiet. I come down to the courtyard in my old clothes; the white ones are too burned, all holes. Through a doorway I see Mirabel kneeling over the beds, pushing for roots, for the parts that may have remained alive; ash over everything, on wet knees, the palms of hands. The ground is bald; it has burned backwards out of form. The trees are white; like brushed ivory they stand in the dawn light.

It is a strong blue day. The marks on my hands are livid burns. I saw a tree on fire. I saw an animal fall from the sky. I reached out to touch.

I go to the orchard. The women are still finding the birds, hobbling on raw feet across the stone or on their stomachs, dragging their lame wings with holes and open gaps. Roofs with the buttresses caved in. They have oiled cloth and wrapped them in it, pink and flayed, some already blind.

The Fool should be here, he would know. I ask a sister where he is and she passes swiftly, turns her face away as if she has not understood. But I am not speaking clearly – the air is still smouldering.

They will die certainly. They must die, says a nun. The women are feeding them water with their smallest fingers, drop by drop. The miniature ribs rise and fall.

Calyssa is out gathering feathers. Nobody dares to touch her. Industriously, with the mark of the holy on her, ash on her cheeks and forehead: Ash Wednesday is months off, but we have burned; we have been touched by the fiery bush of the Lord.

She is picking, picking: the blue largest, the ones that traced the great curve of flight, taut as bows, she finds in puddles, in soft patches of ground. What will she do? Will she assemble identity, lay them on their native clothing and hope for new growth? Thin feathers, down; the softness has been torn out of them.

I come to kneel beside her, as she places them on a cloth on the wet ground. I lay a hand upon her back.

I am so sorry, I say. And our griefs touch, embrace, plait together and hold fast.

You were right. Perhaps it is our sins. Her voice is thick. It comes from another place: it has risen a long way to speak through her, through mud and the gristle of guts and layers of winter geology. That conversation, half a life ago: when the illness was still breaking us. *Our sins have brought this upon us.* She pauses. *Ruth is alive?*

Yes. Her sight is gone, perhaps. But she survives. I rest my other hand on my old knee.

Mirabel saved her. Her voice shudders.

Yes. The strong white hands coming and rolling Ruth in snow. My lit taper of a woman. What would I have done if she had died?

She should be abbess. She is touching the beak of one bird. *She has proven it.* Her sadness is gruelling. It is dragging her through her own body, and destroying it. *I am being punished. God has blasted me — it is as clear as day to me.*

Calyssa, you are a human woman, your sins are not so great. Her suffering makes me ache since I am so close to it. Since she has no children and only these birds, and they are so delicate, they cannot hold such love, and must die.

313

Perhaps there are other sins I did not know. Perhaps I have not confessed. She reaches and clutches my hand now. It is cold, and oiled. *I cannot be abbess if I am so soiled.* Her face is half bird: in its grief I see it breaking, into the pinions of feathers, and abandoning human solidity for animal riot.

I will send for Brother Manfred. I want to kiss her upon the palms, I want to draw her a bath and strip her down and oil her feet and hands until she is calm. (Why? Why a bath? I wonder at my own mind, at its opening traps and peculiar holes.) I want to soothe.

Why myself? Calyssa is saying. To me, blankly, her voice loose as if the meaning is coming out of the bottom of it. She is looking at the feathers on their cloth. Not one is undamaged. *What did I do? You are an adulteress. Your sins are far greater than mine. Whose burdens am I carrying that He scourges me so?*

I open my mouth. *What did you call me?* I am the only one who has heard. I must have misheard. I would have her speak again. But she is silent. She has turned away.

Adulteress? No. No.

A bird stirs and calls. It knows first light means itself, means the rising of its purpose; it calls, and moves in its oily skin. If all the birds die there will be no more dawns. They speak it out of themselves, pull it forth. Grant us a stay from endless night, O Lord, give us the mouth of the bird. Calyssa is praying, her eyes tight.

I am swaying; I will fall.

*   *   *

The bath. It was Regan, I had forgotten; or no, had never forgotten, daughter, I had gouged it from myself, and dug it into a grave, and buried it. But it grows; it grows.

314

Regan had disobeyed. I do not recall. Your disobediences, their small affrays and offences, slip from me, darlings; the emotional taste is long, the clear reasoning short. That she was scolded, and at fault, is true.

Some heat. And Lear was curdling, too. This was a bad season, the girls reaching early womanhood and its fretting sulkiness, the old court greying and threadbare, and still no boy-child. Long wars abroad. We'd fought that day, he and I – quietly: we were vicious, we landed small and private wounds in whispers in the royal chambers. Could prove our lethal vitriol with single syllables. A political skill, that.

What was it? I had resisted some suggestion because of the manner of his address, which was rude, he had riled; we had bitten, spat.

And so I retracted – and would not deal with them, either of them, and lay with my ladies in my solar, and refused my obligations for the evening. *The queen is ill. The queen has business.*

The banquet requires a lady. A visiting dignitary had come. Some advantage pursued with sugar sculptures of cathedrals, four lutists, the last smoked beef of the year.

Send the girl, then. Let her suffer it. Dark smoky halls with cold food and mumbling witless men. I had no patience; through the years I can still touch it, that irritation, the low wash of it in my skin. And the bodily satisfaction of thrusting my play and saying, *Look, there, I am finished with you all.*

Regan was dressed for it. Brilliant, arranged despite herself, so that under the gold and silk she was taut, and threatened to come apart. *Mother, do not make me. I loathe it.*

You loathe it! You are a princess. You must play to the masses. And kissed her, scraping a mark upon the wall of her forehead: my will. Child on whom much is written, and cannot be erased.

It was Kent came to me hours later and said, *There has been an incident*. Dark breaking into the morning. I had been dreaming. I raised on one arm. I saw his face, the set of his teeth, and felt choked. Men at his elbow, who did not belong in the apartments of the queen, but had burst through the pale tissues and were hovering. Grey-eyed. My women were in the corners; my women said nothing.

What is it? Is the king—

And felt the first touch of the drowning that would be, when Lear died. I had stepped into tide, I was foaming.

No. A brief confusion. Kent would not move to me; in the face of miserable violence it was his own backbone that stood, and would withstand. *It is the lord his guest. The Lady Regan gave the alarm and cried out; and the men have found them in the barn.*

Clarity passing over. Thunderstorm.

Everybody out. Bring Regan here. I dressed myself and waited alone in terror. For what I would find.

Oh, my girl. They brought her with ladies, who were shedding themselves, to be helpful, in their anguish. Trampled flowers. She holding her torn dress across herself, sore-mouthed and bloody. Her legs were bare. Still I see her legs, no stockings, bitten away, and red, even in the dark, so red. My daughter, my lovely bird.

I took her and she was not shaking.

A lady gasped, *Will I tell the king?*

His two beauties. His merits in the king's game, already promised and denied to powerful men, on the grace of their high-born virginity, their lineage of innocence. White blooms, tossing in the garden. I laid fur on her shoulders, which were bending. Both slippers gone.

No. She will sleep with me tonight. Bring me water. And lavender and comfrey. Say the girl has fallen down the stairs, she has some wounds. Regan's lips formed but she did not speak. The ribbons fell and rose in her hair, which was untouched and floated above her neck in splendour. Men were mysteries. Her body he had claimed, but the intimacy of her hair, stiff as a frozen garden under golden net, he would not dare.

And so, Kent said. Meaning the man himself, meaning the other side, which must be dealt with. Already the lavender was brought and the maids were breaking it, tearing flowers off, so that their hands and the room smelt oily and soft. We watched. Regan was cooling, the heat drawing away from her skin.

I breathed. *Tell the king the man insulted a servant, threatened violence. Drew his sword.* Unspoken, I added, Break his limbs, his lungs. Send him out of this place maimed, castrated, blinded, to curse the sky and beg. He nodded, left. There would be word later: *done.*

Her sister appeared. Was shooed away. What did they tell her?

Regan would not move as I peeled off her gown and her strips of stocking. Had relinquished her body, I thought, and moved free, to some hidden part, that was vanishing. Her soul spent the night in the wood, perhaps, in the heart of a tree. Meanwhile her open back with its ridge of spine, the bruises on her small breasts just forming, just becoming dark. Her hair still oiled and set for the occasion, which I could not let down without a maid. I put her in the basin, half warm, a bath for a baby; and I bathed her, with warm cloths. Blood and blood.

Sssh. I have you. I have you. Raise your arm for me. Good girl.

The bruises were scrubbed until she cried, and I could not stop. I kept rubbing them – all my robes sodden. My arms ached for days. I would raise them to replace a comb and there it would be, a cry out.

I was never told how they killed the dignitary. Imagined his head, its slam as it hit the wall, the ground. The feet of my servants, of Kent, cracking his ribs. Leaving his corpse to be crow-picked. Justice, in its own unseen way.

13.

I lie with Ruth all night. When she moves I grasp for her hands. I will not let her touch her eyes.

The abbey is battered. As if war, and great casualties of soul are lying in the garden. The ground gives up footprints, handprints; every mark is bare upon it; its silver takes the light imprint of wind. So vulnerable. I am filled with shame for it. I want to cover it, to let it wait for the next rain.

There are beetles in the air this morning. Soon it will be Lent, and spring.

The birds died gently. Which of these is meant to seem crueller? The garden is gone, the aviary empty. *Perhaps the abbey is cleansing itself of vain things* is the dark whisper down the nuns' corridors. I hear it passing outside my door. Nobody will say, *Calyssa*. Nobody will say, *Contest*. Nobody dares draw it down into their mouths from the air, where it hangs.

Yes, the little birds did die, and the women went to bury them, bearing cloaks and small pieces of worsted from the mending. Buried in their cages – Calyssa had them brought from her rooms and cleaned, white cane and ribbon, little palaces. Each bird, the novice Sister Mary Luisa would say later, was wrapped in cloth and placed in its own cage, then lowered into its hole in the soil, and the structure filled. *Though it was all in vain*, said Mary Luisa, *for the dirt filled the inside of the cage, too, up to the top, and covered the poor birdies, and it was such a shame.*

No, though I could not explain it to her — how Calyssa was returning to them their levitation, their air, even in the deep crush of soil, with the struts of the cages holding around them; this gift, so that they were suspended as in life in the density of the earth. *The ribbons were showing at the top of each cage,* said Mary Luisa. *She would not let us bury them.*

And then Calyssa went to her rooms, and will not speak. And her women spread and pray, and will not look at me. The contest has ended. She has given up her claim. It is over.

Mirabel passes and nods to me, shouldering anew a bucket of manure from the stables. It is a nod of mutual promise: *My competitor fell and this is mine now. I will be abbess. You can rest.* Then proceeds, one shoulder hunkered under the steaming bucket, to spread upon the cooling ground, and heal it.

★　★　★

Things move on. Women breathe in corners, wounded, but we recover. And Lent will come, with its empty eggshells and its happy poverty; and the bishop; and I will go out into the world alone, leaving Mirabel studded here as abbess, like a jewelled quince in a pie.

When Ruth sleeps I sit in the kitchen. I beg and make cunning, meek noises until the cook gives me a honey cake, and I put it on my tongue, close my eyes. I am near toothless now and the sweetness swells the gums, pools in the loose clefts that stud my jaw, swilling with syrup. I am made into a hive. I am hum and broken comb and gratitude.

Pleasure. *Queens live lives entirely made of pleasure,* a girl said in my childhood convent. As if power were never discomfiting, as if luxury were always simple. And yet I had luck: it laid its pollen on my skull; I was a blessed woman. I had my children and none died in the cradle. I had two husbands and I lived past their span. I was imprisoned and frequently thwarted but still there is this, the golden cake, the beginning rain.

It begins again. I am going to go. Am I? Out to the graves. Alone.

Abbess Mirabel could have me, beloved, on her arm as a falcon, observing the country, the lie of the cloud. But will have forty new nun-daughters to occupy her! And Ruth, now. Who must stay here, and have cups lifted to her mouth. I must tell Mirabel to be kind, to give her the best meat at feasts.

Well, when news comes of my death, wherever I am, there will perhaps be weeping for me here, and prayers for my salvation. It is pleasing; it is as it should be.

There is something; I am stirring.

Adulteress. Calyssa saying it, weeping over her birds. I had forgotten it. It fell away from me. Now it rises. The cook plunges a hand into the flour-bag.

Why? Wherefore? Adulteress! It is so astonishing I lose hold of it periodically, like a ferret that will not tame, that slips from fingers and finds shadow, wild ground.

I have been called many things, but not this. Never this.

Cordelia, ghost, do you know? But you are quiet. You have never spoken to me, only hovered on the edge of vision, a planet beyond cognition, thrown out of astronomy.

Your new babe-body the size of a rabbit, the light passing through you. Lear came to see you, after it was sure you would live. Steadied himself on the cradle. Hands spanned with gold, up to the nails, ring upon ring of fealty as he clamped the side. Did you look at him, girl, and know your fate? But you could see nothing; your eyes were sucking, they collapsed light into them, and love, and the tributes of kings.

Well. Here is the final child. And a girl at the last. He was unsteady and at last beginning to age. I saw it then. Youth flowing from his body, preparing him for bright shin-bones, half a burned skull, dots over his hands. The ink of passing years.

Our last princess, I said. I am so tired, the memory floods me; I am a bark drowning under.

You were awake, Cordelia. We watched you struggle in your cloth, fattened slightly from the milk and heavier now, less transient. Your brows had grown, and given you a contemplative face. It made you seem inevitable.

He was white-faced. *Perhaps after all this I will die, and you will be queen, and all you four rule together. Four women making up one man.*

You must not speak of such things. You are strong yet. I meanwhile was dripping blood beneath my clothes, was all liquid. Tidal. I was struck by how strange to me Lear's face was, his neck. That I once bit it, that we exchanged anything of our bodies, seemed as unlikely as demanding plums of a statue.

He passed a hand over his face. *Another girl. It makes me feel weak. And she looks like myself, I think. Though it is difficult to tell. Regan says she doesn't.*

She does. You did. Already parts were floating to the surface, your face. His nose, the angle of his lip. So that I looked at you and was flooded with love, not just for your own self but for the king who'd given it, who'd whispered, *Yes,* to my womb and brought you forth.

He was talking as if to himself. *People say such strange things.* So rarely we were alone. In the birthing room in the accident of our isolation — but not accidental, he must have arranged it, have somehow deprived himself of guard and knights and the boy who held his robes. The strangeness of it made the hair rise on my skin. Two bodies, a child. The space between us unbroken by anything but God's air.

What do they say?

Nothing. Nothing of any importance. But this girl is a strange one. She survives. As I survive. He touched you upon the forehead. You lay cool, with the dark stars of young eyes.

She will be a great queen one day. The great queen-daughters of Lear. I was astonishingly sad, the fact of you lay so heavy on me. To kill our one chance, our final gasp at the future, simply by the fact of your body, yourself.

Queens are foolish. Still I had such hopes, the gods know I had hopes.

I know, Lear.

He said my name and held out his hand to me, and I kissed it. The knuckles thick, by that time, and himself becoming seasoned, I saw; the boy having passed off from him, and faded, irredeemably, into air. And then he left us, Cordelia.

The women around me in the kitchen are murmuring. I have been talking to myself, to the air.

Are you well? says the cook, and I say, *Oh? Yes. Quite well.* I cannot decipher her look; it is as if I am transmuting in front of her, translating my body into another language, something she cannot touch.

The ghosts rush from me and away, fire-edged. I am alone. Twice queen, twice married, three times alive: one life for each child, running on parallel tracks, until fire bursts through and all three dissolve together, into one.

★   ★   ★

Days later Lear came to me. Why did he do that? Daughters, do you know?

Talk to Lear of loyalty, spouse. Give us your assurances. You are in faith, you know your vows: recite them.

I had been awake half the night. My milk was inflamed. *What brings this on? I am insulted.*

How did your first husband die? Did you have a lover? Quick, tell me.

This was fresh, and absurd. *You know I didn't. Starvation and madness. He refused to eat. Kent knows, ask him.* God help us, he was an idiot sometimes. *You are tired, I am old, can we have peace?*

He could catch himself in an idea like a trap. Treason, sedition. Young, he'd fought claimants for the crown every season, ground their skulls into dust. Now he usually sat in comfort – but out of the night, sometimes, the worry spilled. And men were culled, and their houses set aflame, and he was comforted.

I do ask Kent, I ask and ask. Doing circles around the room, as if this were a theatre and he were onstage, prowling. *You are loyal. You tell me you are loyal?*

In every sense. You know this, King, in your heart.

Yes. It is not possible. I am misled. I will consult.

He left me, feeling the victor, and yet lost, in a battle I had not understood. The Fool, old too, grizzled at his side, not speaking. Unclear, and yet I am pushing. I sense there is clarity, I sense it is coming. I walk into the drowsy evening.

Adulteress. Ash, in the darkness.

14.

The bishop is coming as the quarantine ends. There is word, a letter over the wall. Little Brother Manfred almost ran through the cloister yesterday evening shouting, as if bearing alchemy, as if it were Christ returned. Poor man, he took the burning of the chapel as a personal message from God, and now acts proud and penitent by turns.

I am awake in the night. Ruth is sleeping in my bed with poultices over her eyes. I will not let her stir. Many nuns have come with soothing herbs for her, with butter, and little prayers. They are so kind. I stand off, and let them sing to her, and wash her all over with their love.

Why were you in the chapel? one asked me this evening. Too tired to reproach.

I thought I heard a woman crying, I said truthfully. *Perhaps somebody trapped.*

But there was nobody?

Nobody. I bowed my head.

You could have been killed. Her companion lifted her head. Mirabel's girls, I thought, the two of them. But my eyes were clouded. I did not know. She was smoothing Ruth's grey hair.

I know. But I am old as the Earth. You young girls — you have so much more trouble to cause the Lord. And Brother Manfred besides.

They smiled. And were so young; and could not be killed by

a fire that was meant for me, that was sent by my daughters to whistle over my bones. It was not intended. They left me a cake when they departed, told me I must eat.

The ghosts whisper. One could listen to them sing all night. I am not afraid of madness: it is easy, so easy. But so difficult to make others understand. It is thin, the time, now. Could put a finger through it to the next day, the next. Things are loose, are unstitching.

Daughters. I want to step through this slender part to where you are; it is so tempting, like gold upon my eyelids, the soft touch of first love. The pull of memory arcs my spine; it hooks onto all my gut and humours. But I will not be mad, not yet. I must remain solid a little longer, a little. To escape this place, to come to you. Then I can come apart, in flowers and beads and dried wax, and all the pieces of me.

Mirabel came earlier, too. *So I will be abbess,* she said simply.

Yes, I said. And strove with my body to feel pride for my friend. *I am sorry about your garden.*

I have heard you are perhaps not well. Would you like to stay in your rooms, rather than come to the investiture? It is a long ceremony. Her face flat as ever; she is a muscle of will, she will outlast. She is folding, eternally, her robe. Am I well? The nuns talk; they will have seen that I am becoming protean, and have ghosts leaking out of my mouth. But I control this.

I am well. I have not thanked you for saving Ruth. Who sleeps still. And perhaps has the same dreams as myself; perhaps princesses riot and pinch her. I hope not. Daughters, be kind.

It was my duty. No further plea of righteousness or love, she is simply herself, in the machinery of her body, until it fails beneath her and her soul rides out alone. Daughters, you could have been so good.

Yes. I will rest before the bishop arrives. And wave her away.

Yes, the bishop will be here, they are putting saffron in cakes in the kitchens. Yellow up to their wrists. It will be Mirabel who eats the cakes and becomes abbess; the abbey knows this. She has walked with me in the garden, and been my friend; and saved Ruth, though not her eyes. It is sufficient. I strive to feel at peace in the sight of God. It is good, and correct.

And yet, and yet.

Adulteress. Calyssa is a question: her face opens a gate in the darkness, and I cannot close it.

There are parts here that must be uncovered. There is a vein that must be bled; and the substance gathered as it falls, though it be black as Hell.

★　★　★

Calyssa's night cell is abraded clean. Raw — I have never been in a space more raw. The walls scoured (for the smoke, for the staining) so that the whitewash in patches gives up stone. She herself is alone under the empty rafters, their hooks swinging.

They told me twenty cages, twenty-five. Her hair is down, and may even grow visibly, in the darkness. The furrows of old plait run down it like water.

Face to the wall. Eats little. Breathes less. Black, black. *Are you awake?*

I am. Her voice flat. A palm against a stone. She is Regan: she shimmers in and out of form. No, I am precise, I know my position.

Do you know me?

I do.

Behind the hair her face is half turned from the light. She could be anybody. No, I will speak.

You spoke to me, on the day of the fire. No answer. *You called me adulteress.*

326

I am sorry for it. She speaks slowly, as if dead. *It was wrong of me. I earned this with my own sin; it is not yours.* I understand her. Grief makes us wild; it darkens us as the blood gathers in our throats.

What did you mean? Adulteress. Why did you say it? The night is varnishing us; I can feel it fixing us in place, the stars above us trickling through the sky. I recognise that it is time, time itself. And am enamelled into this tableau, one hand extended.

If you want to confess, Brother Manfred should come.

She is hesitant. *I was out of my head. I did not know what I was saying.*

Tell me, Calyssa. I am insistent.

I have given up the contest. I will not be abbess. Let me be. Glittering; a bunch of bones held together. She is fixed by time, too. Like clay.

Is that what it will take? Well, then.

I say, *I will make you abbess, Calyssa.*

Opening my hands, since what can it matter? What, in the end, does it truly signify which head bears the mark to lead a bunch of women? Compared to the fate of queens, it is feeble. Miniature, like the workings of clocks. *I will give you the office. It is what you want. If you tell me what you know,* I say. I had come prepared to give this; I know as I say it. It is my barter, my last gift.

She looks at me. Hope has spilled into her. *It is that valuable to hear a rumour?*

It is everything. I must know, I say.

She turns her head to face me. Skull aflame, there is a lantern in it. Her will has risen. The bark of hair falls back.

My girls. Regan in the basin with bruises on her neck, her stomach. Goneril in the dark garden clutching my hands. I never see them beautiful. Always I see them like this.

I must convince her. *I will write that I promise to give you the office, because you have given me a great service.* Luring, luring: flesh before the beast, seed before the bird. *Here. I will do so.* The paper quivers. We are united by blood: I am piercing her; it will begin to flow. Cold, cold, in the morning, Lear whispers.

I write it clearly.

And Mirabel? she asks. She has pity — it flows over her face. Mirabel, who believes herself to be abbess already, who walks with the word written on her head. Perhaps she will not understand; but I dismiss her.

I have given my word. It is written. So. It is your stage. Talk.

She is unblinking. If I had taken her dignity, she could have hated me, and so been more capable of wounding. As it is I am begging her to skewer me with knowledge that will perhaps kill, and she hesitates.

She says slowly, *It was years ago. Brother Manfred and I were summoned and went to minister to a woman who was dying. The abbess was busy with the abbey estate, so I went in her stead. It was many miles. I remember the cart near broke an axle on the road, and the hired hands hammering at it, outside the window, as she lay dying on the small bed.* She is watching the wall. The shadows on it. *The priest left to take food, as we thought it would be hours yet, and I sat by her. She turned to me and said, I have looked at the Devil and served her. Her name she said was Magdalena.*

Magdalena! *I see you know her,* says Calyssa.

Magdalena was the name of a woman in my service. I keep my voice soft as fur.

Calyssa is speaking. *I told her that the Devil worked in ways beyond our imagination. She was streaming sweat. And she said, Ah, but this was a queen. Who was a demon, who would do anything to gain ascendancy for herself.*

Magdalena never liked me, I say, smiling. Which is true.

Calyssa breathes, as if about to spit out something sour-tasting.

And then she said that it was unholy, that a queen would try to have a child from another man's seed, in pursuit of her own ambition.

Ghosts split apart. Light thunders down.

The nun shuts her eyes and continues. *And I said that is terrible. And Magdalena said the queen was so wicked, flaunting her lover Kent. But she was discovered, by Lear's gracious daughter Regan. Who was so beautiful. And so the wicked woman was sent away to die.*

And what did she say then? I am desperate, I must know.

Magdalena said she was afraid to meet the queen in Heaven, if she died now, as she must be dead after those years in the abbey. I told her she would not meet her, for such a woman would not be known to the graces of God. And she was comforted, and died shriven. That is all.

I am looking at her in silence.

In the dark I am thinking. And Calyssa watches, coiled.

Then I begin to laugh.

Queen? You are well? It is Calyssa, anxiously. Breaking through the caul of thought. *The abbess did not know. Neither did Brother Manfred. Only myself. And I believed you knew. You did not know?*

No. You thought me an adulteress all this time? It seems ridiculous that this small nun, this holy bird-woman, would be layering sin upon me, for years. And never spoke.

I did. Or perhaps I did not. She is speaking so quietly, her hair loose: it would be beautiful in high plaits, in the Frankish style, with bright threads of gold. Daughters, you remember, looking as if the very crown sprouted from your skull, as if it grew like horn. *I am not a worldly woman. I do not know the laws of the body, or what queens do. I know very little, I think. And so I would not judge you, for what you had done.*

I can tell you now that I am innocent, and not once an adulteress. Not in word, in thought or in deed. I smile without waiting for a reply. *Well, now you are the judge, and I the defendant. And all the plaintiffs dead. How do you find?* Despite my lightness I feel arid, burned.

But fifteen years here for nothing? It is horrendous! She looks shocked, and unbearably sad. The injustice of men rolls upon her, the breaking wheel of the world. Lear, watch: watch as this good woman suffers, and feels the width of her faith thin, perhaps for the first time. Because of you.

God has His own methods of justice, Calyssa. You will be abbess; you will need to trust that the balance will arc over centuries, and right itself in the end. The daughters are silent. Lear is nowhere. For the first time in many nights there is no whispering.

She has seen my face. *I ask forgiveness. I have hurt you.*

I have hurt you too. So I give it. I extend a hand. She sees, and kneels, and receives my hand upon her hair, which is weighted, and oiled in the darkness. And is cut free of all her sins. And is Goneril, Regan, my daughter, coming to be blessed before sleep.

Good daughter, I say.

What? she says, but I am gone, I am going home.

★ ★ ★

Lear's gracious daughter Regan who was so beautiful.

Regan, oh, Regan. What did you do? My beautiful girl.

In the cell Calyssa was Regan; I was so sure and would have reached to touch her hair, which was no longer glossed and made into a mass, a floating ship of flowers and glints of light, but loose, and undone. It was not, and it was.

Regan, in your bedroom I came to you. You were not bloodied, days after. We had burnished you so that the bruises sank, and you were again white as the pith of a fruit. The king was told, *She fell down the stairs;* and *The lord gentleman was a thief and was beaten for it;* and in his blithe progress did not connect the two facts, but let them float through the body of the place unmolested. Lear could never be taught to anticipate misfortune: even after four hundred warnings it still broke over him, like a boy over-turning a jug of water.

So, Regan, you had escaped, and unblemished. But had sent for me.

I will tell the king. I want him to know. Yes, that petrifies you.

For she saw the thought that split my face from the inside. As if I had been present at the birth of something: a miracle, or a vision of Hell, perhaps. I watched her being born, and was silent.

You wanted my begging but talked. *It was your fault. You sent me to the dinner, and sat me neatly beside and told me to eat quiet mouthfuls and go for walks if a gentleman asks, after meals — walks! — and so look. And so it's ruined, and you are the cause.* Your soul I saw had flown back into you, and was burning at the edges. Ancient Greek spirits had whispered to it, perhaps, and formed it into something gigantic, smelling of marble sacrificing-stones and bronze weaponry. So you were beautiful and your lips were dark, against your face, like the outline of a ridge.

So you'd murder your own life. I was loving but would not let it enter my voice. You would kill tenderness — there was no touching you. *Because I had, I admit, a bad temper and you had a dark day. You want to kill your father, and your future husband, and leave them lying about on my pillow every morning for me to wake up beside.*

I would kill you, but I'm sure the Devil would come after me for being mean to his servant, and you'd sit grinning at the table as before. You were only a child. I was endeavouring not to be cut through, though my throat began to ache.

Careful with the Devil, he'll hear you, I said. *And your father will listen to the news, and know you are ruined, and — what? What will happen? Explain it, Regan, as you are four hundred years old and know everything.*

He will know it is all your doing. You were growling.

And then? You give me too much blame. I did not set the hound to kill the hare. Now the hound itself is dead, as you well know. The lord had crawled halfway to the road before dying in blood-spasm, Kent had told me quietly. Smashed beyond the recognition of God. *And now you are spoiled. Lying on the snow with your neck gashed. What will the hunter do?*

You were choking; and in your fury I saw the impotence of all women, against the rationality of men, and the savagery it excuses. *He would still love me,* you said.

Yes, I said. Lear's love for daughters undone by anything except crimes against himself. *But your father is honest. He will not give you to any man so you'll be nun-bound, Regan, or else kept here, folded in the cupboard with the preserves, to serve your father until he dies. You will be daughtered always. That's the price.*

At least you own that you allowed it so he might beat you too. You smiled, and saw visions, doubtless. Agony wants not relief but to observe equal pain in other deserving places.

I gave you my pain freely. Opened my palms so that it might spill, that you might prick them. *He might, and I would bleed in the courtyard under a whip, and be disgraced by my daughter's disgrace. But after that I would be married, still, and queen, still, and possibly give more children, still. This is not enough to undo that.*

Is it not? Against your thrashing I was immovable, and it was bleeding into you. You were surfacing, coming into clearer thought. Two structures rigid against force, against men.

What did I say then? *I give you freedom to punish me, Regan, as you want, but not yourself.* Not pleading, but soft. In the coaxing of a wounded deer. *Live. Tell nobody. Bite it down, girl, take it into the world, and release it on some wild moor if you like. But survive.*

Yes, I will punish you, you whispered then. *But I will not tell.* I did not know — how could I know you were embroidering this future from that moment, like a bridal-belt, to put around my neck, and strangle me? I had invited, I had declared you just, so it was visible in that room, unseen: my destruction, in black blood, under your blade, Regan.

We were silent.

Will my husband know I am not a virgin when I marry? you said quietly then. Collapsed, a little; the vengeful god slipping away from the small girl, the curve of her stomach against linen, smelling of honey. So our selves become green shoots even through hammered metal.

No. We can find a story for him. Thrown from a horse, perhaps. We will find you a horse. Hymen-myths, which are the duty of mothers. *And you are so beautiful he will love you anyway.*

Vain; glittering through you, a seam of silver.

We did find the horse months later, an angry bay mare, and so you were thrown, into convenient brambles; and in the arc of your body there was the cycle of Fortune, rolling. You to the top, myself closer and closer to the bottom. *Oh, she near broke her neck but she was saved, it was lucky*, I would tell the Duke of Cornwall over wine, when he was courting you, and he said, *I am very glad*, and we turned to look at your glorious skull in the ballroom, your face's startling planes.

The glimmer-stream of your hair is the light, Regan, the dark is your mouth opening. I walk into it, I walk into your body, I am engulfed. So you punished. So it is.

★   ★   ★

Ruth, out of the bed, hears my breathing as I return, and takes my hand. *My lady, sleep. You have been walking all the night. I am afraid for you. You are sad, you are sick, sleep.* I breathe but am silent.

Lear. What a fool.

My body has known two men. In between these two points there could be no third. What else could fit in the space filled by two kings? Of course others would not understand this. That Lear was all men, that no other male existed! He swept the landscape before him. He laid it bare.

But it would hold; for him, the story would hold. My body and Kent's, cooling like honey in a bed, as we attempted a son that would inherit all. And Lear outplayed, outworked. The world folding on him. Older Lear saw conspiracy in the fold of a curtain, a whisper behind a tree. He would believe his little daughter, creeping to his ear.

It was as I taught him. Lear, I am undone by the success of my own vocation. Better you did not tell me, better I never knew – because I'd come to find you, throttle you at the neck, till the blood ran out of your ears.

I look at Ruth and want to tell her, but cannot, as she is no mother. What we pass down is mothering, and bear it between us like a burning tree. Mother on mother on mother, pressing through the earth. And each daughter making it new, taking the weight, declares as she rounds herself and makes a new sum (nought, one, twice herself) that she will be as the others were not. *I will not do this to my own daughters*, the mother says. *I will be better.*

Did they have daughters? I ask Ruth.

What? Lady, please. She is weeping. I do not know why.

The messenger, did he say? Did my daughters have girls?

They were childless, Lady, there were no daughters.

Nonsense. How could they die if there were no daughters to kill them?

I do not understand.

Regan will tell you. Regan is so beautiful but I worry for her. Magdalena says she will not have a child, does not want one. I do not know how to tell her father.

Oh, sleep, sleep, Lady.

I relent then. And let her half get up from the bed, with her eyes held shut, and fold me in fur, and cover her mouth with her sleeve while she cries softly. I reach out and hold her face, between my hands, until she is quiet and the air is still.

★   ★   ★

In the shadows the Fool sang, *A willow, willow, willow. A pretty maid rode and gave me a ring, a willow, willow, willow.*

A sweet song. What do you say of a king who sees plots against himself in every shadow? Is there a tune for that occasion?

He was silent.

No riposte? The parts of this drama are terrible. I must send for better ones.

I have no daughters, no sons. I sold them all for a white jerkin and a tilting-horse. Still, Highness, I greatly pity you.

Nobody pities the queen.

He left me.

15.

I wake from blank cold dreaming.

Early. The nuns are singing. It is matins, and the air is thick with the shards of sleep as they push their voices through their slumber, propping themselves against the cold pews.

Shouldering up into knowledge. *Adulteress.* That Lear died, that my daughters died, thinking me faithless. That they went into the ground slaughtered without the knowledge that I was true, that I held fast, that I had never broken. It is unholy that I cannot plead, that their eyes are stoppered, their ears filled with moss and dark water. Bread of my bread, my girls.

It is as bad as the first night. Where their deaths crashed over my skull, and I was drowned. But I know more, now; I have aged, it seems, one hundred years. Who knew little nuns could teach so much.

Kent was not in my dreams. Such a sour idea. Kent my lover! Kent who only ever loved Lear, and would lie at his door at nights against ghosts. And from this Cordelia! It is – it is an intimate slur. Regan, you strange girl. When I find Kent, wherever he is, he can tell me all: how he claimed our innocence. How he fought for me. Oh, Kent, oldest friend.

My head is as clear as wine. The night passes off me and I am ringing, like a bell. The bishop comes now. I am ready.

★ ★ ★

The bishop comes. Stallions at the gate, storm grey, which must be the fashion. Four, of a single sire. The gate is cracked; the quarantine is over. As a hymen breaks. Regan, Regan. I will wear the grey cloak, and meet him with the other women.

Greetings to you. May the Lord bless and keep you.

And to you. Has the carved face of a man of cultivated pleasure. Aesthete, weighing his rings. *We heard of the death of the abbess with sorrow. But,* spreading his hands, *there has been an accident.*

The razed ground as we stand in an arc to meet him. Ash, still, and the scorch of stone rises through his hair. For days he will smell it. Passing a hand under his face he will pause and remember.

A candle. Mirabel is on my left. *It is all managed.* Calyssa says nothing. And is dulled, her hair scraped back under her habit once again. Looks blurry against the starkness of the dirt, which shows deep shadows.

I would clasp at Mirabel now and say, *You will not be abbess, and it is all for the best,* but I cannot: the light is diving into me, and my daughters, and sickness, blood-tasting, and Lear is walking along the edge of my eyeline; I can see him, he is half turned, his hair pulled through with water. So I am silent.

Well. The bishop claps, has men, who rise to him. Watching this I feel the click of some dim thing. Desire. *Tomorrow we will perform the ceremony for the new abbess.*

Has travelled long, to come to this, and carries his weariness obviously: give me wine, give me scented wood for a fire. Pushes his arms deep into his sleeves. What can he sense? The women gazing, the exhaustion. The abbess's white soul, the souls of my ghosts.

We take him to the old abbess's rooms (still warm, still possessed with the scent of sickness). I linger.

Calyssa will be abbess. It is decreed. I give him her name, her rank. It is arranged. I have done well, daughters. I have made the last step; I am close to you now.

Thank you. He takes note, then looks at me. Stark glance, appraising. In it many scales, many weights.

I meet his eye, his measuring; I have known all the calculations. I could turn you out by the lineament you wear next to your skin, the hidden crystal crucifix under your cassock, given by a wealthy woman. I know you, to your bone. *Do you know who I am?* I say.

You are wearing the charms of a dead woman. Girdle, necklace of power. Pearls, with Lear's crossed dogs, his emblem.

I smile.

He sighs. *I wonder where you found them. She'd be, what? Over fifty. Older than Lear.*

Years older. It is a new thing, to discuss myself as if absent. Lear never had the knack of it. Planetary king, so afraid of his own death. The thought clamps down; it is pain.

And dead, of course. A sinful woman.

I am not offended. I think of this. Sin not as a choice but as a pooling thought that spills outwards from a body. A nun reading by a candle raising her head for the sudden flicker of an idea. I ask, *Was she so terrible, then?*

Only a devil could breed those daughters. One good child, perhaps, but even God makes accidents. He is tired — I can tell by the weight of his head as he moves it. Nods at me. *That necklace came from a naughty, naughty woman, sister.* He puts out a hand, would touch it, the weight of the stones over my neck.

I move away. *God forgives.* And bow, and leave him.

★   ★   ★

So: Calyssa is settled. *Te deum.* Takes the oath, and rises queen. No, not queen, abbess. We perform the vows in the refectory, with a hastily produced altar, old embroidered cloths found in a chest. I am weeping, as I never could when my girls took a throne.

Mirabel's face when Calyssa's name was called was hidden. Smoke, from massed candles. The women looked to her, but she was still. The unreadable stone of her body. They looked to me, but I was glittering, pitiless. A relic left upon the plain, to be rent in half by ancient weather.

I feel a fierce dark sadness for Mirabel's hopes, which are torn apart now. But it is done.

And I will go. I will go, after they have settled, after the light has paled and the singing is done. I have been too long here. The ghosts whisper, *Rotting.* I can already feel the journey shaping around me; the horses that'll warm me when I am cold. Perhaps I will build a little hut by the graves, and live nestled in the folds of my memory, hibernating among layers and layers of daughters and husbands, emerging only for holy days. Ancient priestess, with a mossed roof, and dogs. Yes.

As the prayers go up I am whispering to myself. Ruth, bound around the face like Lady Justice, who has come to witness with her body if not her eyes, leans and touches my lips, and I stop.

★　★　★

The ceremonies go on till the early morning. Afterwards I come to see Calyssa. She is in the abbess's apartments now. Gleaming in the accomplishment of her hopes.

I come to pay my respects.

Yes. Her face is glimmering with energy still. She welcomes me: I am kingmaker, the engineer of her visions.

You will be tired. I am generous. *We may discuss plans later.*

Plans? She looks puzzled. The abbess-chain drips along her robes; her forehead is still damp with anointing. She is ruffled, fresh, as if just baptised, as if emerging from the water.

Be settled first. I will let her rest in this new dovecote, and expand.

Oh, I am settled already. I knew this office better than she did. I must send messengers, the quarantine has delayed so many plans. She is talking to herself, fast, as if held back for a long period and now released. The ambition, met and filled, is to be replaced with larger vessels, demanding other sacrifices. Women like this are never sated by a prize, not for long.

I say, *The spring is coming down. I think the roads will be clear soon.* Beetles, and mud bubbling, rising to swallow the ash in the garden. The world is rioting down, daughters, and your bodies will be growing bulbs and fingerlings of green, and breaking out through the ground; you will be living.

The roads? Why the roads? Has turned; I have her attention fixed.

I know three horses cannot be spared so long. But I could take two. I smile. *Lear will be pleased to see me. He'll make those old dancers come up again. I hated them, their legs were too thin.*

Lear? Lady. What are you saying?

The wind is fresh. I come to hold her arm so that she moves to the window. I feel her yield. The abbey beneath us still burns with lights: many women drinking, blessing themselves, feeling the dip or swing of their hopes. *Sun for a few days, at least, so it will be a good journey to start with. Did I say Lear would be pleased to see me? Of course he will not. He is dead.* It is strange that I made that mistake. But perhaps not so strange: she would understand, if she had met him. He was the substance of all. Though gullible. And killed me for it, but I would not die.

She takes me, and directs me to a chair. *Come, sit here.*

Yes. She gives me a cushion; and I fold my hands over it. Greedy, yes. Old, yes. The ghosts are raucous, and pleased. Or that is the birds – they sound similar. The birds are dead too. They are part of the same chorus.

Now tell me clearly. What is it that you want?

I must have my little house by the graves, you know. And perhaps my daughters. Who might be kind enough to visit, if I have enough baubles for them, and a little entertainment. It will be a fine summer. I think there will be many good days. So I must go. This fills me; I am bursting, the hope of it, the great wave of the future. Breaking over my head. *I will ask. They may have had children, you see. They said they didn't but I don't believe it. To have had no daughters! Girls lie all the time, you must understand.*

Are you sleepy perhaps? Calyssa asks. *Are you dreaming?*

No, no, I am quite awake. She is very young. Why is everybody young, and myself the only one privileged to age? *I will leave Ruth with you, you understand.* I am whispering. *She is old, she is infirm; it may be difficult, and she deserves to rest.*

I will do my best for Ruth, Queen. Her hair hidden now beneath her headdress, so that she looks gentler, more tamed. Though around the edges light flickers. *But I do not feel— Well. I must do what is best for all the women in my charge. I wonder if you realise that.*

I do. You are a wise girl. No men are likely to gull you. Don't get yourself married. I'll not see your heart broken up. This room, the flowing lights: time is broken apart. It is moving freely, and I am falling through it.

Oh, Queen. Her hands are held to her chest. *You will not go. I cannot let you. You are dreaming, you are not well. You must stay.*

Oh, bad girl! *I will help you see.* I take her face. I hold it. I press it to my own, hard as death, until she cries out.

Stop it. She pulls my hands off, at the wrist, and is not Regan. I had thought she was. I had been gripping her like stone.

Other women enter. *Get off her.* They take me by the arms, I am laughing.

Be gentle with her. She is dreaming, says one.

I am to go on a journey, I say to the women. Generous. *Calyssa does not understand. But I will.*

Calyssa has marks across her cheeks, but the confusion passes off her, she is restored again. *Queen, can you understand me?* Comes to press her hands upon mine. I feel their weight, the loam of her palms. *Please. You are my child, my charge. Take direction. You are loved here. But I cannot permit you to leave these walls, not when you are ill.*

Goneril yells, and will bite. Small teeth, a mark round as a crown. Though it is myself, and the ring of red is on the arm of Calyssa's woman, her skin-taste is on my tongue. She screams, like the birds caught in frets of fire. More women are appearing; the world is crushing in upon me.

I gave you all of this, I call to Calyssa, across these protective bodies.

And in good time you gave it. Take her out, please. And turns to bathe herself, to be revealed, as a pearl out of a stone. I hate her: the walls of her fold in and reveal intimate flesh. See, daughters, the incarnadine innards of blessed women, see what we will discover together.

The women steer me down the stairs, into the garden.

*   *   *

I am out — in the evening light, unsteadily. I stagger. Were bones crushed in me? Am I walking on sand, on smashed soles? I can barely go upright.

Mirabel is sitting looking at the burned garden with her hands crossed in her lap. That patch at least is green, at her feet; it has the light fragile hair of shoots, and will be bravely thick with them. I must tell her. I walk to her, and smile.

I am leaving.

342

She looks at me evenly. Has balls of seed in her lap. Has never drawn a breath that does not come from some deep place. Never breathed hard under a man.

I will be going to the graves, and my own little house. Perhaps I'll be leaving even tonight. And would ask her to come, perhaps. She may come. I could have a garden, for her, a court garden, rare trees, and biers of rose, under which I could shelter.

When Michael died I walked in the palace garden and cried and cried. The frost was on the leaves, I laid paths through the white grass. Later when I looked back I had paced arcs and rounds and twists, like a swooping swallow above a field.

Mirabel still looks. Unmoving.

You could express good wishes, I say peevishly.

You are not a stupid woman. Are you a stupid woman? she says.

I am not. I am surprised. The ghosts are rioting now – the light sends them sparking.

She has the bare still gaze of an animal. *You are. You are old and have less solid brain than a rotted bread loaf. You bit Sister Mary Luisa's hand.*

She deserved it, I say, with dignity.

Well, the abbess has decreed that you are here till death, and you had better get used to it. Something moves in her, something I have not seen. Vicious.

Scrape, on the stone. It is not truth; it must be.

But you will allow it, I say. *You will help me.*

As an abbess I may have helped. But you chose elsewhere. Violence shudders her voice, the only part of her that moves. I am afraid, for the first time. *After the shit and foulness of your contests. And the wreckage. What a thing to ask of me.* And wanted; and is thwarted in her want, and so turns, a furious animal, and devours. I see.

I had to choose. You do not know. It was for my girls, but you are my friend. You will understand. Would reach to hold. This human woman, who loves me.

343

I am your friend in God. But otherwise, no. She gets up and shades her eyes against the torches. *Green, nun, light. Be grateful, woman, and don't snivel. Here there is food, and a roof, and we'll keep you well enough. Better that than running around naked on a heath. Which is where I would leave you. If I had my way.*

The world trembles. Here is the noise of the ground, which rises.

Now I must pray. And leaves me.

Oh, here is my poor lady, says the cook. *Come, don't cry. I have a honey cake for you. There's a good woman. Open your mouth. There.*

16.

Spring breaks open.

I go out to watch every day, now. I walk past the fields of whispering grass where men and women with kerchiefs and bare arms are bending — over what? To sow something? Perhaps I have been told, and it has fallen out of me — to the crossroads. There is a low stile and a scoop of shade. I go bareheaded now, in the nuns' old robes, as things are denser, the air is fleshier, the light a bronze caul across my hair and face. I do not fight this density but move deeper within it, sensing its smoothness, the heat of the mud path through my sandals, the sky and pollen and smell of coming wind.

The holy women watch me pass silently; some cry, though I do not know why, and some come and kiss me upon the hands, and tell prayers upon me. Mirabel's face is turned away.

I laugh, and am gentle. They are filmy, they do not signify.

There is such singing, from everything, everything. As when I took all the packets from my bedroom, in my arms and my skirt, and conveyed them to the river, feeling myself under an impulse I had ignored; and now it cracked out of me, yolk out of shell, and was revelling, and the new grass-growth stippled the melted ground. So I took the packets, and pulled them open on the dry bank (a place of history, which had names and deeds attached, but could not care; and simply brooded in the sun, as the mirror of the river observed itself placidly), and made a gift to the water. Handfuls and armfuls, from the sodden packets, given in great arcs: scissors, a shoe embroidered (I saw as it flew out of my hands) with a bird, by some small ancient maid, cracking leather red as a mouth, gold and gold and gold. I was immense; I was the goddess who grants all boons. In the fresh crash of tide they blushed and dulled, and attained new life: after decades of eminent stillness they were moving, flipping over rock-moss, caught twinkling in the throat of an eddy. Elation! The shoes tossed and showed themselves fitted to some water-nymph, who danced and turned their velvet nap to silver. I was releasing.

Three little plaits of hair – which prickled in my palm, which was whose? – swam out of my dipped hand, into the copper depths, and became sea-grass, or a gift for a tench. Names had fallen out of me, and freed themselves. Well, it was good, honest work. And so I came back dripping in ochre mud, grinning for a miracle, as people will after seeing a martyrdom.

I am on the fence, now. There is cake in my pocket, which the cook put there; and a nun took me to the gate, and saw me out, holding my hand, so I might not slip in the spring-mud. And fastened my veil. A dark-eyed girl. They care for me. Though they do not know the enormity of it – the woman they touch, the country of her.

Some days I forget for whom I am watching. So people pass on horses or carrying vast hocks of straw and ask, and I say, *My husband*, or *The nuns*, or *My girls*. They look as if to see me clearer through the dust. But I am vanishing from them, half bird, already spooling out of vision, out over the fields of yellow and gold.

One man comes to the gate. The day is high and the sprays of white are in the hedges, shimmering and agleam, and I am looking at them when his shadow comes blue upon them and upon me. And he says, *Who are you watching for?*

And I because I am caught in the flowers, in their buzz-brightness, I say, *My husband.*

And he says, *Which one, Berte?*

And then I know that it is Kent.

★　★　★

Are you a vision? I say.

Does it matter? His high brow is dark with mud, or with some passing thing, a sorrow, or thought.

No. No, not now.

He walks with me through the walls, into the gardens. There is green, the season is moving through. I knot flowers to my hair often, though Ruth takes them out, Ruth who cries, who is always seen weeping, I know nothing of her. It is such a brief spring. It is Lent; I remember. Calyssa wears the abbess-crown on her blonde hair in the chapel, and is gentle, lets the women give up only small sweetnesses, tips of pleasure. The plant and root she leaves. It has been a hard winter; she is wise, she is wise. Easter will wash us all in honey; we will roll away the boulder and say, *Huzzah.*

Though not myself: I am reborn already, every day. I am profuse with past selves, all at once. Every moment in every moment.

Was Lear mad? I ask Kent. There is no blood in him now. If I took a spear to his breast now there would be only a dark smudge, air, nothing.

He was.

Did he speak of me?

No. Only once. To swear on your grave that his daughter was a bastard. Not Cordelia, the eldest. Goneril. He shades his eyes to the light. There is nothing dishonest in him; he was skinned of it long hence. I am watching him, as if to consume. *He thought you dead years ago.*

I know. There is something. I pluck it. *I thought he would remarry, for sons.*

He was encouraged. But would delay, and dally with his daughters. They enlarged, or perhaps his life shrank.

Goneril and Regan did not allow it, then. I see it. The grown milky girls, at his knee, at his bed, wives and wives.

No. There were eligible ones, good girls. But they clung fast.

Mirabel's nuns move past, in the physic-garden. Hands full of weeds. The factions have declared truce; the bitterness of what was has gone, has lifted away. Out of the cages new birds sing, now. And Mirabel grows her water-garden under the eaves; it was long-planned, and lilies will come. So women flourish, when laid bare, and scoured to the soul.

You are tired, I say.

I am. I have ridden long. Strangeness comes across his face. *I was summoned.*

Tell me.

Later.

Entering the abbey is like breaking through the waves, and we ride together, coasting upon the tide, flourishing our bodies; and the nuns come forward to meet us, as the flat blank coast welcomes the foam.

*   *   *

Inside, after he has rested. Ruth has brought water, for me. Brackish with the dark of winter leaching out. Her eyes remain in winter, white-glossed, and will not grow again. She sat where the packets had been and mourned, but I could not hear what she prayed.

I watch. His beard is thin; it carries moisture from the bowl. The nuns were bright and giddy to him; the masculine arrow-point of him pierced their throats – they see men as great boars perhaps or whales. Brother Manfred's manhood they forget, easily, as if he had laid aside all sex except what was necessary for God. So Kent was palmed through many white oiled hands, and blessed solemnly, while I stood apart, flickering.

His old white lips. Gouges across him; age has scored him down and down. *How did you find me?* The question comes out of me. It is a bud out of my mouth.

I was on my last errand. He pauses. His voice has a withheld thing. As when Goneril hid a filched pear behind her back. *You will be angry.*

I would not be angry. Which is true. Those weights I carried I have laid down. They have passed through my hands into the joyful water.

I was going back to the lands that were Lear's to lie down in the peat, with the grey sky above me, and sink under the moss. He lowers his aged head. *To die.*

Yes. He loved him like a brother, like a wife. I know.

And then I received a letter from an abbess. Passed from many people, so that it found me late. Saying that there was a woman, a queen, who asked for me, who said she was Lear's wife, and would be pleased to know my fate. His hands hold themselves together, in strange prayer; his voice is suffused with astonishment. *She told me to come here.*

The dead abbess's eyes, in the orchard. Green-dark as water. Who had promised to find him. Whom I had not believed. So, ghost, you do your honour: though you raged out of form, some semblance of your will did its work. I feel a swell of deep pleasure. My lovely friend.

I take his arm. It is a shade; it is light as cloth. *She is dead. They are dead. Kent, how have they all died?*

He looks at the rafters, their hanging ribs. *I came to find this place, and wondered if perhaps it was a mistake. And then I met a bishop on the road, and asked him of the abbey.* He smiles. *He told me of a fire, and a strange belt on an old woman. Stones, he said, pearl-white. And the crest of the dogs, in gold. And I knew.*

Yes. By the fire of my room I hold Lear's crest in my hands to show to him. It lives at my waist. Smooth gold dogs, still, their hair pressed along the metal in waves, with wide-awake jewel eyes. *I was to give them to my granddaughters, when they married. Such good stones. They are heavy, you know.* Ruth is snuffling; out of sight.

I know. Lear wrapped them under my chest plate when I came overland to fetch you. They wore a hole through my shirt, I had a bruise to the bone. He is holding his chest. Poor man, bent over as in a storm.

I am smiling. *You were kind.*

And for years, after all, you were here. Simply here. Barely four days north. He looks at the walls, the high cloisters, and yet there is a gauze over his eyes. Like Ruth, like her starred eyes thick as shell.

What tender children I had, to put me here. I am spiteful.

Tender indeed. His hand on my arm trembles. *I wish you had known Cordelia. She was very like you, when you were young. Kind. And headstrong.* Her ghost cools between us, with folded lips.

Now, I explain, *I am as old as God.* I could tell him that I feel the thrust of the spring earth, the green of the uncoiling season, in my gullet, and am tide, am break, am the whim of the shifting world. But hold: he does not need to know it, not yet.

I can hear his smile. *You are younger still than I am, Mistress.*

Am I? I have been married twice. I have three daughters. They are wonderful daughters and healthy, though they behave strangely, and Cordelia is so ill for a child. Do they fare well?

He has my hand and holds it, a moment. *Yes, Queen.* It will stay light until late; the walls are full of sun and half blazing. *They do.*

Good. Lear wants them married, you know.

I do. I must see the abbess.

★　★　★

350

In the evening Calyssa comes at last to my room as I lie and try to sleep. He has been sitting at the bed-foot, guarding the royal bed; he is eighteen again, I am fifteen, Michael is coming at last, the women will be here to dress my shoulders, the blond-fur brush with the silver handle to drift powders over my skin.

No. It is Calyssa. The Lent services are done. Her face is ivory, I watch it through the door. I look to Ruth to tell her, then cover my mouth with my hand and make a soft sleeping noise. Secret, the ghosts whisper, secret.

You are welcome, Lord. She has manners; she comes to them gracelessly, but she has them. Will flow into them with more ease as she grows into her abbess-shape.

He rises, bows. *You may not say so. I am a dark cloud moving over the land, the news I bring.*

They are all dead, then? As the messenger said.

All. In him the deaths smoulder. He too has ghosts. His voice is heavy. *I tell you, Abbess, I would best not have lived to see it.*

Not ivory, Calyssa, no. Perhaps something thinner, so that the light gets in and you can see the thoughts inside her head, black as beetles.

Has she been wandering since that time? he asks quietly.

Not since. Recently.

You should have seen her in her youth. Thin as an eel and all eyes, but cool-headed as stone. They talk around me as if I were a tree, or a dog. And indeed are wise: I am heavier than all women; I am pressing through the layers of time, which are white and transparent; and beneath are more layers, petticoats, packed against my body, bodice made of a hundred linens sewn tight. Each layer a year. A queen's dress.

You are the knight Kent. She hears Magdalena's voice in her head. Reaches towards truth, towards the famous, the slandered.

The unhappy Kent, yes.

I have heard of you. Of your service to the king. And of your ill-usage.

He passes a hand over his forehead, a gesture decades old I know without seeing it. *God help us, I swear it not to be true. I never touched her.*

I know. She is steady, worthy: a jar into which virtue might flow. She wishes to receive him, and hold his old head against her breast.

And all the time Regan whispering, whispering.

Good. He is tired. *Fortunately the Lady Cordelia showed excellent sense and grew with both her father's profile and his stubbornness.*

Yes. The messenger said so, how much she mirrored him. Lear must have had guilt in him, in his gut, at that. Black bile. When she looked over a shoulder and he saw his own face, and knew. Too late; too late. Perhaps she was better than her sisters for it; perhaps he treated her with gentleness, for suspecting her so long.

Fifteen years for a falsehood, says Calyssa. *It is so much. No wonder she has broken apart.* They sit together; I see their silhouettes upon the wall in long silence.

Hmm. Mad she might be, but broken, I'd be surprised. Cleverer than any woman I know. And most well-positioned here, I see. Kent is looking at the appointments of the apartment. Tapestry still smoke-smelling, but rich, yes. Enclosed in an egg, I am: little queen-yolk.

We care for her well. Calyssa's voice is quiet. *We have kept her safe. Though she has wanted to leave, since the news came. To tend their graves. A noble impulse, but—*

That would be a sight indeed. And beneath her. She was always too loyal.

It is true. It slices into me, I am halved, quartered. One quarter for each death. Cordelia, Goneril, Regan, Lear. I gave up myself, groin to chops, for you. I would have laid down my old bones on your death-mounds, and wilted into poppy-heads, into grass. It is too much. It is. At last I see.

He was afraid of her, says Kent sadly. *A greater queen than he was a king, and he knew it.* Moves out of sight towards the fire. *So our gifts doom us.* The birds crackle, in the dark.

I see Calyssa reach for his shoulder. *You are not to blame.*

It is my fault. He holds her hand as if it is a burning brand; and he must hold it and outlast the suffering. *I could have saved her.*

How?

I arc my back. I want to hear. Give this to me, Lord. This is the part I need.

He wanted to kill me. He is whispering. *To escape I told him that the queen attempted to seduce me, that she used wine and all her charms, and I barely managed to resist.* Breathing. Up, down. *He believed me. So it was forgiven, and for years I hoped that the queen was dead, so that she could not tell, and I could have peace. God forgive me.*

A breath with the long shudder of weeping in it. The room is close; it smells of damp.

Traitor Kent. At last I see.

I see my shape in Lear's mind, as if through a mirror. Floating, and stained, from the hands, from the belly. A monstrosity. Betrayer of his love, his vows.

The graves are quiet, on the coast, with sea-flowers perhaps and grasses, from the spring, and poppies. I feel the soil upon the heads of my girls, the softness of it covering their eyes; and I let go.

Calyssa is calming. *You should pray. We have a confessor, and the Lord will listen.*

I had one lord, Lady, and he is deaf to anything. But I will come. She sleeps.

Years, and years. They leave. It is Michael's footstep on the stair; it is the maid; it is Magdalena; it is Kent, rising from the water, who saved but was not loved for it, and hurt for it all his life; it is Goneril with her blue dress on saying, *Mother, where does the wind go when it dies?* It is and it is and it is.

* * *

The solution is so clean, so simple.

I do not sleep. There is so much, so much in this. The women will sing soon, to greet the dawn, and take it into their bodies.

Many things are crumbling in me, but it is no hardship. Old friend, under the tossing white roses: threading first husband, second husband, Fool, onto a necklace. Oh, small callow boy, wearing my pearl-loop over the heather; carrying your service to me on the weals and furrows of your body, the golden dog-shape scraping at your rib. Its soft weight upon your neck, indenting. So I thought this was promised, that the fealty of you was eternal. But you would be broken, Kent, like all men break.

The nights are still cool, or I am preserved in cold, flinted to my bone, now. Land-queen, becoming geology. I am less flesh with each day, I gather earth, mossed granite, long sweet limestone. Behind my eyes are ancient lochs.

I hold the pearl-belt, its moons, at the fire. Gifts, the flow of bone into blood, vows, oaths of love: the things that bind each to each. The rope is still knotted, the weight falls from my palms. Across my hips it has lain years, a reminder of all my promises: I was loyal, I was that selfsame queen, and deathless in loyalty.

The fire when I haul the pine-logs upon it sparks and cracks; the sap glistens. Water, perhaps. It is my hands, which held daughter-heads and pulled them from my body; those hands. They place the pearls in the blue fire-heart.

Slow, slow, the pearls roll and unwrap in the heat, petals of lustre, frilling off. All of them worming back into blackness, returning to a dark seed. Pearls burn in quiet, which is a new thing to know; they release small voices in pops and scratches. Gold, the symbol-dogs waver in flame, as if dashing through wheat after the last rabbit, the final prey of their hunt. Eyeless, now, the small rubies have fallen away. All is blind.

Oh, Kent, I will not die. I alone have everlasting life. I burst with daisies and marjoram, the flesh of my thighs is bee-luscious. All the girls and Lear may sit into silent earth and be glum, but my place is riotous. I am myself; I may be insane, and old, and the nuns may weep, but they are my loves, and my daughters, and I rule what I rule. This glorious place, in spring. My own body. At the last.

I have escaped all that would silence me, Kent. I am simplicity itself.

17.

The ghosts know some words now. Such as *glory be* and *halle-lujah* and *bless our royal father the king. Beast* and *wither* and *naught.* They are moving into language; or I am retreating.

Kent, when he speaks (as he is now speaking, as the earnest face looks at me over his plate of bread in the sheeny bright morning), is one of the chorus. He is yellow at the temple as sour flesh.

Goneril's Albany is lord now. I came from him. And thought you would perhaps like to return. We could sit in the corner of his court — two old rogues. Or else — or else you could come back to the old places. He is far off; his voice has winds in it, the taste of stone, of wild hair in my mouth on the crags. *It is a new chance! Redemption! We must seize it.*

Talk a little slower, now, I say.

Perhaps we could go further, to the little chapel where you were married. And then keep travelling. As long as our hearts hold.

He has a burden he must take. His own heart. But mine is not his to carry: it is an explosion, it is awake every instant. I wish to tell him but do not.

Instead we go into the gardens.

It is growing hotter, he says. *Every year the heat reaches shallower. I dare say this year it will barely reach my bones.*

Mirabel is walking the paths; the spring-god gives her bounty; she is bound. I see her old now, the slip of wind passing over

356

her body in tenderness, as she stakes the waving peas. The ash-boughs have given up their blossom and dampened; and now in some stumps comes white wood-flesh, emergent, as I have wished. I who am flush with all things. Mirabel is not real, though she believes she is; I turn away.

You are so young still, Kent. You talk like an old man. I smile.

I do. And you, you do not feel old, despite being old as God?

I feel as I am. A queen. I am nothing but a queen. See. I hold up one finger. The solitary, the twice-queen. There were crowns, there was such richness. *Nothing. And I may yet have a son. I may yet. Perhaps if Lear and I go again on pilgrimage. It is only two years, three years? Ah, Kent, you must have hope.*

Yes, Berte. Puts his hands across his eyes. When he lifts them all is wet. *I do.*

I know that I am wandering. This fact cracks open in me, like an apple, and is no disturbance, and moves with the passage of all ghosts, as they touch me, *But I know, too, that I will not come to Albany with you, Kent. Or to Dover, or to the old places, not now. That time is over.* I know this. A great many things lopped off at the ends; and I am old; but it is a good world, a pleasurable world. *Which is all right, because I have no friends outside this place, not now.*

You are wrong. I am your friend. Kent's angled glance.

The pearls burn and burn. Though I saw their smallness in the ash this morning, miniature, they are still burning; around my body there is hard blue flame. When they paint me in the frescos, they will have to lick lapis lazuli, dilute it with oil, and show me wavering, in blue; stepping out of the landscape, rimmed with sky-colours. My body enormous, my mouth shown open, smiling.

No, boy. I smile at Kent. This small man, who saved himself, and left me to die alone. *You were my friend, and then you told the king I was a seductress and a traitor, to save yourself. And so.*

The pause bleeds. The ghosts are bleating, wanting something. *Damn you. You always know.* His face contorts. Selfish, men. Always selfish. The things I could tell: about their insides, about how their love turns and folds back upon them. Knowledge is all I have.

I know everything, Kent. How could you think I would not? There is so little hidden from me. I discover. Penetrating. Though I lose so many things, there are others I gather. I am replete with all I need.

I want — I beg your forgiveness. It was so hard— His eyes brew tears.

I know. Lear, wizened, hard-toothed. He must have been corrosive, without sweetness. No rope to hold him back. No wife-love to restrain him. No wonder Kent said, *Yes, she climbed into my bed, yes, she is a monster, yes, lock her away until she withers.*

Then you will forgive? He looks as if he may kneel. Here, in the wet courtyard, with the rose-red stone. As if time is nothing, nothing; as if all is a moment in a garden, at seventeen.

No. No, you must go on without that. I press his hand. *You will go, Kent, and I will think of you here, and pray for your soul.*

You are cruel.

Yes. I bend my head to it. *I am cruel, and so are you. I have always known myself, Kent.*

After all this. His wavering little voice. *You won't kiss my hand?*

His greying hand. Wavering in my own, spotted like a trout with age. It is so many hands. It contains them; little daughter-fingers I have pretended to eat, king-fingers I have accepted inside myself, to pluck out my love.

I laugh. *Dead women cannot forgive people. And I am dead.* The darkness of it. *A whole life: that is enough. I have given enough. Ask no more.* Young Kent. He will lay down his clattering bones on the slate earth of his master, and die wild, and pass into stone, which is always the servant of water.

A bird calls. The self, and the conscience, and the love of

children, all shrivel. Only soul and will remain, and are blooming. I feel their soft sepals and calyxes tremble against my skull.

And, I say, catching the end of a thought as it slips out of vision, *there is no time. It is getting close to summer, now. Have you noticed? The apple-blossom here. The sheaves are magnificent, like bowers of milk.* Milkbowls. Lapping fingers. The many pleasures of it.

I have not. Show me.

And so I take him into the orchard. The drag of blossom: the trees are bent-backed with it, carrying it in hats, veils, trailing sleeves. Even in the winter they hold this, memory of the weight of their delight. Waiting, simply, to spring forth into their first age. I am tree-woman, I am sap-throated. I would root myself right here, in the grass.

I take off my shoes. Walking over the petal-crush, flowers under the foot of the twice-queen. Little Goneril, asleep with pear-blossoms in her dress, her arms. *It is so lovely. The loveliest place I have ever seen.* Scent falling. Blessed, and blessed.

So you have escaped. You, out of all of us. The luck of it, Kent says, into the silence. It is not bitterness as he says it, but simplicity; and also wonder. At the power, the fortitude of me. *You are happy, here?* he adds.

I am. A full life, daughters, kings, the expanse of it, shining. Luck, which has drenched me. I accept all; it gathers, it shifts on the wind, and flows.

He is under the tumbling apple boughs, looking at me, and he is crying.

I put my thumbs to his face. We are under the bower of high-blooming roses, yes, and I am happy, with my childhood friend. *Do not weep, man. The cook will make you baked apples, and there will be music, for the evening, before you go.* There is no resentment, or violence, that remains, only the glint of light across branches. Luck, and luck, and luck.

He kisses my hand. Slow, ceremonious. *Berte.* I do not take it away.

Is that my name? I seem to lose it. I reach for it sometimes and there is nothing. Hands empty; hands full of water, of girls' hair. I smile. *Well, it does not matter. Nothing will come of nothing.*

Perhaps not. No. I wish— He has bent his head in deep emotion. The heart is full, and presses. *You and I shall walk in the gardens for a little while, then, Twice-queen. Before I begin the last journey.*

Are they not beautiful? The gardens are gorgeous. Crusts of white, on the burned trees. The ghosts will knot them and wear them as garlands on their bright hair.

I will not see their like again.

Will you link arms with me, Kent? I survive; I am luck herself; I am summer's end.

Yes, Berte. Yes.